Secrets of the Bull

Other Books
by Rick Steber

Rendezvous
Traces
Union Centennial
Where Rolls the Oregon
Heartwood
Oregon Trail – Last of the Pioneers
Roundup
New York to Nome
Wild Horse Rider
Buckaroo Heart
No End in Sight
Buy the Chief a Cadillac
Legacy
Forty Candles

Tales of the Wild West Series
Oregon Trail
Pacific Coast
Indians
Cowboys
Women of the West
Children's stories
Loggers
Mountain Men
Miners
Grandpa's Stories
Pioneers
Campfire Stories
Tall Tales
Gunfighters
Grandma's Stories
Western Heroes

www.ricksteber.com

RICK STEBER

SECRETS OF THE BULL

– A NOVEL –

TWO STAR

Published by – *TWO STAR* –
An imprint of Bonanza Publishing
PO Box 204
Prineville, OR 97754

This book is a work of fiction. Names, characters, businesses, organizations, places, events, and incidents either are the product of the author's imagination or are used fictitiously. Any resemblance to actual persons, living or dead, events, or locales is entirely coincidental.

Cover design by Gary Asher
Book design by Jody Conners

ISBN: 978-0-945134-36-7

PRINTED IN THE UNITED STATES OF AMERICA
FIRST EDITION

DEDICATION

For my boys, Seneca and Dusty

FOREWORD

In 1923 the famous western painter Charlie Russell was asked to speak before the Great Falls, Montana Booster Club. He sat in the crowd and listened to one pompous speaker after another sing the praises of the white man's efforts to bring civilization to the western lands. Finally, when Charlie was called on to speak he stood, ripped up his prepared notes and spoke from his heart. This is what he said:

> *"In my book a pioneer is a man who turned all the grass upside down, strung bob-wire over the dust that was left, poisoned the water, cut down the trees, killed the Indians who owned the land, and called it progress. If I had my way, the land here would be like God made it, and none of you sons-of-bitches would be here at all."*

SOURDOUGH PANCAKES

3 c. sourdough starter
1 egg, slightly beaten
2 tbsp. cooking oil
½ c. milk
1 tsp. baking soda
2 tbsp. sugar

Directions – Mix sourdough, egg, oil and milk. Gently fold in remaining ingredients. Drop batter on hot, well-greased griddle. Cook until golden brown. Serve while warm.

CHAPTER ONE

BIG FRANK BATTLE LEANED AN ELBOW AGAINST THE HOOD OF HIS battered, flatbed truck and gazed with arrogant pride over *his* empire: *his* secluded valley, *his* sprawling ranch, *his* livestock. He had not the slightest inkling that before this particular morning played itself out, his body would fail him, the power he loved to wield so fiercely would crumble to dust and all the ugly secrets he had managed to keep hidden these many years would be laid bare to the world. A blood clot, a puny thing smaller than a BB, was about to kick loose, pump through his blood stream and wedge itself tight as a tick at the base of his brain.

Frank felt an odd sensation in his neck, automatically assumed he had slept wrong and rolled his massive shoulders side-to-side the way an old range bull will do, trying to work loose that bothersome kink. The soreness persisted, slowly intensified, and Frank stepped to the cab of his ranch truck, flung open the door, dug around under the seat and produced a whiskey bottle. He unscrewed the lid and tipped the cold glass to his lips. Alcohol traced a coarse passage, and for the moment, that seemed to soothe, or at least to mask, the first shallow evidence of the physical pain that would soon kill him.

Earlier, Frank had launched his morning as so many others before it: rising in the dark, dressing, ambling down the hallway in his stocking feet, pausing at the door of his wife's bedroom, moving on. He rubbed his dry hands together, trying to work some warmth and feeling into them. As he came down the long staircase, the ankle he broke when a horse fell on him clicked each time it flexed.

Frank made his way to the immense rock fireplace where he bent to stir the remains of a fire with a blunt poker. He grabbed two chunks of dry pine from the wood box, one in each meaty hand, and tossed them on the bed of coals that flushed bright orange. Wood ignited with a hungry growl and Frank, shimmers of light dancing at his back, made his way to the kitchen where he flipped the switch to start the coffee machine. He slid his frame onto a straight-backed chair. Rawhide lacing groaned. He balanced his forearms, thick as tree trunks, on the smooth surface of the oak table and breathed in the rich aroma of coffee as liquid dripped with measured regularity into the glass pot. The refrigerator hummed and shut itself off. In the other room the fire snapped and popped and there were creaks and groans, as if the great log house was alive around him.

A lazy memory drifted to Frank of a bull elk he had happened upon a few weeks earlier, during fall roundup. He visualized the way the sly old fellow dropped as low as he could, almost to a crawl, tilting his nose in the air and laying his impressive rack of antlers along his flanks, as he slinked through the lodgepole thicket. That bull was undoubtedly still in the same vicinity, and for a few enjoyable moments, Frank contemplated going after him. But a successful hunt meant packing out a thousand pounds of meat. He'd have to do the work himself since the cowhands had been laid off after roundup and J.B., the only hired man left on the place, was just too goddamn old to be good for much of anything. Besides,

Frank owned a cattle ranch and did not need the meat. He concluded that old bull was just fine where he was. Next year he'd be that much bigger.

When the coffee was ready, Frank poured the entire contents of the pot into a Stanley thermos and on his way out he tossed a couple more quarter-rounds onto the fire. In the mudroom he shoved his feet into shit-caked cowboy boots, shrugged on a horse blanket lined Levi jacket and crushed his Stetson on his head. That hat, custom made from ten-X beaver felt, had a wide brim and tall crown. It had once been adorned with a twenty-dollar horsehair hatband that long ago sloughed off. The brim now drooped and the crown, worn through in several spots, was stained with equal amounts of sweat, manure and corral dust. Frank stepped outside into the darkness. He emerged as a simple cowhand might, but Frank Battle was worth a fortune, damn near every cent tied up in land and livestock.

The air was cold, and coyotes cried back in the hills. Overhead a puff of acrid smoke billowed from the chimney like devil's breath and lively embers corkscrewed into the dark sky to join forces in a profusion of glittering stars. Cow dogs materialized from under the house, nipping and growling at each other.

"Sons-a-bitches," groused Frank. He kept the dogs only because it was a western tradition to have a few on a cattle ranch, but he had never found a dog that would consistently work cattle. The closest he had ever come was Blue, named for his one blue eye. He was a Border Collie and Heeler mix. On command Blue charged into any thicket and brought out the cows he found. The trouble was, he applied the same standards to every situation and was just as apt to run the next bunch of animals through a barbwire fence. Blue was seldom called on to work but was allowed the distinct honor of riding with Frank. He jumped onto the back of the three-quarter ton flatbed as Frank climbed in, slamming the door that squeaked on dry hinges. The starter whined like a liquid on high boil and then the engine coughed, sputtered, caught and growled noisily from a busted exhaust. Frank could have afforded a brand new rig but this one ran good and that was all that mattered to him.

Up on the ridge, near the rimrock outcropping, Frank herded the truck into a turnout, pulled over, doused the headlights and shut off the engine. The interior of the cab was as dimly lit as a cocktail lounge, and mostly by feel, Frank managed to pour himself a cup of coffee that he sweetened with a shot of whiskey. He sipped on his candied coffee and smoked an unfiltered Lucky Strike cigarette, holding it oddly because he had lost his index finger and part of his middle finger in a roping accident. He smoked until the red coals nearly ate into his nicotine-tanned skin, then spit into the palm of his hand and ground out the cigarette, casually flipping the butt out the narrow opening where the window was rolled down for ventilation. He wiped his hand on his pants leg.

Over the rounded tops of the Blue Mountains the sky slowly began to radiate a thin silver glow, but Wood River Valley remained filled to the brim with darkness. As the new day plodded forward with the steadiness of an advancing army, Frank sipped and smoked and waited for nothing in particular to happen. The gloom reluctantly gave way to a gray vagueness, and along the eastern lip of the horizon a false sunrise began to tickle the underbellies of a few clouds with a pink blush that fractured into deep ridges and made the sky look like a washboard scrubbed with blood. Time spun in lazy revolutions. Another smoke. Another cup of coffee. Another shot of whiskey.

Through the smoky haze and the mud and bug-smeared windshield Frank watched as the clouds, stretched thin by the pull of the jet stream, took on the richness of hammered gold, quickly tarnishing as a tiny yellow crescent emerged over a distant mountain. Pine trees stood skylined for a lingering moment. Frank's lips touched dry cigarette paper. He inhaled deeply, holding the smoke in his lungs before blowing a white cloud straight out. He tried to work out that persistent kink in his neck, took another medicated shot of whiskey, and shortly afterward, felt strangely flushed. He removed his hat, ran the fingers on his good hand through his thinning hair and replaced the hat. The sensations he was feeling were damned peculiar but did not detract from his enjoyment of the view. Directly below was the head of Wood River Valley and the Home Place, with its row of Lombardy poplars—branches nearly stripped of leaves and bare-boned—towering over the mammoth log house. Clustered nearby was the substantial tin-roofed barn, the shop and numerous outbuildings, all arranged in a haphazard symmetry.

Beyond the Home Place the ridges curved around the valley in a loose embrace, like arms affectionately slung around a lover's shoulders, and brilliant splays of sunlight reached out to touch the valley floor where nearly a thousand head of pregnant Hereford cows grazed contentedly on the late fall grasses. These were Frank Battle's cows, a lineage built over time and prized as among the best of the breed. Any cattleman worth his salt would feel privileged to have a Battle bull cover his cows.

And now Frank's gaze carried from the creases of the canyons and the folds of the ridges to Sugarloaf Mountain rising from the foot of the valley. Its sharp triangular peak, kissed with a dusting of fresh snow, stood in sharp contrast against the green of the valley and the cobalt sky. If Frank squinted and strained his eyes, he could just barely make out the squat chairs and thin black cable of the ski lift extending above tree-line. He rolled down the window, cleared his throat and spat.

At night, given a little more snow, the slope would once again reflect a neon-pink blush from those damnable, high-intensity lights that allowed city folks to ski after dark. Frank viewed the luminous mountain as a cancerous growth of outside influences meddling in *his* world, intruding upon *his* private domain. The developers had bullied their way in, built a ski resort, changed the sleepy little town of Emerson into a resort community and then, to flaunt their muscle, installed lights on the mountain. In the past, Frank had forced himself to tolerate the pinpricks of light from arcing satellites and the pulsating green and red from passing aircraft. Those encroachments were bad enough, but lighting up a mountain was more than Frank could stomach. He hated it, hated it with a vengeance.

A year before, when Sugarloaf Ski Resort first opened, Frank contemplated shooting out the lights. But he had put off his assault and then the season was over. He told himself this year he might very well keep his promise, and unlimber his .308 Winchester with a scope as fat as a Coke bottle, work his way within range and open fire. He flashed a wicked grin because he knew if he did such a thing, he'd be the talk of the town. Hell, Paul Harvey would probably make mention of it on his radio program. Let those college-educated bastards who flitted about the cheerful shops of Emerson, sipping expensive coffee and spending money easily earned from real estate investments, worry about a madman so crazy he attacked a goddamn mountain.

Frank resented the new blood that had come to Emerson—a town spawned a hundred years before for the benefit of ranchers and loggers—turning it into something it was never intended to be, upscale and trendy. In Frank's view, more people living in and around Emerson meant increased pressure on surrounding private ground. This troubled him greatly. But, with a simple turn of his head, he dismissed the impending threat and concentrated on the forest where scattered islands of tamarack, their needles changing to pale copper, stood out against the deep green of the ponderosa pine and Doug fir. Here and there a carpet of vine maple could be seen glowing scarlet. The draws were outlined with nearly naked quaking aspen; only a few leaves of summer remained, clinging to the slender white branches, shimmering in a morning breeze that stripped the frosty leaves and sent them floating toward the ground like dazzling, golden feathers. Soon enough winter winds would arrive, bringing cold from the Arctic region and a strange quiet would descend over this land as lazy snowflakes floated through the tall evergreens, covering the red volcanic soil with a blanket of virgin white. Winter brought with it a sky two or three notches bluer, and at night stars seemed so close a fellow could almost smell them burning up there.

Frank attempted to draw a breath but a fiery sensation in his chest caused him to stop short of filling his lungs. He exhaled, tried again, this time with better success. The burning persisted and caused him to knit his brow in concern. He pushed on the door handle, threw a brawny shoulder into the metal and the door reluctantly gave way, squeaking as it swung open. Frank walked to the back of his rig, stood there and pissed. Blue rose from the spare tire lashed to the bed, came over and tried to lick Frank's face. Frank pulled away from such a deliberate show of affection. As he fumbled with the buttons on his Levi's, he scolded Blue, "Knock it off."

He moved forward and was aware of a peculiar tightness that seemed to be centered in his chest. He stepped around the door and leaned his weight on the truck's hood, thinking maybe he could feel a bit of the engine's warmth still lingering in the metal. Back in the timber a flock of crows called with caustic voices: coarse, dry, irritating. Blue whined.

"Shut the hell up," groused Frank. The dog shied submissively and curled onto his bed on the spare tire. Frank tried to avoid facing his pain and turned his attention to surveying the countryside and the reddish brown and white dots that were *his* cattle. Frank, his hired man J.B., and a couple of part-time buckaroos had spent the best part of the past month riding hard, wearing out one saddle horse after another, pushing these cattle off the mountain pastures and into the barbwire delineation of the valley floor. The yearling calves had already been weaned, sold and sent to buyers in California, Texas and Idaho. What remained were the bred cows, the replacement heifers and the bulls.

The legacy of the Battle family in Eastern Oregon dated back to 1872 when Lewis Battle, Frank's grandfather, traveled horseback from Illinois in search of opportunity. He arrived in the Willamette Valley on the day he turned 18, only to discover he was late and all the good land had been claimed. He doubled back to the east side of the Cascade Range, and out on the broad panorama of the High Desert he chanced upon Sugarloaf Mountain, discovering the hidden valley that lay in its shadow. With a few barrels of whiskey Lewis stole the headwaters of Wood River from the local Indians.

A man could lay claim to only so much government property and other land-hungry pioneers soon arrived and staked their homesteads on the broad meadow of the valley floor. In turn, Lewis's son Harold added to the original holdings by crushing these homesteaders: intimidating those not determined enough, smart enough, or mean enough and, one-by-one, they relinquished their 320 acre desert-entry homesteads, their cherished slice of the American dream, and the land was added to the Battles' holdings.

Frank took over from his father and channeled the river and drained the swamp to not much more than a puddle of water interspersed with a few willows and cattails. He fenced and cross-fenced the valley floor, and when land bordering the ranch came up for sale he promptly bought it. Over the years he had managed to add nearly four sections to the Double X.

Frank's father and grandfather had fought Indians and homesteaders for the land. But the majority of Frank's quarrels had been against nature: the tussock moth that burrowed under the bark and killed the trees, coyotes that came for an easy meal at calving time, infestations of field mice that arrived after the coyotes were poisoned and plagues of grasshoppers that stripped the grasses. Lately the conflicts revolved around the onslaught of developers wanting to turn his valley into ranchettes and golf courses, hunters demanding access and having no hesitation about trespassing on private property, environmentalists using the endangered species act in an attempt to save any acre that did not already have a house built on it, and federal bureaucrats who imposed a series of ever tightening limitations and regulations.

The Forest Service and BLM had become so regulatory and restrictive that a few years back Frank lost his temper. He turned back his permits that granted grazing rights on public lands to the Double X. This prompted the district ranger to accuse Frank of cutting off his nose to spite his face. Frank told him, "Buster, as far as I'm concerned, you and every other asshole bureaucrat like you, can go piss up a rope."

In the long run, Frank's outburst was extremely costly, but earned him a tremendous amount of respect. If he had chosen to cash in on his popularity and run for a Senate seat, every last cattleman would have cast a vote in his favor. The trouble was, the cattlemen were no longer in the majority on the vast grasslands of Eastern Oregon.

Frank was bound and determined to hold onto the ranch at any cost. That philosophy was burned into him the same way the Double X brand was burned into the left hip of the thousand head of purebred Herefords ranging his 64,000 acres of deeded ground. Nothing was more important to Frank than land: not Iris, his wife, or even his boys, Cole and Ty.

Even though Frank had run the boys off rather than turn the ranch over to them, he still remembered the good times they had shared. Back in the distant past, after fall roundup, the three of them had engaged in some spirited competitions on who could kill the biggest buck. Cole, the oldest, was a determined hunter, a hell of a shot and a chip off the old block. He proved what he could do every time he tacked a big set of horns to the side of the barn. On the other hand, Ty could be a piss-ant about that sort of thing. If a big buck wandered within range he might pull the trigger. He never went out of his way and often passed up a trophy for a forked-horn. It was Iris who claimed a spike or forked-horn was preferable to an old buck, saying the old bucks tasted like boot leather. Ty sided with his mother—he always sided with her—preferring tender steaks to bragging rights.

If Frank were to choose his favorite time of the year, it would certainly have to be fall, when the cattle were gathered and he could catch his breath a little before winter and the cycles of feeding and calving began. But he had not always been a dyed-in-the-wool fall man. When he was younger he preferred spring, when each new day was a challenge to see just how much he could accomplish: drag the pasture and break up the manure, seed the meadow, clean ditches, work cattle and horses to top off. Everywhere fresh opportunities were exposed. But over the years Frank changed. He became more content in fall, when the roundup was over, pregnant cows filled the valley and the barn and outside stacks overflowed with seasoned hay. Frank stockpiled and hoarded hay. He reasoned a rancher could never have too much hay. The snow might come early or last longer than usual. To run short meant having to buy expensive hay, or feeding less, and then the cows were not in the peak of condition at calving time.

Frank's contemplations were interrupted by a sharp jab of pain centered somewhere in his large chest. It was the type of pain that will cause a man to think of things unaccomplished in his life, things he had let slide. A peculiar thought came to him. He recalled a headgate that needed fixing. Last spring, when a Chinook hit and the snow came off in a hurry, the headgate had washed out and water gouged a mean scar on the hillside, sending topsoil scurrying toward the distant Pacific. To control the flow of irrigation water he had jerry-rigged a headgate, putting off the proper repair until later, until there was more time.

Time. A cloud passed in front of the sun and a raven appeared as a black shadow angling across a remote corner of the sky that had lost its luminescent quality and become pale and somber. The coyotes, as they trickled down out of the hills toward the floor of Wood River Valley, gave a series of sharp yips. Frank breathed in, but he could no longer differentiate the delightful blend of sage, sweet and tangy, the pureness of evergreen, the rich perfume of damp earth.

Frank's left elbow tingled, as if he had hit his crazy bone, and he reached to touch it. As he did, a terrific jolt clobbered the back of his skull and forced him to fall face-first across the hood of his truck. His heart pounded and his eyes bulged. He saw the powder blue of an acetylene flame cutting a wide swath through his brain and pain, so intense it screamed like a siren, gripped him hard. Nothing existed except that pain. Frank expelled a guttural humph of air, eyelids slammed shut, knees went weak and he instinctively flung a forearm across the fender and managed to catch himself rather than fall to his knees.

When Frank opened his eyes the world was blurry. His left leg refused to obey and his left arm hung uselessly at his side, but after awhile, his leg muscles seemed to firm up enough that he attempted to move. Sheer determination propelled him into action and dragging his bad leg after him, he reached the door, held onto it with his right arm and managed to slowly pivot around it. Lurching backward he was somehow, amazingly, able to pull his hulking frame up and onto the seat, hauling his left leg in after him, resting, breathing hard, sweating profusely, striving but failing to grasp what was happening to him.

Once, on a cold February morning while roping a yearling bull that needed doctoring, Frank took a sloppy dally. The stiff rope trapped two fingers and popped them off like they were beer caps. Frank picked up his glove, swung by the house, grabbed a fifth of Jack Daniels to cut the pain, put on a clean shirt since the one he was wearing was a might bloody, and drove himself into town. He handed the doctor his glove with the fingers still inside but the doctor said it was no use, sewed up the stubs and that was that.

Frank tried to reassure himself that he would make it out of this current predicament just as he had so many times in the past, but the sounds he made were incoherent and the words a mangled and pointless series of grunts, sobs, and pitiful moans. Spittle that he could not feel ran down his chin. His right eye blinked. His lip on the right side twitched. In stark disparity, all the muscles on the left side were slack and lifeless, causing his face to droop like an empty gunnysack.

With his right leg Frank stomped down the clutch. He reached with his good arm and tentative fingers, shaking with exertion, touched the key, grabbed hold and twisted. The starter groaned. The dependable old engine kicked to life. He pulled his foot off the clutch and the truck jerked into forward motion.

If Frank had somehow been able to drive himself the fifteen miles into Emerson and reach the hospital, it would have been heralded as a miracle. He nearly pulled it off. But as the truck descended the grade, coming off the shoulder of Sugarloaf Mountain, he slumped to the right and passed out onto the seat covered with a threadbare Pendleton blanket. The flatbed drifted into the oncoming lane near Tucker's Market, where the special of the day was boneless rump roast for $2.39 a pound, sideswiping a parked car that belonged to Oliver Swindel, a direct descendant of one of Emerson's pioneering families and the man who owned and operated Swindel's Funeral Home.

Thankfully the collision redirected the truck and changed its aim. If it had continued on a steady course, the widow McCaffrey, toting an armload of groceries, would surely have been killed as she stepped into the street. She heard the wild commotion, looked up and dropped her sack onto the pavement. It burst open scattering a one-pound box of brown sugar, a dozen eggs, a pound of butter and a bag of Nestle chocolate chips. She had planned to bake Mr. Pavlinac a batch of cookies. He owned Sugarloaf Feed Store and had recently lost his wife, Beverly, to breast cancer.

The truck tires crushed the dozen eggs and chocolate chips. The flatbed continued on, crossed Main Street and aimed itself directly at the plate glass window of the Department of Motor Vehicles. At that hour there were no customers pulling numbers and standing in line. The lone DMV employee had punched the timeclock and stepped out for his ritual cup of coffee at the Café Paradiso. He was sitting there now, munching on a bit of biscotti and washing it down with polite sips of French vanilla coffee.

Blue, a split second before impact, abandoned his perch on the spare tire, jumped from the speeding truck, tucked into a tight ball like an experienced gymnast and somersaulted across the hard asphalt. He came to rest against the stone masonry of the Purple Sage Gift Shoppe. Considering the violence of the collision, he was damn lucky to only suffer a couple broken ribs, a lacerated hip and a broken incisor. He limped away into an alley where he immediately began licking his wounds.

Meanwhile, the DMV window shattered with a tremendous avalanche of noise, sounding like a busy bowling alley on a drunken Saturday night. Frank's flatbed came to rest in the waiting area. Steam hissed from the busted radiator. Sheetrock dust and tiny bits of hay drifted around the room and slowly began to settle.

From the safety of the café, the DMV employee continued to sip coffee, eat biscotti and watch as the aftermath of the tragedy played itself out. He saw reflections of swirling red and blue lights even before the police car came into view and slid to a stop; the policeman throwing open the car door, jumping out and racing through the opening. He wrenched at the door of the flatbed. An instant later the ambulance arrived and volunteer EMTs placed the victim on a stretcher and took him away. Thirty minutes later a wrecker arrived and removed the truck. And then, showing a slight bit of imagination and more humor than government workers are generally given credit for, the DMV employee walked across the street to his office, made up a sign and taped it to the remnants of his front wall, proclaiming, "Drive-thru Temporarily Closed."

CHAPTER TWO

ABOVE WOOD RIVER VALLEY A PAIR OF BALD EAGLES COASTED ON outstretched wings, riding an updraft, searching for an easy meal. Maybe they would locate the crippled blue-winged teal hiding in the cattails along the river that hugged one side of the valley or the mule deer pulled down by the marauding cougar during the night. The cougar had eaten his fill, had covered the kill with leaves and duff as best he could and was now holed up in a nearby lodgepole thicket. There was meat to be gleaned from the carcass of the deer if the crows and magpies did not find it first.

At the Home Place, while two loaves of bread baked in the kitchen oven, Iris Battle worked in the living room. She was a thin woman dressed in a drab, loose-fitting housedress. A dust rag was slung over one shoulder and she busied herself by straightening the snow-flaked doilies on end tables and on backs and arms of chairs. She had crocheted them all. Seeing them arranged so perfectly gave her a feeling of self-worth. She viewed her delicate handiwork as tiny islands of refinement in a room dominated by manly things. Frank's presence seemed to be everywhere: big leather chairs and sofas, colorful Navajo rugs and saddle blankets, a buck-saw, deer and elk heads, sheep and moose horns and even the wide horns from a steer that had once roamed the ranch. It eluded the annual roundups for 13 years before Frank caught it out in the open and gunned it down. The horns, mounted on a myrtlewood burl, were colored almost ebony, but the tips had been polished a glossy white. The horns were mounted as a testimonial to the undeniable fact that, in the end, Frank Battle always maintained the upper hand.

There was also a collection of Winchester rifles hanging on pegs, Charlie Russell prints and photographs of favorite horses, cow dogs, rodeos, roundups and brandings. Lying on the sugar pine slab that served as the mantle of the grand lava rock fireplace, a place where Frank laid things of importance, was an accumulation of items including stacks of livestock papers, magazines, wooden matches, horseshoe nails, a silver bit, a rasp, a hoof pick, several buck knifes, seashells from some long-forgotten trip to the coast and the book *Lone Cowboy* by Will James. A five of hearts had been slipped as a marker between pages sixteen and seventeen. A layer of fine dust and smoky ash covered all these things because Frank had made it clear that Iris was never to touch anything on the mantle. She obediently complied.

Scattered around the room were objects advertising the Double X brand. The XX was etched into mirrors, arranged into the design on a stained glass window, braided into a throw rug and burned into the top of several small tables along with the brands from homesteaders run out, or bought out, by the Battle men. Iris dusted where she could, picked up the clutter, but mostly she avoided changing anything. This was Frank's room and when he was home this was where he took up residence, sitting in his big leather chair, a floor lamp puddling light around him as he sipped whiskey and read newspapers, livestock reports, cattlemen and stockmen magazines, journals and an occasional book. Each evening he sat here and read until he fell asleep.

On her way to bed, Iris sometimes gently placed an afghan, one of many she had crocheted over the years, over her sleeping husband. Later, Frank would snort himself awake, toss more wood on the fire, traipse upstairs and go to bed in his room; Frank and Iris hadn't slept together in more than three decades.

Iris looked at Frank's chair and tears of sorrow, weakness or something, but certainly not love, welled up, and she removed a crumpled tissue from the pocket of her housedress and dabbed at the corners of both eyes. She was the one who had made the decision to stay with Frank. She had done it for her boys, she told herself, and how many years had it been since she laid eyes on either one of them? Some days she dwelled on her misery, not today. Giving in to her depression would only rekindle her resentment.

Frank was the one who had driven them away, the boys. And what about the baby? The daughter Iris had lost. She could not endure the terrible weight of any of those memories; no, not today, and so she moved in the direction of the kitchen, breathing in the aroma of baking bread as it rose from the oven and filled the room with its warm, yeasty fragrance.

Iris had never felt at home in this imposing log house, built by Lewis Battle, Frank's grandfather. But she did derive a sense of comfort here and supposed, in a way, the house was like the weight of a heavy blanket on a cold, stormy night, giving her solace, a feeling of warmth and possibly even belonging. And besides, Iris recognized she was tied to this log fortress, and to Frank, by her own sense of responsibility and a hundred other irreconcilable emotions.

Iris removed the bread from the oven and set it on racks to cool. She opened a cupboard, got down a drinking glass, and poured herself four fingers of wine from a gallon jug she kept under the sink. She swirled the red liquid around a time or two and took a long swallow with a desire that had nothing to do with simple thirst. She exhaled, turned on the hot water in the sink, took a jar of jam from the counter and held it under the faucet until she suspected the lid was loose. She was beginning to use a corner of her housedress to open the jar when the ringing of the telephone startled her.

The conversation that followed was one-sided. Iris listened as the doctor did the bulk of the talking. He said he was sorry to have to tell her this, but Frank had suffered a massive stroke and had then wrecked his truck attempting to reach the hospital. He said, "I don't know how a man in his condition could have driven so far."

"What is his condition?" Iris asked, her voice flat and unemotional.

There was a pause, as if the doctor was searching around, attempting to choose the right word or combination of words, selecting, "Gravely critical." He waited a heartbeat or two before continuing. "But, you and I know Frank's a tough, old bird." Again there was awkward silence. "I think you ought to know, Iris, so you can prepare yourself, if Frank does somehow manage to pull through, he isn't going to be the same man he was. He could possibly be paralyzed, and since he was without oxygen for a significant amount of time, there could be considerable brain damage."

Iris took this news with a slight bending at the waist. She knew, without the doctor having to spell it out any further, if Frank did live, it would be her lot in life to care for him. She wanted Frank to just die and get it over with, and immediately hated herself and felt guilty for thinking such a morbid thought.

"Well," said Iris, "Thank you for calling and telling me." She promptly depressed the disconnect button and carefully returned the receiver to the cradle. Continuing her deliberate movements she stepped to the radio transmitter, took hold of the handset and calmly, almost dispassionately, spoke into it, "Base to J.B. You there, J.B.?"

After a short delay came the dry nasal twang of the hired man's voice, "Yes ma'am. I'm here."

"I need you to run me to town."

"When you want ta go?"

"Right away, please."

J.B., perhaps reading a slight bit of urgency in her voice, wanted to know, "Iris, is everything all right?"

"It's Frank," said Iris.

"What's the matter?"

"Doctor said it was a stroke."

"Where is he?"

"Hospital."

"How'd he get there?"

"Drove himself."

"Wonder why he didn't... is... is he gonna be okay?"

"We can talk on the way."

"Be right there."

J.B. pushed himself off his bunkhouse cot and stood. He was a bowlegged little fellow with a lot of strut left in him, although he gave the impression he had long ago used up all the good years he had coming. He had shrunken away from his extremities. His feet, hands and head appeared to belong to a much larger man. He hurried to fasten the top snap on the throat of his work shirt and checked to make sure his sleeves were snapped too. He tucked the tail of his shirt into his pants.

From even a cursory glance it was obvious that J.B. was a throwback to the kind of cowboy who existed in the days before barbwire broke up the open range. The closest he came to technology was a transistor radio. If a person had to guess, you'd have to figure he kept it tuned to a country-western station; day and night the voices of Patsy Cline—*Back in Baby's Arms* and *Crazy*, Bob Wills & His Texas Playboys—*San Antonio Rose*, Hank Snow—*I've Been Everywhere*, Ray Price—*Heartaches By the Numbers*, Loretta Lynn—*Don't Come Home A Drinkin'* and Eddy Arnold—*What's He Doing In My World* filling the narrow confines of the bunkhouse. But J.B. thought country-western was too sad and too damn predictable. He was a classical music aficionado and kept his radio tuned to public radio. He believed the most exciting era of classical music occurred between Bach and Beethoven. One time a cowboy, when learning about this unusual facet of J.B.'s personality, asked what was so special about Bach? J.B. grew real serious and said, "Because his music floats like a feather that can't feel the pull of gravity."

J.B. wasn't savvy to modern things or modern ways. He had never heard of the Internet, had never purposely taken a hike through an old-growth forest, though he had ridden horseback through plenty of them. His idea of a cup of coffee was a handful of Folgers tossed in a pot of boiling water with the grounds strained through his teeth. His only concern in life was to make sure the cows and the calves of the Double X spread were in good health and had plenty of feed. He had a couple nasty habits: packing a pinch of Copenhagen under his lower lip and occasionally smoking a hand-rolled cigarette. He was shy to a fault, unless he was drinking, and then he could be the life of the party with stories of what a randy son-of-a-bitch he used to be.

Better than four decades before, J.B. had been a card-carrying saddle bronc rider. Then he got busted up at Cheyenne when his draw went goofy in the chute. It was the end of an illustrious rough-string riding career. Never again did he crawl on a rodeo bronc. Instead, he came to work for Frank and stuck through all the intervening years because he never took Frank's tirades personally. A fence might not be fixed according to the way Frank wanted it fixed, or a sick cow might not be getting well fast enough to suit the hotheaded bastard, and Frank would go off, taking it out on J.B. The hired man never backed off or backed away. He stood his ground and took it, even when Frank emphasized his words with firm knuckle bumps on J.B.'s breastbone, and when Frank had shot his wad, J.B. would give a simple shrug and say, "Okay, boss. If that's the way you want it, that's the way we'll do 'er."

It seemed that, once or twice a year, the pressures of everyday life on the Double X built to an intolerable level and

J.B. went on a rolling toot, the spree typically ending in some small town jail—usually within about a hundred-mile radius—with J.B. flat broke, hung over and remorseful. He'd call the ranch collect. Frank always bailed him out because J.B. was considerate enough to delay his drunken escapades until after calving, or haying, or branding. Besides, J.B. was a hell of a horseman and Frank knew he'd have to hire two men to replace him.

J.B. now hurried from the bunkhouse to the garage, swung open the double doors and there, looking as out of place as the pope in a whorehouse, was a maroon Mercedes sedan. Frank had given the car to Iris as a gift. It was meant to impress the bankers and neighbors and was as show-offy and unnecessary as the mink coat he had given her one Christmas. On that occasion, Iris opened the package and set it aside, saying, "Where am I going to wear a mink coat?" Ever after that mink coat remained in her closet, preserved inside the protective bag it had come in.

Iris did not drive, had never driven. Frank would not allow her the privilege of driving. He said if a woman learned to drive how could a man ever expect her to stay home? J.B. drove Iris whenever she had some place to go, even though it looked ludicrous to see this old pinch-faced cowboy in his battered hat herding a $90,000 foreign automobile down a dusty, one-lane road.

J.B. pulled the Mercedes around to the front porch of the mammoth log house and honked the horn once, polite-like, to let Iris know he was there. She emerged from the house in a freshly pressed brown dress. She was not one to adorn herself with more than was necessary, never bothered with the frivolity of makeup, except for a thin coating of lipstick on her otherwise pale lips. The closest she came to owning jewelry was a pair of stainless-steel pruning shears she kept on a high shelf in the pump house. She did not wear her wedding ring, had not worn it in years. J.B. knew why. He knew most of the secrets, and what he knew he kept to himself.

Iris tugged the wooden door shut, and as she turned, her big purse swung around, upsetting her balance. J.B. watched this clumsy stick-woman lurch across the broad porch and begin to descend the steps. He recalled when she was a good-looking gal with a wondrous smile and a terrific sense of humor. Back then she had dangerous curves, straight white teeth and thoroughbred slim ankles. He remembered one time in particular, when it had first occurred to him that there is no sadder sight in the world than a pretty gal weary in life and trapped in marriage. He had teased her that day, saying, "Why don't you and me run away ta some South Sea island?" She had smiled at him, but there had been more ache and pain than laughter in her blue eyes. J.B. knew she had squandered her youth and beauty and everything that made her who she was, given herself over, become another of Frank's possessions. And to top it off Frank never did appreciate her. She was no better off than one of his brood cows.

Several more thoughts bombarded J.B.—what would have happened if he and Iris had run off to that South Sea island? What if Frank did kick the bucket? No great loss to humanity, but who in the hell was going to run the ranch and look after Iris? Just then Iris opened the door and slid onto the front seat, bringing with her the heady perfume of freshly baked bread.

The ride to town, once Iris had exhausted the little she knew about Frank's condition, was mostly quiet. J.B. was not one to pry or make idle chit-chat and try to pass it off for conversation. Mostly he concentrated on the muffled noise of tires skipping over washboard and the occasional sharp chunk of gravel flipping up and striking the metal of the expensive automobile's underbelly. He thought some about Frank, confrontations they had had over the years and how the old sombitch always tried to build himself up at everyone else's expense.

J.B. had been brought up to believe a man should treat a woman with respect, that he should never cuss in the presence of a lady or be a bully, boastful, or arrogant. Frank broke all the rules. A few times it seemed Frank had actually considered someone other than himself. Those times he was generous to Iris, he made certain everyone was aware of it. Fancy car. Mink coat. In J.B.'s eyes Frank was a rotten bastard, although when he wanted to be, he could be gracious and charming. That was his worst sin of all—Frank knew the difference and chose to be the way he was.

As Iris rode in an insulated cocoon of near silence, she dreaded what the future might hold but slowly came to the realization that the unknown could certainly pose no more unhappiness than the known past. She had been unhappy for many years, so very many years.

Upon reaching the hospital J.B. stopped the car, got out and held open the door for Iris. She thanked him politely, slid the strap of her purse over one shoulder and moved in a steady line toward the double glass doors that opened automatically. She entered the hospital, hesitated briefly while inhaling the bitterly scathing smells of pain, fear and strong disinfectant, and then moved on with blinding purpose. She passed the nurses' station, momentarily abandoned, and kept walking down a long brown hallway until she reached a stainless steel table on wheels that announced the intensive care unit. This was where she found Frank. He was lying on his back and it seemed to Iris as if he wore an expression of contentment, or perhaps simply placid disinterest and it made Iris wonder if, having come so near to the end of his life, had he finally found peace of mind? This thought annoyed her. She flashed on their shared past, pivotal moments, and replayed them: Frank driving her sons away, the death of her infant daughter, Ruth Ann, her little grave atop a rise overlooking Wood River Valley marked with a white marble slab that bore a lamb and the words "*Baby Ruth Ann – Resting In Peace.*" Beside the headstone was an old Mason jar, half-buried in the dirt, that occasionally accepted a bouquet of wildflowers, although Iris did not go to the grave very often any more. Maybe Frank should not be forced to shoulder the total blame for the death of his daughter, but to Iris, his unwillingness, or his inability to console and comfort her when she needed him the most, was almost as bad. And there were other times when Frank's frightful anger had flared. Iris made a concerted effort to force away these memories because she had become such a skillful expert at forcing them away.

The hospital bed seemed too small for Frank's large frame, even though he also gave the appearance of nothing more than an empty shell of the man. Iris stood there staring and what she wanted, more than anything, was to put the vast differences between herself and her husband into something simple, and tangible, and concrete. After several long moments of thought she concluded that if the two of them were at the beach gazing out over the wide expanse of the Pacific ocean, she would be fascinated by the way the individual waves rolled in, changing colors as they progressed, green giving way to a sheen of translucent turquoise and then to frothy white as each wave spent its energy against the shore. In addition to the obvious beauty of the ocean she would also have an appreciation for everything unseen below the surface; the layers of water and vegetation, the buried mountain ranges and flooded valley floors and all the creatures both large and small. On the other hand, Frank would most likely look upon the vastness and see the water stretched taut all the way to the curved horizon. He might imagine himself in a boat, battling the elements –tide, waves, wind—but it was not in his nature to contemplate anything more than the obvious.

Iris had a hunch someone had joined her. She turned and saw J.B. standing in the doorway. He was holding his hat to his heart, head bowed as if in prayer, and she went to him, reached out and patted the back of the hand that held his hat. She said, "J.B., let's go home."

CHAPTER THREE

THE CLASSIC 1962 CORVETTE CONVERTIBLE, WHITE AS DRIFTED SNOW, top down, 327 engine rumbling sweetly, snaked through the Terwilliger Curves heading south on I-5 away from downtown Portland. Cole Battle, his sports jacket carelessly tossed on the passenger seat, steered with one hand and used the other to loosen his red tie and unbutton the top button of his pale blue dress shirt. The radio was on, and in spite of the wind and the noise of traffic, he caught bits and pieces as the newscaster droned on about a civil war somewhere in the world, another terrorist bombing in the Middle East, one more plane crash—all presumed dead—and a human interest story, a tragedy really, about a Southern Oregon farmer who shot his Farm Home Administration representative dead because he could not stand to have the land that had been in his family for three generations taken away in foreclosure.

Cole was wearing tan slacks and Larry Mahan cowboy boots. He wore boots because he felt comfortable in boots. He was built like a wrestler, thick in the neck and strong through the shoulders. His complexion was ruddy, attesting to the fact his job did not permanently confine him to an office. His most striking feature was his eyes, the color of Crater Lake on an overcast day, a gift from his mother's genes. He was clean-shaven and had a head of thick brown hair with only a slight trace of gray beginning to creep in around the temples. He was in terrific shape for a man who had recently turned forty.

Cole, since departing from his father's ranch in Wood River Valley, had done well for himself, carving out a career in real estate. His specialty was brokering deals on ranch and farmland, taking big tracts out of production, carving them up and selling off pocket-sized parcels to people with money who built trophy homes for recreation or retirement. He was good at his job: ambitious, determined and self-assured.

In the suburban home he shared with his wife and daughter there was but a single reminder of where he had come from. On a shelf in the hallway was a small, framed black-and-white photograph of Cole, his father Frank, and younger brother Ty, all dressed in cowboy hats, bulky coats, wool pants and boots. They were mounted on saddle horses. The dark gray of their noses and cheeks attested to the fact the day had been bitterly cold. Stocks of carbines peeked from the top of saddle scabbards. In the background, and giving the appearance there had been a deer lynching, were two monster bucks and a forked-horn suspended from a pole meat rack. Cole would say, that moment forever frozen in time, life was as good as it was ever going to get. Secretly, he longed for the life he had known on the ranch, but deep down he knew he would never again set foot on the Double X, certainly not as long as his father was alive.

"Anybody home?" Cole called to an empty house. He wondered where his wife, Donna, might be and why his daughter, Kendra, was not home from school and wished he had stayed in town and gone to the Multnomah Athletic Club to work out.

The answering machine beeped, indicating there was a message waiting, but Cole ignored it, knowing it would not be for him. Any of his friends or business acquaintances knew to call him on his cell phone. This message might be for Donna, one of her many acquaintances trying to get together with her for lunch, or a store clerk saying such-and-such an item had arrived and would someone please pick it up at their earliest convenience, but more than likely it was one of Kendra's classmates. Lately a boy had been calling and if Cole happened to answer, the boy immediately hung up. This pissed Cole off and once, armed with Caller ID, he turned the tables, called the boy and told him, "Don't call my house and hang up like that. It's not good manners. If you wish to speak to one of us, at least have the decency to ask for that person."

When Kendra, a cute, leggy, active 14-year-old, found out her father had pulled such a stunt she confronted him, and though Cole stood his ground, Donna intervened, siding with Kendra and telling Cole, "You were out of line. Totally." Cole knew the deck was stacked against him. He shrugged it off.

The answering machine beeped again as Cole continued through the house to the bedroom. He changed into running shorts and a sleeveless shirt. He told himself he'd go for a six or seven miler and maybe, when he got home, Donna would have dinner started. He stepped outside into the late afternoon sunshine and began running.

Donna returned home from an afternoon shopping escapade and immediately started dinner, fixing something quick and easy. She had clam sauce simmering in a pan, pasta ready to submerge in boiling water and the garlic bread, wrapped in tinfoil, warming in the oven.

Most mornings Donna worked at a neighborhood espresso bar, not for the little bit of money it paid, but because it gave her a regular routine and allowed her opportunities to meet people and mingle. She was on the board of several community groups, including the Lieser Hospital Foundation and the Friends of the Library, and she liberally volunteered her time at Kendra's school. She derived enjoyment from surrounding herself with creature comforts and regularly shopped at upscale specialty stores. In the afternoons she liked nothing more than to indulge her various appetites with finger foods, Brie cheese on sesame crackers, sipping fine wine and visiting with old, and new, friends. She was also into New Age music.

Donna wore her strawberry blond hair—the color assisted by Clairol's Caribbean Sunset to help promote the golden highlights—shoulder-length. She was a good fifteen pounds heavier than she wanted to be, but refused to exercise, saying it was boring. She had made several stabs at dieting—NutriSystem and WeightWatchers to name a couple—but did not possess the self-discipline necessary to carry through a lifestyle change for more than a loss of five or so. And she always gained the weight right back.

When Cole returned from his run he passed through the kitchen, pausing to give Donna a quick, meaningless peck, while making sure he kept his sweaty body away from contact with her or her clothing. Continuing on toward a quick shower he tasted the residue of wine from Donna's lips and guessed it was Columbia Crest merlot.

Going down the hallway he called back, "How'd your day go?"

"Fine," Donna threw after him. In truth, she had no idea how her day had gone. It was as if, years before, the real Donna had wandered off into the woods, and by now, she had been lost for so long the search had been called off and everyone had given up looking. Suddenly, remembering the message on the answering machine, Donna stopped stirring the sauce and questioned how long it had been, how many years, since she had heard Iris's voice. When they lived together in the big log house she had gotten along with Iris. Iris was easy to get along with. She was milquetoast. Frank insisted she be milquetoast. What bothered Donna was why any mother would allow anyone, especially her husband, to cut her off from all contact with her son and his family? Milquetoast. And now, out of the blue, she had called and left a message.

Donna turned the burner to low and went to the bathroom, opened the door and stepped inside. Cole was already in the shower. She could see him through the frosted glass. The sight of his naked body used to excite her, but it didn't any more and hadn't for a long time. She flipped a switch on the wall and called, "You need to remember to turn on the fan. The steam causes mold to grow. It's hard to scrub off."

Cole, eyes closed and head soapy, replied, "Okay, Honey."

Rather than waste any additional time in this humid environment Donna hurriedly delivered the news, "Your mother called and left a message."

Cole stopped washing and just stood there with his hands on his head, waiting, and finally he asked, "What did she say?"

"Wanted you to call her as soon as possible. Said it was important."

On the way back to the kitchen Donna was remembering the day they had departed the ranch, driving away, Kendra wrapped tightly in her arms. Donna had forced herself to hide her joy at leaving. In her opinion, the years they spent at the Double X, were too solitary an existence to suit her, too confining, way too stifling. She had had nobody to talk to, no friends and no opportunities to socialize.

What had she thought it was going to be like? After all they lived in the same house as Cole's parents. What she had not realized, not at that point anyway, was the effect leaving would have on Cole. He had been forced to give up the one thing in his life he had a real passion for, and when the split occurred, neither his wife, nor his mother, had been willing to stand beside him and fight for what was right.

Donna knew it was because of Cole's sense of obligation to her and to their daughter that he was compelled to live where he did not want to live and work at something—although he was remarkably good at it—that was, to him, meaningless and unfulfilling. She had witnessed, once they were off the ranch and settled in Portland, the way Cole seemed to drift. Then finally he picked up the pieces and challenged himself by carving out a career in real estate. Hadn't Donna been the one standing at his side encouraging him every step of the way? She wondered if he now resented her for that.

There were many nights when Cole was away on business or indulging himself outdoors—hunting, fishing, running rivers—that Donna lay alone in bed and wondered what part *she* had played in his being forced to give up his dream. How might *she* have changed the outcome? What if *she* had been more content at the ranch, less consumed by motherhood when Kendra came along, and perhaps, when the quarrels emerged between Cole and his father, more assertive, more supportive, more sure of herself, perhaps offering to serve as a mediator to make it all work. What *she* could have done, and maybe should have done, when viewed from a distance, was ambiguous and confusing. She was never able to reach a satisfactory resolution to any of her questions or doubts.

What had become unmistakable, although Donna refused to acknowledge it, was the intense love she and Cole had shared in courtship and the first few years of marriage, had, somewhere along the line, come unraveled. Only thin shreds of it existed to loosely bind them to each other.

Cole emerged from the bathroom barefoot, dressed in a pair of sweat pants, pulling a T-shirt over his head. As he came into the kitchen he asked, "Did she sound stressed?"

"Did who sound stressed?"

"Mother."

"Not particularly. Pretty straightforward. Just said she wanted you to call her."

"How long 'fore dinner?"

"Fifteen minutes. You have time to make your call, and then, please set the table? Oh, by the way, Kendra won't be eating with us."

"Where is she?"

"Susan's. They're going to a movie."

"On a school night?"

"I told her she could. If you don't want her to, you call and tell her to come home."

Cole knew better. "Forget it," he said, opening the cupboard door and pulling down a pair of plates decorated with tiny flowers. He didn't like the distinctly feminine floral design, and in the past, made the mistake of telling Donna they were too frilly for his taste. She had taken his comment personally, threw a dishtowel in his direction and told him he could cook his own damn meal.

Cole set the plates on cloth tablemats and thought how little influence and power he had in his life. In business the final results depended upon the whims of buyers and sellers and the cooperation of the governmental entities involved in rural developments. And in his family life, which Cole acknowledged with a growing sense of apprehension, he was losing contact with those he loved the most. He was unable, or unwilling, to invest the time and energy it took to make a marriage work, a father-daughter relationship grow strong and stable, and a household to function as it should. In his own way, without fully realizing what he was doing, he was cutting himself off from those around him, from those he loved. His father had done the same thing.

It seemed as though the only time Cole felt any sense of personal enjoyment and satisfaction was when he was playing. He was an expert fisherman, could land a green-butted skunk on the breaking edge of a submerged boulder, a terrific marksman with both rifle and shotgun, and an avid kayaker. He had run the Snake, Salmon, Fraser and Rogue rivers and every year he applied for a permit to challenge the mighty Colorado. He treated himself to salmon fishing trips in Alaska and British Columbia, hunted pheasants in South Dakota, moose in Alberta, elk in Wyoming and mule deer in New Mexico. Every rapid he confronted, every animal he killed, every fish he caught, was nothing more than a shabby substitute for what he really wanted—to ride roundup, calve-out, brand, feed cows, bale hay—live on the Double X and be the boss of one of the biggest cattle outfits remaining in the Northwest.

XX

Donna was thankful she had Kendra in her life. Their relationship was more than mother-daughter. They were best friends too. While Donna and Cole ate dinner she made a stab at conversation, announcing, "Kendra's class is studying the Oregon Trail. They're planning to raise money for a field trip to the Interpretive Center at Baker City." As soon as the words were out of her mouth, she regretted saying them because she knew even the mere mention of Eastern Oregon caused Cole to think about the ranch. He hadn't returned his mother's phone call, and although Donna really wanted to know why he was putting it off, she didn't dare ask.

"Please pass the salad. So, ah, what's the fund-raiser?" said Cole.

"They decided on selling oranges."

Cole nodded, "Like Fred Meyer doesn't sell oranges?"

"These are special. Bigger. Sweeter. More expensive."

XX

Cole commented, "Good clam sauce, Hon. So what's your part in all this?"

"You're really not interested, are you?"

"Sure I am," shrugged Cole, but he really wasn't, and he was already allowing his mind to wander, organizing a list of what he needed to pull together because he was leaving early in the morning to fish the Wilson River for fall Chinook. With the recent rain he hoped the water was up a little and had good color. After dinner he'd call Jerry, his business partner who had fished the Wilson on Wednesday. Jerry would know.

Donna continued talking, telling Cole how much money the PTA planned to contribute, how much the kids were required to raise, and that she planned to chaperone the field trip to Baker City. Cole offered nothing in response. The silence stretched between them tight as a barbwire fence.

"Care for anything? More ice water?" asked Donna. She rose from her chair and moved toward the bottle of wine on the counter.

"No thanks," said Cole. He followed her with his eyes and what he accepted was the sight of a woman on a steady march toward middle age. She had recently announced she was contemplating going on a grapefruit diet. When she had asked him what he thought about it, he had told her, "That's fine." Later it came out she was upset with him because she wanted him to say she was perfect the way she was. Cole thought to himself, in such a situation, there was no way for him to prevail. He could not win with his wife, and he could not win with his daughter, who was no longer Daddy's little girl and had not been for what seemed like an eternity.

Cole finished eating, and as he pushed himself back from the table, he knew he and Donna needed to spend more time together. Not just a meal or an evening stolen from their predictable lives. He'd like to spend a week with her at a remote cabin, miles from electricity and telephones, where they could hike and fish and in the evenings cook dinner over a wood stove. On the other hand, he knew Donna would prefer to spend that same week at a luxury resort and fritter away the afternoons lounging by the pool, tanning and reading a good book. In the evenings she preferred to dress up and go somewhere fancy for dinner.

Cole reasoned it would be a good idea if he were to send flowers to his wife; better yet he should bring home a bouquet and surprise her. He was excited with the possibilities and thought he would do it tomorrow. Then he remembered he was going fishing in the morning. That thought brought to his mind his favorite spot on the Wilson River, just below the railroad trestle, and he saw in his mind the way the current came looping around a bend and dropped into a deep hole.

The last time he had been there he hooked a 32-inch steelhead so fresh from the ocean she still had sea lice clinging to her quicksilver sides.

He slowly became aware of Donna standing at the head of the table. Her hands were on her hips and she was leaning slightly forward in an aggressive manner, demanding to know, "Cole, have you heard a word I said?"

"I was thinking," he said, "that you and I really ought to get away next weekend, do something, just the two of us."

"Are you forgetting Kendra's volleyball tournament?" Her words carried an edge of impatience.

"Oh," said Cole. He knew if he stayed home next Saturday, he'd be in the dank gym. He was supportive of his daughter and tried to encourage her. At least he did when it was convenient for him. He helped clear the table, excused himself and went to the garage where he began putting rods, reels and tackle into his aluminum drift boat.

XX

Donna rinsed the dishes and placed them in the dishwasher. She listened to Cole moving things around in the garage and it sounded to her as though he was getting ready to go fishing. She remembered a particular incident at a cocktail party they had attended. Cole was talking to a group who had never been fishing and spent 30 minutes describing a particular spot he liked to fish on the Deschutes River, portraying in lively verbs and vivid adjectives how the sunlight sparkled and the riffle ran in varying shades of blues and greens. There was actual eagerness and enthusiasm in his voice.

"I fish a very light rod, a G-Loomis 10-foot, five-weight. A light rod makes you feel light. And when you see that silver flash of a steelhead, in the crystal clear water of the Deschutes, and he takes the offering you tied with your own two hands, I'm not kidding you one bit—takes your breath away—a pure shot of adrenalin."

Donna wanted to know why it was Cole did not get excited that way about her any more. She could not grasp the parallel lines, the threadlike intertwining and brittle divergence that existed between the thrill and challenge of hooking and landing a big fish on a hand-tied fly and the predictability of a stale marriage plodding along in a dull rut of indisputable sameness. She dried her hands, and before stepping into the living room to read the new John Grisham thriller—she was beginning chapter ten—she called into the garage, reminding Cole one last time, "Don't forget to call your mother."

CHAPTER FOUR

TY BATTLE WOULD HAVE BEEN THE PERFECT MOUNTAIN MAN, wandering from one stream to the next in search of beaver pelts and new territory. But he had been born more than a century too late to join Ashley and Henry and had instead become a modern-day drifter. He moved according to the season of the year and the availability of work: driving combine in Eastern Washington, mining in Nevada and again in the Badlands of South Dakota, selling windmills in Kansas, capturing wild mustangs in the Owyhee country, bucking hay bales, riding roundups, building fence and working cattle. He chased a vague dream that a new opportunity or a good-looking gal—one or the other and it didn't really matter which—awaited him on down the road, around the bend, over the next hill.

As Ty steered his two-toned, brown and tan Chevy pickup along a narrow ribbon of Idaho asphalt, he glanced out the cracked side-window, watching a V-wedge of Canada honkers move down the mottled gray sky. They were an uncompromising arrow pointed due south. Ty deduced these geese didn't need weather forecasts, detailed maps or any GPS bullshit to tell them where they were and where they were going. They relied on a natural, god-given sense of direction and a strong charge of wind under their wings. He grinned and thought he was like these high-flying geese, feeling uneasy as an early fall storm came sweeping down out of the north and migrating south—Nevada, Arizona, New Mexico—hell, he might even dip down into old Mexico and spend another winter lying around on an unsullied Baja beach, sipping pina coladas and feasting his hungry eyes on pretty senoritas frolicking in the surf.

When he returned his gaze to the highway it had begun to mist lightly. Up ahead a couple hundred yards, straddling the yellow center stripe, was a turkey vulture hunkered over a roadkill. It gave a nonchalant stare, ripped loose a piece of flesh from a flattened jackrabbit, and without seeming to hurry, hopped to the shoulder of the road. Here the big, homely bird made his stand, eyeing the approaching pickup with a cynical stare, turning his head as Ty passed. It seemed the bird knew that, a hundred miles down the road or a thousand miles down the road, he'd find Ty, nothing more than red meat on blacktop.

Gripping the wheel with one hand, Ty rolled up a sleeve of his work shirt, switched hands and rolled up the other. He wasn't wearing a watch and didn't give a shit about time. On the day he left the Double X ranch, departing in a seething cloud of angry dust, he tossed his watch out the window, and in all the intervening years, had never been tempted to replace it. He figured when he worked, he worked. That ball-buster of an old man who had raised him instilled that solitary principle in him. He remembered Frank grousing his advice, "When you take a job you give the man a full day's work for a day's pay. That way you never have to back up to the pay window."

Conversely, when Ty played, he put every last ounce of energy he possessed into having fun. His schedule of work and play left precious time for sleep. When Ty was young that didn't seem to matter, but he'd discovered that by the time a fellow tips the scale over thirty, he can't run as hard. And if he tries, he doesn't run near as long.

A couple times a year the lack of a watch caught up with Ty. He just couldn't grasp the concepts of springing forward or the falling back. If he were an hour late for work that was easy to fix, he'd work an extra hour, and if that didn't square things he'd draw his wages and head on down the road. Not that changing locations ever untangled what was wrong in his world. He had spent years staring down the road, and more than once, had seen his own reflection staring back.

On this day it seemed as though distance revealed itself in the methodical rhythm of spinning revolutions, miles added onto miles. Every mile headed south. He was jerked out of his spinning orbit of monotony as a copper-skinned Firebird, an older model with fading paint, came wheeling up from behind, pulled out and around his Chevy and stormed past in a sizzling torrent of speed and suddenness. Ty managed to catch a quick impression of the driver and what stuck with him was of white skin and flowing hair the color of a lion's mane. Definitely female.

The driver horsed the Firebird back into the right lane, and just like that she was gone, replaced by a fine mist that drifted back and caused Ty to turn on the wipers. They smeared the windshield glass, and he squinted at the mess while listening to the repetitive slap of wiper blades and the swish of wet tires. He checked the interior mirror in a vain search for answers as to why this gal, any gal, would pass him in such a rush. After all, he liked women; they typically sensed it and liked him back. He prided himself on the fact he was handsome enough to turn a pretty gal's head.

The face in the mirror had spent a lot of time feeling the bite of the hard wind and the sharp-edged shine of sunlight. The skin was a tad leathery and there were creases in the soft tissue at the corners of his eyes. The blue irises held about an equal amount of truth and regret. Ty broke into a grin and kidded himself the lines were smile-lines. He gave his reflection a carefree wink, licked his lips, rapped the glass with a knuckle and said aloud, "You handsome devil you: don't you ever die."

Ty wished he'd come to a town or at least a gas station with a convenience store. He could sure use a beer; in fact, several beers would kinda take the edge off the travel, grease the miles, make 'em slide under his belt a little easier. Before the sun was too far down, he wanted to be in Caldwell, a distant suburb of Boise. He was planning to spend the night with his best friend from back home who lived there.

Ty busied himself by visualizing his fingers wrapped around a cold bottle of beer and this triggered him to contemplate hangovers. He rarely got a hangover from drinking beer, sometimes from whiskey or tequila, but rarely from beer. Someone once told him a lack of hangovers was a bad sign because drinkers who didn't get hangovers were more prone to becoming alcoholics. He didn't want that to happen. The chance he could become an alcoholic scared the piss out of him. Every time he really started to consider he might be headed in that direction, he'd go on the wagon and not drink for a week or two, proving he was the one in charge. He believed he could walk away from alcohol any time he wanted, never look back, but of course he never did because beer joints and honkytonks were the parameters of his social life.

The road followed the shoreline of a lake. The wind had gotten the water all worked up—whitecaps danced across the pale turquoise sheen—and when Ty returned his attention to the highway he noticed fresh skid marks smeared across the surface and plunging off into gravel on the lake side. He let off on the gas and started through the gears, downshifting, allowing compression to do the braking. The Firebird was there, right side up, in the skinny strip between road and lake. It faced the road and was sitting at an awkward angle. A thin ribbon of steam rose from a busted radiator. A gal was perched on a corner of the hood. Her long tawny hair blew sideways in the wind.

Ty overshot the mark, finally stopped, backed up and swung onto the shoulder of the highway. He turned off the engine but it dieseled on fumes, shuddered and died of starvation. He kicked open the door, pulled free and began walking in the direction of the wreck. The gal had her knees hauled up to her chin and her face buried in her hands. Ty walked to her and stood. She was sobbing quietly into her open palms.

"You hurt?" he inquired.

She must have heard him approach because the sound of his voice did not startle her. She shook her head. The sobbing ended. She mumbled into her hands, "A little shook-up."

Ty removed the bandanna from around his neck. He offered it to her by laying it against the back of her hands, saying, "Could you use this, Ma'am?" She took it without looking at him and held the material to her eyes.

She was wearing a cotton blouse, lilac blue, and jeans, women's jeans that had sparkles sewn into the denim, and cowgirl boots. He could see she had attractive fingers and well-kept nails, but not exceptionally long nails like pampered women tend to cultivate. Her blond hair was a windblown mess and when she finally did look up, Ty saw a pretty face with eyes the color of emeralds, lips full and plump with refreshing little upturned creases at the corners of her mouth. Her nose, although a little too long for her face, was her cutest feature because freckles were speckled across it, splashing onto her cheeks. Her skin held a lingering trace of summer's sun.

Ty guessed she was his age or a year or two older, mid-thirties, most likely. In some indistinguishable way she reminded him of that actress, the one who stole the car and tried to outrun the cops, what the hell was her name? He could see her face, although if memory served him she had been a redhead, and so he dismissed the association as quickly as it had occurred to him. He swung himself up and onto the hood and sat beside the woman.

XX

Her first impression of the Good Samaritan, this woman who had a face as distinctive as an actress, was a tear-smeared visual of a man with boyish good looks, wearing clothes that had a comfortable, lived-in look: faded jeans and plaid work shirt, sleeves rolled up. He was tall and rangy, a cowboy from the looks of his soiled cowboy hat, but oddly, he wasn't wearing cowboy boots. If she had chosen to break the ice by asking him why, Ty probably would have explained to her that a workingman wears lace-up work boots, buckaroos and truck drivers wear cowboy boots.

She felt kindly toward this stranger for a number of reasons. Obviously, he had stopped to lend assistance, but also he had been so kind and patient, offering his kerchief and sitting with her until she finished her cry. And yet she was guardedly aware of a sixth-sense, a suspicion, that led her to believe he might also be a little risky—like the red paper on an old stick of dynamite, the way it curls around the edges and hints at unpredictability. But what the hell, she wasn't intimidated easily and besides, a slightly volatile man held a certain appeal. It always had for her.

Having finished her cry she regained her toughness and handed Ty back his kerchief, offering, "Sorry 'bout that."

Ty, feeling the damp fabric with his fingertips, said, "Nothin' to be sorry about, it'll dry." He wrapped the bandanna around his neck, tied a knot, and in the wind, his neck felt simultaneously warm and yet cool. He sensed a sudden closeness with this woman.

"Goin' a little fast, I'd say."

"Reckon so," she muttered.

"You came around me like a bat out of hell. Goin' to a fire?"

She flashed a grin, showing straight teeth. "Fellow at a gas station up in Jackson Hole said I needed shocks. Figured he was either trying to get into my wallet or my pants. Brushed him off. Next time I'll pay a little more attention to free advice."

Ty was curious. "Where you headed?"

"Boise."

"Job or family?"

"Figured Boise was good as anywhere."

"Guess so," said Ty. He introduced himself and held out his hand. She took it and said, "Tracee."

"Tracee," repeated Ty. "Tracee, with no last name."

She nodded.

He mused aloud, "A gal who likes to keep herself at arm's distance. Interesting, maybe, but not very friendly."

She ignored his comment and thanked him for stopping.

"Sure thing," said Ty, sliding off the hood, standing and stretching. If he did not move every so often his back stiffened. The only way he could unlimber was to have a chiropractor realign him. That was forty bucks down the drain. He'd much rather spend the money on beer or gasoline. When he finished the stretch, he returned to his normal posture, slouching slightly, thumbs tucked into his belt, fingers making an oval frame around a silver buckle with a golden bucking horse.

Tracee noticed. "You rodeo?"

"Done a little. Never was all that serious. Hit a few jackpot shows. Won some day money, couple buckles. Never one to try and hit the big lick, go on the circuit, anything like that." Ty glanced at the buckle and down beyond to his Levi's. He saw a reminder of where, at his last job, the barbwire he had been stretching ripped a gash in the fabric just above his knee. He wore Levi's because he preferred buttons. They were safe. Not like Wranglers with a zipper that could rip off a man's dick.

Tracee ran her fingers through her long hair, attempting to untangle it, but the wind made that impossible. She gave up and turned her attention elsewhere, patting an open palm against the hood of the Firebird. "Think it can be fixed?"

Ty looked at the path leading from the car to the road, taking notice of the streak of paint and conspicuous scrapes across the surface of rocks and fair-sized boulders. He tilted his head and arched an eyebrow in an effort to give an exaggerated visual appraisal of the car. He breathed in a combination of antifreeze and hot oil. He shook his head. "If I was to make an educated guess, I'd say you got yourself a busted radiator and a broken oil pan, most likely a bent frame, trashed motor mounts, rear end's history and the tranny's wrecked to hell and gone. If I owned the son-of-a-bitch I'd pull the plates and registration, take what I could carry, leave the rest to rust."

Tracee gave an exaggerated laugh, slapped her thigh and exclaimed, "Then by God, that's just what I'll do." She slid off the hood, took hold of Ty by the arm and purred, "How 'bout it, cowboy, wanna give this girl a ride to Boise?"

Ty acted painfully shy, "I don't know you very well, Miss Tracee with no last name."

"Well," she said mischievously, "I got a case of beer in the trunk—twenty-four temptations to help pay my way. Besides, I'll help you drink 'em."

Ty responded immediately, "Deal." He said the word with authority, the way he might instruct a man shuffling cards to include him in the game. And, in a way, that was exactly what he was doing. Including himself in the game.

Ty rolled down the window, and with an expertise that comes from years of practice, deftly tossed a pair of empty bottles—one after the other without breaking either—into the bed of his truck. Tracee pulled a tall-boy from the open case on the floor at her feet. Using the tail of her blouse for leverage she twisted off the cap and handed the bottle to Ty, repeating the process, and when she finished, she stuffed her loose blouse down the front of her jeans. Ty eyed the maneuver. It made him grateful for times like this, and for all the first-class moments in his life that involved fun-loving girls, golden sunsets, happy laughter, cold beer, and some decent runs of luck. Watching the fabric disappear into the waist of her jeans suggested to Ty this might be the start of a hot streak. Anyway he was feeling pretty damned lucky.

Tracee turned, brought a leg up and tucked it under her round rump. She said, "So, from what you've said, sounds like you've tried your hand at a lot of things and never stuck with any one thing in particular. Ever suppose if you had, you'd be a millionaire by now?"

"Don't interest me," said Ty.

"What?"

"Being a millionaire."

"Why not?"

Ty, while tipping the bottle to his lips, contemplated the question. He allowed the cold liquid to slide down his throat and found he couldn't come up with a ready answer.

Tracee, thinking she was being perceptive, said, "What are you running from?"

He lowered the bottle and licked his lips. "I ain't running from nothin'."

"Well then?"

"It's been my experience, money only ties a fellow down. I like my freedom way too much to sell out for cash, not even a million bucks."

They passed a farmhouse. A woman was hanging clothes on a line. Ty pictured Tracee there, in a pale dress, holding wooden clothespins in her mouth, stooping, lifting, pinning frilly panties on a sagging clothesline. He abruptly announced, "If we come to a likely spot, I'm gonna stop. I'll spring for dinner. You hungry?"

"Yeah, I could probably eat," she said. "But I pay my own way."

"Miss Tracee, I can tell from our conversation you're an independent gal. I admire that in a woman. Now, you may be used to standing on your own two feet, but I'm the one who asked you to join me for dinner. I'll take care of the bill."

She flirted a little, smiling and batting her eyelashes.

He patted the seat beside him. "Wanna slide over here close? Play like I just picked you up from your momma's house and we're fixin' to go see a movie at the drive-in picture show. We'll get a tub of buttered popcorn, a coke and a bag of Whoppers."

"A real date? I don't think so," Tracee said, acting more bashful than she had intended. The beer made her want to giggle.

"You mean you're the type of gal who climbs in a rig with a stranger, drinks beer with him, talks his ear off, laughs, jokes and has a grand ol' time of it, but your strict sense of morality doesn't allow you to slide over a tad and sit next to him?"

Dragging out the words and being silly, she said, "Maybe I will, after I get to know you a little better." She lit a cigarette, puffed it, eyed Ty and had more than a hunch he was the type who devoted a substantial amount of energy to the fine art of gentle seduction. This wasn't a negative, not in her mind, because she enjoyed playing the game, knowing full well the predictable progression of words and actions, and that sex would be the end result. Then she smiled as she reminded herself she was only catching a ride with this stranger. But Tracee was never quite sure what she might do if the mood, or the man, struck her fancy.

"What you smiling at?" asked Ty.

"Nothing," said Tracee. But she was imagining herself in bed with Ty.

The moon emerged and played peek-a-boo between storm clouds. Ty and Tracee rode along through the thick of the evening, drinking beer and talking casually until, finally, the pickup's headlights flashed across a sign advertising, *"Paradise Bar & Grill – Best Steaks in the West."*

"Jesus H. Christ! About time," said Ty. "My stomach was beginning to think my throat had been slashed." He guided the pickup off the highway and down an oiled road, pulling to a stop in front of a board-and-batten building with a wide porch and a tall false front. A number of haphazardly parked pickup trucks and a few cars were strewn around the parking lot.

Tracee asked Ty to turn on the dome light. She fished a pink ribbon from her purse, and using the light and the interior mirror, tied back her hair and applied a thin layer of red to her lips. Ty went to the back of the truck, took a leak and stepped around and opened the passenger's door. He took Tracee by the arm and escorted her the short distance to the steps, up onto the porch and through the wooden door.

The interior of the Paradise Bar & Grill was divided into two main rooms with a kitchen scabbed on the back. The small dining room, a place where out-of-towners could sit and enjoy a meal, was dimly lit with glowing candles in red glass containers at every table. The other room—dominated by a cherry wood back bar that the owner was fond to brag had, "Come 'round the Horn in 18 and 77, brought up the Columbia River to Umatilla Landing and hauled 300 miles across the mountains and over the desert by wagon to get here,"—was a smoke-filled cavern where locals congregated to drink and shoot pool. A number of professional alcoholics were sprinkled along the historic bar while two men wearing ball caps advertising fertilizer companies shot nine-ball on a pool table.

Ty nodded toward the bar, visible through a set of swinging double doors, and announced, "We eat in there, they'll wanna serve us greasy burgers or pizza, but that sign out front, 'Best Steaks in the West,' gave me a hankerin' for a big, fat, juicy steak. What say, Miss Tracee, we just stay here in the dining room and have steak?" She concurred with a willing nod.

They were the only customers in the dining room. Ty pulled a chair away from a table and held it for Tracee. He removed his hat, dropped it crown down onto a free chair and sat across from her, inquiring, "What cut do you prefer—New York or a filet?"

"Doesn't much matter to me," said Tracee. "I'm so hungry I could eat a horse."

The waitress, menus clutched to her chest, appeared. Ty ordered a couple beers. When she attempted to hand him a menu, he waved it off. "We can dispense with those, Ma'am. Just tell me, what's your best cut?"

"Depends," said the waitress. It was obvious from her demeanor she had been slinging hash for more years than she cared to remember. Now she just put in her time, and at the end of her shift, methodically counted the money in her tip jar, went home and put her feet up on an ottoman.

"Well," drawled Ty, "I like meat that's thick, well-aged, a good bit of marbling but not a lot of fat. That's how I like it."

"New York then. Just got 'em in today," the waitress said. "So mister, you a butcher or a cattleman?"

"Neither," said Ty. He was looking directly at Tracee and a smile was beginning to spread across his lips. "I'm just a man who knows what he likes."

"How'd you want it cooked?"

Ty abdicated to Tracee, indicating he was going out of his way to be a gentleman. She responded, "Medium, medium rare."

Using a stubby pencil, the waitress made a notation on her pad and asked if Tracee wanted soup, navy bean, or a tossed green salad, and did she want her potato mashed, baked or fried? Tracee wanted the salad, ranch dressing, and a baked potato.

"Sour cream and chives?"

"Please."

Without waiting for the waitress to recite the stock questions Ty told her, "Kill it, pass it over the fire, everything else the same as what the lady's having."

The waitress did more scribbling and exited, passing through the double doors into the bar. She came back a few moments later, carrying a tray with two beers in frosted mugs. Sounds from the bar were audible. Snippets of Elvis's velvety voice crooned, *"Are you lonesome tonight? Do you miss me tonight? Are you sorry we drifted apart?"* Glasses clinked against the bar. The cue ball caromed off a sloppy rack and into a side pocket. A man cussed, "Goddamn it!"

Ty took a sip of beer and eyed Tracee. Her face was giving off a ruddy glow. He thought it was probably from being in the wind or maybe the beer. Either way he liked it because it made her freckles stand out all the more. Already he found he was fond of these freckles, and enjoyed the way her hair was gathered in a ponytail, away from her face. She looked pretty. He leaned forward and told her so.

Tracee smiled. “Thank you.”

“I wouldn’t say it if it wasn’t true. One thing about me, I’m always brutally honest.”

“I believe you.”

“And you know, it’s a pleasure to find a gal who can take a compliment.”

“You dish out a lot?”

“Only when they’re warranted. Most gals, you compliment them, and they make some lame excuse why they don’t look better. I like it when....”

The waitress set a plate of chilled vegetables, surrounding a small bowl of ranch dressing, on the table midway between Ty and Tracee and gave a perfunctory, “Enjoy,” as she spun on the balls of her tired feet and departed.

“God I hate it when a waitress says that. ‘Enjoy!’ Hells bells, of course I’m gonna enjoy. I’m the one starving.”

Tracee put her hand over Ty’s hand. She smiled, “No need to get worked up. Relax, Honey.”

Ty’s anger dissipated like steam from an opened pot and he shrugged, “I’m hungry, that’s all. Hey, Babe, we havin’ fun yet?”

Tracee slathered a mushroom in the white sauce and popped it into her mouth. She chewed a few times, swallowed, lifted one eyebrow and said, “I am. How ’bout you?”

Ty bit into a piece of crisp celery. It broke with a sharp snap. He talked around the bite. “’Bout as much fun as two people can have with their clothes on.” He toasted her with his mug, “Well, here’s to whatever’s down the road.”

“To the road,” she echoed. They chewed and drank.

The waitress brought the salads and finally the dinners. The meat sizzled and she cautioned, “Careful. Hot.”

Ty reached for his fork and knife. He closed his eyes as he breathed in, savoring the tantalizing aroma of cooked meat.

He opened his eyes and said to Tracee, "I feel like a film crew should be here shooting this for an upcoming segment of, *Lifestyles of the Rich and Famous.*"

As they were nearing the last of their meals, the waitress inquired if she could get them dessert. Ty patted his belly and said, "Not for me. I'm stuffed." He nodded in Tracee's direction. She shook her head and chewed her final bite.

The waitress laid the bill on the table. Ty leaned to one side and pulled a money clip from his pocket. The clip gave the appearance of pounded gold nuggets but actually it was brass with a thin plating of gold. Brass showed through in several spots. Ty checked the tab, peeled off several bills and laid the money on the table. Then he led the way to the big room where he ordered another round of beer. He asked Tracee, "Wanna shoot some pool?"

"I'm not very good," she replied.

"Don't matter," he said, strolling to the pool table. He lay quarters along the rail. The locals had just completed their game. They looked at Ty as if he had committed some terrible indiscretion. He smoothed it over, saying, "Mind if the lady and I challenge?"

The two men turned their attention toward Tracee and watched as she swung her bottom up and onto a high stool. One of the men grinned and said, "Sure, we'll shoot ya-all a game."

The first game was played for fun: all the others, four more, for money. Five bucks a rack. Tracee managed to knock a few balls down but it was Ty who won the games. He was the type of player who, if the competition presented him with the slightest opening, could, and would, run the table. On the last rack he broke, shot all the striped balls, the eight, and then ran the solids in descending order, calling the number of banks and the pocket as he walked around the table chalking his cue.

As they exited the Paradise Bar & Grill, Tracee playfully punched Ty in the ribs and said, "You're a showoff."

He laughed and pressed two five-dollar bills into her hand. "Your cut of the hustle," he said. She protested, but allowed him to tuck the bills in her hind pocket as they hurried toward the truck.

A cool, hard-driving rain was coming down, threatening to turn to snow before morning. While waiting for the defroster to clear the foggy window, Ty asked, "Wanna buck this storm or catch a room?"

"What do you want?"

"I'm in no special hurry. Catch a room, I guess."

Tracee slid over next to him, pulled the knot on the ribbon and shook her hair free. "I don't know you all that well but suppose I can trust you as much as any man."

Normally, when on the road, Ty saved money and slept in his truck. But this night he stopped at the Best Western on the freeway exit at Burley and got a room. He pulled a small overnight case from under the tarp in the bed of his pickup and handed it to Tracee, asking if she needed her suitcase, too. She said she didn't. He grabbed his canvas war-bag and what was left of the case of beer and led the way upstairs to the room. Once inside, he turned up the thermostat and flipped on the television. Tracee ducked into the bathroom. When she came out, Ty was sitting on the edge of the bed with two beers open and waiting. He handed her one and proceeded to play with the remote, flipping through channels, looking for something, anything, that might prove to be halfway interesting. Tracee sat beside him, their sides almost touching but not quite. They sipped beer, jumped back and forth between David Letterman and bull riding, and talked during commercials.

After finishing her beer, Tracee excused herself, took her overnight case and stepped into the bathroom. After a few minutes, Ty depressed the orange power button on the remote. The sound died immediately and the picture winked off, but the screen glowed for a long moment. He lay back on the bed with a satisfying groan and listened to the shower in the other room. He visualized hot water streaming over white skin, water bumping over breasts and the ridges of ribs, traversing taut stomach muscles, gravity dragging water down, down long, shapely legs. In that instant, Ty felt absolutely right with the world. He was happy to be sharing a room, and a bed, with a woman he scarcely knew. For him there was no past, only this sliver of time in the present and the growing anticipation of what was to come.

As he waited, Ty felt a pressure in his groin begin to build for the want of this gal. Just when he thought he could wait no longer, the bathroom door swung open and Tracee appeared like a lovely butterfly emerging from the confines of its drab cocoon. She was wearing an oversized T-shirt with a San Francisco 49ers logo emblazoned on the front. She did a quick pirouette for Ty's benefit. The shirt adequately covered her nakedness but, on the bottom, the margin of error was exceedingly slim.

Ty grinned. "Niners never looked so good." He beckoned her, "Come here, woman." He wanted to watch her cross the room and see the way the parts of her body moved independently and yet were connected in a swaying swirl of erotic motion. But she stood transfixed in the doorway, not moving, eyeing him. Ty wasn't sure where it was coming from but felt a sudden coolness come over the room.

XX

Tracee, naked under the smooth cotton knit jersey, in a motel room along the interstate, with yet another stranger, felt a ripple of awkward embarrassment, vulnerability, sadness, something, and told herself if she could summon the willpower she'd get dressed and leave this place with some shred of dignity and pride still intact. Who was she kidding?

XX

Ty got up off the bed, went to Tracee, pulled away from her face a few loose strands of wet hair, bent and tenderly kissed the V-spot where neck melted into shoulder. He felt the warmness of her skin, smelled the heady fragrance of freshly applied perfume, sensed the hard thumping of a runaway heart, and just below the surface, the long muscles of her sensuous neck fluttered and twitched. He took all these as positive signs of impulsive acceptance and steadily worked his way upward until at last, he took an earlobe in his teeth and began nibbling it. One hand remained at the small of her back. The other traced a passage up her spine. His fingers found, and intertwined themselves in the long strands of her damp hair. He pulled back and kissed Tracee on the lips. Her muscles went slack, eyes snapped closed and any lingering effects of reluctance on her part seemed to melt away like soft steel under the heat of a welder's torch. Ty eased her toward the bed, laid her gently down and quickly got out of his clothes.

Tracee's sexual awakening occurred the summer she turned 16. Her mother worked swing shift at the plywood plant. Her stepfather, having lost his job, mostly sulked around the house and acted strangely any time Tracee was alone with him—stopping whatever he was doing to watch her walk across a room, patting the cushion beside him on the couch when he was watching television wanting her to sit with him, tickling her when they passed in the hall, sneaking up behind her when she washed dishes and trying to hug her. He gave Tracee the creeps and she tried to avoid him. The bulk of her time she spent with a boy from school who worked pumping gas at the Union 76 station. They talked and played cards between customers. After his shift ended they'd usually walk to the football field, lie on the grass, gaze at the stars and kiss. Sometimes she allowed the boy to feel her up but she was deathly afraid of becoming pregnant, and for the longest time, refused to have sex with him. And then, one evening before his shift was over, she went to the restroom and bought a condom.

Tracee had sex with the boy, not for love, uncontrollable lust, or even a sense of obligation, but merely out of curiosity. She wanted to know what it felt like to have him inside her. What surprised her most about the experience was, in the heat of his climax, how much wild, animalistic passion he exhibited. And then it was over. They got dressed. He made some lame excuse and left. She lay there alone, on the fifty-yard line, under the canopy of twinkling stars, the cool, moist grass pressing against her backside and for the longest time she could still feel where the boy had been between her legs and smell the faint residue of gasoline contaminating her skin.

After that experience, Tracee was driven to seek encounters with other schoolboys. The driving force, whether she admitted it or not, was her desire to be needed by a guy. Tracee's father had abandoned his family when she was five, and after that there had been a steady string of men her mother paraded through the house to her bedroom. Then she got remarried and that man proved to be a piece of work, a pervert who wanted to diddle his own stepdaughter.

On the day she graduated from high school Tracee left home. She continued hopping in bed with men, men she hardly knew, doing it for the same reason she had engaged in sex with boys. But now she often blamed her loose morals on alcohol, or marijuana, or cocaine, or loneliness. Each man, to get inside her cheap cotton blouse and tight fitting jeans, fed her ego, telling her she was beautiful, wonderful and sexy. In turn, she pleasured each of them in the vain hope that when the frenzy of the moment was spent, there would be something worthwhile, something lasting: a sense of fulfillment, acceptance and love, for her to hold on to. There never was.

Once Tracee thought she found someone special and married the man. His name was Jeremy. He was the manager of a Subaru dealership. But after less than a year Jeremy came home and announced his secretary understood him way better than Tracee ever could. He moved in with his secretary. When that affair cooled Jeremy came crawling home, begging Tracee to forgive him and take him back, and regrettably, she did just that. Tracee became pregnant. Her husband left again, this time running off with a girl from Seattle he had met in a bar. Tracee had the kid, a boy she named Stormy.

And now Tracee found herself in the Burley Inn Best Western Motel, crawling under the sheets with yet another man. She found herself somewhere between giving in to the pleasures of sexual indulgence and having the strength to stop this headlong plunge. She felt the warmth of Ty's lips, and they certainly did excite her. His hands slid under her T-shirt, touched her breasts, squeezing, kneading, the nipples crushing under his thumbs and forefingers. She was tempted all the more.

She knew this man was hungry to have her. She wanted him too, and yet, some shred of moral courage came to the forefront. She told herself she couldn't keep doing this, giving herself to every man she met, and if she did, she acknowledged she would, after it was over, once again feel cheap, used and ashamed of herself.

Just before she was swept away by his appetite for fulfillment, she began to summon every bit of strength she could muster, every atom of resoluteness and determination she possessed, to push him away and save herself. She cried out, "I can't!" Tears cascaded down her warm cheeks. "I just can't."

A distance opened between the man and woman in the bed, a distance that lasted only an instant, and then Tracee threw herself at Ty like she was a drowning victim and he was her savior. She encircled him with her arms and legs and sobbed violently onto his bare chest. Outside the wind blew harder, drew back and tried again to blow the building down. Hail pinged against the window.

Ty didn't know how he was supposed to respond. He had been with hundreds of women and none had ever reacted to the prospect of lovemaking in such an emotional manner. Tracee's salty tears, like incriminating accusations, collided against his bare chest. All he could think was this was a married woman and that she had suddenly been struck with a sense of tremendous guilt and shame.

The act itself, sex, was not something Ty placed a particularly high value on. Either a guy got it, or he didn't. And now he lay in this motel bed wondering if he should maybe not be remorseful for every meaningless dalliance he had engaged in without having given the least bit of consideration to his partner and her feelings. Almost as soon as it hit him, he abandoned the idea. After all, he was well-practiced at the casual bonding of recreational sex, and in his mind there should be no more meaning attached to it than a bull breeding a cow on the open range.

Tracee held onto Ty until gradually her violent quaking subsided and then she rolled onto her back. He leaned toward her, held her face in his calloused hands and began to soothingly kiss away her tears. She eagerly accepted this display of tenderness and, in time, repaid it with an affectionate kiss of her own.

The consequence of this kiss was both miraculous and intimidating. One moment she was limp to his touch and the next leaning into him, grinding against him with desire, sharing an urgency neither of them could have anticipated or prepared themselves for. It was Ty who broke away. He held her at arm's length and looked at her tenderly. In response she sat up, pulled the flimsy T-shirt over her head, tossed the garment onto the floor and lay back on the bed to receive him.

Light filtered into the room from the bathroom, illuminating golden freckles splashed between full breasts. Dark nipples stood as stark contradictions against the pink blush of the surrounding skin. And when Ty looked into Tracee's green eyes he saw only her unreserved acceptance, and he leaned forward and flicked his tongue over a nipple. It immediately stiffened and as a shiver raced the length of Tracee's spine, she gave a little gasp. Unspoken lies passed between the two of them: there were to be no consequences, no permanence, no right or wrong, only this precarious sliver of time and the insatiable appetite they held for each other.

Ty rolled on top and thrust himself inside her. Their hips began a slow dance, in perfect unison, and while the tempo was establishing itself, Tracee kept her eyes open and intently watched Ty's changing facial expressions, from a near grimace to one of infinite pleasure. He moved with proficient purpose, did not hurry, and as the clock on the nightstand decisively celebrated each passing second, she found herself going to a place she hardly ever visited. Blood rushed to her core and she sensed the weightiness of it there, the delicious feel of expanding warmth. She allowed herself to be swept away in the hard charging current of her impending climax as she felt him grow longer and thicker inside her body. She tumbled over the edge, arching her back, thrusting forward and elevating her pelvis to receive him even deeper, digging fingernails into the soft tissue on the sides of his back, moaning and finally screaming aloud with rowdy shrieks of pleasure.

Only after she had passed the apex, and was gradually sliding down the incline toward normalcy, was she aware of her lover as he rolled off to one side. She reached a hand to stroke his hair and face, whispering, repeating over and over again, "Oh, my god! Oh, my god! Oh, my god." Finally, speaking slowly, breathlessly enunciating each word, she acknowledged, "That was absolutely fantastic."

They lay together in the dim light, listening to each other's raspy breathing, and the wind moaned around the eaves as the full fury of the fall storm hit, rattling the window glass and causing the door to bang against the jamb.

By morning the storm had blown itself out. Tracee awoke and Ty was not there. She immediately castigated herself for having chosen wrong, once again, in a lifetime of wrong choices. Then she noticed the canvas bag on the chair by the bed and heard the scuffing of boots outside on the walkway. She pulled the top sheet loose, wrapped it around her nakedness and eased back a corner of the curtain. Ty was standing there trying to balance white Styrofoam cups with steam rising from them while digging in his pocket for the room key. She opened the door and stood mostly behind it.

"Morning," she said, trying to make her voice sound light and airy.

"Mornin' back at you," said Ty. He stepped through the doorway, handed her one of the coffees, dug in the pocket of his vest, produced packets of sugar and powdered cream and offered them to Tracee. "Didn't know if you doctor it or not," he said.

"Thanks. Black's fine." She stood on her tiptoes to plant a kiss on his cheek and returned to the bed, drawing the sheet tightly around her. Ty followed, sat beside her, asked a little self-consciously, "How you feelin' this morning?"

She beamed. "Wonderful."

He surveyed her, announced, "Some gals need time in the morning to look presentable, but you look great just the way you are."

"Doubt that," she countered.

"Hey, you took compliments a whole lot better last night."

"Maybe you were more sincere last night."

"Naw, just horny," he told her and laughed.

She made a playful swing at him, spilled coffee down her front and gave a gasp and a yelp. Ty took her coffee away and set it on the television. He grabbed a towel, pulled the sheet away from her and dabbed at the brown liquid. A few moments later they were having sex.

Xx

Ty awoke for the second time that morning to find Tracee nestled in the sheltered crook of his arm. He could feel all the wonderful points of contact where her body touched his—her face on his chest, the way one of her breasts was pressed into his side, the soft texture of her belly lying against his hip, the searing heat of her inner thigh cocked over his leg—and while he could take pleasure in the sensations there was a force at work inside him telling him to get up, get dressed and get the hell out of there.

Normally, the fear of even a casual commitment drove Ty away like a thief in the night, but he found himself content to lie quietly beside Tracee, so as not to wake her, while trying to make some kind of sense out of their lovemaking: the contrast of her guilt and her passion, her tears of unhappiness and her tears of joy. Making love to Tracee had been like walking across Death Valley followed by dancing on the summit of Mount Everest. He questioned whether she was like that with every man, or was he something special?

Xx

Tracee was awake but refused to open her eyes, figuring why take a chance on spoiling this warm sea of satisfaction where she found herself floating. She lay concentrating on the thunder of Ty's heart and the sounds of blood being driven through his arteries, looping around and returning in veins to be recharged with oxygen. She dwelled on the memories of his kisses and how his tenderness had consumed her. She thought there had never been anyone as sensitive, as gentle, as attuned to her and her needs as he had been. But still the question nagged her; was she making the right choice? One part of her said yes, but another part knew better.

Ty took a quick glance backward, through the open doorway, at the bed. The sheets and blankets were tossed in a heap on the floor. He flipped the key on the mattress and pulled the door shut with finality. They had stayed thirty minutes past check out. As he came down the stairs and headed toward his pickup, Ty reminded himself that whatever happened in the past, no matter how enjoyable it might have been, was in the past.

Out on the road the wipers had a hard time keeping up as a curtain of rain descended from a cloud as thick and lightly colored as alkali soil. In less than a dozen miles the cloud wore thin and bands of brilliant yellow sunlight splayed through the moisture and turned the muted grays and browns of the landscape into a vivid panorama of lively colors. Ty drove with one hand on the wheel, the other resting on Tracee's thigh. She scooted to the far side, cracking the passenger window and lit a cigarette. She proceeded to indulge herself, blowing swirls of smoke out the narrow opening.

"You don't smoke all that much," stated Ty.

"No, not really," said Tracee. "And when this pack's finished, so am I. It's a nasty habit. I'm sorry I ever started."

"You been quittin' for a while?"

"Most all my life, it seems. Picked it up when I was 16. Anymore, it doesn't give me much pleasure. Usually smoke when I'm either happy or sad."

"Which are you now?"

"Little of both."

"Why?"

Tracee did not answer right away. She finished her cigarette, tossed the butt out the window and scooted over near him. His right hand, once again, automatically went to her thigh, and he began massaging the familiar contours.

"The why is probably more than I care to get into at this particular point."

"Okay, I understand."

"Understand what?"

Ty forced a smile. "You were a little emotional back there, in the motel. And, if I'm reading you right, you probably don't want me to think you hop in the sack with every Tom, Dick and Harry who picks you up alongside the road."

"Wipe that smirk off your face," said Tracee.

Ty turned, raised his eyebrows, looked at her and knew better than to say anything more.

Tracee scooted away from him and went on. "You don't know shit about me or what I think."

"Whoa there, Princess," said Ty, feeling as though he had to defend himself. "Don't get yourself worked into a lather. I was just kidding."

"You couldn't handle the truth."

"I'm a big boy."

"Well then, let's just see.... Maybe I was sad because I know what's gonna happen. You'll drop me off in Boise and that's the end of the story. Or, you might swing by in six months, or a year, and you'll remember what we did and want another roll in the hay."

"What's the problem with that?" said Ty.

"I felt we had... a special... something... that you.... Just forget it." She stopped talking, slid as far away from him as she could get, lit another cigarette and smoked it. The engine purred contently and the spinning tires whooshed against the damp asphalt. A magpie flew in front of them and a semi passed in a swirl of wind that provoked even more misconceptions and half-truths.

Ty thought he might want to talk, but was finding it difficult to separate what he had to say, and his intentions, from the irrelevance of what he considered nothing more than acrid corral dust. When the dust began to settle, he cleared his throat.

"I've enjoyed being with you, your company. We had a fantastic time last night, and again this morning, too. Anyway, I did. I'm not trying to speak for you. But it seemed like you had a good time. What I'm trying to say, I suppose, is that I don't want to just drop you off and take a chance of never seeing you again." He allowed the words to tumble into a canyon of silence and lay fallow for a good long while. "On the other hand, I do value my freedom. I don't want you, or anyone, to make me feel like I've got hobbles on. I can't. I don't. Hell, I guess what I'm trying to say is, if you want to stick with me we can go on down the road together for a ways. No strings attached."

Tracee laughed.

"What's so goddamn funny?"

"You are," she said. "At the restaurant you were such a silver-tongued devil, and when you got me in bed you said all the right things, and now, now...."

"I stumble around like a one-legged man in a china shop, bumping into things and knocking china left and right," interjected Ty. He was laughing. They were laughing. When the laughter ran its course, he asked her, "So, wanna ride with me for a while?"

"Where you headed?"

"Arizona. New Mexico. Old Mexico. Somewhere warm."

"Suits me," said Tracee, but the smile faded. "One little problem. I want you to know I never lied to you, but I didn't quite tell the truth, either." She removed a Kleenex from her pocket and began twisting it into a tightly wound rope. "The reason I was going to Boise was to see my boy. He's five years old. His name's Stormy. You'd get a kick out of him. He's the cutest kid." She was looking directly at Ty, trying to get a read, but his face was as blank as a hunk of common slate.

"What's your last name?"

"Coleman," she said, and her voice sounded far away.

"So, Tracee Coleman, why didn't you tell me about your kid?"

"We were having fun. Just never got around to it."

"Who takes care of him?"

"Momma does."

"When we get to Mountain Home we'll stop, and I want you to give her a call," Ty said. "We'll swing by, see your boy. After that, you make the decision. It's up to you. Do what you gotta do. I'll understand."

Linda, a relatively young but tired-looking grandmother, stood washing endless circles on a clean plate. She watched Stormy through the wavy window glass playing in the trailer court driveway. He was decked out in the gunfighter outfit Tracee had bought him. His six-shooters were slung low on his five-year-old hips. A red straw cowboy hat with a fancy chinstrap shaded his steely-green eyes. He was facing off against Ty. They were engaged in what could pass as a re-enactment of the shootout at the OK Corral.

Stormy drew his toy revolvers and gunned down Ty in a merciless barrage of make-believe bullets. Ty stumbled sideways, clutched at his heart, fell to the little patch of grass that passed as a yard and lay twitching in pretend death. Stormy jumped up and down in glee, becoming so excited he peed his pants.

Linda rinsed the plate with hot water, placed it on the dish rack and proceeded to dry her hands on her red-and-white checkered apron. She blew back a hank of loose hair from her face and turned toward Tracee. "Where did you pick up this one?"

"Why do you always have to be so negative?" Tracee scooted the chair away from the kitchen table. "The long and short of it is I stopped by to see Stormy, and I wanted us to talk. I don't wanna fight. Can't we ever see each other without fighting?"

"Where you and this fella headed?"

"South."

"Takin' the boy?"

"Don't think so. Not right now."

"What you gonna do?"

"Get somewhere warm."

"How's he make a livin'?"

"He can do 'bout anything."

"Sounds like the last one, and the one before that, and.... None of your men friends ever got a regular profession. Closest you come was that husband, the one who left you. And the mechanic, the one who beat you."

Tracee abruptly stood, placed both hands on her hips and lifted her elbows. Her electric green eyes flashed. "God-damn-it! Stop it! He treats me good, Momma."

Hostility, like a thin, taut band connected them. The clock over the stove counted measured beats. Tracee broke the tension by turning away, crossing the room and plopping down on the sofa. It was Linda who, at length, picked up the conversation. She asked, "Been with him long?"

Tracee pouted. "Does it really matter?"

"The way I figure it, the two of you just met up."

Tracee blew air into her cheeks.

"Looks a little young for you."

"He ain't," said Tracee.

"What, five, six years difference?"

"Try one or two."

"He have a name?"

"Ty Battle."

"Sounds like a rodeo rider."

Tracee heaved an exaggerated sigh.

"Now, if memory serves me, you had yourself a bronc rider, had a bull rider, too," said Linda. "This one must be a team roper. Header or heeler?"

"I ain't gonna play your game, Momma. And I'm not gonna get mad neither, no matter what you say."

"Your track record with men ain't all that good."

"Yours either, Momma," said Tracee, her face reddening. "How many times you been married? Five I know about."

"We ain't talkin' 'bout me, we're talkin' 'bout you, darlin'," said Linda, and then the fake smile she was wearing, and her vindictiveness, suddenly melted away to nothing. "I just hope to hell this one treats you better than the others have."

"He will, Momma." Tracee got up off the ratty sofa, went to her mother and gave her a one-armed hug. "We gotta get goin'. Take care of Stormy for me, just for a little while more, please. Maybe in a month or two I'll be on my feet and can take him off your hands."

"When he's with me I know he's being fed and taken care of. He ain't no trouble. Go. Get the wild oats out of your system."

Tracee looked back and waved. Her momma was standing on the steps of her singlewide and little Stormy, still in his soiled pants, was standing beside her, grinning and giving a big, animated goodbye wave. She wondered what the boy might be thinking as he watched his mother and her current boyfriend pull out of the drive, and out of his life, one more time. She didn't want to think about that. She withdrew a tissue from her pocket, daubed at her eyes and blew her nose.

Ty reached over, patted Tracee's thigh and told her, "You got yourself a real cute kid. Yep, real cute."

Tracee tried to hold back the tears but could not stop them. All she could remember was the way her son had clung to her so desperately, not wanting her to leave him again, but she had pulled away from him. It took her a very long time before she quit crying.

Caldwell, once a lively farming community with tractors coming and going and an occasional cattle drive down Main

Street, had been discovered by speculators and developers who prized the easy freeway access and still relatively inexpensive land. Town had been reborn as an ideal bedroom community. Houses were springing up like colorful flowers appearing after a desert rainstorm: T-1-11 siding slapped over down-and-dirty frames, painted happy colors and sold to commuters who didn't mind the short drive on I-84 to their jobs in Boise.

Jim Garrison, Ty's best friend—they were classmates all twelve years at elementary and high schools in Emerson—lived in Caldwell. Jim had a thirty-year mortgage on a house so poorly constructed it might last fifteen. He worked as a customer service representative for Les Schwab Tire Company, which meant he changed tires, fixed flats and lived under the weighty expectation that if he worked hard, kept his nose clean and was a good family man he might, some day, get a shot at a store manager position where he could make really good money and enjoy the fruits of a million-dollar retirement package. He was required to be clean-shaven and have a close-cropped company haircut. The skin on his hands was constantly cracked and imbedded with someone else's road dust.

Jim was married, going on ten years now, to Dorothy, his high school sweetheart. They had three kids, Brett, Mike and Matty. And they had a yellow lab, Teddy, a calico cat, Tabby and a stainless steel Weber barbecue that stood, like a monument to the family's success, on the back deck. A Slip 'n' Slide was staked on the lawn and would probably freeze in place unless it was rolled up before winter hit full force.

Jim guided the silver Camry, with 210,312 miles registered on the odometer, into the untidy garage. It had been another long day at work. He killed the engine, tripped the remote, and as the garage door jerked its way to the ground, he stepped inside the kitchen, grabbed a beer from the refrigerator, leaned over to untie his laces and kicked off his boots. He went into the front room and fell backwards into his easy chair, the one Dorothy kept covered with a beach towel so his work dirt would not ruin the fabric. He could hear the kids playing in their bedroom, and from the sounds of sloshing water he guessed Dorothy was running yet another load of dirty clothes through the endless cycles of wash, rinse and spin. The doorbell rang. Jim just sat there. He did not move.

Dorothy called, "If that's the paper boy, I've got money for him."

The bedroom door swung open, banging violently against the stopper as a pair of towheaded boys blasted across the room, dodging toys and clutter scattered across the carpet, and raced to see which could reach the door first. Dorothy again called to Jim, "Hon, could you check Matty, make sure she's still on her blanket?"

Jim turned his head, saw their youngest stretched on the pink blanket near the doorway to the laundry room, called, "She is," and took a long gulp of beer.

Brett and Mike came running in and leaped onto their daddy's lap. Jim, who had been taking a drink of beer, had to protect his lips, as well as his privates. He set the bottle on the TV tray, roughhoused with the boys and asked, "Who was at the door?"

"Don't know," said Brett.

"What do you mean you don't know? Who was it?"

"Cowboy," said Mike.

"What'd he say?"

"Said, 'Is your daddy home?'"

Jim smiled, "What'd you say?"

"Said, 'Yes sir, he is.'"

Jim chuckled, "And then what?"

"I close the door, come in here to be with you, Daddy."

Jim groaned, boosted the boys off his lap, got up, went to the door, opened it and exclaimed with a roar, "Ty Battle! Now ain't you a sight for sore eyes! Where have you been keeping yourself? How goddamn long's it been? A goddamn year, anyway."

Jim and Ty awkwardly embraced. They pounded each other on the back a time or two and pulled away. Jim noticed the blonde gal standing behind Ty and extended his hand in Tracee's direction, introducing himself, and then reached back, flung open the door and said, "Where the hell are my manners. You guys come in. Get out of the cold." He ushered them inside as he called, "Hey, Hon, we got any more beer?"

Dorothy, hands on hips, looking frazzled and unhappy, appeared in the doorway. She gave Ty, and then Tracee in turn, the once over and with a quick reversal tried to make up for her disapproving look with a flippant apology, followed by an excuse. "Sorry for the clutter. These kids are impossible." She scooped Matty off her blanket and held the baby like a shield in front of her.

It was obvious Dorothy was less than thrilled to have Ty and his latest girlfriend drop in out of the blue. It seemed to her that whenever Ty visited it took another chip off the enamel of her marriage. One time Ty had taken Jim drinking, and they ended up in a fistfight with a crew of oil drillers in a topless bar in Jackpot, Nevada. Another time they dashed across the border to attend a cockfight in Oregon, only to have it raided. That little episode cost $700 in attorney fees.

Even when Jim didn't get beat up or thrown into jail there were always consequences to pay when he ran with Ty Battle. It seemed to Dorothy that Ty boasted about his freedom, made being foot-loose and fancy-free sound so goddamn appealing that, for weeks after, Jim pouted like a caged hyena rather than getting down on his knees and giving thanks to the Almighty for everything he had: a loving wife, three adorable kids, a roof over his head and steady employment. Hell, shouldn't that be enough to keep any man content?

Dorothy, well versed in her responsibilities as a dutiful wife, went to the refrigerator in the garage, got more beer and doled out bottles to her husband and their guests, asking Ty in passing, "Will you be sticking around for dinner?"

"Just passing through. Stopped to say howdy, that's it. Don't want to interrupt anything important. We'll just drink a beer, and then we gotta run."

"They'll eat," Jim insisted. He gave a snort. "Couple more mouths to feed ain't nothin' 'round here."

Dorothy shot Jim a sidelong glance because Jim never used "ain't" unless Ty was around. This only confirmed Dorothy's feelings that Ty was a bad influence on her husband.

"Let me help," offered Tracee. "What can I do?"

"Peel potatoes, if you want. They're in the sink," said Dorothy. "I need to change Matty. She's messy, again."

While Tracee worked in the kitchen she listened—around the boys fighting over a toy—to snippets of conversation between Jim and Ty. Jim said Ty's mother had called several times. Tracee was unclear what was being said about those calls, but she gathered Ty's father had either been stricken by a serious illness or involved in a terrible automobile accident. She wasn't sure.

Later that evening, after they were on the road heading toward Nevada, Tracee tried to find out. She asked Ty, "Is your father sick, or was there an accident?"

"Both."

"Aren't you worried?"

"Not particularly."

"Why not?"

"Not my concern."

Tracee proceeded cautiously. "If you want, we could swing by, see how he's doing."

Ty violently slammed an open palm against the steering wheel. "I don't wanna be around in case the son-of-a-bitch wakes up. No way."

Nothing more was said. The miles—punctuated by headlights illuminating infrequent, floppy-eared jackrabbits racing from one barrow pit to the other, a night bird flaring its wings, the eyes of a coyote slinking through the sage—rolled out behind them. Tracee toyed with the thought this man next to her, this man she found herself desperately clinging to, just might not be the top prize at the carnival.

CHAPTER FIVE

THE CORVETTE PULLED THROUGH A TIGHT CORNER NEAR THE SUMMIT of Blue Box Pass on the southern flank of Mt. Hood. Cole guessed it had been something like a dozen years since, in a swirling whirlwind of accusations and anger, he had pulled out and left the Double X forever. But now he was headed back to the Home Place.

Coming out of the corner and entering a straightaway, Cole tromped the gas pedal. The four-barrel kicked in and, strangely, the throaty growl of the engine reminded him of his old man's voice—distinctive, raw, guttural, overpowering. The thought of that voice triggered a memory. Cole was just a kid and was riding horseback through the tall timber. He came across an orphan heifer calf with a misshapen head. The little thing was covered with mud and manure and evidently had lain beside the body of her dead mother until hunger drove her to try and find a replacement. But the cows with calves of their own must have refused the deformed orphan, and she had probably attempted to nurse limbs and even fence posts, anything that remotely resembled a teat.

Cole gathered the calf in his arms, slung her over the saddle in front of him and packed her on his lap to the barn. He put her in a stall and was attempting to bottle-feed life back into her when Frank stumbled on the scene. Cole recalled the way his old man stood there at the edge of a shallow pool of light shaking his head, grunting out a few words in that gravely voice of his, "Jug-headed son-of-a-bitch."

"She's taking the bottle good," Cole said.

"Knock that lame bastard in the head."

"No, Dad. I couldn't."

"Then get to the house. Do your homework."

Cole had wanted to defy his father, wanted to save the deformed calf, wanted to make it a pet. But he dared not challenge his father. The calf was not up to the strict standards of the Hereford breed, and Cole knew that in his father's mind there was no place on the ranch for an inferior animal. Resolutely he walked away. Only when he reached the stairs leading to the log house did Cole look back. He saw his father, an eight-pound mall slung over his shoulder, walking into the barn. He knew.

Cole figured that, at that time, he must have been seven or eight years old because school had started, and he and his mother and baby brother were living in town, only coming home, weather permitting, on weekends. On the way to bed that evening, Cole had gone to where his father sat in his easy chair in front of the big stone fireplace. He manufactured the nerve to ask what happened to the calf.

Without looking up from his magazine Frank growled, "Culled the leppy son-of-a-bitch." For him the malformed orphan was not worth wasting any more words on. He went right back to reading.

"She was mine."

Frank tossed the magazine aside, and with one big meaty hand, he pushed the sleeve of his shirt up a forearm thick as a tree trunk, switched hands and duplicated the motion. In another setting such an action would have caused a normal man to shy away but Cole stood his ground. Frank looked his son straight in the eye and told him, "Ain't no 'mine' on this ranch. I make the decisions. Decide what breeding stock gets kept, what gets culled. Get to bed."

Cole went to bed, but he never forgave his father for killing the deformed calf, never forgave him for a lot of things.

The speeding Corvette topped the backbone of the Cascade mountain range and slipped along the side of a long canyon, through the timbered fir and cedar ridges and out onto the broad gray apron of the High Desert. Cole breathed in the tangy aroma of sage and juniper and was reminded that he always felt best on the east side: riding horseback, working cattle, feeling free and unencumbered in the wide-open spaces. When he was younger he felt his destiny was to take over the reins of the family ranch, just as his father had taken over the ranch from his father. Sons were meant to take over from fathers, to carry on the western tradition. When Cole came home after college, and a couple years spent working selling feed for Purina, his bride Donna in tow, that thought was definitely in his mind; taking over from his father.

As it had turned out, Frank had no intention of giving up the reins. His thinking was he had been born on the ranch, and by God he'd die there. He'd never give up his authority. Not to Cole. Not to Ty. And he'd never sell out. Never.

It had taken time for Cole to understand his father and the forces that drove him. When Frank's character flaws had been revealed they had lodged in Cole like shrapnel from some nearly forgotten war. And now he was coming home for one reason and one reason only, to help his mother through a difficult period. He told himself he never blamed her for the sins of the past. She was not responsible for him leaving the ranch. She was a bystander, nothing more, and she undoubtedly had reacted the same way when Ty left home the summer before Cole got there. What Cole never understood was why the hell his mother ever stayed with his father. As far as he was concerned, the only logical explanation was she viewed all those years of living with Frank as an investment. But that was bullshit too. No amount of money or worldly possessions would cause a woman to reject her flesh and blood. He'd have to ask her, just come right out and have her explain her thinking, and her actions. He'd do it at some point, when the time was right, not right away.

Cole felt that he had no choice but to let go of the past. The past was poison. He tried concentrating on the present and that was nearly as bad. He wondered how he might react if his father lived and was a cripple, giving orders from a wheelchair, as growly as he ever was. What if he was little more than a mindless vegetable staring at the ceiling, uncommunicative? Cole forced himself to quit thinking such morbid thoughts.

When Iris had asked Cole to come home, a tiny black corner in his personality had been revealed. He was secretly pleased she had chosen *him*, wanted *him*, had faith in *him*. Her request was acknowledgement, Cole thought, that he was the one person who had the skills and the resolve to tackle the responsibilities of effectively operating the Double X in Frank's absence. He felt a stab of pride and pictured himself as an absentee landowner, hiring a crew of good men and overseeing the operation of the ranch from Portland. He could return on weekends and holidays, occasionally bringing along his wife and daughter to enjoy the fruits of the rural lifestyle. And as the Corvette sped through the soft afternoon sunlight, he recalled men he had known who might be willing to pitch in and lend a helping hand, both in the short run, and if need be, in the long haul. Faces and names came to him—cowboys, buckaroos, top hands—men who could be asked to fill in and do the job without requiring a lot of *"micromanaging."* That term, *micromanaging*, was not a ranch word. He had dragged that in from the city. And now he found it amusing and began to laugh.

XX

Sugarloaf Mountain, its perfect pyramid glistening white, came into view and Cole recalled a hot August afternoon many years before. He had stood with Frank in the harsh sunlight—light so coppery it seems as if it has been hammered flat on an anvil—and Frank kicked the pointy toe of his boot into the dry, gray dirt in the hay field and said, "City folk got no goddamned idea how fragile it all is. Do they ever stop and think that everything they eat is dependent on six-inches of good topsoil and rain when we need it? Hell no. They just assume it's gonna be there, that it's gonna go on, last forever. They got no clue. No goddamn clue at all."

Cole had every intention of stopping at the family owned house in town, figuring his mother would most likely be staying there, but instead drove directly to the hospital. He hardly took notice of the dramatic changes that had come to the town of Emerson and the building boom that now threatened to burst the community apart at the seams with newfound prosperity.

Cole found an open parking spot in front of the hospital and took it. He went inside to where, with directions from a nurse, he was quickly able to locate his father's room. He thought he had prepared himself for the moment when he first saw his father, but he never could have. His father's hard-chiseled features were rounded and softened. He laid passively, his muscles slack and pliant. Tubes pumped oxygen into his lungs and other tubes dripped liquids into his arms. Tubes carried fluids away. Gunmetal gray sensors were stuck to his bare chest and a heart monitor recorded jagged outlines of orange mountains and deep ravines. Rhythmic pings echoed each feeble heartbeat.

The sight of his father, nothing more than a helpless, hapless empty husk of a man, brought Cole up short. He stood staring, tried to draw a breath, failed, knew he had to get away and stumbled from the room, down a brutally long hallway, reached a set of double glass doors, bullied his way through and stepped into the merciless glare of the setting sun. He managed to suck in several huge gulps of clean, fresh air and that helped revive him. A small wind rustled the few remaining leaves on a mountain mahogany tree. He noticed the tree had been planted too close to the sidewalk and the roots were beginning to buckle the concrete. Cole recognized that his father was never going to make it, and probably wouldn't last through the night.

"I need a drink," Cole muttered. He'd prefer a straight shot of whiskey in the type of bar where a man could get a drink and something pickled to eat from a glass jar. He got in his Corvette and headed toward town. As he drove he glanced in the direction of Sugarloaf Mountain, knowing a ski resort had been opened there, having read about the development in a trade magazine that touted Sugarloaf Resort At The Mountain as the next elite resort community. There had been a light dusting of snow on the mountain from a recent storm, and Cole saw the new chair lift, Rainbow, running down the white slope like a complicated metal zipper. Clustered around the base of the lift, and clinging precariously to the flank of the dormant volcano, were sprawling log mansions with massive lava rock fireplaces and stick-framed homes with natural wood siding and exposed foundations covered with washed river rock. These were second homes. Vacation homes. Trophy homes. Speculation homes. Homes owned by investment bankers, company executives, doctors, lawyers, developers and airline pilots. The service workers: waitresses, bartenders, cooks and dishwashers, clerks, secretaries, teachers and firefighters could never afford to live in such lavish homes. They would be relegated to affordable housing built down-slope on the least desirable ground, land without much of a view.

As Cole drove along Main Street, he witnessed further evidence that the once sleepy little town of Emerson had undergone a complete transformation. The *Corner Café* was gone and a new building was springing up from a muddy hole in the ground. Cole remembered the atmosphere of the old café, the wonderful smells of sizzling bacon, bubbling sourdough pancakes, sputtering eggs, and the way the racket of conversations ebbed and flowed as ranchers and loggers sipped coffee and exchanged idle banter. Every morning the locals, along with help from an occasional passerby, formed and reformed into groups like so many drifting clouds on a hot summer day. The gossip mill worked overtime. Most community scandals were flogged to death within a day or two, and even the steamiest of details were talked to death and never lasted much longer than a week.

The old brick building that had been *Miller's Hardware* was now a mini-mall containing several businesses, including *Red Cloud*, a Native American craft store, *Kathy's Kitchen*, specializing in the sale of expensive jams and jellies, and *Angie's*, a candle store. *Ed's Shoe Shop* had become *All Creatures Great and Small*, a dog-grooming boutique. *Pioneer Saw Shop*, where loggers had lined up every afternoon to have chain saws sharpened and made ready for morning, was now the *Cosmic Coffee*, a specialty store advertising "Gourmet Coffees Made With Organic Coffee Beans." And what had once been *Dillion's Saddle Store* was now the office of a massage therapist specializing in Rolfing.

Cole asked himself where had the cowboys, with a swagger to their step and toothpicks clenched between their teeth, gone? Where were the loggers with their red suspenders and snagged tin pants? Who were these folks parading around in expensive gear, looking as though they had just stepped off the pages of a *Columbia Sportswear* catalog? Had Emerson become the new Aspen, Sun Valley, Telluride, Park City? Apparently this new breed of inhabitants had elbowed their way in and pushed out anything that did not fit their strict idea of progressive prosperity.

It seemed to Cole that in his absence a hundred years of history had suddenly vanished. Gone was the boulder with the names of teenagers killed in car wrecks a week or two before graduation. Did anyone living here remember that Bobby Kennedy had passed through town on the campaign trail in 1968, that the football team had won the state championship in the late 80s, the names of soldiers who gave their lives fighting for freedom? Gone, every bit of it gone like so much dust swept under a rug. Cole longed for the old days. He wanted things to be as they used to be. The way he remembered.

Iris's father was a bandy-legged, second-generation moonshiner who suffered the inglorious misfortune of having fallen in love with his own merchandise. Before he set himself on a course to drink his life away, he bought a 320-acre homestead in Wood River Valley and managed to win the heart of a good woman, the schoolteacher, Ria Kirkmeir.

This union produced Iris. From her mother, Iris acquired strength, stability, creativity and unflagging tenacity. She could trace a few of her trifling, less desirable qualities to the genes provided by her temperamental, scatterbrained, impassive and ambitionless, alcoholic father.

It is hard to say which genes caused her to change her mind about remaining at the town house, but she made an impulsive decision and called J.B., asking him to come to town and drive her back to the ranch. Before she left the town house, she tacked a note on the message pad beside the door instructing Cole to come to the ranch.

It felt very strange for Iris to be making decisions. She had spent so many years standing in her husband's shadow that now, with him all but gone, standing in the direct light of freewill was a strange, almost frightening, and yet liberating experience for her.

In a bar decorated to resemble a ski lodge, Cole fortified himself with a single drink, whiskey and water. Once he consumed it, he promptly drove to the squat town house, a three-bedroom home originally built by a logger but owned by the Battle family for several decades. Here he found the note his mother had left for him, directing him to come to the ranch.

By the time Cole reached the western boundary of the Double X, the last vestige of twilight had pulled a murky curtain over the landscape. The Corvette's headlights threw a wall of illumination on the green Powder River gate hanging from an impressive log structure, two upright logs teed into a top log from which hung a juniper slab with the XX brand burned into it. Tacked to one of the upright logs was a sign, shot to hell, noting, *"No Trespassing – Survivors Will Be Prosecuted."*

The combination to the lock was emblazoned in Cole's memory—his father's lucky number, doubled—1313. He opened the gate, got back in his car, bumped over the cattle guard, closed the gate, locked it and started down the gravel road. After less than a mile he stopped to put up the Corvette's top and turn on the heater to ward off the cold. As he went about these tasks he chastised himself. What the hell had he been thinking? Not thinking straight, that was for sure. He should have left the Corvette in the garage and driven his Ford pickup. He blamed his faulty judgment on his mother's call. The news of his father's condition caught him off-guard and he chose to drive an impractical rig without giving it a second thought.

The Corvette's headlights opened a narrow slit in the darkness. From the shadows pairs of eyes gleamed like live embers and sometimes the ghost-like images of deer were visible. Another time a coyote stood in the middle of the road, defiantly holding his ground until, at the last instant, it leaped aside, flipping up its white-tipped tail and loping away through the sage.

Cole reached the great two-story log house and the present crop of dogs came out to bark and challenge him. He got out of his car and when the dogs couldn't intimidate him they quit barking and slunk away. He walked toward the house and the light on the porch illuminated marbles imbedded in the steps so many years before. Cole and Ty had pushed some of their best marbles—Rainbos, Corkscrews, Teardrops, Purple Dots, Oxblood Swirls, Bumblebees, Red/yellow Comets and fancy Cat's-Eye shooters with wavy blue and red and green veins that shimmered in the sunlight—into the wet concrete to form their initials. Iris had come along later, before the concrete set, and added R. A. B. for Ruth Ann Battle, even though she never lived past infancy.

An awkward sensation rippled the skin on the nape of Cole's neck as he realized, if Ruth Ann had lived, she would most likely by now have completed college, been married and given Iris a passel of grandchildren. He shuddered as he contemplated the disconcerting force that drove his mother to push the marbles into the wet concrete. He looked up, saw his mother's expressionless face, eyes as dark and deep-set as the bore of a double-barreled shotgun, perfectly framed in the window.

Iris was confused, unsure of the visitor's identity. Then she recognized it was her oldest son. Moving with conviction, she rushed to him and threw her arms around him in a tight embrace. For the past dozen years she had wanted to hug him like this, and never could; Ty too, and poor little Ruth Ann, never again.

"Thanks for coming," she moaned into Cole's chest.

Cole felt his mother's skinny arms tremble, and tried to step back. She clung to him for an uncomfortable amount of time before finally acquiescing and allowing him to hold her at arm's length.

He could see the past twelve years had definitely taken a toll on his mother. She was thinner, more haggard and much older than he had her pictured in his mind. The west wind whipped at Iris's stringy hair and she brushed it away from her face without lifting her eyes. A gust blew harder and the tall pine tree at the front of the house bent like an old man. Cole concentrated on that whoosh of wind through the clusters of needles and thought how strange it would be if he was that tree, rooted to the same spot year after year, having rivers of change eddy around and never being able to take an active part in the flow of that change. He had left a wife, daughter and his business behind in Portland, had driven three hundred miles, and now he was not at all sure of his place.

Xx

Iris felt Cole's gaze and was unnerved under the weight of it. She looked up at his face and smiled because he was so handsome and poised, like a leading man in a movie. She rocked back and forth slightly and wondered how many years had it been since she went to the show-house and saw a movie? She didn't know.

"Let's get out of this wind," she said abruptly. "Come in. It's so good to have you here. Thanks for coming. I know you're busy. I know you have things to do. I know it's hard for you to break away and come chasing way out here at the drop-of-a-hat but...."

"Mom," said Cole in a reprimanding tone, "You're chattering like a crow." He laughed.

She brushed at her hair. Her eyes were moist, and though she felt an inclination to cry, she did not. They stepped inside and she asked him if he would like something to drink. He told her, "Sure. I'd take a beer if you've got one."

Xx

While Iris headed to the kitchen, Cole wandered into the front room, pausing near his father's chair, listening, thinking he could actually hear the slow breathing of the old house but decided it was nothing more than the sleepy drone of one last fly trying to hide indoors and cheat winter. He caught the familiar scent of Hoppe's solvent, a sentimental fragrance every hunter picks up quickly and never forgets. Now he recalled Frank sitting in his leather chair, leaning forward, muscles in his forearms flexing as he pumped a cleaning rod in and out of the barrel of his lever-action 30-30. At his feet patches had accumulated, from nearly white on top to light gray, and toward the bottom, a swatch of gray-black. There was the soft swish of cloth polishing cold metal, and of course, the heady scent of Hoppe's solvent.

Iris momentarily showed her face in the doorway and said, "Going to the pump house. Be right back." She ducked away.

"Want me to go?" offered Cole.

Iris had retreated to the far side of the kitchen and hollered, "Heavens no. You had a long drive. Just relax."

It had been one of Cole's chores, when he was a boy, to fetch whatever his mother needed from the pump house: a jar of home-canned pickles, tomatoes, applesauce, plum or chokecherry jam. He recalled the forceful pull needed to open the solid door, the foot-thick walls filled with sawdust, shelves stacked deep with the harvest of summers past. He could almost smell the dankness of the dirt seeping up from beneath the rough-cut board flooring and feel the way the clamminess clung to his skin. If the electric pump happened to kick on while he was there, and it seemed like it usually did, it always startled him. He had a recollection of small green frogs that somehow found their way inside the pump house and spider webs, too. His mother's voice called, "I'm back."

Cole looked at the big leather chair and saw the permanent indentation where the horsehair stuffing of the cushion had been molded to his father's backside. The surface was ruddy, slick and shiny under the glow of the floor lamp.

Remnants of a fire glowed in the fireplace. Cole moved the screen, set it aside, stirred the embers and laid several pieces of wood on top. He bent and blew on the coals until a tongue of fire leaped upward and licked at a layer of glistening pine pitch. He replaced the screen and stepped away. An odd sensation swept through him—here he was, back at the Home Place, and he seemed to fit right in. He thought if circumstances had been different, if he had been able to take over and his father had gracefully stepped aside, this would have been his life.

Frank Battle was never the type of man who could gracefully retire, dress in Bermuda shorts and take vacation cruises on luxury ocean liners. Nor was he like other stockmen who had been able to give up working and go into something different: raising flowers, woodworking, making saddles or rawhiding. Cole always figured his father might enjoy breeding quarter horses and traveling up and down the west coast to watch them race. And, if he had gone from cattle to racehorses, it wouldn't have been like he stepped down at all but more like a lateral move.

Cole was a firm believer in lateral moves. Back in high school, and when he was the star running back at Willamette University, his favorite play in football was the slant off-tackle. The hole opening fast; Cole with the ball bursting through the line of scrimmage, making a quick lateral move and popping outside to daylight.

In Cole's opinion this was exactly what his father should have done, moved laterally until he found an opening, then take it. But he never did. He kept the ranch and drove Cole away. He had done the same thing to Ty.

Cole now recognized that the living room was like a museum devoted to Frank Battle. It exalted his many exploits and achievements. There was an ancient photograph of Frank spurring a buckskin bronc named Hellcat at the Myrtle Point rodeo, an enlarged photograph of Frank applying the XX brand on the flank of a calf, a certificate proclaiming Frank Battle a

Diamond Pioneer and another acknowledging the Double X as an Oregon Century Ranch. There were plaques from the Oregon Cattleman's Association, Eastern Oregon Livestock Association, Oregon Veterinarian Examining Board, National Hereford Association and another for recognition as a leader in the biological control of tansy ragwort. Also, gathered in this room were western artifacts including Charlie Russell calendar prints, deer heads, elk heads, Navajo rugs, snowshoes, spurs and rawhide ropes. Cole took it all in and realized this room had stayed as an unyielding constant. Just the way his father insisted it remain.

Iris arrived carrying a cold beer in one hand and a water glass filled with red wine in the other. She handed Cole the beer and led the way to where two leather couches were arranged facing each other. The leather had come from Double X cattle and bore the brand burned into the tanned hides. She took a seat and Cole sat opposite her. He settled himself and took a long, satisfying drink of beer, allowing the cool, amber liquid to drain down his parched throat. Coming over to the High Desert from the Willamette Valley, where the humidity was typically high, always irritated his throat for a day or two.

Iris sipped her wine and when Cole placed his elbows on his knees and leaned forward, eager to tell her, "I stopped at the hospital and saw him," she was thankful she wouldn't have to either make up a lie or wade through the awful truth—that Frank was in a bad way, was more than likely never going to get better, and in fact, he was not long for this world.

"Didn't look good," said Cole.

Iris nodded.

"Don't suppose there's much we can do."

Sip. "Not really." Sip.

"What about sending him to Portland? The cardiology department at Providence Hospital has one of the best reputations on the coast."

"The damage has been done. Doctors say the clot stopped the blood flow; say there was considerable brain damage. Even if he does make it, he'll never be the man he was. They wanted to put him on life support. I said no. He wouldn't want to live like that."

"He's tough."

"Yes," said Iris. She forced a stubborn smile.

They drank in unison. Cole's cell phone suddenly rang, and it startled them both. Cole recovered, said, "I'm amazed. I didn't figure there'd be reception way out here." He dug in his coat pocket for his phone.

Iris offered, "They put one of those translator things on top...."

Cole, opening the phone and looking at the screen, interrupted his mother and said, "It's Donna." He put the phone to his ear. "Hello.... You caught up to me.... Here at the ranch.... No, just got here.... stopped by the hospital.... Not good. They wanted to put him on life support. Mom told them no. She did the right thing.... Don't know, but it's not encouraging. There's been brain damage.... Don't know that, either. Well, enough of that. How are you doing? How about Kendra? She get that paper she was working on turned in?"

Cole, after a long pause, finished by saying, "I don't know. When things are on an even keel. We'll have to wait and see. I'll call tomorrow.... Probably in the evening. Why, you going somewhere? .... Well, whatever. If I can't get in touch with you, I'll leave a message. If there's any change I'll let you know right away. Talk to you soon, 'night."

Iris thought Cole's side of the conversation had lacked even a hint of affection and certainly no reassurances of love, but she did not mention that. After living within the tight confines of her own troubled marriage, she'd be the last to point an accusing finger at anyone else. She sipped her wine and watched the dancing flicker of the firelight, concentrating on the soft ticking sounds of the wood as it burned.

Cole finished his beer and announced, "I'm gonna bring in my gear. Where do you want me?"

"Your old bedroom. I made up the bed just before you got here."

Cole laughed, and the sound of it, deep down in his chest like a logging chain being dragged around the bottom of a 55-gallon drum, reminded Iris of the way Frank had laughed in the early years. She was perplexed and maybe even a little annoyed at the memory because she could not remember the last time she had heard Frank laugh. It had been some time.

Iris liked to remember Frank when he was a young man. He cut quite a dashing figure riding horseback to her parents' homestead. Later, after her family had sold out to Frank's father and her family had moved to Emerson, Frank used to drive the stock truck to town and they would go on dates to the picture show or to the Idle-A-While Café for cheeseburgers and cokes.

Cole started to stand. Iris said, "There's something I need to talk to you about. Sit back down a minute, please." Cole allowed gravity to take over. He settled his body back onto the couch.

"I spoke with Bob Sandlin, the attorney, your father's attorney," said Iris, and then she purposefully took the conversation in a different direction. "You've had yourself a long day, wouldn't you like another beer?"

"I'll get it," said Cole.

Iris raised her empty glass. "Please," she said, "The bottle's on the counter. I put more beer in the refrigerator, top shelf."

In the kitchen Cole noticed the calendar on the cupboard door with reminder notes his mother had scribbled: "make relish, apple pie, extension 1:00." His eyes followed the stretched-out beige telephone cord to a nearby painting of a single iris, so recently painted he could smell the thinner that had been used. He poured wine from the gallon jug and got himself another beer, bumping the refrigerator door shut with his hip the way Iris always did, or anyway used to do, and that thought amused him.

He re-entered the big room and handed his mother her glass of wine. She was still seated on the couch but had turned sideways and had one arm slung over the back. With the light behind her, her face was masked and it was hard for Cole to distinguish her features. He had the unsettling impression of her as a rocky outcropping, her body composed of sharp, knobby features set at crazy, odd angles.

She bent toward him. "Your father," she said and paused. He wanted her to go on, to say what she had to say. Quit stalling. When he was a kid, and he did something wrong, Iris ordered him to go cut a willow switch, and when he returned with it she had had him sit and wait for his whipping. He never minded the whipping near as much as waiting for the whipping. She finally picked up the conversation. "You need to know this—your father placed a stipulation in his will—that, in case of his death, or if he was incapacitated, physically or mentally…." Again she paused, collecting her thoughts before continuing. She took a sip of wine for fortification.

To Cole the words she had already spoken seemed to be blending together like watercolors bleeding into a loose, colorless wash. He was gripping the bottle of beer harder than necessary because it allowed him a point of reference, something solid on which he could hold onto and focus his attention. He waited in nervous anticipation for the next few words, for the proverbial hammer to fall. The blow was coming. He knew it and tried to brace himself.

"There was a bunch of legal garble-de-gook, but here's what it boils down to—if Frank dies or is unable to take care of the ranch, then the responsibility falls to us. The provision he made, according to Mr. Sandlin, is that you and Ty must return to the ranch and we operate it for one year. At the end of that year we must show a profit. If we can't show a profit, if we lose money, the ranch is gifted, lock, stock, and barrel, to Oregon State University."

Cole was dazed. "What's that mean?"

"We get nothing. We're cut out of his will."

"I can't believe it," said Cole. "He wouldn't do something like that."

"He did."

"What would you live on?"

Iris shrugged her bony shoulders, shook her head and said, "Nothing. I'd have nothing."

Cole exhaled a puff of air and snapped, "Christ! I can't believe he'd pull such a stunt." Two thoughts struck him: First, that Frank did not have the decency to provide for his wife, and second, that Frank, with one foot firmly planted in the grave, was still calling the shots, would call the shots for the next year. If his rules were not followed to the letter, he'd reach out and deprive his family of what rightfully belonged to them. This ranch had been in the Battle family for three generations. All the history was going to be thrown away and handed to a state university that would probably unload the property to the highest bidder.

Cole had absolutely no idea of how he should respond. Frank had taught him it was unmanly to reveal genuine emotion and all his life he had stoically shouldered conflicts and stood his ground. But in this instance he uncharacteristically threw back his head and laughed. And when the laugh ran its course, he wiped his eyes with the heels of his hands and commented, "Just like that son-of-a-bitch. Think he'll do one thing, and he does the exact opposite. Always was one to enjoy throwing a monkey wrench in the gears. Couldn't stand to have anything run easy. Buck the system. Be in control. Make the decisions." Cole took a long swig of beer. "But why Oregon State? He never went to school there, did he?"

"I suppose because it's an agricultural college," responded Iris. "I think Frank always wished he could have gone to school and have had some fun before getting tied down to the ranch. He never had that opportunity. His daddy put him right to work."

XX

Cole found sleep exceedingly hard to come by. He concentrated on the quietness, comparing the solitude of the Home Place to his normal life in the city and its dizzying array of sounds, its frenzied pace, its push and pull of traffic and overall crush of humanity. Finally, and for the first time in a long, long time, he began to feel a part of something, the quiet, the land, this ranch. He was satisfied in the knowledge he could saddle a horse, ride into the hills and immediately be surrounded by those elements he loved the most: fresh air, open country, mountains, forests, meadows and miles and miles of pure solitude.

Cole recalled a time when he was in high school. He met a very old man at the main gate. The old man claimed his family had taken one of the original homesteads in the valley and that he had spent his youth on the place. He said he wanted one last look around before he died—wanted to see the virgin land he plowed under, the open range he fenced, the paradise he helped to conquer and transform into a ranch. He was filled with remembrances of the valley and described how tall the meadow grass had been, the thundering flocks of waterfowl that arrived each spring and fall, the vast array of wild game, the blueness of the skies, the length and coldness of winters, the wildness of it all and the isolation of the early days, when it took a full day's travel in a wagon to reach Emerson.

"No matter where I went, and at one time or another I've rambled all over the world, I always thought of this valley as home. Still do," said the old man. "I give thanks to the Creator for allowing me one last visit."

Cole had felt sorry for the old man. He thought he was owed a look around and invited him in, telling him, "Be sure to close and lock the gate when you leave." Cole knew if his father caught the old man on his property, he'd run him off because he didn't have a sentimental bone in his body. But his father was in the mountains putting out salt for the cattle and would not return until nightfall.

Like that old-timer, Cole could now feel how much he was locked into the geography and history of Wood River Valley. When he was young, the valley's hold on him was so powerful he never even imagined living anywhere else. He just assumed he'd go away to college, marry and return to live and raise a family.

But in the past dozen years, Cole's life had taken some radical twists and turns. He found himself thinking about his successes in real estate, buying unprofitable ranches and farms, breaking them into smaller tracts and selling them for fast profits. Others in the industry, noting his success, his cowboy boots and western bent, referred to him—mostly behind his back—as the "Real Estate Cowboy."

Cole had never stopped to scratch below the surface of his chosen profession, to scrutinize the way he made money from the sale of rural land, but he began to now. Those techniques he had devised and refined did not involve raising a single cow or calf. Their only purpose was to put money in his pocket. He knew that the sad truth of contemporary life was that a ranch was worth far more if the cattle were sold and the land divided and purchased by urbanites to build expensive homes and use on selected weekends and a few short weeks each year as a retreat from their typical confinement. He could not fault people for wanting to get away, and in fact, he had used escapism to his advantage, persuading the wealthy to share in the dream of owning a chunk of ground off the beaten path, allowing themselves to participate in the slow pace of a country lifestyle and take pleasure in postcard-beautiful scenery, panoramic sunsets and serenading coyotes.

His first few years of selling real estate he had sold to individuals but he soon learned it was more lucrative to package land and unload it on investment syndicates, thereby forcing them to be the ones who dirtied their hands developing the property. Let someone else gouge the earth, carve the roads, lay the drain fields, dig for water and rape the land in the onward march of inevitable progress.

It was obvious to Cole that ownership of a land, especially ranch land, was cyclical. People quit eating red meat and ranch land becomes devalued; this corresponds to the gentrification of the west. It happens like the slaughter of buffalo led to the near extinction of the Indians, the discovery of a handful of nuggets at Sutter's Mill coincided with the California Gold Rush, the promise of free land lured a quarter-million pioneers over the Oregon Trail. Some things happen and it kicks off a chain reaction. That's what makes history.

And then, lying there in bed, Cole knew he had never faced up to the truth, that his job as a real estate cowboy made him no better than a land whore. An expensive, high-classed whore to be sure, but all the same, he knew none of that land he bought and sold and pulled out of production would ever again graze another cow or grow another bushel of grain, and that each new parcel he sold would become tied up as tight as a national park. He felt a stab of guilt for his part in the debasing of the West.

Cole quit castigating himself and turned his attention to his mother, picturing how weary and frail she looked when he first saw her from the porch, framed in the window. Now he tried to imagine her in her room. As far back as he could remember she had had her own bedroom. Growing up it never seemed odd. He assumed all married couples slept separately. He wondered if she still had her old-time Philco table radio and could visualize it sitting on her dresser with the once shiny wooden case turned dull and filmy, creased with tiny hairline cracks, the top marred by where some hot object had once been set and had burned a perfect dark brown ring into the veneer. His mother had enjoyed listening to a radio station from San Francisco that played hits from the Big Band era: Glen Miller, Artie Shaw, Paul Whitman, Duke Ellington. When Cole was a boy, some nights if he had a bad dream, she'd invite him into her room to sit on her lap as she rocked in the rocking chair. They listened to the music while out the window the Big Dipper tediously swung around the North Star. Those were pleasant memories, and Cole, beginning to feel secure and loved, allowed sleep to tiptoe into the room and take him by the hand. His last conscious thought, as he drifted toward sleep, was an image of his mother kneeling in the garden, weeding amid the hollyhocks and snapdragons, bees and hummingbirds winging in and out of the flowers, insects filling the air with a steady drone.

By morning the initial shock had passed and Cole now regarded the news his mother had delivered the night before as a golden opportunity to prove himself. He could be the one who saved the ranch. Sure, it might prove to be one hell of an ordeal, but never in his life had Cole Battle ever shied away from taking on a challenge. He joined his mother in the kitchen, and they drank coffee and visited. Cole outlined his plans for the coming year, saying he'd get word to Ty, convince him to come home, and he was sure J.B. would stay on board.

"The three of us can handle the bulk of the work," said Cole. "If we need outside help working cattle, making the drive to summer pasture, riding roundup, that sort of thing, we can hire a few buckaroos. I do know this, if we hang together as a family, we can come out of this on the topside. Without a doubt we can."

Iris, eyes red-rimmed from a sleepless night, remained stoic, saying, "Honey, you do what you think is best." She rose from the kitchen table and went about cooking him breakfast on the wood stove—hotcakes, sausage and eggs how he liked them—the same breakfast she had fixed all the years Cole was growing up.

After eating Cole felt energized. He went to his room and called his business partner, explaining his predicament. He said it looked as though he was going to have to stay longer than anticipated. He detailed what he declared were his father's "unreasonable restrictions" and finished by saying, "If our real estate partnership can't withstand me taking a year-long sabbatical, I'm amiable to having you submit an offer to buy me out." Cole's partner reassured him, said not to worry, that they would work through this current situation.

Cole's next call was to Donna. When he shared the news with her she was upset and abruptly tried to end the conversation by saying, "I was just going out the door."

"Tell me what you think," urged Cole.

"You've never asked my permission on anything. I know you. You're going to do what you think you have to do. "

He complained, "Hey, I'm caught between a rock and a hard place. If I let the ranch go, we lose everything. Millions and millions. And what's gonna happen to Mother? What will she live on? What can she do? Where will she go?"

Donna snapped, "This isn't about your mother. You've always wanted that ranch. Now you've got it. I have to go. Goodby." She hung up, breaking the tenuous connection between the two of them.

CHAPTER SIX

IT TOOK JIM GARRISON MOST OF THE EVENING, BUT HE FINALLY LOCATED Ty Battle at the Bulls Head Motel in Winnemucca, Nevada. The clerk rang the room. There was no answer, and Jim elected to leave a message, telling the clerk it was a family emergency and urgent Ty return the call. He left his number.

It was after midnight and Jim was asleep in his lounger when the phone rang. Jim never heard it. Dorothy had to get up, answer the phone and bring it to Jim.

She shook her husband awake and told him, "It's Ty." Jim took the receiver, and though his words were slurred from sleep, he managed to ask if Ty had called his mother.

"Hell no. Not yet. I told you I'd take care of it. So, why bother me?" said Ty, sounding belligerent.

Jim was coming awake now. "Not an hour after you left, your brother called. He's been looking everywhere, trying to track you down. I told him you just left here. He was all excited about that."

"So, what's the big emergency?"

"I told you what your mom said when she called. It was about your dad. This is a big deal or Cole wouldn't be following up, be so anxious to get in touch with you."

"The old man must have kicked the bucket?"

"I don't rightly know. Cole wouldn't say. I told him I'd find you. Didn't figure you'd get too far. Winnemucca was a safe bet."

"I'll tell you what's up. Cole plans to divide up the Home Place in five-acre lots and sell them off to rich Californians. He needs me to sign off. That's it, isn't it?" asked Ty.

"Don't have a clue. But you need to talk to him. Promise me you'll call the ranch and talk to Cole, or to your mother."

"Okay. I'll do it."

After hanging up Ty gulped the drink he had set on the nightstand, and for emphasis crushed a cube of ice between his teeth. He glanced in Tracee's direction. She was stretched across the bed, elbow tucked down, head resting on her hand. A tangle of hair made a delicate curtain around her arm. She wanted to know, "What's up?"

"Cole. He wants to talk. Big deal." He sighed, "Shit on a shingle!"

Tracee, knowing it would be best if Ty waited until he was sober, suggested, "In the morning, cowboy. You left something turned on over here and you need to take care of it right now before it burns." She made a clumsy grab for him, caught hold of his belt and pulled him toward her. He fell backward onto the bed. Tracee proceeded to unbutton his shirt, and as she did her slender fingers wandered through the hairs on his bare chest. She leaned forward and lightly bit one nipple, then the other, taking them between her teeth, flicking them playfully with her tongue. Ty moaned, began to relax and any thoughts he might have had of calling his brother were soon forgotten.

After having sex Ty promptly fell asleep. But Tracee lay awake, breathing in the musky aroma of sex that hung in the warm room like ozone after a lightning storm. She wondered what was going to happen to her. Were her plans to go to Mexico with Ty about to change? Her thoughts shifted to Stormy, and she felt a physical ache in the pit of her stomach over the continuing separation with her son. What would she do? What could she do?

Cole called the bunkhouse and told J.B. the news. Less than five minutes later the local radio station J.B. had been listening to interrupted a Brahms concerto to report that legendary cattleman Frank Battle had died.

In the forty-odd years J.B. had worked for Frank, he never found a single good reason to like the man. But he did respect Frank's ability to run a ranch. He was a good man with cattle and horses and with numbers. He had an uncanny ability to manage and coordinate the various facets of the daily operation of a working cattle ranch. But when it came to relating to people, Frank wasn't worth a tinker's damn. That's what J.B. thought, and he figured the saddest part of Frank's death was how Iris would respond to the loss. He wished he had an excuse to talk with her now, but really, what good would that do? He had not the slightest inkling of what he could say to her that would ease her burden.

While the on-air personality related the history of Frank Battle, listing his involvement in the cattle industry and his numerous accomplishments, J.B. fixed himself a bite to eat. He opened a can of hash and poured the contents into a shallow pan. He set the pan on the hot-plate burner and cranked the dial to 10. As he stood waiting for the hash to heat he could feel the floor through his wool socks and the way the cold, clammy linoleum wicked upward like the flesh of something dead. He made his way to the slump-shouldered Kelvinator refrigerator, removed an open can of tuna and peeled back the hunk of tin foil covering it and stood spooning tuna fish onto a saltine cracker and eating it opened-faced as an appetizer. When the hash was good and hot, he gave it a flavor boost with a light sprinkle of salt from a Morton's box, pepper from a pepper tin, a shot of Tabasco sauce and a liberal dose of ketchup. He ate with a spoon directly from the pan. Afterward he was still hungry. Again he went to the refrigerator, took out a roll of liverwurst and thought to himself how odd it was that one man's death could have such a profound affect on another man's appetite. He leaned against the sink, pared off several slices of liverwurst with his pocketknife and ate until he stopped feeling the desire for food.

J.B. ate most of his meals this same way. It saved on having to wash dishes. He could not remember the last time he had a sit-down dinner; at a table with a knife, fork and spoon, a folded napkin on his lap and a china plate. It was some time back. He was sure of that.

On gimpy legs J.B. shuffled across the open room and took a tentative seat on the edge of his bunk. He began to read the week-old local newspaper, looking for a name he might be familiar with and not finding a single person he recognized. J.B. gave up, folded the newspaper and set it aside. He raised his eyes and stared at the brown oil burner that clanked periodically as heat, escaping up the pipe, caused the metal to alternately expand and contract.

What would happen to the ranch now that Frank was gone? Whoever took over might not have a place for a broken-down buckaroo. J.B. thought of himself somewhat like a faithful old ranch truck that had given years of dependable service and now was old and wearing out. Maybe it was time to scrap him in the junkyard since any repairs would be growing progressively more expensive. Last winter he had suffered a bout of bursitis, and the doctor put him on medication. Then he had to have his remaining teeth pulled and false ones fitted. What was next? Cancer? His ticker?

Never one to dwell on depression, J.B. tried to shift gears but came full circle. He realized he had waited all his life for a good woman to come along. A woman like Iris. Now it struck him as ironic that she was finally a free woman, and he couldn't do jack shit about it—just his no-account, miserable luck. Frank should have had the decency to die a couple decades earlier and given J.B. a shot at happiness. Goddamn that bastard for living so long.

XX

As they drew near to the western boundary of the Double X Ty was keeping a wary eye on the army of charcoal-bottomed clouds blowing in fresh off the Pacific Ocean, rolling in with only a slight intention of bringing any moisture to the High Desert. He noticed the hillsides were thin of grass and ready for a blanket of snow to be pulled snuggly over them. He stopped at the main gate, opened it with the same combination as always, drove his pickup over the cattle guard and went back to close the gate. A squalling wind made the buckshot riddled, "*No Trespassing – Survivors Will Be Prosecuted,*" sign flutter. Ty told himself if his old man had caught someone pulling such a stunt, shooting up a sign, they sure as hell wouldn't do it a second time.

Back in the pickup Ty spoke quietly to Tracee. He did not want to awaken Stormy who was curled in the seat, feet against the door, using Tracee's leg as a pillow. Ty related an incident that was supposed to have happened years ago when Frank came upon a trespasser during deer season. The story had it that Frank made small talk with the man, about the weather and the condition of the deer herd, and then switched the conversation to inquiring about the man's rifle. Frank innocently asked if he might take a look at the weapon, and when it was in his hands, he promptly broke the stock over a boulder and handed the pieces back to the man, snarling, "You son-of-a-bitch, you're trespassing. Now, get the hell off my land. If I catch you on the wrong side of my fence again, swear to God, I'll break your rifle and ram what's left up your ass."

Ty said, "I never knew for positive if that was just a story that circulated but, given the old man's temperament, it probably did happen."

Tracee whispered, "Wouldn't take too many incidents like that for a rancher to build himself a reputation."

"No it don't," said Ty.

They rode in silence. Ty drove along the red cindered road that wove in and out of stately pine trees, crowding close to the edge of a broad valley where horses stood ass-end into the wind, tails blowing between their legs, and hawks sat hunched on fence posts, feathers plumped. Clusters of brown cows with white faces slowly turned their heads to watch the pickup chatter across the washboards. Fences and cross-fences, built of sturdy juniper posts strung with five strands of prickly barbwire, marched straight across the open ground and disappeared into the timber several miles away on the far side.

Ty pointed out an old Fresno, a farm implement that had once been pulled by horses and was designed to move dirt around and dig irrigation ditches. It sat rusting in a fence corner, and Ty claimed it was parked there when the first tractor with a blade was brought onto the ranch.

"What year was that?" Tracee inquired.

"Dunno for sure. This valley has always been thirty or forty years behind the rest of the world. Along in the late '40s or early '50s, I'd guess." Ty nodded toward a pile of blue-gray boards, scattered and trampled by the cattle. He said, "'Bout all that remains of the old hay slide." He went on to explain the slide was a complex affair that involved several hired men, long lines, nets and a drive team to pull hay up the slide. He told about stacks of loose hay dotting the valley floor but claimed he never saw the slide in operation, that by the time he came along Frank had long since switched from loose stacks to wire bales.

Within a couple miles they came to a number of long stacks of baled hay, fenced off with wooden panels to protect them from deer and elk. Ty bragged, "Every summer I bucked bales. I've stacked more hay than Carter has liver pills. It takes a fair amount of skill to make sure a stack remains standing and doesn't fall over."

Tracee laid her head against Ty's shoulder. "What's the secret?"

"Well now, it's sorta complicated," said Ty. "Basically you interlock each layer. The sides have to remain as straight as a brick wall. The ends require special attention. You gotta tie them together so they don't kick out and you taper inward as you build up."

Tracee glanced again at the stacks. They were covered with brown tarps, and she could see nothing of their construction, only that they seemed to be hunkered down out of the brutal wind. The sun managed to find a narrow slot in the pallid sky and sent a dazzling arrow of light shooting down, turning everything it touched to gold. Tracee breathed, "Isn't that incredible!" Stormy stirred but did not awaken.

Ahead, a row of tall Lombardy poplars appeared. Tracee wished she could watch the green leaves shake against a bluebird sky and hear the soft rattle of the wind in the trees, but the leaves were gone and bare branches stood like bleached rib bones caught in a spotlight. The long slanting shafts of light shivered once, disappeared, and the naked branches turned moody and sullen.

Behind the poplars an array of cars and pickup trucks had been indiscriminately parked between a huge, tin-roofed barn, a scattered collection of outbuildings, and an imposing log house that stood like a sentinel at the head of the valley. White smoke boiled from the lava rock chimney, only to be whipped away by the insistent wind.

As Ty was finding a place close to the house to park, he told the story about the old Swede who had built the fireplace, claiming the Swede started each morning by cracking the lid of a quart jar of moonshine, and then sipping it throughout the day; his workmanship never faltering. Each rock was artfully and meticulous placed and the chimney straight and true. Ty said, back when the stone fireplace was built, the rumor in Emerson had been it was so gigantic a horse and rider could turn around in the opening while a line of chorus girls danced on the hearth.

Over the years other gossip had made the rounds, too: that the Battle home had solid gold faucets, that an elevator had been installed, that the floors were teakwood imported from the Philippines. The truth was: Ty's Great-Grandpa Lewis Battle and a dozen men built the house. The outdoor privy was eventually replaced with indoor plumbing. Along in the '40s the local REA cooperative brought electricity to the ranch. Grandpa Harold bought a radio and in the evenings the family sat around and listened to *Amos and Andy, Fibber McGee & Molly, Red Skelton, Jack Benny, Ozzie and Harriet, Sherlock Homes, Groucho Marx* and *Gunsmoke*. Over the course of several Christmases Grandpa Harold gave his wife an electric stove, refrigerator, washing machine and iron—every year another labor saving appliance.

Ty parked and said, "Might have missed the funeral, but guess we're in time for the wake." Actually, Ty was relieved he had missed the funeral. He tried to imagine what it would have been like if he had been a member of the congregation. Walking past his old man's casket, even though the sun would be angling through the tall stained-glass windows, would have been like walking in the darkest and dankest air possible. He could all but feel the sympathetic vibrations of the organ music, see the showy flowers and watch them wilt, hear the drone of some preacher relating the positive impacts Frank Battle had made on this world. Ty figured if he had been there, more than likely, he would've been overcome by a compulsion to jump to his feet, interrupt the service and shout, "Bullshit!"

Ty climbed from the pickup and stood arching his back, cracking his spine. He let out a sigh and turned to face the valley: where the majority of the cottonwoods had long ago been felled, where the meandering Wood River had been controlled and channeled and ditched, where the wild camas that once provided sustenance to the native people had been plowed and planted to grass, clover and alfalfa, where fences and cross-fences looked like bad sutures across the face of the land. And overlooking all of this artificial civilization and cultivation was the showy white sentinel, Sugarloaf Mountain.

Ty shook his head and muttered under his breath, "Tame the land—what a crock. Give it time and it tames you."

"Where are we, Mommy?" said Stormy, sitting up, wiping at the sleep in his eyes.

"We're at Ty's ranch," Tracee told him. She pulled her boy off the seat and stood him on the ground. She held his little hand while wrapping her free arm around Ty's narrow waist, remarking, "You never said it was anything like this—so beautiful—the mountain, the valley, all those cows. I've never seen such a huge log house."

"Better get used to it. Gonna be home for a while, anyway," said Ty, making it sound like she might be facing a lengthy period of incarceration.

It had been Ty who decided to give up going to Mexico and return home to Eastern Oregon. He made that decision while talking to his brother on the phone. What probably swayed his thinking was Cole claiming Ty was needed if they were going to keep the ranch in the family. But what really tipped the scale was Ty knowing, if they failed, his mother would be left destitute, without so much as a pot to piss in. Another important element in the equation was that Frank was no longer of this world. Ty had made his decision to come home and there was no turning back. He asked Tracee if she wanted to tag along, said she could help with the cooking, do a little of this and a little of that, and even suggested, since they were going to be settled in one spot for a while—at least through winter-feeding and spring-calving—that maybe she might like to bring her son along. Upon hearing Ty's suggestion, Tracee gave a shriek of joy, but elation was quickly tempered by reality and she asked, "Sure no one will mind?"

"Not at all," said Ty. "'Sides, Mom might just enjoy havin' a rug rat runnin' around. Yeah, she might at that."

In that instant, Tracee was convinced Ty was everything she was looking for in a man. He fit the bill to a T.

The wake for Frank Battle was in full swing with music—several guitars, a fiddle and at least one harmonica—loud voices, and raucous laughter. It was the kind of party where booze flows freely, and before the night plays itself out, there more than likely will be a few conspicuous seductions and a brawl or two. Some people will go home with their feelings hurt and others might use the occasion as the launching point for a running drunk lasting several days, or if they have a good head of steam up, they might carry on for a week.

Ty, Tracee and Stormy approached the big house and were met at the top of the steps by a woman. It never registered with Tracee who this wisp of a woman might be. She was very plain. Her brown hair was mousy and the skin around her eyes was as thin and transparent as a petal stolen from a flower, faintly bluish. She wore little or no makeup. Her complexion was ashen and there was a cool mist of perspiration coating her face, making her forehead look like a shiny rock at water's edge.

"How you doing, Mom?" said Ty, giving her a quick embrace.

"It's been a rather difficult day," understated Iris. The strain was evident in her voice. She turned her attention to Stormy, managed a thin-lipped smile and asked, "And who do we have here? What's your name young man?"

Ty raced through introductions. Stormy announced he had to go potty and they went inside. Ty pointed the way and Tracee, with Stormy in tow, made her way through the crowd, up the stairs and down the hallway. She found the bathroom. It was old-fashioned with floor-to-ceiling cabinets made from knotty pine and a toilet with the water reservoir mounted high on the wall and a chain that was pulled to flush the bowl.

As they returned to the party, Stormy desperately clung to his mother's leg. They moved slowly, passing a group of men who, Tracee guessed, were most likely businessmen. They wore dark suits and were engaged in a dialogue about celebrity golf tournaments they had watched on television. A cluster of nicely dressed women chatted about how grand it was to finally have a health club in Emerson. Tracee kept moving forward, maneuvering her way toward the stone fireplace where a group of old-time cowboys had congregated and were busy swapping stories. She found a spot away from the flow of traffic where she could listen in on their conversation.

One cowboy was saying, "Remember the time Fuzzy Potter brung that roan mustang name of Skeeter off the range and sells 'im to Frank as green broke? Come that next spring, I'm givin' a hand brandin', and this here kid from Alabama or Tennessee, somewhere like that, shows up an' wants a job. Don't 'ave squat fer experience but Frank hires him, warns 'im, says, 'Don't never get on a horse if you're scared 'cause a horse can sense it.' Puts him on ol' Skeeter. We go maybe a mile and all the time Skeeter's gettin' more an' more fidgety. Frank tells this here kid he better get aholt of that horse or else it's gonna shit him. We didn't go but a little bit fer Skeeter blows sky high and that kid sails off, hind laigs kickin' like a migratin' bullfrog—lands face down. Frank he rides over, asks the kid if he's gonna get back on and the kid he says, 'No sir, I don't believe so.' He walks clear back to his rig an' gets gone. That was the last we ever seen of him."

"Every once in a while a kid like that'll come in," said another man. He smiled. "They learn in a hurry there's a heap more to bein' a cowboy than just settin' astride a horse with yer feet danglin' down."

Tracee listened to one tale after another. One was about a fellow who went into the business of raising fighting cocks and when that story was finished, a cowboy wearing a plaid shirt in need of ironing, claimed, "I raised me a few of them fightin' roosters. They was flat mean. Come close an' they'd puff up like a green bronc on a cold mornin'. One time I was watchin' and this here bald eagle come down and grabbed one of my roosters, flew back up on the ridge an' was commencin' ta eat him, but in nothin' flat that proud eagle was screechin' like a plucked jaybird. An' before it was over that rooster made the eagle fly him back to the barnyard, set him down gentle-like, an' apologize fer the inconvenience."

Tracee could have listened to the windy yarns all night but she wanted to find Ty and finally spotted him across the room shaking hands with a man who appeared to be in his late thirties or early forties. The two men seemed a little standoffish, and yet there was a certain familiarity they shared. Tracee sensed they wanted to be together, but weren't quite sure how they were supposed to act in each other's company.

"That's Ty's brother, Cole," said Iris, coming up to Tracee, nodding in the direction of her sons. " I'll introduce you. Cole's six years older. That's quite a bit of difference for boys. But they always did get along."

"Let's give them a few minutes alone," said Tracee. "They haven't seen each other in a while."

"Suit yourself," said Iris. She stepped back and melted into the party, socializing with people, making it a point to thank each and every one for taking the time to come to Frank's wake.

Tracee stayed where she was and became engrossed in the comparison of the two brothers. Each, in different ways, was attractive and they shared poise, self-confidence and certain mannerisms—hand gestures, nods and shrugs—and yet they were strikingly dissimilar. Ty was lean, with muscles like braided rawhide. He had an oblong face, like his mother, and was dressed like a working cowboy. Tracee figured Cole must look more like his father. His facial features were hard-edged and defined, with a jaw so square it had to have been chiseled. He was built like an athlete who had participated in a contact sport and wore nice clothes; a western-cut sports coat, pressed shirt and gray slacks. When Tracee spotted Cole's cowboy boots peeking out from the cuff of his slacks, she thought, "You can take the man out of the country, but you can't take the country out of the man," and she had to laugh.

XX

Ty leaned in close so his brother could hear over the noise. "Where's your family?"

"Back in Portland. They're real busy. Had commitments they couldn't get out of, not on such short notice, anyway," said Cole. He quickly changed the subject. "So, what do you have to say for yourself? Where you been? What you been doing?"

"Mostly just wandering here and there like a pony with his bridle off," answered Ty with a grin. He had half a mind to let it go at that but took a pull off his beer and that recharged him. He went on talking. "Was around Billings for a while driving combine, got mixed up with a pretty little squaw off the Crow reservation but they let her old man out of prison and I figured it best to move on. Shoed horses around Sheridan for a spell but they don't wanna pay nothin'. Farriers are a dime a dozen. Ended up at Red Lodge riding roundup for the TY outfit."

Cole, making sure the conversation moved forward, said, "On the phone you said you were headed for Mexico."

"Yep, winters are a lot easier to take the farther south you go."

"I'm sick as hell of the rain on the west side. I'd take snow over rain any day of the week," said Cole.

"You don't have any idea," responded Ty. "Down south, nothing but miles and miles of white sandy beaches and not a soul around to ruin it. It never rains. Water's warm as a bath. Ten bucks lasts all day and most of the night."

"Not much chance you'll see Mexico this winter," said Cole with a cruel grimace.

"What a shame." Ty was not smiling. "What about you? Had any fun lately?"

"Got in a lot of fishing. Went to Alaska three times this year. Maybe one of these days we can slip away and give it a go."

"Be a hoot," said Ty, "but it looks like the old man made sure we got about as much chance of going to Alaska as we do Mexico—zero. He always was one to roll his own hoop. Now he's got us rolling it for him."

Johnny Ritter was a buckaroo. He had worked for Frank Battle, mostly spring and fall, for the past couple decades. He was in his mid-30s, was raw, unrefined and yet ruggedly handsome in an original sort of way. His face looked like it had been marked for life by having every hard lesson he ever learned hammered into it. He wore his scars like badges, was proud of them, and he was a good talker, loved the ladies and fancied himself a bit of a rounder.

Johnny took notice of Tracee the minute she walked into the room. He momentarily wondered, coming in with Ty, was she an acres-and-dollars type of gal, a hanger-on looking to cash in on a rancher's inheritance. He quickly put that out of his mind and focused on her good looks and eye-catching figure. She had a kid in tow, and to Johnny, this proved she was willing and able. His lazy stare wandered up and down her lanky highway, lingering with pleasure at her most interesting intersections. To Johnny, timing was everything and he patiently waited for the right moment.

Tracee trundled her boy upstairs and put him to bed, returning to the party alone and standing at the fringe of a group of old cowboys. Johnny sauntered over and greeted her with a delicate tip of the brim of his cowboy hat, and in a friendly manner, said, "Howdy ma'am." He introduced himself, asked her name, made general small talk about where she called home, what jobs she had worked and the party. All the while, he leaned in close under the pretext of trying to hear, and be heard, over the noise.

Tracee leaned back against the wall. She had men like Johnny hit on her damn near every day and knew all their subtle, and not so subtle, tricks. She was determined not to give him any false sign of interest but when he persisted she thought she just might fish for a little information. "Mr. Battle must have been well-liked for this many people to turn out in his honor."

Johnny, his lips only inches from her ear, responded, "Not necessarily. Put it this way, Frank was an important man, had power and wasn't afraid to use it. Got what he wanted. Take that back; *took* what he wanted."

"What did he want?"

"Everything. Wanted it all. Land. Cattle. Money. People. He demanded respect, got it because he had the special touch. Every time cattle prices fall a lot of ranchers go belly up, not Frank. Hell, he always increased the size of his herd, bought more land and when prices did come back, he was the one in the driver's seat. Controlled his outfit with an iron fist. That's the reason them boys of his never did have a fair chance."

"How do you figure?"

"Don't need to say much about Ty. He probably told you what happened when he lit out of here. As for his brother Cole, now he's older than me. You know, I seen him play football. Had it all. Size. Speed. Cut on a dime and give back change. Power to burn. Small college All-American. Willamette or Lewis and Clark. One of them private colleges over in the valley. Can't rightly remember which. Heard the Dallas Cowboys wanted him to play for them. Don't know that for a fact but he was one hell of an athlete. Probably the best ever to ever come from around these parts; big fish, small pond.

"After college he came back, was gonna take over the ranch from his old man. That's what he had figured. But his old man worked the shit out of him and cut him loose."

Tracee wanted to know, "What happened?"

"Don't rightly know. Probably got sideways with his old man, easy to do, but I always suspected it might have been woman problems. Cole's wife, now she was one fine lookin' lady, probably still is, but she didn't fit in all that well, not around these parts anyway. She was a city gal. Sometimes them city gals have trouble handlin' country life. Know what I mean? Can get a little lonely out here in the puckerbrush." Johnny paused, allowing that to sink in, adding, "Say, I do like your perfume."

When Johnny failed to get any reaction whatever from Tracee—he had been expecting a pleasant thank you, maybe a demure smile, but nothing—he took a step back, leaned an elbow against the wall, and tried to imagine Tracee in a different outfit, something skimpy. She had such fair skin he guessed she took a tan like butterscotch. He wished he could find an excuse to touch her.

"Hell of a thing Frank did, forcing everyone's hand. Don't know how it's gonna play out, what with Cole coming back now to run things. Guess maybe he can make a go of it if he ain't completely citified. He might wanna remember 'round this neck of the woods we trap coyotes and hang the pelts on the barn to dry. Cut and burn wood. Every two years we gotta move the privy. We raise chickens, collect eggs, butcher the roosters, smoke ham, make jerky, put up wild strawberry jam. Don't know if Cole can relate to that kind of shit no more."

Tracee said, "This ranch has been in the Battle family for a long time." She made it sound like more of a question than a declaration of fact.

Johnny picked up on it. "Long, long time. Story goes Frank's grandfather got his first one-sixty from a sodbuster after the Indians killed his wife. The fellow wanted out and Battle supposedly swapped a beat-up McClellan army saddle for the land claim. Sodbuster walked out of here, saddle slung over his shoulder, lookin' for a mustang to ride. That's one story. Another is the old man stole it from the Indians. Paid them with whiskey. Hard to tell where truth starts and stops.

"But now if you want to uncover the skeleton in the closet, and if you want the straight skookum, you best talk to J.B. You'll find a little Jack Daniels works wonders to loosen his tongue." Johnny gave Tracee an expressive wink, continued, "He's the hired man, claims he's been in these parts since Sugarloaf, the mountain you passed on your way in here, was nothing but a hole in the ground."

Tracee laughed. Johnny felt good that he could make this pretty gal respond to him and it gave him the confidence to make a bold move. He reached out, touched her forearm and said, "Sweetie, I've been hoggin' the conversation. Sorry 'bout that. So, why don't you tell me a little more about yourself? You here to stay or just passing through?"

Tracee felt a strange coolness on her arm where Johnny's hand had rested for those fleeting few seconds, and when she spoke her tone was not as trusting as it had been. "Not much to tell. Be here through calving season, that long at least." She turned to face him and reclaim the upper hand. "So, Johnny, you been here your whole life."

"Yep, and proud of the fact. Graduated out of high school in Emerson, that was all the formal education I figured I needed. Never had no desire to go to college. Don't seem right for an 18-year-old still wet behind the ears deciding what he should do with the rest of his life. Figured I'd stick close to home. Mostly I buckaroo. Come winter I feed cows and break a few colts on the side. Ain't no big-time wages, but I make enough to get me by. I'm my own boss. Found out a long time ago, in this line of work, it's best to stand up for yourself, don't complain, keep your eyes open and your mouth shut, never brag about anything you can't back up. If I was to move to some town and go to work in the mill, I'd be just another flunky pushing through the gate in a baseball cap, getting a paycheck handed to me every two weeks and running out of money before the next payday. My way's a whole lot better. I get crosswise with the boss, and I'm on down the road. There's always another ranch in need of a buckaroo."

Ty wandered into the kitchen to grab another beer, and in his absence, Cole watched Johnny Ritter try to make time with his brother's girlfriend. It amused him because he considered himself a pretty good judge of character and was sure he saw something in this woman that a drifty cowpoke like Johnny Ritter would never see. He hadn't even met her but he told himself what appealed to him was the way she carried herself, with dignity, composure and a certain amount of charm. She seemed to be the one in control, the lead actress of the little drama with Johnny, and then Cole laughed at himself for his patronizing attitude and had to admit she was attractive as hell, and yeah, he could see why Johnny was making a run at her.

Tracee broke away from Johnny, went to the kitchen and in her wake Johnny stood rooted to the same spot, intently watching her walk away, seemingly fixated on the way she filled out her Levi's in just the right places. When he finally did manage to rip his eyes from her backside, he looked up and met Cole's fixed stare. He reached to the brim of his cowboy hat in salute and moved away in search of easier pickings.

Ty stood outside on the porch listening to the river of unsteady feet inside: the moving, shuffling, rumbling, bantering. In his mind he compared the crowd to a ball of snakes on that first warm day of spring, the way they tangle and untangle around and over and through each other.

The solitary voice of an owl, calling from the poplars, drifted high and lonesome across the cavernous valley. The wind had blown itself out and a chunk of moon, the color of weak iodine, played peek-a-boo behind wispy clouds, leftover fragments from the fast-moving storm. A thin skin of moonlight bathed the hills, rock ribbed and ancient, and cast an eerie glow over the deep, dark woods beyond.

Up the hill, at the edge of the family burial plot, the backhoe, its work completed, sat parked beside a pile of freshly-turned earth. The body of Frank Battle lay there. Ty could not see Blue, but the dog had found his way home and now lay curled on that mound of dirt. Even though Frank was gone, old Blue wanted to be as close as possible to his cold body. In time the ground would settle, a tombstone would be erected at the head of the grave and Blue would grow old and die.

A quick mental picture came to Ty, an image of his old man hunched over the kitchen table, eyes puffy, face bloated, drinking whiskey. And Ty realized his memories, and the memories of those in attendance at the wake, might endure for a while but would surely be lost within a generation. With Frank's death there was the opportunity for new blood to take up the reins and forge the future of the Double X ranch. It seemed to Ty that a grand parade had been called, and he was afraid of missing it and afraid of catching it, too. He cursed himself, knowing he could be in Mexico warming his ass, swimming in the tepid coastal water, making love to Tracee on a secluded beach, kicking back and taking life easy. Instead, he had come home, and now that he was here, he was not sure of much of anything, much of anything at all.

Ty took a seat on the porch railing, and even though he rarely smoked, he lit a borrowed cigarette. As he inhaled smoke into his lungs, the point of the cigarette went from green to silver and then shined with a pinprick of red in the ebbing sea of darkness and scant moonlight. For an instant, Ty's face was illuminated. He turned away feeling anxious and unsettled. He did not like the idea of being tied to this ranch, nor did he look forward to having to try to mesh his personality, and his basic needs and desires, into the complex web of family relationships. In the past there had been no place, and no woman, to hold him for long. He liked it that way, and asked why in hell had he hog-tied himself with commitments to his brother and mother, to the ranch, and to Tracee and the boy? On one hand he felt as hapless as a deer hunter who dresses in fluorescent orange in a futile effort to keep from being mistaken for the quarry. And on the other he was sure, if he looked, he'd find a bull's eye painted on his back. He had set himself up as a target for failure. He knew that.

Ty reasoned that if given free rein to run the ranch, he could do it. And if such a situation had presented itself he, more than likely, would have been content to stay inside, lift a glass and drink a toast to his old man. But he was the younger brother, standing outside, with only the thin outline of a bloody moon to keep him company.

There were still a few hangers-on who refused to allow the party to die a natural death, and their erratic noises filtered through the floor as shrill as a prairie dog town at first light. Iris stood in front of her bedroom window, body draped in a blue flannel nightgown, her reflection hinting at a thin but modestly good figure for a woman her age, a woman who had borne three children. Her legs were straight, hips wide with a smooth curve to the waist and her breasts, though small, had continued to hold their shape. But what did it matter how she looked and whether some man might find her attractive? Iris would never be with another man. She told herself that and sighed deeply. She pulled back the covers and crawled into bed. She drew the blankets over her and lay very still. It was strange, after having lost her life's partner, that she did not either have a sense of overwhelming bereavement, nor the exhilaration from having the jailhouse doors kicked down and unconditional freedom granted her. In truth she felt very little of anything at all. In her marriage she had been forced to build so many walls around her emotions that she had become immune to any feeling, any feelings whatsoever. Not sadness, not joy, nothing. And yet, a single tear formed and began to slowly slide down her cheek. By the time that tear had dried, she was asleep.

The following day, after the mess from the wake had been cleared away, Cole, Ty and Iris sat around the kitchen table discussing Frank's will and the challenges facing the family. Cole took the initiative, "We can sell some timber, turn this into a dude ranch for the summer, take on fee hunters come elk season. We're not without options and opportunities."

Iris set him straight, "According to Mr. Sandlin, we are required to operate this as a cattle ranch, like it has always been run. The court will appoint an appraiser, and he will set the starting base according to the current market value of the cattle. Over the course of the next twelve months, with all expenses factored in and the income of the sale of the calves recorded, the same appraiser will compare the value and determine if we made or lost money. If the calves don't gain weight like they should, that counts against us. If we have a bad winter and have to buy hay, if we have a late spring and can't turn out when we normally do, if a cow dies, if we lose too many calves, if we get rain and the hay molds, if, if, if.... The long and short is, we have to work the ranch, and in the end, we must show a profit. If we fail, Oregon State University takes title to the ranch. We lose everything. That's the way Frank set it up. It's a done deal, black and white."

"It doesn't matter if we're the best ranchers in the world," complained Ty. "If the beef market drops we can't help but lose money."

"That's right, Honey," said Iris.

"Why the hell would he do something like that?" said Cole.

"You know your father. He had some strange quirks."

Ty was agitated. "Damn sight more than a few strange quirks. The man was crazy."

"We can't change facts. All we can do is move forward, make an honest effort, try," said Iris.

Cole turned to Ty, "What's your take? How do we make it work?"

"Can't go hiring a lot of outside help. Have to do the bulk of the work ourselves. Cut expenses wherever we can. Jerry-rig things together. Get by on the cheap. Pray like hell cattle prices don't go in the shitter. Pretty much it in a nutshell. As far as I can see we got no alternative, do we?"

"Nope," said Iris, but as she continued to talk there was a peculiar enthusiasm in her voice. "If we work as family, everyone pulling together, we can do this. We'll be all right. It's mainly up to you boys. I'm sure that's what Frank had in mind. He always did like to test a person. See what their limits were. I think he'd roll over in his grave if the college actually ever did take over."

"I'll get hold of Sandlin. See if there's any wiggle room," said Cole.

"Think you'll find it just like I said. Cut and dried. Frank liked to keep things on the straight-and-narrow, no room for interpretation, simple and straightforward," said Iris.

While the Battle family was involved in their meeting, Tracee took Stormy outside. He was a bundle of pent-up energy, wanting to see the horses and the barn, sit in the truck, crawl on the hay swather, and when he had his fill of all these, some of the excess energy still had not unraveled and Tracee led him on a hike. They angled up the hill to where they had a good view and sat on a flat boulder. Stormy promptly laid his head on his mother's lap, and within a few minutes fell asleep.

From her vantage point, Tracee could look down and see the family cemetery and even a dog lying on the mound of fresh dirt. She had seen other dogs on the ranch but didn't remember this particular one. She made a mental note to mention the dog to Iris.

If Frank had been alive, he'd have marched up the hill to challenge Tracee. He'd stand in front of her wearing his western-cut shirt with pearl buttons, tugging at his pants, kicking at the dirt, legs apart, arms hanging loose, looking tottery and crotchety but with no signs of ever giving up or giving in. He'd demand to know why she was parking her carcass on *his* land.

But if Frank had allowed himself the opportunity to get to know this woman he'd have liked her, and probably engaged her in a long-winded discourse, undoubtedly getting around to one of his pet peeves—complaining about the interlopers who had moved into Emerson. He'd say they come from the Willamette Valley, and California and Washington, driving their automobiles across the whiskey-colored plains, and in an hour's time cover way more ground than a man on a good saddle horse could travel in a long day. He might even criticize some of the locals—in particular the wives of the old ranchers who had worked themselves into an early grave, and even before their husbands bodies were cold these women were dumping the cows to the highest bidder and selling out to a real estate broker. And while the broker was busy carving up the land, the widow was hightailing it for a condo in Boca Ratan and living the good life.

In his booming voice Frank might have railed, "This here country's always been bone dry. No one but a fool expects more 'an a foot of annual rainfall. But that goddamn ski resort comes in, I know what they're up to, hell yes I do, they seed the clouds. They goddamn do! And why? So they can have a few more inches of precious snow, that's why. What I get are stock ponds gone dry, grass shrivelin', hungry cows an' country that wants to go back to sand dunes an' rattlesnakes.

"I go to town and don't even know where I am. Nothing is where it's supposed to be. What really frosts my balls, I go to the store an' they wanna know whether I want paper or plastic. They smile sweetly, say, 'Have a nice day,' when they don't give a good goddamn whether I have a nice day or a lousy-assed day.

"Them rich folks drag their sorry-assed kids in here an' ever' last one of 'em is fat. Add a dozen together an' you couldn't get an honest day's worth of work out of the bunch, not in a month of Sundays. Hell, back when I was a pup, my schoolmates were skinny, quick ranch kids. They looked like slim-stick kindlin'. Any of 'em drop his drawers, take a shit 'hind a clump of sagebrush, an' nobody's the wiser.

"Look around an' see if you don't agree—most all these newcomers deserve to be ridden bareback by the devil wearin' pointed can-openers for spurs. Tell me if it ain't so?"

A couple hundred feet above where Tracee and Stormy now sat, Frank had often parked his truck at the pullout, watched dusk tumble from the sky and a globe of light, like an incandescent jellyfish, form on the flank of Sugarloaf Mountain, poisoning the emerging darkness with the weak orange glow signifying the encroachment of civilization. But Tracee had never been subjected to Frank's uncompromising abrasiveness, and she was perfectly content to drink in the pleasant sights of mountain, valley and forest. With her son resting his head on her lap, she was thrilled with the solitude and more happy and content than she ever remembered being.

CHAPTER SEVEN

COLE NEEDED TO GET BACK TO PORTLAND. HE HAD PENDING REAL ESTATE matters to hand over to his business partner, would trade his Corvette for the practicality of his pickup truck and was looking forward to spending the long Thanksgiving weekend with his wife and daughter. But more than anything, he was hopeful he could convince Donna and Kendra to return with him to the rural vistas of Eastern Oregon. It seemed reasonable for them to move into the town house in Emerson. Kendra could attend school there and Cole, feeling it vitally important they remain together as a family, had resigned himself to traveling back and forth to work at the ranch. But Cole's plan was tenuous at best. Soon winter snows would close the road, isolating the ranch, and calving season would occupy nearly all his time.

Upon reaching the summit of the Cascades—the snowfields on Mt. Hood shone like reflective mirrors in the late afternoon sunlight—Cole picked up his cell phone, saw he had good reception and called Donna. He promised her that, after making a quick stop at the office, he would be home in time for dinner. But time got away from Cole. He was delayed by road construction and heavy traffic and when he did get to the office there was a lot going on, and to get away from the hubbub, he and his partner went to a nearby brewpub where they talked business and fishing. Dinner had come and gone by the time Cole reached home. Donna voiced her displeasure by remarking, "At least we know where your priorities are." Cole, to his credit, did not rise to the bait and simply sat with her and watched television before excusing himself and going to bed.

The following morning Cole expected to awaken to bustling activity and the air charged with the delicious smells of baking turkey, but there was nothing. Donna informed him she wasn't cooking and had made plans for them to have Thanksgiving dinner at a friend's house.

Cole hid his disappointment and held off saying anything about the possibility of having her and Kendra moving with him to Eastern Oregon. Finally, and rather thoughtlessly, he broached the subject when they were getting ready to go out for dinner. Donna was taking a shower. Cole walked in, went to the sink, lathered his face and began shaving. Raising his voice so Donna could hear him over the noise of the shower he said, "What would you think about living in Emerson? After school is over, you and Kendra can move to the ranch for the summer. Sound good?"

After a long moment and no response, Cole stepped to the shower, rapped his knuckles on the glass partition, saw her nakedness as a blurred image, asked, "Did you hear me?"

"I heard."

"Well?"

"We'll talk later."

Cole finished shaving, got dressed and was sitting on the edge of the bed pulling on his boots when Donna, dressed in a fluffy pink bathrobe, wet hair wrapped in a white towel, marched into the room and took a commanding position directly in front of Cole. In an edgy voice lacking any thread of compromise, she announced, "Kendra and I will not move to

Emerson or to the ranch or anywhere else. This is our home. We're staying here." She turned away, went to her closet and began pawing through clothes looking for the outfit she planned to wear.

Cole, feeling wounded, said, "I thought we were a family; I thought you'd support me in this. It's not like I have a choice. This is something I have to do. I want you and Kendra with me."

"Maybe you should have thought of that before you jumped so wholeheartedly at the chance to go back to the ranch. You made your choice. Live with it," said Donna. And with her outfit draped over one arm, she left him and went to the bathroom to dress.

That evening, after returning to the house, Kendra went directly to her bedroom. Cole and Donna spent a grueling hour in an intense and futile dialogue where neither of them was really wrong because neither, in their relationship, had been right in a long, long time. Donna was defensive. She kept nervously smoothing her gray skirt over her legs. At one point she asserted, "I have absolutely no intention of pulling Kendra out of school and forcing her to move away. Anyway, I never liked living in Eastern Oregon. It's too far from anywhere."

"Emerson's a nice town," countered Cole. "We own a house there."

"Peyton Place. Where everybody knows everyone else's business. No thank you. Not interested."

"It's not like that. Emerson's changed. It's become a resort community. It has trendy stores and everything. You could find something to do, maybe even open a little coffee shop," suggested Cole. When that failed to excite Donna, he appealed to her practical and sensible side. "We stay a year and then decide, as a family, what to do. Think about it—if I turn my back on it now, we lose the ranch and we lose millions and millions of dollars. And what about Mother? What's gonna happen to her? You want her to move in here with us?"

"Where was she when Frank ran you off?" Donna's words cut like a serrated blade. "Where has she been for the last twelve years?"

"That's not fair," complained Cole.

"Fair. Was it fair when I fell in love with you and foolishly believed everything you told me? You painted this idyllic picture of what our life on the ranch would be like: this bucolic existence of contented cattle on pasture, spirited horses galloping in the mountains and wonderful dinner parties with interesting people. I bought into it," said Donna. "And even when I realized it wasn't true, none of it, I still tried to make it work. But I never took any pleasure in living at the ranch.

"Face it Cole, you made a mistake. You married the wrong woman. You should have married a local girl who'd have appreciated that primitive lifestyle. That's just not me. I enjoy social interaction, culture and all the amenities city living provides. You think you have to rescue your family, fine, go rescue them. This is your fight. Just don't drag me, and your daughter, into it, okay?"

That night Cole and Donna slept in the same bed but as far away from each other as humanly possible. In the morning Cole, so as not to awaken his wife, rolled out quietly and pulled on his clothes. As he did, he surveyed the room and saw, on prominent display, photographs of Donna's mother and father, her brothers and sisters and nieces and nephews. Lined up on the dresser, like toy soldiers, was a collection of Terry Lee dolls. And there was the special Madame Alexander doll with her painted bisque face, circle hoop slip under a satin, corseted, midnight-blue gown, looking every bit like the belle of the south. Books given to Donna by her mother dominated the bookcase—*A Girl of the Limber Lost,* the Nancy Drew mystery series and *Peter Pan*. There was an ornate jewelry box—a gift from Donna's father—and Cole could almost hear the tune *La Vie En Rose* that played each time the lid was lifted. There were decorative perfume bottles, an arrangement of dried flowers in a vase that had been passed down through several generations, and in the corner was a cuddly teddy bear dressed in a striped vest. It occurred to Cole he did not exist in this room, that he never had.

He headed for the kitchen, making a side trip to the bathroom, and as water dripped through a coffee machine, he stepped outside to retrieve the early edition of the *Oregonian* from the porch. He sat at the table drinking coffee and reading the fishing report on the sports page until he heard the TV switch on in the family room. He investigated and found Kendra, wrapped in a blanket, mindlessly flipping through channels. Cole tried to talk with her about how he was involved in attempting to save the ranch. He stressed how important it was for the family to stay together and concluded by saying, "I want you and your mother to move to Emerson. You can live in the town house. They've got a new school there. It's real modern. They have a terrific computer lab. Be something a little different for you, a challenge in some ways, but you'd adjust. I think it'd be fun for you and certainly a worthwhile experience and help broaden your horizons from just living the city life."

Kendra never bothered looking away from the television. She said with a snarl, "What about my friends? We get to do what? Text message each other?"

"You're being a little melodramatic. You'll make new friends. I predict that, within a week, you'll be voted the most popular girl in school."

Kendra shook back her hair in the same irritating way her mother did whenever she was upset or things weren't going her way. "You want to take me away from all my friends and force me to live somewhere I don't know a single person. What's reasonable about that?"

"We'll be back and forth. We're not going to sell this house or anything. Sweetheart, the ranch has been in my family for more than a hundred years. I've got to be there. I'm the one who has to run it. Come on, all I'm asking is for you to give this a try."

"What'd Mom say?"

"She's thinking about it."

Kendra finally turned her head and looked at her father, seemed to look straight through him. She said, "That's not true and you know it."

Later that day Kendra went to a movie with a friend and Cole tried, one last time, to convince Donna to move to Emerson. She stubbornly refused to consider it and the resulting quarrel was an ugly affair. During the most heated part of the exchange, Donna dredged up every disagreeable memory and unpleasant incident that had occurred during their married life, and hurled them at him as if they were sharp barbs. Her final accusatory volley was to say he had no right to try and impose his dominance over her and to force her to do something against her will.

Cole made a sweeping gesture with one hand, in an effort to encompass everything in the well-appointed house, and asked, "Aren't you happy with what I provide?"

She replied, "You tell me about being happy. You run off to all these places. You hunt and fish and run rivers. You do what you want to do. And now you've got the ranch. You should be the one to define happiness. Are you happy, Cole?"

Cole didn't know how to respond. He looked at her and tried to remember the last time they made love. He could not recall when that might have been. He pulled himself off the sofa, went to the garage and pulled a cloth cover over his Corvette. He loaded his Ford pickup with three duffel bags of clothes, fishing rods, tackle and his hunting rifle. This, he figured, were the bare essentials, all he really needed. He opened the door, stuck his head inside, told Donna, "I'm going," and drove away without showing an ounce of affection or regret in going.

XX

When they had first arrived at the ranch, Iris had dictated that Ty take his old room, the room where he slept when he was a kid. Tracee and Stormy were relegated to one of the guest bedrooms. Tracee thought forcing her and Ty to sleep in separate rooms was old-fashioned but concluded, if Iris wanted to stick her head in the sand, it was her prerogative. She would accept it. Ty offered to talk to his mother but Tracee gave him a playful jab in the ribs and whispered, "Don't worry, mister. I can still get to you."

One day, while Tracee was doing a little snooping around the massive old house, she opened a door and found what appeared to be a nursery. There was a crib and a pink bassinet, a Winnie-the-Pooh bear and an array of dolls, stuffed animals, a mobile with cutouts of Mickey Mouse and other Disney cartoon characters, a miniature Ferris wheel and cute little dresses, hats and mittens. Tracee slowly backed from the room, and using both hands, firmly and quietly pulled the door shut behind her. Later she asked Ty why there was a nursery when there weren't any babies in the house.

Ty merely shrugged. "Oh, you stumbled onto Ruth Ann's room. It's been the same ever since she died. Mom never did change it."

"Don't you think that's kind of bizarre? How long's that been?"

"Since before I was born," said Ty. He grinned. "You'll find out, around here there's lots of things that could be classified as bizarre, or at least a little strange."

XX

Tracee helped Iris prepare Thanksgiving dinner. She basted the turkey, tore breadcrumbs for dressing and rolled piecrusts. Stormy was content to play with a truck in the living room, driving it around the furniture, making *varooming* noises. Two hours before dinner, with nothing more for her to do, Tracee bundled Stormy into warm clothes, and they went for a hike. They went to the barn and climbed into the cavernous loft where they lay together, breathing in the smells of summers past that sagged from the mound of baled hay. Below them, in the alleyway, horses materialized out of the darkness to bury their warm muzzles in the manger. Their rhythmic chewing echoed in the barn as bars of sunlight leaked between weathered boards and amber particles of dust and powder-dry manure hung suspended in the dank, still air. A hardy moth flitted in and out of the sunlight looking as though it could be a burnished needle tediously weaving an elaborate tapestry. A horse shivered, another coughed and others stamped the thick board floor and swished their tails to keep away a few persistent flies. A big bay gelding stood spraddle-legged and pissed a forceful stream. When he finally finished, he gave a satisfied groan and farted. Tracee and Stormy held their noses against the acrid stench of hot urine and giggled.

Seconds tiptoed away and soft, absorbing sounds came alive: sparrows flitting about the eaves, mice burrowing into the hay, a cat meowing faintly and a light drizzle from a wayward cloud affectionately drumming the tin roof. And all the while, overhead on a rafter, a pair of cream-colored barn owls sat perched, motionless, except for the shifting of their yellow, watchful eyes.

When Stormy began to fidget, Tracee took him by the hand and they slipped down from the loft and peeked inside the tack room where dim rays of truculent light revealed the history of a working cattle ranch. There were reatas coiled like sleeping snakes, leather chaps, widowed gloves, harness leather, driving lines, hames and collars. Conflicting and incompatible smells rose; from leather, oils, horse sweat and from an assortment of livestock medicines and liniments. Tracee closed the door without ever setting foot inside the room.

They hiked to where Wood River murmured around a bed of rocks, and stood above a tranquil pool where they watched quick minnows flash silver and plump tadpoles burrow into the brown mud. Along the fence line a few cows lifted their white faces, eyed the intruders with measured indifference and spoke in low and throaty tones.

Tracee led the way to where spring runoffs had gouged away the topsoil, and in the gully were the littered remains of old car bodies and tires, furniture and appliances, rusting cans, broken bottles, sodden magazines and many other household and ranch items that had been discarded there over the years. While they scanned the useless treasures the misty rain gave way. The gray sky broke apart and the sun began playing hide-and-seek, disappearing for long moments and then burst through and shining down from blue holes between feathery-edged clouds. Ravens called from deep in a white-barked aspen grove. High overhead a flock of Canada geese, having rested in the valley on the way north, followed the arrow point of the leader on a due southerly course, soundlessly traversing the sky. A gust of wind swept through the treetops. Two trees rubbed together, screeching until the gust pushed past, and in an old snag, a hungry hawk leaped light-boned from a brittle limb and began circling on outstretched wings.

Tracee, holding Stormy's hand, pulled him up a long hill coated with leafy manzanita. A white-tailed rabbit hopped into view, made a quick cut left and disappeared. Quail, with a sharp whirring of wings, burst from the cover and flew away, scattering, landing on the run and darting into hiding places along the willow-lined creek. Almost immediately they began calling to one another and Tracee tried to imagine the quail's dialogue as individuals revealed their hiding places. She wondered if there was a reason they did this and figured it had to be so they could find each other and reform the covey as soon as the danger passed.

"Mommy, I'm hungry," said Stormy.

"Okay. Let's go back."

Upon returning to the house, and stepping inside, Tracee and Stormy were engulfed in a pleasant wave of warmness and a host of wonderful smells from cooking food. But dinner was far from being ready to serve and Stormy insisted on eating. Tracee heated a can of alphabet soup and Stormy played with his food, dipping out letters on his spoon. When he could not find the right combination to form his name he complained.

Iris slammed a cupboard door, and in a voice hard-edged with annoyance, scolded, "Stop your whining!"

J.B. showed up for dinner at the big house wearing his best shirt, although even his best was paper thin at the elbows. His hair was wetted down and neatly combed. There was a hint of brown stain at one corner of his mouth, evidence of where a spittle of Copenhagen-laced drool had been backhanded. While Iris said a prayer of thanks, J.B. bowed his head and joined the tips of his fingers together. Pale blue veins stood out on the backs of his hands like secondary roads on a map.

After the big Thanksgiving dinner had been consumed, including pumpkin pie and apple pie for dessert, Tracee offered to clean up and do the dishes. J.B. made up an excuse, said he had to be getting back, and returned to the bunkhouse. Iris poured herself a glass of wine and was content to sit in front of a window, sipping wine and gazing over the valley. Ty and Stormy played checkers.

When her work was done, Tracee curled up in a chair and though she wanted to watch the spirited game of checkers, her eyelids began to flutter. She pulled a colorful afghan over her legs. Firelight danced on the open hearth, heat shimmered and the flames crackled. Occasionally a log shifted, sending a shower of sparks leaping up the chimney. Under the floor the dogs squirmed and whimpered in dreams of chasing deer or turning back a pack of vicious coyotes. Tracee slept.

The year's calf crop had been sold and the cattle that remained on the Double X—seven hundred brood cows, a hundred 2-year-old heifers, the same number of replacement heifer calves, and fifty bulls—were scattered over the meadow and marsh, grazing in separate fields. The grasses were brown and withered but held sufficient nutrients to sustain life for a few more weeks.

The week after Thanksgiving the weather turned cold. Snow crept down the sides of Sugarloaf Mountain and each morning the line of demarcation was drawn a little lower until, one morning, the tops of the hills surrounding the valley were white with a skift of snow. Still the valley floor remained untouched. A few elk and deer followed the snowline and moved down to forage alongside the cattle, taking the opportunity for an easy meal even though they could have subsisted at higher elevations.

Before long snow would drift the road shut, cutting off access to town and isolating the ranch for several months, although, in case of a dire emergency, the road could be plowed open with the Caterpillar. But fifteen miles was a long way to walk a Cat, and besides the wind was likely to come up and drift the road over again just as soon as it was punched through. While travel was possible, trips were made to town for many last-minute necessities and for Christmas shopping. A close tab was kept on expenses and nobody went overboard because, come next fall, a few dollars one way or the other might make the difference on whether the ranch was saved or lost.

On one trip to town, Ty told Tracee that every day stolen from winter, when the cattle did not have to be fed, allowed a rancher to slip a little more profit in his pocket. He explained cattle lack the pawing instinct. Once the snow was too deep for them to push it aside with their noses, they had be cared for, fed and babied, or they would starve. He said, "Each pregnant cow requires twenty pounds of hay per day, more in colder weather. If we have to buy hay at market prices, counting the cows, heifers and bulls, it could cost between a grand and fifteen hundred bucks each and every day. That's why we're putting off feeding until we absolutely have to."

A week before Christmas the first substantial storm of the season blew in. Fat snowflakes drifted light-footed through the limber pine but the snow was timid, or the soil too warm, and did not stick. Soon small islands of white appeared where stumps and rock piles had thrown an arc of shade, and finally, as the temperature dropped a few more degrees, snow began collecting in the openings between trees. On the meadow, the cattle moved toward the edge of the sheltering timber where they stood with their heads down while snow accumulated on their backs, turning their coarse brown hair white. Wind whistled through the treetops, and blowing snow obscured the ruddy red of the ponderosa pine bark and drifted over the blue-green hues of lichen clinging to outcroppings of lava rock. Underground, in the hidden world of unconscious sleep, squirrels and chipmunks, badgers and sage rats, bear and timber rattlers settled in their beds, floating on a river of delirious hibernation.

By morning the wind had died but it was still snowing lightly. Ten inches of wet snow had accumulated, and yet, in places, sere grasses poked through the thick layer of white like errant whiskers. Cole and Ty stood together on the edge of the porch, shoulder-to-shoulder, surveying the staggering, silent world. Ty hunched his collar tightly around his neck and endured the cold without enthusiasm. Cole tipped his head back, allowing the wet flakes to land on his warm skin, instantly turning to water and sliding down his cheeks like sad tears. He looked at the milling cows, nervous and hungry, and then up into the western sky hoping to see that the storm had passed and behind it a flourish of blue sky dragging in warm, dry air. But the falling snow cut visibility to almost nothing. Not even Sugarloaf Mountain could be seen.

"At least the skiers are happy," offered Cole.

Ty responded, "Glad someone's enjoying it."

"We gotta do it, don't we?" said Cole.

Ty shook his head up and down. "Once we break that first bale we're committed—two hundred bales a day, seven days a week. No holidays."

"What do you say, should we get to work?"

"Do we have a choice?" said Ty.

"Nope. Suppose we don't." Cole stepped off the porch and into the snow. The brothers headed in the direction of the forty-year-old International truck. It had always been referred to simply as the "feedwagon."

Cole had been anticipating the arrival of this day and had prepared for it by getting the International ready to run: putting in a new battery, changing the crankcase oil, adjusting the points, resetting the gap on the spark plugs, draining the gas and adding fresh. He had wrapped heavy-duty tire chains around the dual tires knowing when the feedwagon was loaded with hay, it could easily pull its way through 18 or 20 inches of snow. More than that and a pathway had to be cut with the blade of the Cat.

J.B., coming from the bunkhouse, had the shortest distance to go and reached the feedwagon first. He climbed in, pulled out the choke and pressed the starter with the toe of his boot. The old engine coughed a couple times, choking on a rich mixture of gasoline and air, but caught and blew a plume of white out the exhaust. Cole slapped Ty on the back and told him, "Runs like a champ don't she? We're burnin' daylight, let's get-er-done."

The feedwagon was maneuvered close to one of the stacks, the heavy tarp rolled back and while Cole kicked hay off the stack Ty restacked the bales on the bed of the truck. When the truck was loaded they rode the top while J.B. slowly drove toward the feed grounds. The driver's door was soon splattered with tobacco juice from J.B.'s nasty habit of spitting out the window.

Upon reaching the feed grounds a handful of cows, evidently sent by the herd to investigate and see if the rumor of free food might just prove true, crowded around. One old cow stopped dead in her tracks, turned her head toward the timber, and with her long tongue extended, bellowed assurance that the feedwagon had indeed arrived and dinner was soon to be served.

The valley erupted with bawling and bellowing. A long, reddish line of Hereford cattle angled toward the feedwagon. Here and there clusters of disbelieving cattle stood apprehensively watching the procession but quickly lost their shyness, and with udders and bellies swaying, trotted to catch up with the others.

J.B. drove the old International in a big circle while Cole and Ty worked to disperse the hay. They wore gloves to protect their hands and leather chaps to save the knees of their Levi's. Using a hay hook to maneuver the bales and dikes to snip the wire, they skillfully flaked hay onto the ground. The cattle lined out behind, bawling until they had a mouthful of hay and then were content to quietly savor the sweet flavor of summer. When the last bale had been fed, J.B. returned to the stack for another load and the process of feeding was repeated for the heifers and bulls.

While the cows could be fed on the ground, the bulls and the second-year heifers, kept in separate fields, required feeding in hayracks. The bulls cleaned up the hay better that way. As for the pregnant heifers, having their first calves as 2-year-olds, their feed needed to be adjusted to assure their calves would be smaller, making for easier delivery. There was also a group of recently weaned heifers that were fed in racks. In another year they would take their turn and be replacements for old cows, dry cows or dead cows. A cow that lost a calf might be given a grace year, but if she lost her calf two years in a row, or if she were 10 or 12 years old, she served no useful purpose on a cattle ranch and was shipped off to be made into Whoppers or Big Macs. The mother cows were content to have their feed dumped on the ground, and on the coldest days, they cleaned up their allotment within a few hours and always demanded more.

J.B., in the broad spectrum of his lifetime spent working cattle, saw this as just another day, assigning it no more significance than flipping over a new month on a feed store calendar. For Ty the day signaled the real starting point of what he viewed as his self-imposed sentence. He was stuck and would have to remain on the ranch through the winter, through calving and at least until the cattle were turned onto summer pasture. Cole was the direct opposite of his brother. He extracted a great amount of pleasure from this day, signaling the start of the structured routine of feeding out, the cold stinging his cheeks, the tang of cows and fresh manure, the fragrance of dry hay and the amusement derived from watching cattle push each other to get at the hay as it rolled off the truck and plopped onto the ground. All of these sights and smells and sounds were liberating to Cole because he knew he was needed, and absolutely essential to the process of running a cattle ranch.

Through the long winter Arctic storms would roll in, one after another; clouds sucking moisture over the Pacific, bullying ashore, ripping open on the jagged peak of Sugarloaf Mountain and dumping snow in Wood River Valley. From this day forward, each day would be a familiar circle of sameness. There were cattle to feed, horses to feed, wood to haul, fires to build, meals to cook, eggs to gather, cows to milk. Each day the four adults and a child, now snowbound together on the Double X, would face the same two nagging questions—was this to be the winter to break all records for cold and longevity? And, was this the winter that would cost them the ranch?

XX

With Christmas fast approaching Cole found a beautiful fir in a clearing where the sun had coaxed each sashaying bough into a graceful green arc of perfection. He cut it down with a bucksaw and brought it to the house where everyone joined in, helping to decorate it. Stormy hung ornaments on the lower branches and asked Ty or Cole to give him a boost to reach the higher branches. With Ty lifting him over his head, Stormy topped the tree with the snow angel. Iris plugged in the lights and Tracee exclaimed, "Wow, I've never seen a more beautiful Christmas tree!"

Presents purchased weeks earlier were brought out from a variety of hiding places and placed under the tree. Stormy searched through the packages and each time he found one with his name on it, he shook it and tried to guess what was inside.

On Christmas morning Stormy discovered Santa had been there during the night and brought him a small train that puffed white smoke. He played with the train and sipped hot chocolate with tiny marshmallows bobbing on the top while the adults enjoyed Tom and Jerrys. Tracee sat cross-legged on the floor and read names on the packages. It was Stormy's job to take each package to the appropriate person. Tracee received a wool stocking cap from Cole, a matching scarf from Iris, and Ty gave her a red flannel nightgown. Cole and Ty received identical presents from Tracee and Stormy, down-filled vests. Iris gave them wool socks and insulated shirts. In return, the boys had purchased a blender for Iris. Tracee, having been told by Ty that his mother enjoyed art, gave Iris a set of watercolors and a thick tablet of art paper. It was Stormy who really cleaned up on presents, getting a well-balanced mix of practical warm clothes and winter boots as well as a teddy bear, a toy backhoe and truck and a plastic pony. He liked the plastic pony best of all and took it everywhere with him.

J.B. came to the house for Christmas dinner and Cole presented him with a wrapped gift, but J.B. was bashful about opening it and said he would take it back to the bunkhouse. Cole chided him, "Come on, you gotta open it," and called to Stormy, "Better give J.B. a hand." Stormy was only too happy to oblige, ripping away the paper and handing the box to J.B. who pried off the lid and found a pair of sheepskin lined work gloves. He grinned and said, "Just what I was needin'," and he really meant it.

Several times during the day, and into the evening, Cole tried to call home to wish Donna and Kendra a merry Christmas. All he got was the answering machine and hung up each time because it seemed too impersonal to just leave a message. He wondered if the presents he ordered for them had arrived. It was not until two days after Christmas before he was finally able to make a connection and then Donna was evasive about where she had been, simply saying she and Kendra had spent the holiday with friends at a cabin on Mt. Hood, and oh yes, they had received Cole's presents. She thanked him and inquired what he thought of their gift.

He said, "I don't have any idea. We're snowbound. Don't you remember what that was like?" When she didn't respond he said, "So, what is it?"

"A photograph. We had it taken by a professional. It's real good of Kendra, not so good of me. We hope you'll like it."

"I'm sure I will."

Cole spoke with Kendra. He asked about school and what she was doing. She volunteered very little information, and when Cole hung up, he felt lonely and totally disconnected from his family on the west side of the mountains.

A new year brought with it no change in the daily routine. The only difference seemed to be that, on the coldest days, more hay had to be fed to keep the cows content and the babies in their bellies growing. At night the cows wore trails in the snow moving back out of the reach of the cold north wind and into the shelter of the trees where they stood together sharing each other's warmth under the sloping rafters of a pine bough roof. With the arrival of each new day they moved over the crunchy snow to stand broadside to the warming rays of the feeble sun, attuned to any movement from the house or barn, waiting for the familiar squeak of a cold hinge, the banging of a door, the grinding of the starter, the roar of the engine and the sight of the feedwagon lurching toward them. Then they flowed toward the gate and stood impatiently calling, a cloud of steam rising from their shivering nostrils. When the feedwagon did reach the cows, they parted just enough to allow it to pass, surging in behind like an undulating reddish-brown tide while, in distant fields, the bulls and the heifers bellowed with hunger.

It used to be that Frank, J.B. and at least one hired hand, sometimes two, took turns driving and feeding out. Cole told J.B. he was making a change and promoting J.B. to the permanent position as designated driver. That suited the old cowboy just fine because the bales were too heavy for him, or he was too frail for the bales, or a combination of both. He took his new responsibility seriously and each morning had the truck idling and waiting at the stack for Cole and Ty when they showed up. The feedwagon was loaded and J.B. drove to a clean area, shoved the transmission in granny and steered in a big circle while Cole and Ty staggered around on the flatbed, manipulating bales, gathering a growing bundle of cut wires in one hand, flaking hay over the side with a gloved hand, the wire cutters, a hay hook or the toe of a boot.

It did not take long before Cole began to recognize subtle differences between individual cows. Some cows accepted the hay gratefully and were content to stand in one spot and munch until every last leaf and stem was devoured. Cole greeted these cows with a friendly, "How you doing, Girl," or "Mornin', Sweetheart." Other cows were chronic malcontents, butting other cows out of their way and sniffing the hay as it came tumbling off the wagon, moving on, aspiring to discover the perfect bale, never satisfied with the hay in front of them. Cole might address one of these cows by telling her, "Stop that you old biddy." There were always a few cows that stretched their necks to steal a bale, pulling it off the wagon with their teeth. Every time a bale landed on the ground Cole or Ty had to jump down, break that bale and scatter it, working fast and then run to catch the feedwagon.

After the last scraps of hay had been gleaned from the snowy crust, the cattle, singly or in groups, moved back toward the timber, pausing on their way to drink from an open spot in Wood River. They might have an itch and rub against the rough bark of a pine tree, or stand with a friend and discuss the fine hay they had devoured that morning, or belch up food from their false stomach and grind it between ivory molars before finding a patch of clear ground under a tree, and dropping hard to their knees, flopping to their bellies and passing the remainder of the day lying with their legs tucked under them.

When the wind drifted the snow, or a new storm dumped another heavy load, the Cat was fired up and used to open areas for feeding, as well as trails so the International could be driven from the stacks to the feeding grounds and the feed racks. The Cat, although cold-blooded and hard to start, was absolutely essential in the process of getting hay to the cattle.

Tracee passed January devoting most of her free time to Stormy. They read books, played games and sat in front of the big windows watching birds at the feeder. They looked in a bird book and read about the birds they were seeing: Oregon juncos, purple finches, pine siskins and chickadees. Nuthatches, small white and bluish-gray birds, were frequent visitors and amused Stormy because of the way they were able to defy gravity and move headfirst down tree trunks or hang precariously from the undersides of limbs. When the stellar jays arrived with their raucous calls and weird shrieks, scaring the other birds, Stormy rapped his knuckles on the windowpane hoping to drive them away. Sometimes magpies, aglow in iridescent black and white plumage, appeared in search of something to scavenge. But repulsed by the offering of cracked corn and sunflower seeds, they flew away with harsh, unhappy cackles. Each afternoon a covey of quail materialized to scratch at the snow below the birdfeeder, looking for leftovers, and occasionally, a gray squirrel leaped onto the feeder, loudly scolding any bird that tried to crowd in for a few seeds. From time to time, the dogs left their hiding spots under the porch and house and emerged to bark defiantly at the squirrel, and in response, the squirrel raised its tail and chided the dogs until, tiring of the game, it sprang onto the branches of the big pine and climbed up and out of sight. After the dogs returned to their warm beds, the squirrel reappeared and continued to dine on cracked corn.

Tracee helped with cooking and housekeeping, and little by little, assumed many of the outside chores. She looked forward to escaping from the house, pulling on a pair of oversized black rubber boots and a heavy coat, bundling Stormy in warm clothes and tramping with him through the snow to the barn. And while she worked, Stormy played in the hay. One time he sat so quietly that the owls, believing they were alone, turned their attention to a foolhardy mouse that scampered into view. One of the owls sprang from its perch on the rafter, glided for a brief moment and then, with a flash of white and the sharp popping of wings unfolding, seized the tiny mouse in its talons. The mouse shrieked and squirmed, thrashing about wildly. The owl ended the struggle with a sharp peck to the base of the mouse's brain. And when it was over, Stormy ran to his mother and related every last gory detail to her.

One of Tracee's chores was to tend the flock of chickens. She packed a pail of warm water to the chicken coop, fed the birds and gathered the few eggs they were able to lay during the cold days of winter. Tracee learned how to milk the Holstein; J.B. taught her. She took the morning shift and it amused her to think of herself as having become so thoroughly domesticated to ranch life. But she found, when she rested her head against the side of the cow, pulling and squeezing the teats from index to pinky finger and listening to the long rips of milk hitting the side of the steel pail and the froth building until it muffled the sounds, that this was a very tranquil time of the day for her. After milking, she called to Stormy and he usually made a game of hiding, forcing his mother to find him in the myriad of hiding places. When she found him, she tickled his ribs and they wrestled and played until it was time to go inside.

Iris, who had painted with acrylics and oils but had never tried watercolors, was thrilled with Tracee's Christmas gift. She set up a makeshift easel in her bedroom in front of a north-facing window. Here she sipped red wine and painted, mostly flowers, usually of irises, her namesake flower. Her paintings were of unfurling buds with definite feminine characteristics, much like a Georgia O'Keefe painting. Once in a while she diverged to paint a landscape or a ranch scene, but even then she managed to slip in at least one iris, sometimes only a tiny flower beside her name.

Tracee complimented Iris on her control of the paint and the washes. Iris shrugged it off, saying she had learned the technique when the boys were growing up, and they had all lived in town. She had watched an artist on television, hardly ever missed his show and retained most of what he taught because she loved art so much.

When Iris painted, she focused her mind and was very much in control of her emotions. Other times of the day she was prone to sudden mood swings. For instance, she might help Stormy grease a baking pan and ladle out spoons of chocolate chip cookie dough to make cookies. Stormy had a habit of taking a little pinch from the cookies and Iris would suddenly snap at him and say, "Quit eating so much dough. It'll make you sick."

Sometimes it was Tracee who bore the brunt of Iris's displeasure. She criticized Tracee for the way she dusted or, if she discovered a piece of bark Tracee had missed when sweeping in front of the fireplace, she called attention to it. And yet, strangely, Iris followed nearly every emotional eruption with a smile, hug or a compliment. It was as though she couldn't stop her outbursts, and yet recognized what she was doing, and tried to make amends.

Iris also confided to Tracee some intimate details she remembered from Ty's or Cole's childhood. "When he was just a little tyke, Cole wore out the inside of his pants riding stick horses," she said one time. Another time she offered, "Ty used to play like he was a mountain man and sneak out of his bedroom and sleep outdoors on a pile of spruce boughs."

Tracee realized Iris was a grieving widow trying to find her way and did not take her criticism personally. She assumed Iris, having had her life change so drastically and now living with her boys again after all the intervening years, was finding it a difficult adjustment. Tracee told Ty, "I'm just trying to be sympathetic and cut her some slack."

XX

A few horses were kept in the corral at the barn, and after feeding the cattle Cole and Ty picked a horse, saddled and rode through the various herds of cattle, looking for sick animals. They drove any that needed doctoring back to the barn, holding them, if necessary, overnight in one of the stalls. As they worked, they discussed the amount of hay that remained and speculated whether it would last. Buying hay was costly, and then there was always the problem of having to open the road to bring in hay to the cattle. They did not want to have to do that. Cole was constantly calculating how much hay remained because he felt it was more prudent to adjust the hay now, rather than to run low when the cattle needed it most, closer to calving season.

XX

Old Blue had given up sleeping on Frank's grave and joined the other dogs roaming the hills, dragging in winter kills and lounging around under the porch ripping off bits of meat and gnawing on bones, crunching them to get at the marrow.

XX

A front moved down from the Gulf of Alaska, and for more than a week the daytime temperature never got above ten degrees, and at night under skies so clear they magnified the stars, the mercury skidded as low as 32 degrees below zero. In the mornings the cattle were humped up, frost clinging to their muzzles, and as the feedwagon made the rounds, the herd crowded close and steam from their breaths made fluffy white clouds.

Sometimes, after the cows were fed, Cole and Ty followed J.B. to the bunkhouse where they sat drinking strong coffee and J.B. spun stories about the old days. One morning J.B. announced, "I ain't agonna accept no pay for this winter. I ain't doin' nothin' 'cept drivin'. You boys buy my grub, that's plenty."

"You don't have to do that," said Ty.

"That's the way it is," countered J.B.

"As long as the Battle family holds title to this land, you've got yourself a job," said Cole. "No need for you to ever worry about that, J.B."

That made J.B. feel good, to know he had the support of the brothers, and that he had a place to bunk and a job for life at the Double X. He figured the Battles were about as close to real family as he was ever gonna get.

Cole and Ty had resumed familiar roles. Cole was the big brother and the boss, but he tried to soften that reality by always making sure he discussed matters with Ty and cut him in on most every decision. He might nod toward a particular cow and say, "Think she looks a little down?" Or he might suggest, "What say we run that heifer in and doctor her eye?" Ty was well aware of what his brother was doing. He accepted it, although in the back of his mind he also understood that when push came to shove, it was Cole who had the final say.

They divided up the tasks as evenly as possible and pulled the load together, and yet, as compatible as they were in physical work, they never meshed in sharing feelings or personal concerns. Cole never brought up his conversations with Donna, and Ty never asked. Cole never inquired if Ty had given any thought to marrying Tracee. Those, and many other topics, were matters that remained private and unspoken.

CHAPTER EIGHT

February weather, in the cow country of Eastern Oregon, is ordinarily unsettled and characterized by sharp and maddening contrasts. The only true constant is wind. One day the gray clouds spit snow, and the next the sun emerges, the sky becomes radiantly blue and by afternoon the top layer of snow begins to rot. The feeding grounds run with rich brown rivulets—a vile combination of water, mud and manure—moving downhill to fill all the low spots and become like messy mirrors reflecting the robust glint of the sun. The cows, their shiny coats stretched over protruding bellies, remain on higher ground, soaking up sunshine, enduring the passing of time until they give birth.

It may even be so warm that the rancher throws off his coat and goes about his work. But come nightfall, or sometimes even by late afternoon, the coat and gloves are once again required. The cold and the warm, the gloom and the sunshine, all extract a toll. It is said, if a rancher is going to go mad and contemplate suicide, February is the month for it to happen.

On Groundhog Day the sun shone but with little effect because the temperature remained so bitterly cold. Cole took a long, hard look at the dwindling piles of hay and wondered if he shouldn't make a few phone calls to try to get a line on more, just in case winter really did hang on another six weeks. He talked about his apprehensions with Ty, but Ty shrugged it off, said they had plenty of goddamn hay, that the weather would soon break. He felt it in his bones.

The following morning, as usual, Iris fixed breakfast. She preferred cooking on the wood stove rather than the electric stove, and although it required a certain amount of skill in building the ideal fire and knowing where the hot spots were, Iris said the wood stove gave food a better taste. She was well-practiced and was constantly moving skillets and pans accordingly; bacon requiring more heat, hashbrowns and hot cakes a steady moderate heat and eggs less.

For Ty, it seemed that lately, a number of things had been tugging on his psyche—the sameness of the daily routine, his feelings of entrapment, wanting to get out from under the weight of responsibilities and his need to see new country, meet new people and live a little. When Iris served his breakfast he stared long and hard at his plate. He imagined he was looking into a dead man's face: two wild egg-yoke eyes, a pancake nose and wrinkled bacon that harkened into a ghoulish grin. He stabbed the yolk of one eye and as the yellow bled into the pancake he felt a pounding ache in his gut, the same way an inmate facing a long stretch of confinement feels when staring through the rigid, steel bars of his cell. Ty wanted to go away, get away, do something different than eat the same breakfast every morning, do the same work, face those stupid goddamn cows, console Cole about the ration of hay lasting the season, play daddy to Stormy, sneak around in the middle of the night to.... He ate with a rush, shoving food into his mouth, and when he finished, he tapped the tines of his fork all around the empty plate like a blind man probing for food.

"Stop that," reprimanded Iris. She dropped a fresh stack of pancakes onto Ty's plate. He shoved the plate away.

"I ain't hungry no more."

"They'll just go to waste."

Ty pushed his chair back and stood. "Nothing goes to waste around here. Dogs 'll clean it up."

That morning, while they fed cattle, Ty told his brother, "Everyone around here is in a such a pissy-assed mood. Mom's got a case, Tracee too, and you ain't your normal, charming self either."

"What've I done?" said Cole defensively.

"Ah, nothing. Forget I even mentioned it."

Cole angled an eyebrow. "Sure you're not the one in a pissy-assed mood? Maybe you got yourself a bad case of cabin fever. Maybe you need to get out."

Cole ran through his mind the many things needed in town, the most pressing being vaccine for the cattle. It was out of the question for Cole to leave right now because if a bad storm blew in, he might not be able to get back to the ranch for several days. Some rare disease could sweep through the herd causing the cows to abort, and he wouldn't be on hand to do anything about it. Besides, if he went to town, he'd have to fight the compulsion to drive to Portland and get things right with Donna. Nothing was ever resolved in their phone conversations but he thought if he could talk with her in person, then maybe they could still work through their problems.

Cole was thinking aloud, "We need to get the cows vaccinated, the sooner the better. If I called in for vaccine they'd have it tomorrow. We could chain my Ford up all the way around and I think you'd be able to bust through the drifts. Hell yes! You go. Take Mom and Tracee with you. Do both of 'em good to get away for a day, not have to cook. They can shop. We're running low on lots of things. They'll have somebody new to talk with. What say? Wanna give it a try?"

"Suppose I could, but maybe you're the one should go."

"Naw, I'll guard the fort. Stormy can stay with me. I wouldn't mind it, really wouldn't, not for one night anyway: be kind of fun for us to have the run of the place."

The pickup engine raced and chained tires spun as Ty hit the tallest snowdrifts with a full head of steam. Little was said as the three occupants huddled in the cab of the jostling Ford, lost in their private thoughts and of what they planned to do when they hit town. Tracee wanted to taste crispy chicken, coleslaw and devour a chocolate milk shake. Iris intended to see all the pretty new things in the stores and get more watercolor paper, paint and a few more brushes. Ty had to have, absolutely had to have, a beer in a bar. That's what drove him—a beer in a bar.

They were able to remove the chains at the Double X gate and drive into Emerson, where they split up, agreeing to meet later at the town house. Ty went directly to the nearest bar. When he finished his first beer, he wanted another. This time he ordered it with whiskey back. The alcohol began its honeyed rush through his bloodstream and before long he had slid into the great mellow distance beyond the point of reason or sound judgment. He sidled up next to a young, leggy gal with a cascade of blonde hair, tipped his cowboy hat respectfully in her direction and said, "You know, Sweetheart, the odd thing about booze is it can make you big, or it can make you small."

"And which are you?" she asked.

"Big," said Ty throwing out his chest, standing tall.

He leaned against the bar, and they talked. The blonde was from Illinois and had come west on a dream skiing vacation at Sugarloaf Mountain. When she asked Ty what he did he said, "I mess with cattle."

"You mean you're a cowboy?"

"Not really. I don't know. Kinda, I guess so. We're gonna be calvin' close to a thousand head. Say, if I was to feed the jukebox you wanna dance?"

"Little early in the day for dancing," she said and got back to the subject she wanted to talk about. "I thought all the real cowboys had been replaced by urban cowboys."

"As long as there's cows there's gotta be cowboys." Ty ordered another round for himself as well as the blonde.

She took a sip of her new drink and said, "I grew up in a suburb of Chicago. My image of a cowboy was the Marlboro man. His only job was to light up a cigarette. If he did any work, it was to swing a rope over his head as a herd of horses thundered down a mountainside. He never, like you say, 'messed with cattle.' And that's what you do?"

"Yep. That's what I do." Ty took a gulp of whiskey and chased it with a swallow of beer. "Let me tell you somethin', Sugar. Messin' with cows ain't near as appealin' as a horse gallopin' down a mountainside. Cows are big, ugly, dumb, clumsy, slow and stupid. They stink. I oughta know, I tend them every goddamn day of the week. Hell, I probably stink."

The blonde did not confirm or deny that he smelled of cattle. She said, "I took a class last quarter, *'The Western Myth and Modern Man'*, and it was fascinating to contemplate the whole abstract view of the cowboy and the way society has elevated him to the status of cult hero. To most people a cowboy is simply a horseman. He rides the prettiest horse, through the most beautiful country, and it is all romanticized and sanitized. Don't you agree the cowboy has gradually been absorbed into our culture as an idealized myth?" When Ty had nothing to offer she continued, "Did you know, Garth Brooks has sold more records than the Beatles ever did?"

The general drift of the conversation made Ty a little edgy. He didn't much go for intellectualized bullshit. He stood a little straighter. "Garth Brooks ain't no cowboy."

"What makes you say that?"

"I seen him on TV, performing at one of his concerts. For Christ sake, he was flying on a goddamn wire over the crowd. Now a bucking horse might toss a cowboy over a rail fence, cow kick him to Timbuktu, but a cowboy sure as shit don't fly on a string like Peter goddamn Pan." Ty knew he was playacting for this girl but he didn't really give a rat's ass. Actually, he liked some of Garth Brooks' music but he lied, "Nope, that fellar's music is to be listened to in cabs of fancy stretched pickups with leather seats, tinted windows and vanity plates while the driver heads down the Santa Monica freeway, making his way home to a spacious two-bedroom spread where the only riding he'll do is to park his fat ass on a La-Z-Boy lounger in front of a big-screen TV."

"So, if you don't like Garth Brooks, what music do you listen to?"

"Real cowboy shit."

"And who, in your opinion, is a real cowboy singer?"

"Someone who keeps the grit between the notes, makes me feel the bite of the wind ridin' out a blizzard, has a twang like barbwire stretched tight, knows from personal experience how lonesome can make your soul unravel. Someone who rips my fuckin' heart right out of my chest. Someone like... Hank Williams singin' "*I'm So Lonesome I Could Cry*."

"That's just what I wanted to know," the gal said and touched Ty's arm with fingertips sporting freshly manicured, Ragin' Cajun red nails. "I came west because I wanted to see for myself what I was missing. The skiing was just an excuse. Actually, I'm not a very good skier."

Ty was drunk and fast becoming belligerent. "Lady, if you want to experience the real West don't go lookin' 'round these parts. Ain't nothin' in this town.

"Here's the way I see things, this is what's wrong. Folks like you jump in a jet plane, seal yourself inside a pressurized cabin, ride to your destination, rent a SUV, drive down a four-lane highway and shoot across the desert. You never get out, never get dirt on your shoes, never know what the country is really like when you get down in it.

"Did you know, every fifteen minutes in Oregon we lose another acre of workin' land to what is called progress? Same thing's happenin' in Idaho, and Montana, and Wyoming—all over the West—and it's a damn solid fact, once a developer slaps up a house, or a factory, the land is worthless as tits on a boar.

"And another thing, I think every developer should be rounded up, taken out on the desert, staked over an anthill, gutted and left to die. But I ain't naive, I know progress 'll keep progressin' an' that sooner or later they're gonna squeeze me out. That's why I keep on the move. So all that shit can't catch up to me.

"Nothin' personal against you, ma'am, but I don't wanna think and I don't wanna talk, I wanna be left alone an' just get drunk. Go the hell away."

Having completed her list of town chores, and celebrated with fried chicken and coleslaw for lunch, Tracee went looking for Iris. She found her at the Frame-Up Gallery, sitting in the owner's office. Tracee wandered around the store and came back. Iris was still sitting where she had been. This time Iris happened to glance over her shoulder; saw Tracee and gave a feeble wave. She said something to the man seated in front of her and a moment later the man emerged from the office, closing the door behind him. He was dressed in slacks, a white shirt and a bolo tie. He introduced himself as Stewart Caraway and said, "Ms. Coleman, may I speak with you in private." He led the way to the storeroom where he quickly and quietly informed Tracee, "We have a problem here. I saw Mrs. Battle slip several paintbrushes into her purse and try to leave the store without paying for them."

Tracee defended Iris. "I'm sure she meant to pay. She just forgot,"

"Ms. Coleman, may I be frank with you?"

It was all Tracee could do not to throw a joke in this older man's direction, say something flippant, like, "I thought your name was Stewart but if you want to be Frank...." But something told her this was a serious situation. She said, "Yes, please be frank."

Mr. Caraway pulled himself to his full five-feet eight-inches of height. "I prosecute all shoplifters."

"This is a different situation than your typical shoplifting case," said Tracee. Her voice was very controlled, very firm. "The Battle family is one of the oldest and most respected in this community. They are the largest landowners in the county. And, also, I'm sure you've heard that Mrs. Battle lost her husband a few months back. If paying for a few paintbrushes slipped her mind, I think it's perfectly understandable." Tracee opened her purse. "How much were the paintbrushes?"

Stewart acted sheepishly. "Seventeen dollars and thirty eight cents."

Tracee handed him a twenty-dollar bill and said, "This will take care of it."

Cole helped Stormy say his prayers and gently tucked the blankets around the boy, kissing him on his forehead and telling him good night. As he started to leave the room Stormy called, "Where's Mommy?"

"Remember, I told you she was spending the night in town."

"What's she doing?"

"A bunch of things. Stocking up on food and such. Maybe she'll bring you back something special. We can call her in the morning. What would you like?"

"Chocolate ice cream."

"Chocolate it is," said Cole. "There shouldn't be any problem keeping it cold." He laughed and tenderly patted the boy's shoulder. "Better get some shut-eye, partner. Morning will be here 'fore you know it. You're gonna help me feed the cows aren't you?"

"Can I drive?"

"We'll see about that." Cole had almost reached the door when the small voice came again, "How many stars are there?"

Cole laughed. "I don't know." He stepped near the window, looked outside and a million stars pricked through the blue-black sky.

"Can I sleep with you?" asked Stormy. "Sometimes when I can't go to sleep Mommy lets me crawl in bed with her."

"Tell you what," said Cole, "You can warm up my bed for me and when you're asleep I'll put you back in your own bed. How'd that be?"

"Good," said Stormy, and sat up with his arms extended, waiting for Cole to pick him up.

Cole and his little shadow, bundled up against the cold, stepped outside into the morning sunshine and went about the business of loading the feedwagon. J.B. was dressed with numerous layers including long johns, flannel shirt, wool Filson vest, insulated Levi coat and a hat with earflaps. With effort, and none too fast, J.B. rolled bales off the stack. Cole loaded them on the feedwagon, and when it was full, he and Stormy rode to the feed ground.

"See those birds?" said Stormy.

"I sure do."

"They fly real fast."

"Do you know their name?"

"Stellar jay," said Stormy. "They steal food and scare other birds away. I don't like them." He paused, but came right back with a series of unrelated questions, fired like quick rounds from an automatic weapon, and Cole laughed, then started trying to answer the boy's questions.

Cole and Stormy, having fed the horses, were coming out of the barn when the roar of the Ford became audible. Cole said, "Your momma's here."

Stormy flew out the door to greet her. He ran to her, and as she emerged from the pickup, he threw his arms around her in an unrestrained display of enthusiasm. He blurted: "I warmed Cole's bed, helped feed cows, rode a horse. Cole fixed me breakfast, macaroni and cheese just like I asked for, and last night we had hot dogs and potato chips. Mommy, did you remember the chocolate ice cream?"

"You bet I did," she informed him.

"Can I have some right now?"

"I don't know why not," said Tracee, and she picked up several grocery bags and started for the house.

Ty pulled himself from the driver's side looking as though he had been dragged headfirst through a long irrigation culvert, and after carrying a couple sacks of groceries into the house, he popped opened a beer and flopped onto Frank's old chair. He gave a forceful groan.

Iris put away groceries while Cole took the bottles of vaccine to the pump house where, with the heat of a 75-watt light bulb and the pump running every now and then, the temperature never dropped below freezing. Tracee brought out an armload of groceries that needed to be kept cool and set the sacks on a shelf. When her hands were free she reached out and touched one of Cole's thick forearms with her long fingers and said, "Thanks for watching Stormy. You're his new hero."

"We had fun," said Cole. "He really is a good kid."

After returning to the kitchen, Tracee pawed through a box of mail, sorting envelopes into piles, and when Cole came in, she handed him his stack with a registered letter on top, saying, "Wasn't sure if I should sign for this or not. I've never gotten any good news when I had to sign but thought you might be lucky—this might be your notification from Publisher's Clearing House, and you're already a winner."

Straightaway Cole saw that the return address on the envelope bore the name of a Portland law firm. His immediate reaction was a sinking feeling; he knew what the letter contained, but managed to hide it and respond. "Not likely."

He took the stack of envelopes and started to leave but added, "The one thing about bad news is, you never have to go looking for it—it finds you."

Cole went to his room and turned on the radio. George Straight was singing, *"I want to share my world with you...."* Cole did something he hadn't done in a long time. He got down on the floor, did fifty push-ups, and still a little breathless, stood, took out his knife, opened the blade and sliced through the thin flap of the registered letter. He read the contents stoically—Donna had filed for divorce.

The news, although unexpected, didn't surprise Cole. He understood his marriage had been at a crossroads, had been for some time, and knew it could have gone either way. If he had stayed in Portland, he thought maybe he could have done something to change the inevitable outcome. He was struck by a compulsion to hear Donna's voice, to talk to her, and punched in her number on his cell phone. She answered right away.

"I got the notification," he said.

She didn't respond.

"For your divorce."

"It was just mailed on Monday," said Donna. Mostly she talked and Cole listened. And it seemed that everything she had to say was very controlled, almost as though it had been rehearsed, delivered with about as much emotion as a doctor describing a terminal illness to his patient.

Cole brought up their daughter, "What about Kendra?"

"You can have visitation anytime you want. She needs to stay where she is, go to school, keep her same friends. Cole, don't fight me on this."

They talked a little more, and it was clear neither wanted to disrupt Kendra's life any more than was necessary. Donna briefly outlined what she needed in a financial settlement. Cole wanted to take care of her, wanted to take care of his daughter too, but most of all he wanted to know, "When did you stop loving me?"

"Please, Cole."

"When did it happen? Why?"

"Let it go. Why is it important for you to determine when, or why, or try to assign blame. We grew apart, okay? And now you've made your choice. Cole, I want you to know, if you do manage to save the ranch, I don't expect anything from it."

With that said, Donna broke the connection and the line went dead. Cole stood with the phone to his ear, still in shock, trying to make sense of what had transpired during their conversation and feeling powerless to change the course of what he viewed as the downward spiral of his life.

Ty stepped outside to get some fresh air. He watched a squirrel run up the big pine tree in front of the house, its tail flowing like water behind it, gamboling higher and higher until it was nothing but a tremble of pine needles in the treetop. A hawk came sailing overhead, and the squirrel came down just as fast as it had gone up. Near the ground it dipped to the underside of a large branch where it clung tightly, so it would not be taloned to death and have a hooked beak rip its flesh into bloody strips. Ty was close enough to see the squirrel's nose twitch and a puff of wind lift its delicate eyelashes. As soon as the squirrel supposed the coast was clear, it dropped to the ground and scampered away. A moment later the hawk, hoping to catch the squirrel out in the open, made a final sweep, flying low over the white valley, banking and casting on new angles in the wind to soar high across the green canopy of the forest and lazily cruise along the hard, distinct edge of the ridgeline.

Cole came and stood near Ty. He might have mentioned most anything—the weather, sports, fishing, alcohol, love, adultery, divorce—but what he chose to say was, "I suppose we ought to run the cows in and get them vaccinated. How you feeling?"

Ty, still suffering from his hangover, said, "Like someone cut my nut sack and shoved my head inside."

Cole chuckled. Ty finally said, "Had this fellow, all dressed up in fringed leather like some drugstore cowboy pimp, buy me drinks last night. He's pushy as hell, has his bullshit down pat, wants to get his hands on this place in the worst way and turn it into some sort of resort dude ranch."

"Double X isn't for sale."

"Yeah, that's what I told him."

XX

Ty and J.B. used the saddle horses to push groups of unwilling cows into the corrals and start them down the long alley to the chute. The pregnant cows protested, swishing their tails, throwing their heads and trying to turn back. They shoved, pushed, crowded against each other and shit green slime down the slats. They were so big their distended sides rubbed the rough-cut boards. There was nowhere for them to go but straight ahead, to where Cole was manning the mechanism at the squeeze chute. Tracee, with occasional help from Stormy, who was more inclined to play with a truck in the mud, worked to load syringes with vaccine. Each cow got three shots: *Scour-Guard* to build antibodies in the rich colostrum milk; *Redwol* to defend against liver disease; and *Staybred* to protect against five strains of leptospirosis, an abortion-causing organism spread from deer to cattle.

The assembly line of cows moved forward. The squeeze chute banged closed and open. Bottles clinked and clanked. Dull needles were replaced. Cows, feeling the bite of the vaccine, bellowed in angry surprise. Always there was noise and movement and a steady rhythm: every thirty seconds another cow. Three shots. Another cow. Three shots. Another cow. Seven hours after the operation began all the cows had been vaccinated and were back on the feed grounds with their full ration of hay.

Tracee finished her evening chores and went to where J.B. was milking. She leaned against the doorway and busied herself by attempting to work one hand into the tight back pocket of her faded and frayed jeans. She wore a light blue man's insulated work shirt and an open Levi coat. The top two buttons of the shirt were undone, and if J.B. had bothered to look he could have seen, in the V opening, the gentle curve of her collarbone, and because she was so thin, the tiny shadows where ribs attached themselves to breastbone. Her neck was lightly punctuated with freckles and a few long creases that come, not necessarily from age, but the skin's reaction to dry, cold air and constant exposure to weak sunlight. Her attractiveness was undeniable, and yet thin crescents under her eyes belied her constant anxiety about the unknown; what would become of her and her son when they had to leave this piece of paradise. She had promised herself she would always be his full-time mother. She would never leave him again.

"You worked for Frank a lot of years," she said to J.B. "You probably knew him as well as anybody. Tell me, what was he like?"

J.B. kept right on milking. He chuckled and the sounds he made were soft like footfalls creaking on snow. "Tell you what?"

"For starters, why was he so mean? Why did he force the boys to leave?"

"That's none of my business."

"I was just interested in what you thought."

J.B. stopped milking. "I'll say this—Frank, he could be a mite heavy-handed. But I got no complaints with the man. He treated me fair and square. 'Cept I never figured he done right by Iris. Talk to her, maybe she'll tell you a family secret or two."

Tracee had succeeded in pulling the dikes free from her back pocket. She asked, "Want me to feed the horses?"

"Suit yourself, Honey."

Tracee went to the stack of hay, cut a bale and forked chunks into the feeder. When she finished she stepped outside, tossed the wire from the hay bale onto a pile, and stood drinking in the beauty of the evening. Sugarloaf Mountain was still edged with the quicksilver of after-glow but the valley was quickly filling with the unpredictability that darkness brings. Standing there in the pale glow, Tracee looked as uneasy as a heron at the water's edge, all sharp bones and blue angles.

The twenty-first of February broke with a bright blue sky that was soon threatened by an unruly mob of surging clouds. They flung themselves against Sugarloaf Mountain like angry waves crashing against a rocky coastline. And in Wood River Valley rain poured down, gnawing at the remaining snowdrifts and sending thin streams of water downhill to form brackish puddles in all the low places. The storm pulled in a blast of Arctic air. A cold north wind sprang to life, and the rain changed to sleet, and finally to snow.

Cole had been intently watching the cows and had recognized many telltale signs that calving season was drawing near—udders pink, tender, engorged; the area under the cows' tails were noticeably plumping; their bellies were enormous and they walked with effort and groaned under the weight—and now he was out in the rising storm, riding through the cattle. The cold brought blood to the surface and turned the skin on his cheeks a ruddy color. He squinted into the wind and to keep the Stetson on his head he adjusted the rawhide bead of the stampede string, sliding it up tight under his chin.

He fixed his concentration on one cow in particular and followed her at a discreet distance as she drifted from the herd, nervously swishing her tail, occasionally kicking at the discomfort in her swollen belly, moving farther back into the privacy and protection of the timber. In a patch clear of snow the cow dropped her head to sniff a pile of pine needles. She turned around several times in tight circles the way a dog will do when looking for a place to lie down, and collapsed with a weary heaviness.

Cole sat easy in the saddle and watched as the first wave of labor rolled through the cow, causing her to toss back her head, extend her neck and give a long, heavy moan. The pain receded but soon returned with a vengeance. Her sides heaved as the tip of a blue-veined, sapphire sac emerged from under her raised tail. When she again involuntarily pushed, her eyes were white with hurt and fear. The sack ruptured, flooding the ground with bloody liquids, and two ivory-colored objects appeared. Another push and slender brown legs could be seen attached to the tiny hooves. The surge of pain momentarily subsided, and the cow laid down her head and all but the ivory hooves retreated inside her.

For many long minutes the birthing stalled, but ultimately the cow gathered her strength and again pushed. The long, brown legs reappeared, accompanied by the tip of a pinkish-brown nose. In a frantic attempt to gain a point of leverage the cow stretched out her neck, shoved against the ground, and with a guttural roar, pushed out the calf's head. She gave a tremendous shuddering heave and expelled her offspring. After that astonishing effort she lay nearly motionless. Her eyes glassed over and her only sign of life was ragged breathing coming in quick pants and puffs.

And there, amid the steaming pile of wetness, through a thin cloud of rising vapor, Cole saw the newborn calf blink long lashes at the soft, snowy light. Its rib cage glistened but did not rise, did not fall. The baby lay suspended between worlds, born but not yet alive.

An ancient and overpowering instinct propelled the cow to rise, and with afterbirth swinging beneath her tail, she turned to the baby. This movement broke the umbilical cord and shocked life into the calf. It gasped a breath of frigid air, blinked its big brown eyes wildly and shook its tiny body. The mother sniffed her calf's sticky hair, glistening and slippery, imprinting the distinctive scent of her calf so that forever after she could recognize it by that first smell. She pushed at her shivering calf to get it moving and its blood circulating. Then, with her rough tongue, she licked away pine needles and birthing fluid, and when that was done, she began to chew and devour the afterbirth.

The bull calf, its lungs not yet free of fluid, gurgled when he breathed. He thrashed wildly and attempted to stand, but it was as though the tiny hooves were slipping on ice and his spindly legs went out from under him. Again he tried and failed, tried again, and again, and again. He managed to gain his feet, only to lose his balance and fall heavily to the ground. Here he lay until his mother pushed at him with her nose and finally, totally unsure of his equilibrium, eyes bewildered and out-of-focus, the baby managed to get his legs under him and even staggered a few steps before crumpling into a gangly heap. But he was a fighter. He got up, and driven by his instinct to nurse, wobbled in the direction of his mother. He nuzzled and chewed on her shoulder and she lowered her head and sniffed, licked and gently directed him toward her flank.

The calf searched along the warmth of her underbelly until at long last he located a bloated teat. He wrapped his lips around it and began nursing, ingesting the warm, sweet, colostrum filled with vitamins, antibodies and sugar. His little tail flicked, as if that motion was the handle of a pump that allowed him to suck even harder. The snow came down relentlessly and the elusive light all but vanished from the day. Wind howled through the supple pines, making the treetops sway like Latin dancers.

When the baby had drank his fill he gave a grateful moan and flopped onto the ground. His mother joined him, using her body to protect him against the harsh wind. She tenderly nuzzled him, and in response he squirmed in close to share her warmth.

Cole lifted the reins, laid them across his horse's neck, lightly touched spurs to ribs and at an easy lope moved in the direction of the barn. Nothing could detract from his happiness at having been witness to the arrival of the first calf of the season—not the reality of the biting cold against his unprotected face, his impending divorce, or even the possibility of losing the ranch.

XX

The men took turns riding through the cows, looking for any cow about to calve, making sure there were no difficulties during the birthing process. They carried a host of items and medications tucked into inside pockets where they stayed warm—colostrum in nippled coke bottles, penicillin and streptomycin medicine along with hypodermic syringes to deliver them, sulfa pills and a bottle of iodine. The iodine, used only when human assistance was required in a birth, was poured on the navels of the new calves to form a barrier against bacteria from the soil. It stained human skin the color of nicotine and could not be washed away.

The men constantly searched for a cow with a full udder, which meant her calf was not sucking, or a calf with mustard yellow on its hindquarters, indicating scours, or one with a bluish nose instead of pink indicative of a fever. It was up to the men to question everything. Why was that cow kicking at her belly? Why was that calf hanging his head? Did that calf look thin? Was that cow lying in the same place as yesterday? Was that calf breathing hard as though it had pneumonia? Why was that cow still bleeding...?

It was never easy checking the cows because of the chaos of healthy calves scampering madly about, often looking for a meal with the wrong cow that, likely as not, kicked at the stranger. When the calf bawled, an angry mother emerged on the run to claim her baby. Within a few days of their birth, the new calves and their mothers were separated and run onto an adjoining feeding ground. Segregation made life easier for the new calves and their mothers, as well as for the men who watched them for signs of trouble. And trouble seemed to occur, time after time, at the same spots, traditional places where a cow having difficulties calving tended to hang up or where a cow with a sick calf might head. The men looked in these places first, and if a calf had scours, they opened its mouth and poured in a liberal dose of *terramycin*, a yellowish powder. If a baby was exceptionally large at birth, the momma was often times unable to stand and required an IV of antibiotics before she regained her strength. And sometimes a calf was stillborn or born with a serious deformity. But all was not lost as oftentimes another calf, a twin or an orphan, could be grafted onto the mother.

Every day the same dramas, as well as a host of new ones, unfolded and played themselves out. Bald eagles and golden eagles were constant visitors. They circled the calving grounds, or patiently stood on the ground or on a snowdrift near a cow that was calving, and as soon as the calf was born and had moved away, the eagles claimed the afterbirth before the mother returned to clean it up. And coyotes came for anything they might steal and sometimes settled for licking bloody snow. There were even some cows notorious for eating the afterbirth of other cows. They were generally the same cows that were impatient to give birth and attempted to steal calves.

XX

Tracee was walking through the snow toward the house when Cole drove in, making a wide swing and backing his pickup to a pen under the barn eave. After he parked Tracee called, "What you doing?"

"Grafting a calf. Wanna see how it's done?"

Tracee walked to the pickup. A newborn calf, legs tied together like at a rodeo roping, was lying in the bed and Cole was busy working on a second calf, this one dead and stretched across the opened tailgate. Cole was skinning the dead calf with his pocketknife.

"This is the unglamorous part of the business, but important all the same," related Cole, skillfully hacking the hide away from purple meat. "Fact of life. Some live. Some die. If I don't do this, a good mother won't have a calf to raise."

He pulled the hide loose from the dead calf, deftly cut a few slits in it as he explained, "This will allow the cow I'm grafting to smell her own calf and at the same time some of the smell of the new calf I'm trying to graft comes up through these openings." He laid the hide aside and reached for the live calf, untying the pigging string that bound it, setting it on the ground and wedging it into a standing position between his own legs. He fit the hide over the back of the calf, saying as he worked, "Trick is to make sure this fits nice and snug. Do me a favor. Take my knife." He nodded toward the back of the pickup. "Cut me four strips of bailing twine, each about a foot long." And when Tracee delivered the twine, he said, "Thanks a lot."

Cole used the twine to secure the hide of the dead calf over the four legs of the live calf, and when he was satisfied he picked up the calf and carried it toward the pen and the cow that had lost her calf. Tracee asked, "What can I do?"

"Just stay clear. This part can get a little dicey."

Cole set the calf on the ground and shoved it forward, directing it toward the flank of the cow. She was tied short to the railing but still managed to reach out with a hind leg and kick the baby away. Cole slapped the cow's side, told her, "Stop that! Be a good girl."

Again he pushed the introduction, taking hold of one of the cow's engorged teats and directing a stream of milk towards the baby's mouth. After a few minutes of fighting, the cow and the calf finally got the idea. The calf found the teat and the cow relaxed and allowed the baby to suck. Cole moved cautiously away, ready to jump back in if the cow suddenly threw a fit. But she did not.

"It usually takes a couple days, but once her own milk goes through the calf, she'll accept it, no problem," said Cole. He stepped outside the pen, swung the gate closed, moved to the cow's head, and disengaged the quick release hondo, freeing the cow. She rolled her eyes and retreated to the far side of the pen, nearly knocking over the calf as she went.

"Easy," Cole told her. He motioned for Tracee to slowly back away. They went and stood beside the pickup where he explained, "After a cow loses a calf, she's a little squirrelly and then gentles down."

"What an education," said Tracee. "Until I came here I figured cows took care of themselves. I never would've dreamed this went on." She nodded to the body of the dead calf. "Will you bury him?"

"Naw," said Cole. "We just dump the carcasses on the ridge. Birds and coyotes clean it up. That's nature's way."

"Look," said Tracee nodding. She had noticed the grafted calf was nursing on his own. Cole closed his knife, gave her a wink and said, "We'll make a cowgirl out of you yet."

CHAPTER NINE

During the night a thaw teased of warmer days just around the corner and by morning a full-fledged Chinook, a wind exclusive to the Northwest states and eastern slopes of the Rocky Mountains, and characterized by a powerful surge of subtropical air blowing in off the Pacific, was licking at snowy Wood River Valley. At the haystack J.B. said, "One time when I was working out of Paisley, a Chinook hit, and the mercury rose fifty degrees in an hour."

This wind would never come close to the record, but it was strong and powerful. Its hot breath melted the snow and caused a piece of loose tin on the barn to rattle and bang. On the hilltop pine needles whistled, and smells that had been hibernating all winter sprang to life: wet pasture, bare ground, manure, moldy duff, sage, juniper and pine. The fragrances were so well mixed between sour and sweet that they charged the air with an almost yeasty tang.

At the house the Chinook produced a humming sound as it strummed against the logs, and this propelled Stormy into action. He asked his mother, "I wanna go outside and play. Can I Mommy? Can I?"

Tracee dressed Stormy for the outdoors and turned him loose with a playful pat on his bottom. He raced across the porch and down the steps. When he reached the ground, he stomped his rubber boots in the spreading puddles and laughed so much the dogs came to investigate and join in on the fun. One of the dogs found a small rubber ball uncovered by the melting snow. Stormy laid claim to it and threw the ball onto the metal roof of the shop. He floundered around in the slop of the thaw trying to catch it when it came rolling off, and each time he managed the difficult feat, he held the ball aloft in triumph, as if he had just recorded the last out in the World Series. He called, "Mommy! Mommy! Did you see? Watch me."

Iris stood in front of her bedroom window observing Stormy at play, and her eyes became misty. When tears came, she made no effort to stem the flow, but at long last she took a deep breath, dabbed at her nose with a tissue and struggled to calm herself. Her gaze drifted up the hill, away from Stormy, to the family cemetery where Ruth Ann was buried. Iris saw her baby as a tiny, perfect angel. But the apparition suddenly changed to something sinister; swelling with colors so intense Iris became scared she might be losing her mind and backed away from the window. She hurried downstairs to the kitchen where she busied herself scrubbing the floor. When the floor was clean, she went around the house throwing open windows, causing curtains to flutter like flags and a warm cross-breeze to flow through the house as freely as it would across an open field, cleansing the house of an accumulation of obstinate winter smells.

Tracee was upstairs but felt the power of the breeze and went looking for the cause. She found Iris wielding a paring knife, the tip wrapped with a rag, scouring the backsplash behind the sink. She offered, "A wonderful day for house cleaning. What can I do to help?"

Iris put Tracee to work with a bucket of hot, soapy water, sponging grease and smoke from the wall near the wood stove. After that they worked together: winnowing the junk drawer and then removing all the dishes from the cupboards and laying new paper on the shelves and in the drawers. As they worked they chatted good-naturedly.

"We used to have an outhouse," said Iris. She chuckled at the remembrance. "It was an awful place, absolutely dreadful; smelly in summer and colder than a meat locker in winter. I tell you it took a great act of faith to expose your bare bottom to that cold, black hole."

They laughed more when Iris told about watching Cole, when he was a boy, riding his stick horse separating particular chickens away from the flock like he was mounted on the finest cutting horse, and how he had been chased back to the house by an angry rooster. She related, "When Ty was young, he practiced roping by riding his horse up to anything not moving and throwing a loop over it—fence posts, 55-gallon drums, even the poles holding up my clothes line. One day, I had a full load of wash on the line, and he pulled down one of the poles. After that I put a limit on what he was allowed to rope."

Iris went on recalling, "The boys rode calves and when they got bucked off, it was most nearly always in the nettle patch. They'd have big welts all over their bare backs. Ty was all the time trying to measure up to his big brother, but Cole was so much older and stronger. I'll tell you this, that Ty never had an ounce of quit in him."

The two women found the work and their conversations to be a liberating experience, and with Tracee lending support, Iris even felt confident enough to attack the mantel, something Frank had never allowed. She put all of Frank's papers and personal items in a cardboard box, and Tracee carried it to Frank's bedroom and slipped it under the bed.

As the day progressed, Iris offered many insights into what her life had been like at the ranch. She avoided going into the details of her family, how it had splintered and how she had grown to despise Frank, concentrating on painting a portrait of the Battle family using only the broadest of brush strokes. There were many gay moments that danced in her memory.

After their work was finished and dinner was cooking in the oven, Iris and Tracee took a well-deserved break. They sat at the clean kitchen table and indulged themselves with big water glasses of red wine. Iris said, "You never said anything to Cole or Ty about what happened in town, the paint brushes, did you?"

"No."

"I thought you might."

"Never. That's our little secret."

"I appreciate that," said Iris. "And, you know, it was so nice to have your help today, nice to have another woman around to talk to."

Tracee felt especially close to Iris. "I'm sorry. I know it would have been wonderful for you if Ruth Ann...." Tracee had wanted to add the words *"had lived,"* but she saw the wave of incredible sadness that swept across Iris's face and abruptly stopped talking. To try and lessen the obvious pain she had caused she reached out and patted the back of Iris's hand.

The solid exterior Iris had built around herself, and had stalwartly maintained for so many years, momentarily breached, and she whispered, "After Ruth Ann was gone, I became so absolutely desperate for intimacy. But Frank—he couldn't, he wouldn't...." Iris gave a fragile shudder, the way she might have done while reading the obituary of some dear friend who had died unexpectedly, and concluded by saying, "A body can't live in the past. I need to learn to live in the here and now."

Iris pushed her chair back, stood and moved away, giving Tracee no more notice than if she had been a lone raven sitting motionless on a fence post. With her wine glass in hand, Iris swiftly crossed to the stairs and continued on to her room. Tracee was left wondering if she had heard right and was thoroughly confused at Iris's statement because Ty had been born after Ruth Ann's death, and if Frank couldn't, or wouldn't, what did that mean?

That night Tracee listened to Stormy mumble his prayers as she tucked him into bed. Then she went downstairs feeling tired but also invigorated by all she had helped accomplish that day. The house smelled clean and fresh and a cheery fire burned in the fireplace, giving off both heat and light.

As she stepped off the stairs, Cole asked, "Wanna beer?"

"Sure," said Tracee.

Tracee took a seat beside Ty, who was slumped on the couch, beer in hand. Cole handed her a bottle, she took a sip and found herself wanting to say something about Iris's strange comment but, of course, never would. Instead she made idle conversation, asking if the big Chinook would leave any snow, and if the cows and calves were handling the warmer weather okay, finally offering for the sake of discussion, "When I was cleaning, I came across an old newspaper in the bottom of a drawer. There was an interesting story, well, kinda interesting, about a woman who died. Her husband was scattering her ashes at sea, and as he leaned over the side of the boat, a big wave washed him overboard and he drowned. Do you guys think it was simply an accident or was something more involved?"

"Don't care," grunted Ty.

"You have to have a response," said Tracee.

Ty shook his head side to side. "No I don't."

Cole found himself recalling his dream from the previous night. He had been going back to that dream all day long like a tongue goes to a broken tooth. Donna was in his dream, the way she had once been—young, spirited, adoring....

"Cole?"

He looked up and replied, "Yeah."

"Where were you?"

Cole lied, "Thinking I should make one last swing, check the cows before turning in."

"I'll do it," said Ty, struggling to his feet. "I need to get out." The truth was he had a bottle of Jack Daniels under the seat and wanted to tip it to his lips and feel the friendly burn slide down his throat and set his stomach on fire. As he moved toward the mudroom he tossed over his shoulder, "Don't wait up."

After Ty was gone, Cole allowed a few seconds to pass and said, "In answer to your question, I don't think it was an accident, and I don't think it was fate. I think he did it on purpose, in order to be with the woman he loved."

"Cole, you're a romantic at heart, now aren't you?"

Cole laughed. It felt good to laugh. He hadn't had much to laugh about lately. He and Tracee sat listening to the truck slog through the mud and splash across the puddles. When the sound was nearly gone, he glanced around the room and said, "You guys certainly did a job on this place. Looks great. I'll bet you're bushed."

"Not really," replied Tracee. "I'm tired but not sleepy. Wanna play a game? How about Monopoly."

"Not in the mood for Monopoly. Probably never would be."

"Everyone loves Monopoly. Why not you?" asked Tracee.

"I've been involved in real estate and just find the Monopoly rules to be arbitrary and silly."

"What do you like to play?"

He shrugged. "Chess. But it's been years."

"I know where the chess set is."

"Get it," he directed.

As they were setting up the board Tracee asked another question. "Why is chess your game of choice?"

"I suppose," said Cole as he deliberately set up his pawns in the middle of each square, "it's because each piece has an established power and there are an infinite number of moves and possibilities. I like the challenge, thinking ahead, planning moves, reacting to threats and ambushes from my wily opponent." He looked at her then, and flashed an impish grin. He never mentioned that, way back in high school, he had become obsessed with chess, had gone to the county library and checked out every book on the subject, and even ordered more through interlibrary loan. He memorized opening moves from the grand masters and could beat most novice players with a quick offensive attack. If he did not win outright, he typically crippled his opponent so severely he was content to ruthlessly trade pieces of equal value, his victory assured.

Tracee had a rudimentary understanding of how the game was played, couldn't remember who had taught her but guessed it was a boyfriend somewhere in the distant past. She permitted Cole to help her with her opening moves. He soon allowed play to progress without comment. Between moves the quiet sifted around them; the only sounds were the muffled snap of the fire and the melodic strumming of the wind across the face of the eaves.

Tracee, or perhaps her feminine attributes, proved a conspicuous distraction for Cole. Each time she made a move she pulled back her hair. That simple gesture radiated a whiff of the perfume she had splashed on after her bath. And Cole, even though he tried not to make an obvious point of looking, was well aware that when she leaned forward she presented him with an unobstructed view down the front of her shirt. He noticed the dappled pattern of freckles splashed against pink skin, and the fact she was bra-less. It crossed his mind she might be doing this on purpose, as a ploy, but quickly discarded that notion as he experienced a jab of both dishonor and jealousy because, after all, she was his little brother's girlfriend. And yet, those quick peeks aroused in him feelings of passion that rose like a deadly swamp gas. He became distracted, quit concentrating on the game and made an incredibly dumb move by exposing one of his castles. Tracee quickly took it, and the complexion of the game dramatically changed. In order to recover, Cole was forced to concede a bishop for a knight and a pawn for nothing in return. But those calculated moves exposed Tracee's queen, and Cole wasted no time in taking it. The game continued, although it wasn't long before Cole announced, almost apologetically, "Checkmate."

Tracee smiled and leaned back. "Good game. That was fun. Now I am tired. But one of these days we'll have to have a rematch."

"Anytime, anywhere," teased Cole as he scooped up the pieces and returned them to the box. And later, when he was alone in his room, just as sleep swept him into its void, he pictured Tracee, separated from him only by the distance of the chessboard—soft hair as flat as primer paint, lips wide and lethal, substantial breasts, delicate earlobes attractively ornamented with silver hoops, enticing perfume, the soft ring of her laughter—but as he fell asleep, her face was replaced by a stark image of Donna. He groaned and rolled onto his stomach.

Tracee lay in bed and watched the night sky outside her bedroom window. Stars glittered and flashed through the thin, finger-like branches of the poplars. A pack of coyotes began to make noise and the dogs emerged to stand stiff-legged and bark at them. Stormy cuddled against Tracee but did not awaken and she gathered him in her arms, held him and stroked his warm face with her fingertips. And when the dogs began to bark even more fiercely, and the coyotes yapped and yammered and raced across the soft snow that was barely able to hold up their weight, she whispered, "Ssshh, everything is gonna be fine," and her little boy believed her and snuggled even more tightly against her.

Later, Tracee heard the pickup grinding along in low gear, splashing through the puddles and pulling to a stop. She listened intently with her eyes closed. The motor turned off. The door slammed shut. Ty's footfalls clomped onto the porch, paused in the mudroom. A moment later stairs creaked under his bare feet. Boards groaned. Tracee got up from bed and opened the door.

As Ty approached she whispered, “Everything okay?”

Ty stopped, shook his head up and down. “Yeah, fine. Got a new baby on thc ground. Healthy. Nursing.”

Tracee, her red flannel nightgown hanging loosely from her shoulders, had heard the slurred words, could smell the residue of whiskey, saw the silly smirk on Ty’s face that confirmed he had been drinking. She leaned into the doorframe, crossed her arms under her breasts and asked, her voice low and throaty, “Want me to come to your room?”

“I’m tired,” said Ty, as if his short declaration was plain fact instead of a personal rejection. He moved forward, his gait jerky, almost lurching. The door to his bedroom swung open and closed firmly behind him. Tracee stared hard at the exterior of the shut door and imagined the squeak of bedsprings accepting Ty’s weight. She wanted to know, when did it end? Her relationship with Ty? It had been such a gradual thing. That much was certain.

Their hot romance, starting with a chance meeting, had been fed by their mutual attraction and the torrid flames of sexual satisfaction that consumed them there in the motel room alongside the interstate in Idaho. Tracee returned to her bed thinking that in the beginning she and Ty had been like a pair of High Desert mustangs running wild and free. But time and circumstances changed that. She no longer saw Ty as the herd stallion, constantly on the move, rounding up mares to breed and living life at a hard gallop. The winter, and the work, had tamed him. Trapped him. He had become more like an unwilling plow horse; resigned to his fate, moody, sullen, and regretting that he was unable to get back to his free-roaming ways.

And Tracee also recognized the changes that had come over her and how those changes now united her so intimately with her son. It was difficult for her to look back and see her former self; hard to recognize how she, or really any mother, would willingly give up a child. But she had, and now that realization made her sad and maybe even a bit desperate, to think she had been capable of such a cowardly, selfish act. She found herself breathing hard and fast, almost panting, and tried to calm herself by concentrating and thinking that what she needed to do was to put all this in a context she could accept. And what was that context? She hugged Stormy, and as love and emotion welled up inside her, quiet tears stung her cheeks. She tried to convince herself she was this person, this devoted mother; had never been that other person, the shameful one who had refused to accept, and take responsibility for her son.

She fell asleep and dreamed, and in her dream she got out of bed, dressed warmly, took a pair of skates and went down to the river where she strapped them on her feet and began to skate on the ice. *Ssshh-ssshh-ssshh-ssshh.* The music of coyotes bounced between ridges and echoed over the snowy valley floor, and even though Tracee had never skated, in her dream she skated fast, crouching low, legs slicing back and forth like brawny scissors. The air's crispness spanked her face and starlight glittered and reflected off the sheen of the frozen river. She muscled around bends that were like loops on a long silver ribbon and glided down straightaways. Her flaxen hair flowing in the wind, eyes watering and she could feel it all, every last nuance and ripple of realization and sensation, and speed, too.

Then she saw herself lying spread-eagle on the ice, facing upward. Her skin, under the blush of the star-studded sky, was as white and luminescent as bone. The coyotes were quiet now. The only sound was of her raspy breathing. She imagined the sky was watching her, judging her, and wondered if the sky approved. She thought it did, but then ruined it all by thinking about that other person she once had been—remembering men, moments, songs, certain colors, distinctive smells, unusual tastes, and like scraps of discarded cloth, moments of dissatisfaction, sadness and loneliness. As she pressed herself against the rigid exterior of the ice she slowly but certainly became aware that only a few scant inches beneath her, was the flow of water, an entire river of change, and possibility. And hope. This acceptance allowed her to forgive herself for her reckless past and to accept the person she had become.

And when she awoke she saw Stormy's face in the starlight. He was frowning, as if worried about something, and she used her thumb to lovingly smooth his brow. She held him close, kissed him lightly and whispered, "Ssshh, ssshh, ssshh, everything is gonna be alright."

XX

The big Chinook blew itself out and the weather became volatile. Fierce storms curled around Sugarloaf Mountain, bringing in blustery winds and sometimes snow, and then the weather mocked the chaos of winter with the brief respite of windless, bluebird-sky days that coaxed the crocus up through the thinning layer of snow with grass-like leaves and showy colored flowers that obliquely hinted at the coming of spring. Waterfowl began their migrations along the flyway: tundra swans pointed white shafts toward nesting grounds in Siberia, flocks of Canada geese broke formation and landed slow-footed on the standing water in the meadow, a wide variety of ducks—mallard, pintail, green and blue winged teal, redhead, wood duck, northern shoveler—became regular visitors. Great flocks of sandhill cranes trumpeted and circled, spiraling downward, and when they reached the ground, the tall pearl-gray birds pirouetted and leaped high in the air in their ritualistic mating dances. Wood River Valley was alive with the raucous crescendo of bird sounds.

XX

Early spring is typically an unglamorous time of year for the cattleman. He is constantly covered with snow and mud, blood and manure and finds himself either too cold or too warm. There never seems to be a happy medium. And each time the fickle weather turns from warm to cold, it lowers the herd's resistance to disease. Deadly bacteria lives in damp soil, and after a storm the weaker calves can be stricken with infectious scours or pneumonia and have to battle against white muscle disease and intestinal problems. Each calf that dies is a bitter defeat for the cattleman, and in the long run, might make the difference between a financial loss, or the ability to actually turn a profit.

It is easy to spot difficulties with cows that have calved. A red flag is a cow with a full udder, meaning her calf is lost, or sick, or dead. If it has been lost, it has to be found quickly and reunited with its mother. If sick it has to be doctored. And if a calf dies, an orphan calf has to be grafted onto the mother. Sometimes a cow has a full udder caused by nothing more than wind and wet weather, making the teat too sensitive for the cow to allow her calf to nurse. In those instances the cow is roped, her teats massaged with Bag Balm and the excess milk stripped by hand. And then the cow is watched until she allows her calf to suck.

The feeding grounds on the Double X were animated with cows milling, calves nursing and calves kicking up their heels in play. Each morning Cole would cast a wary eye beyond the cows and calves to the shrinking stacks of hay. He spent his afternoons calculating whether there was enough hay in reserve to hold them until the grass turned green with nutrients. Ty was quick to voice his opinion, that worry was nothing more than interest on a debt that might never come due.

XX

The 2-year-old replacement heifers had been bred to Angus bulls in the hope this cross would produce a smaller calf, better able to slide out the heifer's narrow pelvic opening. Bankers and government reports listed these crossbred calves as "black baldy" but cattlemen generally bastardized the name to "black bally." These calves have the white face of their mother, and everything that is reddish-brown on a Hereford, because of the genetically dominant Angus father, turns to black. Come fall the hybrid calves would be sold and the following year, having given birth and had the experience of caring for a calf, the new mothers would be bred back to registered Hereford bulls and the purebred line would continue.

Calving heifers requires even more attention than cows. They often have difficulty during birthing, and once the calf is on the ground, the new mother does not automatically have the instinct to care for her calf and allow it to suckle. Until all the heifers had calved, it was understood, nobody at the Double X would have free time to run into Emerson or take a leisurely ride into the woods to see what could be seen. Everyone had to work together, taking shifts, to make sure the heifers and their calves pulled through the birthing ordeal.

On a warm day in March the first heifer dropped her calf and soon after two others went into labor. Tracee, curious what the process was like, tried to talk Ty into taking her on his rounds. But Ty had become moody and distant and guarded his time alone. He told her, “It’s sloppy as hell out there, besides you never know what’s going to go wrong. It’s no place for you.”

Tracee didn’t give up easily, and one night she stopped Cole as he was getting ready to go outside and asked, “Mind if I tag along? I won’t get in your way. I’d just like to find out what goes on.”

“Fine,” said Cole. “If I run into trouble, I can always use an extra hand to hold the flashlight.”

Tracee pulled on Ty’s rubber boots and rode with Cole as he drove to the field. He announced, “It’s too muddy to drive. We’ll have to walk.”

With a powerful flashlight casting a tunnel of light in front of them, Cole and Tracee stepped into the night. Overhead the Milky Way glittered like reflective diamonds, and the blackness of the night pressed ominously around them. The beam of light picked up a pair of narrow-set eyes shimmering like red embers—the eyes of a raccoon—visible for a moment before turning up its bushy tail and scurrying away. Somewhere in the darkness a great horned owl hooted and was answered from afar. The frogs, after a long winter spent burrowed in the mud, were awake and sang in unison until, as if on a prearranged signal, they stopped. Silence prevailed, and then one tiny, croaking voice spoke out and all the frogs joined in, mixing their voices to become a complex chorus that echoed and re-echoed in the cathedral of the outdoors.

The smells of cattle, hay, manure and mud were so overpowering it was more a taste than a smell, and the sounds of animals—feet sucking when they were pulled from the wet ground and clopping on drier ground—were audible. Cole moved through the cattle in a circuitous route, shining the light here and there on individual heifers and sometimes their calves. Tracee had to resist a strong urge to take hold of Cole's arm as she stumbled along in boots that were too big for her feet.

Cole stopped unexpectedly, and Tracee bumped into him. He cocked his head to one side and said, "Listen," and a moment later, "Hear that?"

"What?"

"We've got trouble," said Cole. He moved forward, and Tracee almost had to run, feet sliding up and down in the loose boots, to keep up with him. At last they came to where a heifer was stretched on the ground, covered with mud and groaning and tossing her head. Cole maneuvered around her and shined the light on her hindquarters. He whistled through his teeth. "She needs help. I'll get the calf-puller. Stay put 'til I get back. Don't crowd her none."

Tracee stayed rooted to the spot, watching the beam of the flashlight bounce with Cole's long strides as he hurried in the direction of his pickup. The darkness seemed to crush in around her, and to gain a point of reference she glanced up. The stars were more brilliant and seemed so much nearer than she ever remembered. The cold dampness made her nose run, and she wiped at it with one hand while pulling the coat tightly around her shoulders with the other. The heifer moaned and thrashed, and Tracee wished she could do something to alleviate its suffering.

Off to the west a small section of Sugarloaf Mountain was illuminated, and Tracee's mind went to the skiers who were having fun cutting curlicues in the snow. After one last run they would gather in the lodge to drink hot chocolate or something stronger, spend money and talk about the fabulous powder in Colorado or Utah. Tracee thought that maybe, after she was no longer needed on the Double X, she might apply for a job at the lodge. She wasn't above hustling drinks. She thought about those people sitting in the bar, oblivious to the fact that in the valley below, out in this pool of darkness, a fateful performance was in the process of playing itself out. A 2-year old heifer was having trouble giving birth, needed assistance, and if the calf was not pulled, cow and calf would die.

For the past few months Tracee had willingly confined herself to housework and chores. But she had come to realize she wanted to be a part of it all, to know what was involved in ranching and to have the knowledge to be able to take care of a sick mother cow or pull a calf when it was necessary and she wanted to take personal pride when the baby she helped bring into this world kicked up its heels in play. Tracee could hear metal banging against metal and knew Cole had reached his truck.

Tracee gave an involuntary yelp as another heifer, coming to investigate, brushed against her in passing. The unseen visitor made a low, guttural noise and in answer the heifer trying to calve moaned. Cole's light returned and illuminated the heifer on the ground touching noses with the visitor that had wandered in. As Cole approached nearer, the visitor moved away.

Cole took command: giving the flashlight to Tracee, instructing her where to point the beam of light, laying a gunnysack on the ground and spreading the tools he would need on top of it. He removed his coat, handed it to Tracee, and rolled up his shirtsleeves as far as they would go. He took the calf-puller and placed the forks against the heifer's rump, attached chains to the exposed ivory-tipped feet of the calf and began working the jack handle. As the device tightened, it pushed against the cow's hindquarters and pulled on the calf. On his knees, Cole worked a hand inside the heifer, trying to create room for the calf's head. He sucked in quick breaths and exhaled bursts of leaden vapor that hung in the golden light. Beads of sweat were soon visible on his forehead as he ratcheted the jack a few more times and then leaned back on his haunches, taking a blow.

Tracee wanted to know, "Is the baby going to come?"

"Could go either way," said Cole. "Too much pressure and there's the risk of tearing off the legs. Too little and we lose the calf and the momma. One way or another we got to get it out, that's all there is to it."

He went back to work. The heifer raised her head, her eyes showing white with pain and panic, yet she tossed her head and strained to expel the calf. Cole ratcheted the jack several more clicks and reached his fingers inside the heifer's opening, trying to create a little more space. Suddenly there was a smacking sound, and beneath the heifer's tail a white head popped into view. Cole worked feverishly, pumping the handle to take up the slack, and when the puller tightened, the calf's shoulders were visible, followed in a quick rush by hips and legs and a gusher of blood and birthing fluids.

Cole unfastened the chains, grabbed the calf's hind legs and hoisted the lifeless form into the air with one hand while with the other hand he wiped mucus from around the mouth, pulled out the tongue and stretched the body. He laid the calf on the ground and began pumping the tiny legs up and down like bellows, attempting to inflate the lungs and jump-start the heart. He paused, studying the gaunt rib cage, and for the longest time, there was no movement and then the hollow little chest seemed to expand on its own, and then contract. It was very shallow and ambiguous, and then it came again with more conviction. The baby moved its head, opened its mouth, emitted a puny squeak and began wildly thrashing its long, spindly legs. It tried to turn over to get those legs on the ground.

Cole, his arms and the front of him covered in sticky fluids and pink blood, took a step back, away from the cow and calf. The cow immediately raised her head and began licking her calf. Cole glanced at Tracee, saw tears glistening on her cheeks, knew she shared his appreciation for this moment, and oddly, more than anything, he wanted to kiss her. But he didn't. Instead, he just stood there grinning foolishly.

Four inches of fresh snow covered the ground, and Iris, who had planned to have J.B. run her to town, was disheartened at the possibility of having the trip postponed. She called the bunkhouse, and J.B. told her they better get going before the wind came up and drifted the new snow. That news buoyed her spirits.

And while Iris waited for J.B. the sun found a patch of blue and shone down, reflecting off the brilliant snow that was already beginning to settle. Trees sloughed snow and flexible boughs came to life, springing upward. Squirrels chattered. A flock of violet-green swallows swooped low and were gone. Geese cackled and discussed the pros and cons of leaving the protected valley for the vast stretches of the far northern tundra.

Cole, as he and Ty rode horseback through the cattle, mentioned, "Radio said feeders are down another two cents."

Ty responded, "Question is, not what the market is now, but will it come up by fall when we have calves for sale?"

"Such a goddamn crap shoot," said Cole. "Factor in expenses—taxes, hay, medicine, fertilizer, gas, groceries and all the rest—and the costs go up every year while the price of cattle goes down. How the hell can a rancher expect to ever make a go of it? I say the old man stacked the deck against us."

"Son-of-a-bitch did it on purpose," groused Ty. "He knew what the hell he was doing."

They rode in silence, both lost in thoughts about the old man and how he lied to them, forcing them to work with the hidden promise that someday, if they worked hard enough and long enough, they'd be entitled to a stake in the ranch. Ty finally asked, "Why'd you pull out? You just get tired of the shit the old man dished out?"

"Pretty much it." Cole shrugged. "You know, every suggestion I ever made was crap to that man. Nothing ever suited him. Did he say, even once, 'Now that's a damn fine idea, Son. Maybe we should try that.' Or even a simple, 'Good job.' Hell no; he found fault with everything I did."

"Know what you mean," said Ty. "Nothing ever pleased that bastard."

"Donna figured it out way before I did," said Cole. "She wanted to leave, but I was stubborn, thought I could work through it, that things would get better in time, but they never did. Only worse."

"What was the straw that broke the camel's back?"

"Never one thing for me to hang my hat on; an accumulation of a lot of little things. Just got tired of the general drift. I made up my mind to pull the plug and told him so, but stuck around through haying so he wouldn't be caught shorthanded. Did he appreciate that? Hell no.

"Want to know what he said when I told him I was pulling out? He said, 'Don't let the door hit you in the ass.' Swear to god, that's what he said."

"Sounds 'bout right," said Ty.

Cole asked, "And you? How'd he run you off?"

Ty laughed. "It was Fourth of July. Some friends called and wanted me to go water skiing. I'd been haying for a month straight, said I figured I had a day's vacation coming, asked the old man if he minded.

"He pulls out a goddamn tape measure, asks me what the life expectancy of the average man is. I tell him that I think it's 'bout 73, or so. He sets the tape at 73. Asks me how old I am. I tell him. He holds his thumb and forefinger at that number on the tape and tells me, 'Here's how much you've lived, and this is how much more you're gonna live.' Then he moves to his age and says, 'I've lived all this and only got this much to go. If anyone should take a day off, it sure as hell ain't you.'

"That was it. I packed my bags and got the hell out of Dodge, hit the cattle guard doin' 90-miles-an-hour, never looked back."

"Any regrets?"

"Nope. None whatsoever."

"Ever wish you had some college under your belt?"

"I live like I want," said Ty. "No strings, nothin' to tie me down. No ass to kiss. Go where I want. Stay as long as I want. How about you? Ever wish you hadn't let him drive you off like he did?"

"There've been times, I suppose. If I hadn't had Donna and the baby, maybe I'd have bucked him a little harder. Had to do what I had to do—what was best for my family.

"Suppose what bothers me most, thinking back on it, is that Mom never tried to patch things up, keep the family together. She just stood by and allowed us to leave."

"I ain't gonna defend what she done," drawled Ty, "but think about it—she knew that old bastard way better than we did. She stuck it out. Didn't stay out of love, not unless she loved the ranch more than she hated him. Maybe she figured she couldn't make it on her own. I don't know. But I do know she paid a price to stay, one hell of a price."

Cole, thinking aloud, added, "Maybe she couldn't stand the thought of leaving Ruth Ann."

Winter and spring continued their tug of war. The grasses pushed up only to freeze and retreat. The cows sloughed hair and took on a tattered look, as if moths had been eating away at them, and the restless bulls scratched themselves on the rough bark of the ponderosa and showed their irritation by butting heads. Even the frisky calves were not as playful as they were when the sun shone. And the stacks of hay, once so tall and mighty, had been consumed and reduced to pitiful proportions. If the weather did not turn around, and turn around soon, the Double X was going to be forced to dip into that last reserve, the hay in the barn, and that would carry the herd for ten days tops.

CHAPTER TEN

AT LONG LAST DAZZLING SUNSHINE FILLED THE MORNING, AND ALL the creatures, big and small, seemed to be in the mood to celebrate. The glorious songs of animals and birds filled the valley to overflowing: coyotes ki-ied, squirrels jabbered, a few gluttonous cows bellowed their displeasure at having to wait for the feedwagon, woodpeckers dug spurs into pine bark and kept the beat, *thunk-thunk-thunk*, frogs thundered a chorus from the swampy pasture, male snipes flew high and dove in a spectacular display of aerial courtship, causing the wind to whistle eerily through their set tail feathers, kingfishers called shrilly, meadowlarks trilled, blackbirds staked out their territories and chanted *"oak-a-leo,"* and finches sang like canaries.

Cole missed most of that warm, glorious morning because of a disturbing telephone call he received from Jerry Pavlinac, one of the stalwarts of the Emerson business community who had owned and operated Sugarloaf Feed Store for more than twenty years. He said he needed to talk to Cole, said it couldn't wait.

On the way to town Cole convinced himself an outstanding ranch bill must have gone unpaid and that the money owed was for a substantial amount. He drove directly to the feed store and sat in Jerry's small, windowless office like a fidgety schoolboy, waiting to feel the bite of the principal's paddle.

"I'll get right to the point," said Jerry. But he picked up a yellow No. 2 pencil and tapped the eraser on his desk several times before finally saying, "Over the years I've done a lot of business with the Battle family. More than that, I always considered Frank a personal friend. Not that we were particularly close. Don't know if Frank ever allowed anyone to get too close, but that's beside the point; point is, I have something to say that will undoubtedly shock the hell out of you, Cole." His meaty hands fidgeted with the pencil, rolling it between his palms as though he was in the process of starting a fire from scratch. He looked up to meet Cole's steady gaze. "When your father was alive he took care of things. Don't know how to say this except straight out. Your mother is a wonderful person, a terrific person in so many ways, but she is a kleptomaniac."

Cole never flinched but did draw a larger breath than normal.

"Whenever Iris comes to town she steals things; puts them under her coat, shoves them in her purse or into a bag. She's been sick like this for quite a long time, in fact, for years. Frank told all of us business owners to keep a running tally, and he'd settled up. He always made good, and then some.

"As you know, with the coming of the ski resort and all the development going on around here, this town has really boomed. There've been lots of changes, new faces and new businesses. I've made it a point to speak to these newcomers and tell them, in a confidential manner, about your mother's problem, as well as the fact that your father always bent over backwards to make things right. Now that he's gone, I assume you'll have to be the responsible party."

Jerry produced a number of receipts held together with a paperclip from his desk drawer and handed them to Cole. "This is what I've collected so far, mostly little things, nothing big. Total comes to a hundred and eleven dollars and thirteen cents. If you want, I'll be glad to disperse the payments, give everyone what they have coming, their fair share."

"Thank you," said Cole. "This is a big surprise to me. I couldn't have imagined this was going on. And I do appreciate your understanding. But I feel compelled to take care of this. One more thing, I absolutely guarantee you, I'll make sure she gets the professional help she needs. Hopefully, this sort of thing will never happen again."

"Well, good luck," said Jerry, standing and extending his hand. "And Cole, if you have time, swing by the Frame-Up Gallery and have a talk with Stewart Caraway. He's another newcomer to town. I never had the opportunity to speak with him but guess he had an incident with your mother a few weeks back. Don't know the particulars, but it's my understanding the situation worked itself out."

Cole paid off the receipts for the merchandise Iris had stolen. He thanked each of the storeowners or managers for their understanding. The only problem he encountered was at the Frame-Up Gallery where Stewart Caraway acted like a banty rooster puffing for a fight. He told Cole, "She should be committed."

Cole, in his mother's defense, said, "She's not crazy. She just has a problem." He turned around, walked out the door and upon reaching the sidewalk he was intercepted by a paunchy man with dyed brown hair and dressed in Wranglers, a bright red cowboy shirt and a flashy fringed buckskin jacket decorated with colorful Indian beading.

"Mr. Battle," said the man, holding out a pudgy hand. "My name is Thomas Taylor. Folks call me Doc."

Cole shook the man's hand. "Medical or veterinarian?"

"Nickname. Comes from the fact I fix things need fixin'," said Doc. "Say, how 'bout I buy you a cup of coffee. I'd like us to talk. Can you spare a minute or two?"

Doc led the way to the Café Paradiso where he laid claim to a table, plopped down on a chair and wiggled a pair of fingers at the waitress. She came right over and Doc instructed her, "Two coffees." He nodded toward Cole. "Need anything in yours?" Cole shook his head. Doc said, "Two straight up, Darlin'."

The men made small talk until the coffee was served. Cole took a sip and said, "So, what do you want to talk about?"

"You were in town late last fall and a friend of mine pointed you out. To be perfectly honest, I've been wanting to meet you for quite a spell now," said Doc. "I did have a couple drinks, here awhile back, with your brother. He said you were the one running the show. Didn't know how to go about it, meet you that is, since you spend so much time at your ranch."

Cole's initial impression of this man was that he was a blowhard who seemed to be purposely exaggerating a dishonest western drawl, like a salesman on TV pitching used cars. "Why did you want to meet me?"

"'Cause, you and me, we got a lot in common."

"That so?" questioned Cole. He couldn't imagine what they might have in common. "And what's that?"

"Dirt," said Doc. "Your family's the biggest land owner in this county, and I'm the biggest developer. I'm the one who secured the funding for Sugarloaf Resort at the Mountain and put together Sugarloaf Estates. I don't know if you've had a chance to look it over, but it's one of the finest upscale housing developments you'll find. Top-of-the-line. Investors see the potential here. They're coming in from all over."

Cole blew a slew of wrinkles across the surface of his coffee. "Did you happen to come up here from California, Mr. Taylor?"

"Just call me Doc. Sure enough did. Got my feet wet down there in the big time. And just so you know, in addition to leveraging funding for development I've also been involved in the ranching game. Owned several ranches, I have. Back in the old days folks could manage to scratch a meager livin' runnin' a few head of cows, some sheep, a pig or two, raise up a flock of chickens, plant a garden. Not that way no more. No way it's ever gonna pencil-out. In today's market, dirt is just too much of a priceless commodity.

"Mr. Battle, I'm a man of vision. Real vision. I can see things the common man cannot. When I first came up here, this was nothin' but a two-bit town. That hillside was a place where the locals dumped their garbage. Look at it now, a complete makeover, a shining testament to what can be accomplished with big dreams, guts and a shitpot full of hard, cold cash."

"I don't mean to be rude," said Cole, "but, like you say, I don't get to town very often, and I've got things to do and need to get back to my cows. You being a rancher, I'm sure you understand." Cole pushed his coffee cup away. "What do you want from me?"

Doc leaned close to Cole, lowered his voice and said, "I know about the will and let me tell you this, you have an ideal piece of property, absolutely ripe with potential, for commercial and residential development. All that land in one solid block, unspoiled scenery, recreational opportunities up the wazoo, adjacent to a major ski resort and a topnotch development. My friend, you hold the key to the future. You can't afford to keep all this dirt locked up in order to raise a few brown cows. You have an obligation to share this property with the public, who I might add, will pay handsomely for the opportunity to own a piece of paradise.

"If your ranch is ever gonna reach its full potential, we start by taking out the fences and channel the stream to meander back and forth across the valley floor the way it used to do. On the lower end, closest to the mountain, we put in a 72-hole golf course designed by Arnold Palmer, Jack Nicholas, Tiger Woods, someone of that caliber. Line the fairways with multi-million dollar homes.

"Moving up the valley we stack ranchettes in a series of tasteful cul-de-sacs. In today's marketplace everyone wants *"5 'n' 5,"*—five-acres five-miles from town. Investors demand privacy and solitude, a safe haven, and they're willing to pay a premium to get it. Whatever it takes. And they want to be surrounded by others of equal social standing. That's part of our overall game plan, to have a homogeneous neighborhood of people with high-end, disposable incomes.

"My proposal is, we keep the upper end of the valley for a dude ranch and advertise it as a working cattle ranch. Your big log house will make a dandy guest lodge, a real showplace, and think about the advertising possibilities: *'Live the excitement of real cowboy life, experience brandings, cattle drives and round-ups.'*

"But if we find the cowboy theme is hard to market, we'll switch to buffalo. Let me tell you, a buffalo ranch is an easy sell. But we'll try the cattle thing first.

"Now, with the timber we're not gonna rape it. We'll do selective logging to open it up and allow us the distinctive, magical qualities of offering properties with spectacular views of Sugarloaf Mountain. How does this sound—*Hideaway Cabins*—slap up some prefabs, trim them with decorative log siding, presto! They become instant money-making time-shares and weekly rentals."

In his mind Cole was picturing the steady stream of traffic invading Wood River Valley with a hoard of people milling about, trying to decide should they play golf or tennis, swim in one of the indoor pools, relax in a spa or sauna, ski, bird watch, fish the stream or one of the secluded ponds, hike, bike or ride miles of equestrian trails. There would be something for everyone, an opportunity to meet the wishes of each single member of the privileged clientele. He could almost picture the television advertisement promising beautiful scenery, wildlife and blessed privacy. And the energetic salesman would confide to the viewer, *"This is your once-in-a-lifetime opportunity to become a member of an authentic working ranch—enjoy the secluded valley with your family and friends, breathe the fresh mountain air, stargaze at night. And all from the deck of your own Riverfront Ranchstead or Hideaway Cabin."*

Doc momentarily jarred Cole from his thoughts, "Do you want to know the best part? I have the perfect name for this exclusive development. In honor of your family we'll call it, *'Water's Edge on Battle Creek'*. So Cole, what do you think?"

"You're serious?"

"Ab-so-lutely," said Doc. His face was as flushed as if he'd just run a mile.

"Once again," said Cole. "Exactly what is it you want from me?"

"Cole, my friend, you've been in the real estate business. You know how the game's played, how ranches get bought, divided up and sold off. Just give me your assurance you'll work with me. We can figure out details down the line, but let's get started with me agreeing to purchase your cattle outright, at an inflated price, which will guarantee you show a profit. Once you have clear title, you sell me the property. You, and every member of your family, will never have to work another day in your lives."

Cole scooted his chair away from the round table and stood. He looked down at the man in the red shirt and fringed jacket with the Indian beading and said, "Personally, Mr. Taylor, I enjoy putting in an honest day's work. But right now, rather than risk saying something I might regret later, I'm going to walk away. I'll leave you with this thought—our ranch is not for sale, not at any price."

Doc threw loud words at Cole's retreating back. "I've already spoken with the lands acquisition representative at Oregon State University. He said, after you lose the ranch, he'd be more than happy to work with me."

Ty rode to check for any cows and calves that might have hung up in the timber. Near the back of the parameter fence he came upon a break where a herd of elk had gone through, tearing down several posts and scattering the wires. He dismounted and worked to untangle the mess. He thought about the men before him who had built this fence, hand digging the postholes. On good ground it might take them thirty minutes for each hole. Where the topsoil was thin, it could have taken a half-day to dig around the rocks and punch a single hole through the hardpan, set a juniper post and tamp it in using an iron spud bar, stringing barbwire, tightening it until it sang and anchoring it with staples driven into wooden posts.

Ty pulled a handful of smooth wire from his saddlebag and used it to splice the barbwire. And, as he took up the slack and tied it off, he cursed the time it took to maintain the fences. It was bad enough being stuck here as a general ranch hand, but he knew he sure as hell would never want to shoulder the responsibilities and obligations of owning a ranch; nights spent fretting about unpaid debts, foreclosures, sickness, accidents, rain that did not fall or fell to extreme, escalating machinery costs, rising hay prices, falling beef prices....

He kicked a pinecone downhill and shouted, "Fuck it!"

While repairing the break Ty had noticed the tracks of three cows and their calves that had found the hole in the fence and gone through. Judging from the way the edges were worn down and the inside of the prints had dried, he guessed the tracks had been made during the previous night. Ty accepted it was a rancher's duty to keep the herd together and went after the itinerant cows and calves.

Their muddy tracks flowed along, weaving in and out of the trees, staying up high to avoid the boggy bottom. They seemed to have been moving at a leisurely pace, at times in single file and sometimes scattering out, all heading in the same general direction, ambling along. Ty knew, sooner or later, the cows would try to get onto the meadow and the tender, succulent green grass that was coming up on islands above the water. Ty told his horse, "Stupid damn shitters. Why couldn't they be content to eat hay like the rest of the freeloaders?"

The trail led through one of the many boneyards on the ranch where outdated machinery had been dragged and abandoned. Here were the remains of a discarded hay rake, a land leveler and a gap-toothed mowing machine, the blades rusted all the way back to the guards. Workhorses had pulled the mower, its teeth clattering as it mowed down the grass, the grass toppling over and laying flat. Those mowing machines were dangerous: they routinely cut off the heads of nesting ducks, chopped the legs off fawns, and if there was a runaway, the driver had to make sure to pile off away from the snapping teeth or risk losing an arm, leg, or even his life. The dump rake that had been parked decades ago had only a few tines left unbroken, and the spring seat ran red with rust. A pine tree was growing up through the spokes of an iron wheel. There was a chunk of black harness, a broken singletree and shards of sun-blued glass.

All of the items in the boneyard were remnants of another era. Ty saw the discarded machinery as nothing but junk; not as tangible history, the building blocks necessary to forge a ranch into something from scratch. On this day, Ty was entirely self-absorbed in his own thoughts, replaying his conversation with Cole and thinking back to that Fourth of July when, a few angry moments had forever changed the direction of his life. He had run away from Frank's domination, jumped in his pickup truck and headed out with no thought of ever returning home. That memory came to him in scintillating clarity—blasting through Emerson, the streets mostly empty except near a windowless bar called the Tahiti Lounge, the most popular place in town. Ty recalled, as he passed, a customer threw open the door and stepped outside into the brilliant sunlight. He paused waiting for his eyes to adjust. And by the time he moved again, Ty was beyond town, out on the highway with nothing but bare pavement stretched flat and one-dimensional in front of him.

The day had overflowed with sunshine. Off to the west summer clouds were building above the distant line of the Cascade Range like the billowing sails of pirate ships. Ty cranked down the window and took a taste of the same High Desert air that had surrounded him his entire life, only this time his lungs filled with the intoxicating tang of freedom. He stole a glance in the rear view mirror and saw the little cluster of buildings that were Emerson fade into nothingness.

The road ahead was wide and wind-blasted, lined with tumbleweeds stopped dead in their tracks by fences. The thought of becoming trapped like those tumbleweeds spurred Ty on. He drove through the ambiguous heat shimmers and the drifting shadows of clouds until he had crossed two mountain ranges. In front of him he saw the Pacific Ocean laid in a broad vista of shimmering blue. He pulled off his cowboy boots and walked bare-footed into the cold waves lapping at the tan, sandy shore.

Late that afternoon, Ty located the largest building in town, an appliance center and went in and asked for a job. He was handed an application and told to fill it out. A man wearing a business suit and an imported yellow tie surveyed Ty, appraising how this youngster, outfitted in denim and a cowboy hat stained by every dirty task on a ranch, could ever be an asset to his company. He inquired if the applicant had attended college, even though the answer was inked over every inch of the young man's hayseed carcass.

"Finished high school," said Ty with obvious pride.

Under the question concerning work experience Ty had written. *"Everything from building fence to castrating calves, hauling hay to branding, riding snorty broncs to general all-around cowboying."* The man tapped his pencil and said, "I want to ask you, Mr. Battle, what is the most essential skill you bring to the job market?"

Ty answered quickly. "I'm a real fast learner. You only have to tell me something once, and it's done and done right."

"We'll get back to you when we have an opening you are qualified for," said the man with a smile he normally reserved for puppies he had no intention of keeping.

Ty ended that day at an ocean-side park where he was surrounded by panhandlers. They worked the tourists but never bothered Ty. Perhaps they saw him as one of their legion, but in truth Ty was worse off because he had no experience scrounging for pocket change. At dusk he settled himself on a wooden bench, and later watched fireworks in the distance, listening to the unrelenting rhythm of the pounding surf. Growing tired he lay down on the bench and covered his eyes with his hat to block out the nightlight. It was an uneasy sleep, and he awoke surrounded by a thick, cold, damp fog. He got up and began walking. When he passed a phone booth, he had a sudden urge to call the ranch but knew how the general drift of the conversation would go. Frank, grumpy about having to take a collect call, would want to know, "Where the hell are you?"

Ty never made the call. Standing there beneath a streetlight shrouded in dense fog, he was stung by loneliness so acute he felt it as an actual physical pain. He crawled back in his pickup and drove east until he could once again smell the High Desert sage and juniper. And here, with the emerging sun just beginning to tickle the sky with a palate of soft pastels, surrounded by miles and miles of emptiness, he no longer felt alone. He pulled down a dirt road, stopped and dozed on the seat of his pickup with his feet extended out the open window. A pack of coyotes began to serenade him—barking, yelping—acting as if they belonged locked in an asylum. Ty liked that about coyotes.

After the sun had launched itself into the sky, Ty drove a hundred miles where he caught on working horseback at a sale yard in Madras, pushing unwilling steers out of pens and down the long alleyway to the sale ring.

A high school counselor once described Ronny Case as: *"A troubled young man from a wealthy family, not inherently bad but a more or less misdirected youth who, in his formative years, lacked parental supervision and continually finds himself careening from one small crisis to the next."*

Ronny graduated from high school and refused to find a job, saying it would *"interfere with my playing around."* When his father, a bank executive, threatened to cut off his allowance, Ronny just laughed and moved from his parents spacious home in Portland's West Hills and came to live in their *"getaway"* vacation home. The house was a palatial palace of lava rock and clear, vertical grain cedar built in a mortar-and-tendon style on a prime lot in Sugarloaf Estates. Ronny spent his time skiing, chasing girls and generally misbehaving.

The Willamette Valley youth had a rap sheet but nothing too serious. He had a bunch of unpaid parking tickets, which forced authorities to slap a boot on the front wheel of his red BMW, immobilizing the car until his father paid the fine. Another was an inglorious episode involving street racing, attempting to elude, and drunk driving. Ronny's father, not wanting to have the family name sullied, employed an expensive attorney who was able to arrange to have the street racing charge disappear, the DUI charge dropped because of a minor technicality, and the attempting to elude reduced to a simple speeding ticket. Ronny plead guilty and paid a $175 fine and $25 in court costs. Actually, his father paid for him, once again.

After that escapade, Mr. Case was only too happy to have Ronny move miles away to Emerson. He hoped that his son would tire of the rural life and agree to enroll at a private liberal arts college near Seattle. He had promised to pony up for tuition and other related expenses, but Ronny, with a free ride going and no academic expectations to have to try to meet had no interest in expanding his intellectual horizons. His main ambitions were to do some late spring skiing and to party with his best friend, Win Roberts, who had moved in and was sponging off Ronny.

It was Win who suggested they ride the four-wheelers. But Ronny was the one who brought out his father's hunting rifle, in a scabbard, and strapped it onto his four-wheeler, saying, "We might find something to shoot, or at least we can crank off a few rounds just for the hell of it."

Ronny, dressed from head to toe in camouflage, also tied a cooler stocked with beer onto his four-wheeler. He got on, twisted the throttle and the two-stroke engine screamed in defiance as he shot down a dirt road leading around the flank of Sugarloaf Mountain. Timber flashed past like individual frames ripped from a cartoon, and Ronny's long, stringy reddish hair whipped from under his cap in the artificial wind he created.

When Ronny came to a fence with a sign declaring, *"This is not your land, Keep Out, Double X,"* he took it as an outrageous affront to his entitlement, his constitutional right to ride wherever he goddamn well pleased. He drank a beer and using a pair of pliers he found in the four-wheeler's tool kit, he cut the barbwire. Ronny, followed closely by Win, ran his four-wheeler through the opening and carved a trail downhill, slowing only when he reached the apron of a broad meadow nearly covered with a shallow skin of standing water.

When the other machine came up fast, Ronny goosed the throttle of his four-wheeler and accelerated onto the shallow lake, sending up a glorious, aquamarine rooster-tail that floated in a perfectly graceful arc like a weightless ballerina under a crowning cobalt sky.

XX

The lay of the land forced the wandering cows and calves to climb the side of a rocky outcropping. Ty read the ground, intently scanning for the slight irregularities in the chaos of shale, rocks, dirt and the occasional remnant of a snowdrift.

Each time the tracks disappeared he looked for an overturned stone, matted grass, a broken twig. And if there was no sign to follow, he spiraled out following nothing but his intuition, making his way along the south-facing hillside finding, losing, finding the sign again until at last the trail of the wandering cows and calves moved downhill to the fence line where a tree had fallen and pinned the barbwire to the ground, allowing the livestock to easily cross onto the meadow.

Ty soon came to a decisive intersection—the tracks of a pair of four-wheelers sliding in a wide semicircle and coming in behind the cows and calves—and what transpired, the precise chain of events, was as obvious as giant letters splashed across the expanse of a billboard. Every last detail was indelibly etched into the soft earth on the floor of the broad meadow: The four-wheelers accelerating, giving chase, tires spinning, digging for traction. Cattle spooking, kicking loose gobs of mud that were flung from their hooves like wild accusations, back toward the four-wheelers.

For better than a half-mile the cattle had tried every maneuver to escape the maddening whine of the racing machines. This desperate game continued until a calf faltered, or fell, and was run over by one of the four-wheelers. A chunk of green plastic was ripped from a fender, broke off and was imbedded in the dead calf's skull. This must have infuriated the riders because ahead, scattered over the next several hundred yards, lay the carcasses of three cows and two calves, shot to death. Scattered around the scene were several empty beer cans.

Ty, enraged at such a wanton and wasteful act, kicked spurs into the ribs of his mount, forcing the horse into a hard gallop. He followed the trail of the four-wheelers across the edge of the meadow and up the side of Sugarloaf Mountain, finding where the fence had been cut to gain entry. And even though the sun was beginning to tumble from the sky, he stayed on the trail, galloping into Sugarloaf Estates and halting only when he reached one of the imposing mansions built of native rock and red cedar. Muddy tire tracks, as straight and true as a shot arrow, led to an attached four-car garage. Ty dismounted, dropped the reins, ground-tying his horse, and walked over and peered through one of the narrow garage door windows. He saw a tarp partially covering a pair of four-wheelers. He tried to lift the garage door but it was locked. He went to a side door and it was also locked. With a single powerful kick he broke it open and stepped inside.

The pale sun was seeping through the slender garage door windows, throwing coppery shafts of burnished light around the big room. Ty ignored a red sports car and marched directly to the four-wheelers. He flung the tarp aside and saw that a chunk of the right fender was missing from one of the four-wheelers. He bent to examine it and found coarse red hairs embedded in the green plastic. He was straightening his back when a high-pitched voice wailed, "Hold it right there!"

Ty raised his hands above his shoulders, slowly turned, and there, framed in the interior doorway to the house, was a longhaired young man squinting down the sights of a rifle. The squeaky voice demanded to know, "What the hell do you think you're doing?"

"You God damn son-of-a-bitch," snarled Ty. He took one menacing step forward.

"Don't move. Swear to God, I'll shoot."

Ty stopped. "You killed my cattle. I trailed you here. I got evidence." He lowered the hand that held red hairs clutched between thumb and forefinger.

"Hey dude, I'm no criminal. You're the one breaking the law here."

With devastating swiftness Ty charged the young man with the rifle. There was a blinding flash of yellow, orange and red. A shocking wallop of force slammed into Ty's left shoulder, spinning him around, knocking him backwards and onto the concrete floor. A hard-edged clap of thunder boomed and rolled around the confines of the garage.

When Ty came to his senses, he was lying on his stomach and could feel conflicting sensations—the coolness of concrete and the searing heat of metal that had passed through his left shoulder. He knew he had to move, and with reckless urgency, pushed away from the floor. He grunted involuntarily, nearly toppled over and fell, but was able to use his good arm and the strength in his legs to propel himself onto his feet. He stayed low, moved fast, crab-walked the short distance and ducked through the open doorway. Once outside the fresh air revived him and he questioned whether he had moved with astonishing speed and agility, or had the red-faced kid with the scraggly hair simply chosen not to fire a second round?

Ty's horse was standing where he left it, but its ears were perked forward in alarm. It sidestepped as Ty lurched forward, calling to the horse to whoa, reassuring it, "Easy boy, easy." With his good hand Ty made a grab for the headstall and when he had it, he steadied himself, gathered the reins and clutched the saddle horn. In one swift, continuous motion he stepped into the stirrup and vaulted upward, flinging his leg over the cantle and plopping his butt onto the saddle. A jagged slash of pain caused his face to contort and a grunt squeezed from between his clinched teeth, and yet he was able to tug one rein and lay it across the horse's neck. In response the horse spun in a quick half-circle, and when Ty brought up his heels, the horse launched into a ground-eating gallop.

He held the damaged arm as tightly to his body as was possible and could feel blood gushing from the wound, soaking his shirt and dripping into the waistband of his Levi's. He was light-headed and a little shocky, but reassured himself he was going to make it to the hospital.

With the arrival of darkness, Ty had still not returned. Cole began to worry and played in his mind the countless ways a cowboy could get hurt. Cole went to the barn to check and see if Ty's horse had come in on its own. It had not.

At half-past-seven Tracee took a call from the sheriff's office, and after hanging up the phone, she immediately went searching for Cole. She found him in the barn, saddling a horse to go look for his brother.

Tracee was a little breathless. She told Cole, "I just took a call from the sheriff's office—Ty's in the hospital. He's okay."

Sheriff Dubois, a tall, rangy lawman, had put twenty-six years in law enforcement in Southern California before moving north and finding a laid-back community where he could work a few more years, thus allowing him in his retirement years, to double-dip from two state pension systems. He had been Chief of Police in Emerson for 16 months and was fond of dressing the part of a western lawman, favoring pant legs stuffed into high-topped, hand-tooled cowboy boots, a knock-off Tom Mix shirt and a flat-brimmed, black cowboy hat.

When Cole came charging into the hospital the sheriff was able to intercept him. He extended his hand, introduced himself, adding, "Your brother is in surgery. The doctors say he'll be fine. He got himself shot."

Cole took a step back. "What? Shot? Who the hell would shoot him? Why?"

Sheriff Dubois had spoken with Ty before he went into surgery and now gave Cole a quick rundown of the circumstances. He never let on that he viewed the shooting as a page torn from a Louis L'Amour western. But he could visualize the headline in the up-state newspaper, "*Cowboy Shot In Gunfight.*" And since he was the lead law enforcement officer, he was sure the reporters would want to interview him, maybe take his photograph, and more than likely, his image and quotes would be splashed across the front page of the *Oregonian* newspaper. He'd have to get some extra copies and mail them to his California cronies. They'd get a hell of a kick out of this one. Yep, Sheriff Dubois was going to be receiving a lot of well-deserved notoriety, and while he talked, he checked his reflection in a window and was pleased with what he saw.

Cole was fired up, wanting to know, "Where's the son-of-a-bitch who shot him? Did you arrest him? Is he in custody?"

Sheriff Dubois fingered the points of the star that gave him his power and stated, "I've spoken to the young man's attorney who, by the way, is headed in this direction from Portland as we speak. Mr. Battle, I have rules to follow. I can't interrogate the suspect until his lawyer gets here. But I'm sure when he's had an opportunity to speak with his client, he's gonna tell me Ty barged in unannounced, was belligerent and threatening, and that the boy, fearing for his life, had no choice but to protect himself."

"Bull shit." Cole clenched his fist and his jaw jutted forward in defiance.

"I know, I know," the sheriff said reassuringly. "But we've got to play this strictly by the book. If it all checks out, and I have no reason to believe your brother told me anything but the truth, we should be able to wrap this up quickly. Come morning, I'll want to have a look at the dead cows."

"Forget that. The son-of-a-bitch tried to kill my brother."

"We're going to take things one step at a time. It's up to the DA. If she wants to go for attempted murder, she will. She has a mind of her own. The problem is, your brother had no right doing what he did, sticking his nose into something that should have been handled by law enforcement. If he had a problem, he should have come to me. I could have launched an investigation, and we'd have avoided all this unpleasantness. As it sits, Ty runs the risk of being charged with Burglary II, and that's a Class C felony.

"Better face it, cowboy, this is a brand new millennium. Everybody has rights these days. This ain't the Wild West, not any more."

Tracee drove Iris to the hospital and stayed with her in the waiting area. Iris paced nervously while Tracee held Stormy, who was asleep, on her lap. Cole came in, sat down and spoke in detail about the unsatisfactory conversation he had had with Sheriff Dubois. After telling everything he knew he picked up a copy of *Outdoor Life* and tried to concentrate on an article about hunting whitetail bucks in Minnesota. He could never seem to finish an entire paragraph. Mostly he just stared at the wall and the hard lines etched in the skin around his eyes and mouth were like windows to his worry.

A mind saves things, files them away without the expectation of ever having to bring them to the forefront. But the morphine that killed Ty's pain also forced a bizarre accumulation of distorted memories to come wiggling out of the dark recesses of his mind like worms after a hard rain—jumbled thoughts, impressions, feelings, sensations. He was reciting his ABCs to his mom, swinging his shotgun on a passing duck, changing a flat tire. He was in a fancy house he helped build along the north shore of Flathead Lake, Montana. He floated between rooms, watched the sheetrock gang covering stud walls, installers working on the counters and painters laying down a base coat. He breathed in lingering smells of gypsum dust, muriatic acid and Dutch Boy paint. He saw Frank's eyes, set way too close together, as dark and beady as if they belonged to a bear. There was a river running wide and deep, its waters reflecting sky like shattered glass shivering in sunlight. Beneath the twisting current were bright pebbles. A doll was down there; lying on the bottom, eyes open, staring upward. Ty was determined to save her but couldn't gauge the depth and did nothing. It occurred to him this must have been how Ruth Ann had looked in death.

Iris spent the night at the hospital. Tracee and Stormy stayed for a long time but finally retired to the town house. Cole went home. He had a ranch to run, but he called the hospital several times and each time was assured Ty was doing fine.

CHAPTER ELEVEN

THE SUN WAS A PULSATING BALL OF FLUORESCENT YELLOW, THE SKY A flawless shade of blue and new grasses pushed up from the valley floor were causing an explosion of green so rich and vibrant that if a contemporary western realist were to use these same colors the critics would soundly criticize the painting, saying, *"Nature can never be this vivid, and colors so urgent and intense...."*

Cole and J.B. were riding the boundary, checking the fence line. At one point a doe flushed from a clump of red-barked willows, and the riders moved in that direction. When they were near, Cole stood in his stirrups, and after a moment of searching, located a tiny fawn curled in a tight ball. The dappled pattern of soft brown hair and white spots helped it blend into the surroundings of earth, grasses, wildflowers, sunshine and shadows. Cole settled himself onto the saddle, and signaling with his reins and a gentle dig with his spurs, let the horse know it was time to move.

After fixing breaks and pounding in staples to take up loose wire, they rode on toward the cattle. A few insatiable cows bawled, and Cole eyed them, making a passing comment, "Little thinner than I'd like to see."

J.B. spit a string of Copenhagen-laced saliva and said, "They'll pick up fast once they get on grass. Don't have to worry none 'bout that."

At the fence corner J.B. slid off his horse, and when his boots hit the ground, it was questionable if those bird-like legs of his would hold him. But they did and he managed to open the gate, swinging it wide and tucking it tight against the fence. And while he performed this task, yellow-breasted meadowlarks trilled intricate melodies, red-winged blackbirds called from the cattails and a female killdeer gave a familiar cry and acted as if she had a broken wing to divert attention from her nest in the gravel.

The riders moved through the open gate. The sun was warm, and Cole rode with his jacket tied behind the saddle. J.B whistled between his teeth, some strange melody, and Cole couldn't place what it was, thought it might be an old Tex Ritter or an Ernest Tubb tune, but listened a bit closer and figured it had to be classical music with a dollop of western twang added by J.B.

The horsemen rode into the herd and gently pushed a few head toward the open gate. At first the cows seemed reluctant to leave the feeding grounds. A few head wandered into the field, and upon tasting the succulent grasses, bellowed their good fortune and soon a reddish-brown stream of cattle surged through the narrow opening and spread out over the upper pasture at the head of the valley. Some of the calves became lost in the confusion. They bawled their discontent and ran around aimlessly until becoming reunited with their mothers, punching at exposed and distended udders, searching for and then finding a teat to wrap their hungry lips around. A few frothy gulps eased the pressure on the swollen bags and the mothers were off again in search of more narcotic grass. The babies had little choice but to tag along, trying to grab a meal on the run.

Cole sat on his horse and watched the cattle, and all the little conflicts unfolding and then resolving themselves, and wished his life could have such simple resolutions.

Ty awoke and it took him a moment to remember where he was. His mother was sitting in a nearby chair, dozing, but she came awake. He said, "Why are you still here, Mom?"

"I wasn't about to leave you," she said immediately.

"I'm fine," said Ty. But his voice was thin and his tone unconvincing. He went on, "I'm in good hands. There's nothing you can do. Go home. Get some rest. Come back later."

After an hour or so, Iris relented and had Tracee drive her to the ranch. Once she was inside she went directly to the kitchen. She was going to pour herself a glass of wine but decided against it and instead fixed herself a cup of coffee. She sat down and held the coffee cup with both hands, feeling the warmth against her palms. An unanticipated wave of nostalgia swept over her as she remembered those winter nights when she and Frank were first married, and she had slept against him and felt as warm and comfortable as her palms were feeling against this cup.

She set the cup aside, climbed the stairs, went to Frank's bedroom and sat in the chair with the wonky leg, the one where he had always, at the end of the day, tossed his soiled clothes. It was understood she was to gather, wash, fold and put his clothes away in the dresser for him. And even though it had been months since he had been in this room, she could still smell the odor of his presence—his clothes, body, horse, dog, cattle, oil and grease—and at long last she opened the window and sat in front of it, allowing the fresh air to wash away all those familiar smells of her dead husband.

The chores were done and Stormy was down for his nap, allowing Tracee time to indulge herself with a bath in the big tub. As she submerged herself up to her neck, breathing in the comforting fragrance of lavender, and the goat milk bubble bath, she felt relaxed and soothed but immediately tensed when she heard footsteps padding down the hall. She held her breath. It sounded as though someone, she supposed it was Iris, had opened the door and gone into Frank's bedroom. The door closed. There were no other sounds.

Tracee soaked, washed with oatmeal soap and finally stepped out onto a small rag rug and dried herself. She pulled on the clothes she had hung on the back of the door, tied her long hair, which had become less tawny and more chestnut over the course of the winter, into a pair of stout pigtails that she secured with rubber bands. Wearing her hair this way made her feel younger. She liked that and dabbed on Lady Stetson, two tiny splashes behind each earlobe and a little at the top of her breastbone. She had tried perfumes with exotic names, expensive perfumes, but always returned to Lady Stetson. She was convinced it was her scent.

In many ways Tracee found it complicated being a woman. She had a desire to look her best but applied little, or only the absolutely minimum, of makeup. She did shave her legs and armpits a couple times a week and made a concerted effort to keep herself "fixed up." It wasn't easy to do that while keeping house, cooking and serving meals whenever the men came in, washing, ironing, doing outside chores, being a mom and doing the myriad of other tasks that needed to be done. The work, it seemed to go on and on without end, and Tracee just wanted to be able to finish a job, put it aside, and move on to something new and different. But she couldn't and saw the work she did as lines that curved into a series of tightly interwoven circles. There was sameness, tedium and monotony. There was boredom and repetition. She stood in front of the mirror and thought, "God, I wish I had another woman my age around here so we could just talk."

In spite of the drudgery Tracee found happiness in doing for others. She liked pleasing Ty and Cole. Ty rarely handed out a compliment but Cole was a sweetheart, never missing an opportunity to praise her dinners; although he rarely noticed the dusting, the loads of dirty clothes and mountains of dishes she washed, dried and put away between meals.

What made all the work worthwhile was having the opportunity to play an active role in Stormy's life. Gone was the needy child who had, on her infrequent visits in the past, clung to her so desperately. At the ranch Stormy had blossomed into a confident young man who was perfectly content to entertain himself, or help the men roll bales off the stack, ride around with them when they fed cows, go for walks and have Tracee play games or read to him. Tracee told her reflection that if all this ended tomorrow, and for some reason she had to leave the ranch, she would look back on this time as the major turning point in her life. Before coming here she had been a pleasure-seeking, self-indulgent, immature woman. But now, no matter what happened from here on out, she knew she and Stormy would remain together. He meant everything to her. She would never again pawn him off on her mother. She might not have played a pivotal role in his past, but he was definitely her future.

Tracee blew her nose and flushed the tissue down the toilet. Water roared from the overhead basin, made loud sluicing sounds as it spiraled around the bowl and fresh water seethed into the high cistern, ending with a sharp bang. This must have served as a signal because, as Tracee opened the door and stepped into the hallway, Iris was waiting for her. She was holding a faded black-and-white photograph. She pushed it into Tracee's hands and proudly stated, "Me and Ruth Ann."

The image on the photograph was sharp and clear. It depicted a much younger Iris holding a baby wrapped in a delicate white shawl. The end of the shawl hung down, and

Iris was pulling a corner away from the baby's face, showing her off. Iris was facing the camera. Her expression was triumphant, as if she was saying, "Look at me. I made this adorable baby."

Tracee realized that Ruth Ann had allowed Iris to know the full extent of contentment, and hope, and love. She had never seen that look on Iris's face. Tracee said to Iris, "She was a beautiful baby."

"Yes she was. How could God take her away from me?"

Tracee's thoughts turned to Stormy. What if God took him away? And she began to cry.

Cole visited his attorney in Emerson and signed the divorce papers. They already contained Donna's signature, a flourish of blue ink that wandered above and below the line as though she had been ecstatic in the act of gaining her unconditional release. All that remained in the dissolution of their marriage was the judge signing the decree, a four-week waiting period and it was official and final.

Donna had received everything she wanted, including custody of Kendra. Cole expected that, in time, he and Kendra could forge a relationship based on something with more depth than a reflection of her mother's animosity. He hoped Kendra would want to spend vacations and summers at the ranch.

Upon reaching the street Cole extracted his pocketknife and took a seat on a bench. He removed the small whetstone he carried in a case attached to his belt, leaned forward, spit on the stone and began sharpening his knife. The blade sang against the stone with music soft and melodious: the same swishing sound grain makes when poured into a wooden trough, the whisper of hay sliding off the tongs of a buck rake, the sigh of a horse shuddering away the dust of a long day. Spit. Reverse the blade. *Swish. Swish. Swish.*

Cole tested the blade for sharpness by cutting the tiny hairs along the underside of one wrist. He was not satisfied and kept working the knife against the whetstone. The skin on his hands was browned by the sun, cracked in places, and the nails held a crescent-shaped accumulation of red volcanic soil, brown grease, pale hay dust and white dander from horses and cattle. The blade threw off a thin, curved image of the sun that flashed like lively sparks on inanimate objects: sidewalk, tree bark, brick and grass. Testing the blade once again Cole found it sufficiently sharp. He folded the knife, stood, tucked it in a front pocket and put away the whetstone. He sat back down.

The simple act of honing the blade had helped Cole put a few things in perspective. He acknowledged his marriage had failed, and he shouldered the brunt of the culpability for that. Not that Donna was blameless. It was a simple but true fact that they had grown in different directions. He didn't doubt he still loved her, he did, but he didn't love her with the passion a husband needs to feel for his wife. Love has to be a two-way street. Has to be, he told himself. There is giving, and there is taking. He felt as though, for a long while, he had been giving without receiving anything in return.

What he and Donna shared was a whole lot of history. That history was part of the failings that went back a long way: in Cole's case, to his bitter disappointment at having allowed his father to run him off the ranch. Yes, he had given up, quit, and that caused the direction of his life to suddenly veer away from everything he ever wanted. Donna had pushed him in that direction but ultimately it was his decision. And giving up his dream had alienated him from her. The real travesty, as Cole saw it, was that there was not a goddamn thing he could have done to change any of it. The past and the inevitably of his divorce were like those marbles that made up his name on the front steps to the house. The house could burn to a pile of rubble, but the marbles would remain.

Cole pushed himself off the bench and shrugged off his self-pity and his feelings of abandonment. He walked to his pickup and drove to the sheriff's office. Here a deputy told him that Ronny Case, through his attorney, had agreed to plead guilty to six counts of willful destruction of property and to pay the full market value of the animals he slaughtered. He would be required to complete a one-year probation, but if he kept his nose clean, everything would be removed from his record, and once again, he would be the best model citizen money could buy. Sheriff Dubois suggested to Cole that Ronny's family was worth a lot of money and that Ty might want to consider filing a civil action lawsuit.

Before he drove home, Cole swung by the hospital and visited Ty. He found him sitting up in bed.

"Get me the hell out of here," Ty told his brother. "I'm goin' nuts."

"They haven't released you," said Cole.

"Well Jesus H. Christ, at least go down and get me a six-pack."

Ty had been lucky. The bullet passed though his body cleanly and had not shattered any bones, only chipped one, as it tore through muscles and nicked an artery. Cole left the hospital. On the drive home he felt stress building to an intolerable level: the criminal who shot his brother and killed his cattle was free as a bird. And Cole was deeply saddened and distressed by the finality of his divorce.

In the past, whenever he felt worried or fretful, Cole had conditioned himself to run away and involve himself in frivolous pursuits—hunting, fishing, running a river. This time he sought escape above the Home Place, where Wood River tumbles from the mountains and spends itself in a quiet pool. Cole parked, took his fly rod case from under the seat, opened it, and as Frank had taught him, he oiled each joint by rubbing it alongside his nose before sliding the pieces together. He threaded the line through the eyelets, tied on a tippet and a fly and hiked through the tall grasses to the water's edge. He stood drinking in the natural beauty of this basin where ten thousand years ago, maybe more, it had been formed by fire. Pockets of soil between outcroppings of basalt held delicate native wildflowers and Wood River tumbled over a ledge in a showy curtain of white before settling into the pool that was deep and cold and where big trout held themselves nearly motionless, except for the slight fanning of their fins against the languid current.

A trout, thick-bodied, silver and speckled with a muted rainbow of elusive color, rose and hungrily gobbled an insect on the surface, throwing off a shower of iridescent droplets in the process. Cole was pushed to action. He deftly unlimbered his rod, stripped out line and cast a tiny gray-winged mayfly pattern exactly where the trout had slipped below the surface. He sensed the take before he felt it and instinctively prepared to set the hook.

That evening Cole arrived at the ranch house with four large trout wrapped in wet riverbank grasses. They were gutted and the flaps of their empty bellies lay neatly together like silent lips. Tracee was glad to get the fish. She had been in a quandary about what to fix for dinner. Fish were a welcomed change from the beef they ate all too often.

"Would it be okay if I invited J.B. to dinner?" Tracee asked Cole.

"Sure," said Cole.

Tracee sent Stormy to the bunkhouse with an invitation she had written on an index card. It read, *"J.B., Your company is formally requested for a fresh-caught trout dinner. We eat in an hour. Love, Tracee."*

Tracee cooked a terrific meal: steamed wild rice, green peas and Trout Almondine. Following the recipe she found in a cookbook, she dipped the fish in flour, then in a batter of eggs and cream, then in flour once again. She seasoned the trout with salt and pepper. While the fish cooked, five minutes per side, she lightly roasted almonds in butter and lemon juice in a cast iron skillet. She served the trout, golden brown, with the sauce ladled over them. The fish lay in a long dish, their backs arched a little as if they were in the midst of a final, desperate leap. Cole, remembering the way they rose to his fly and the feel of their powerful runs, savored every bite. In hungry anticipation, before he ever took a bite, J.B. rubbed his rough hands together making a sound like paper rustling. Then he dug in, his knife and fork flashing. Stormy asked where the fish came from, and Cole told him about the hidden pool and promised to take him fishing.

Stormy was excited, "Can we go in the morning?"

"I think Ty's gonna come home in the morning," said Cole. "We can fish another time."

Tracee said, "I'd like to go in with you when you pick up Ty."

Cole nodded, "Don't see why not."

Iris sat quietly staring at the eyes of the fish, sunken in cooking, looking inward like an old man's eyes. With each serving she watched the flesh fall away and when the bones were stripped the spine reminded her of the keel and ribs of a derelict ship. She remained quiet as the others visited and refilled their plates. She was mesmerized as those around her forked the pink coral flesh into their mouths. Her gaze darted quickly, from one face to the next, never resting, always on the move.

CHAPTER TWELVE

COLE PUT OUT THE WORD—THE DOUBLE X WAS HOLDING SPRING branding the coming Saturday—and several cowboys, including Johnny Ritter, showed up to help. Ty, his arm encased in a sling held tightly to his body, was able to ride, but his shoulder was much too fragile for any groundwork.

Ty and J.B. rode horseback through the herd, pushing cattle from the various fields down the lane toward the corrals. Stormy, under strict orders to stay clear of the action, sometimes played in the dirt outside the corrals and sometimes climbed onto the rails to get a better view of the action.

The cows, having run this gauntlet many times before, attempted to break toward freedom while the calves, not knowing what awaited them, allowed the riders to drive them into a holding pen and down an alleyway where, one by one, the calves were forced to take their turn. The lead calf was prodded into a contraption known as a squeeze chute, and when its head appeared at the far end of the device, a lever was quickly thrown. The stanchion banged closed, gripping the calf's neck tightly, while walls of metal tubing came up to cramp snuggly against its body. With the flip of a lever, the table was rotated from vertical to horizontal, one of the ribs was kicked loose and swung out of the way while a loop was attached to the outside hind foot of the calf and ratcheted up, stretching the animal and providing easy access to the lower belly. In a series of rapid procedures an earmark was cut into the bottom edge of the left ear, the tiny protruding buttons of horns were pinched off with a dehorning tool and the wound was smeared with stinky, brown bug repellant. All calves were vaccinated against clostridial bacterin, leptospirosis and respiratory disease. Another shot was administered to make up for a lack of Selenium in the soil. In addition, heifer calves received vaccinations against Bangs disease, and to control internal and external parasites. Bull calves were castrated: the end of the scrotal sack sliced with a sharp knife, the cords crimped, both testicles removed and the laceration powdered with blood coagulants. All calves were branded, a red-hot Double X iron was pressed against the left hip, singeing the hair and leaving an indelible mark on the hide. The loop over the hind foot was removed, the table returned to an upright position and the stanchions released. The calf stumbled forward a step or two then bolted into the open corral, bleating loudly about the rough treatment it had received. All of this happened in less than a minute, and by then another calf was pushed forward into the squeeze chute and the stanchion was being swung shut around its neck.

To an outsider the scene smacked of utter chaos and commotion but actually it was controlled pandemonium, and the success of the operation required that each man perform his independent task with teamwork rivaling the split-second timing of an Indianapolis 500 pit crew.

At noon Tracee, who had spent the bulk of her morning cooking in the house, shifted her attention to a bed of glowing coals in a pit outside the corrals. She tossed steaks on a blackened grill, and the sizzle gave off a tantalizing aroma that had the cumulative effect of causing the riders to dismount, loosen cinches and tie their mounts to a corral rail. Those working on the ground ran a few more calves through and called it quits. Then the men, after pausing to wash their hands and faces in the flow of water that emptied into the water trough, lined up and moved down a table set with a tempting mountain of food: hot rolls, baked potatoes, corn, sautéed mushrooms, chilled butter, sour cream, hot coffee and grilled steaks. They also had their choice of cold pop or iced tea.

The men ate as though they were starving, and now and then, tossed a tribute about the tasty food in Tracee's direction. Most doubled back for seconds, and some returned for thirds. After dinner they dallied for a few extra minutes, visiting and letting their food digest a little before getting back to work. By the middle of the afternoon the men's backs ached from bending over, muscles were sore and hands were developing blisters at the edge of calluses from wielding knives, dehorning scoops, vaccination guns, the squeeze chute lever....

Shadows lengthened and at long last Cole called it a day, telling the hired hands, "Tomorrow we'll save a few head and you can shake out your rope. Everyone gets a turn."

"Looking forward to it," said one of the cowboys with a dusty grin.

"What time?" Johnny Ritter wanted to know.

"We'll have calves ready and the fire hot by seven. Get here before that and the coffee 'ill be on," said Cole. He stood watching as the men headed out. The dust they made in leaving hung in a long cloud that turned golden in the fading sun.

XX

The calves shied and bunched against the far side of the corral as a mounted cowboy swung his lariat. His loop flicked out, popped like a rattler striking and settled smoothly over the head of a surprised calf. In a series of quick movements the horse turned, the cowboy grabbed a dally around the saddle horn, the slack came out of the lariat and the calf, bucking and bawling, was dragged forward. Another roper moved into position behind the calf, and with a big, graceful loop captured both of the calf's hind legs. This cowboy too grabbed a quick turn around the saddle horn with his lariat, his horse set himself and, like a blanket hung on a line to dry, the calf was suspended on the ends of the lariats.

A little slack was given and the ground crew leaped into action. One man flipped the calf on its side and kept it from struggling by pressing a knee across its neck. "More slack," he called, and when the header moved forward the noose was removed from the calf's neck and placed around the front legs. Other men worked to cut the earmark, vaccinate and dehorn. J.B. dipped his open knife blade into a pan of green soap to sterilize it and with a well-practiced stroke, castrated the calf, pulling the testicles free and dropping them into a three-gallon bucket.

Cole reached for a branding iron, lifted it from a bed of coals and applied the red hot metal to the left flank of the calf. Hair caught fire and hissed. Smoke boiled. The calf rolled its eyes and extended its tongue without uttering a sound. The stench of singed hair swirled on a mischievous wind, stinging Cole's eyes, and he blinked and coughed a little but took pride in laying the brand, knowing it would be clean and clearly visible on the hide, but not so deep as to cut into muscle.

Four men took turns roping and when a loop missed, or a roper picked up only one hind leg, the others needled him. But it was good-natured teasing, and the hundred head were soon worked, turned out and mothering-up. With the work behind them the men gathered at a water trough filled with ice and cold beer. They ate Rocky Mountain oysters cooked over the branding fire and washed down with swigs of beer. Stormy drank soda pop and resolutely refused when he was offered the calf testicles. Having seen where they came from, he shook his head and exclaimed, "Don't believe I'd care for any but thank you all the same." That brought a chorus of laughter from the men.

While the men enjoyed themselves, off in the distance, a bald eagle fingered the edge of a dying thermal. Its white head was etched cleanly against the darkness of a building thunderhead that soon rolled over the sky and began spitting rain. It settled the dust and made streaks on the dirty faces of the cowboys but was generally ignored until the beer was gone and then, as the men prepared to leave, Cole cut their checks and they went away. The last to go was Johnny Ritter. He mentioned to Cole, "If you need help turning out, I'd be glad to lend a hand." With that said he took his pay, crawled in his pickup, and in passing, took a sidelong glance toward the house, hoping to catch a glimpse of Tracee. He spotted her on the porch sitting with Iris and gave a snappy wave. Then his pickup and horse trailer were bouncing and rattling down the rutted road, and Johnny was telling himself, when it came to that pretty filly on the porch, he wouldn't mind dippin' into that and gettin' himself a little. He suspected Tracee was way too much woman for Ty, but he reckoned she wasn't too much woman for him.

XX

Tracee and Iris sat together on the porch, on comfortable wicker furniture, and sipped wine. It was evident from the drift of their conversation that Iris either considered Tracee a trusted friend, or she desperately needed to get some bothersome things out in the open.

Iris said, "When I married Frank and moved into the house, Frank's father, his name was Harold but I always called him Grandpa, was still living here. We moved in with him. Took some adjustment from all three of us, it did. This place was too big for Grandpa to live here alone. Grandma had died the year before. It was cancer that took her.

"She's buried on the hill. Grandpa's up there, too."

"When did he die?" asked Tracee.

"Don't rightly remember the exact date, but I had Cole and was pregnant with Ruth Ann, not too far along yet, I do know that."

There was a long pause, and it was as if Iris was either trying to remember or make up her mind about something. Finally she turned toward Tracee and said, "Cole talked to me about what I do sometimes, you know, take things from stores and forget to pay. He wanted me to see a doctor. He even set it up for me. The other day, when I was in town, I went to my first appointment.

"The doctor, he's a psychiatrist don't you know? He told me I need to quit trying to hold everything inside. I have to, what was that word he used? Oh yeah, it was *"unburden"* myself from things that happened in the past. And you know, he might be right. We talked for over an hour. He seems like a real nice fellow. I like him. I think he'll help me some. I'm going to see him again tomorrow."

Iris dropped her voice to where it was barely audible and said, "I know you can keep a secret. Want to hear something? I've never breathed a word of this to anyone. I swear it's true, every last word."

Tracee was a good listener. She nodded her head in encouragement and said, "Okay."

"Grandpa died this time of year, at branding. It was the end of the day, and the men had gone to the bunkhouse. We kept on a full-time crew back then. Grandpa and Frank were alone in the corral. I went to see if they were ready for supper.

"Frank always said it was a horse kicked Grandpa, and that's what killed him. But I saw what happened." Iris took a sip of wine as fortification. "They were arguing, Grandpa and Frank. They argued a lot in those days. Grandpa wanted things done his way. Frank, he had a terrible temper, didn't like being bossed.

"Grandpa thought Frank had treated a calf too roughly during the branding and said so. Frank got mad and told him to go to hell. He turned away. And when he did, Grandpa slapped him across the back with a coiled rope. I will say this in Frank's defense; he acted more out of instinct than anything. He spun around and swung, caught poor Grandpa flush on the temple with his fist. Frank had huge hands, was strong as an ox. Grandpa went down like he'd been shot. He lived for a while after that but never came around. Doctor said his brain swelled. Blood on the brain was what killed him."

"He killed his own father?" asked Tracee in disbelief.

Iris nodded her head up and down. "It ate away at Frank, you know it did, the shame of it. At night he'd have terrible dreams and thrash around like a wild man. Scared me. One night he gave me a black eye and never even knew he did it. I was afraid for the baby I was carrying. And so I set Frank up in one of the other bedrooms. We never slept together again after that.

"Every morning, when he woke up, he had to massage his hands until they loosened up because he clenched his fists so hard in his sleep. He became an angry man, drank more than he should, never cared a lick about anything but this ranch and his damn cattle. He thought if he had the biggest spread and the most cattle that somehow that proved something. That he was worthy, I'd suppose.

"Folks around these parts treated Frank like a king. He had power, standing. Did you know he was president of the state cattlemen's association?"

Tracee was too overwhelmed to do or say anything.

Iris continued, "When we were first married he was a different man. Cole came along, and he was so proud of that baby, so proud. And then there was Ruth Ann. But really, after Grandpa ... after that, Frank was a changed man.

"I will have to hand it to him—after I left home, and everything that happened came to pass—he still took me back. And when Ty was born, Frank treated him like he was his own. No better, no worse, than Cole."

A black cloud rolled in front of the sun, and a light spattering of rain began to fall. Iris did not speak for a long time, and then she said, "I've never told the truth about what happened. Not to anyone. I even tried to hide it from myself. But now I've told you. I feel like a heavy weight's been lifted off me. The doctor told me I don't have to live under Frank's shadow any more. I should live my own life. That's just what I'm gonna do."

Iris and Tracee continued to sip wine and think their private thoughts. They watched the men leave, one by one. The last to go was Johnny Ritter. He waved as he passed. Finally Iris said, "It's gettin' a might chilly. Maybe we should go inside."

XX

That night Tracee had trouble sleeping. She got up and stood at the window watching the cloudy remnants of the receding storm march past a moon the color of a ripe peach. The moon arced into the sky. For a time it became entangled in the leaves of the Lombardy poplars but broke free and rose like a bubble of air from deep underwater. Shadows lengthened, stretched, shrank; changed with subtle allusions of melancholy and became vague and indistinct, finally disappearing as the moon ducked behind yet another cloud.

Stormy sat up in bed, called, "Mommy, where are you?"

"Right here, Honey." She turned toward him, swept him up in her arms, commenting how heavy he was getting. He giggled and squirmed like a puppy.

XX

The meadow was bathed in a snow-white moon and smelled sweetly of grasses and wildflowers. The mother cows contently grazed, and their babies, sick from the shots and in pain from dehorning and castration, lay restlessly on the ground nearby.

CHAPTER THIRTEEN

WITH THE COWS TURNED OUT ON THE VALLEY PASTURE, THERE WAS finally time for the men to catch their breath and turn their attention to other work: tacking down loose tin on the barn, rebuilding headgates, repairing Stormy's swing, the barn was overdue to be mucked out, the tack room required a good cleaning, there were miles of fence in need of checking and repair, equipment had to be made ready for the summer haying season, and the list went on and on. And still the cows demanded attention. Some of the stragglers—cows that refused to calve with the others, were bred late, or not at all—aimlessly milled around, going from one calf to the next, sniffing suspiciously until the real mother arrived and drove the intruder away. These pretender cows were a constant source of irritation and needed looking after.

Cole knew there was plenty to do and yet, in his heart, he was restless and clung to a thin shred of hope that if he could speak to Donna in person instead of over the phone, he might change her mind before the divorce became final. He wanted to believe she was still willing to listen to reason: might be swayed by their fifteen-year investment in this marriage and the love they, even now, undoubtedly shared for each other. The trump card, in Cole's mind, was they needed to stay together because it would be in the best interest of their daughter to have both a mother and father in a stable home. He was convinced if he made one last desperate attempt, he could salvage their marriage and patch their lives back together.

One morning Cole came downstairs, approached Ty at the breakfast table and simply said, "I got business in Portland. I'll be back in a couple days." And without further explanation he was gone.

Ty worked on a fence. A windfall had created this particular break. The next break, and there was always going to be a next break, would likely be caused by elk, deer or wild horses. Ty was tired, and he was tense. The tiredness could be easily explained as he worked long, hard hours. But his tenseness was a little more ambiguous. Although he was pretty sure he knew why; he thought because of his commitment and loyalty to his family that his sacrifices should ultimately add up to something. And yet, they never seemed to. Instead, each day was like another clump of dirt added on top of his grave. That's how he saw it.

Ty further reasoned that if he could explain his family entanglement so easily, could he also justify his continued involvement with Tracee? Such a lengthy attachment with a woman, especially one with a kid, was something new for a love 'em and leave 'em guy. He defended himself by supposing Stormy was involved in the mix. After all, Ty had been the one who suggested Tracee might want to bring him along even though he knew kids had a way of dominating your life, of tying you down and turning you into something you were never intended to be. Ty thought a perfect example to demonstrate this point was that, here lately, it seemed he and Tracee never had any time alone. She was busy. He was busy. It was a rare night, a rare night indeed, when she slipped down the hall to his room. In fact, it was so rare he couldn't remember the last time it had happened. He was forced to face the unadulterated truth—whatever it was they once had, they probably didn't have it any more.

Ty indulged his fantasies by recalling other women who had brought him pleasure. There were many. Each had been good in the short run, but none ever held his interest over the long haul. It wasn't their fault, he knew that, it was something in his personality, probably a phobia or a short circuit that caused him, every time a relationship became too serious, to pull up stakes and move on. He figured he was too wild, self-seeking, self-indulgent, set in his ways, to ever be roped, throwed and broke to ride.

So, he asked himself, exactly when were his happiest moments? Images came to him like Polaroid snapshots—a frosty morning with the sun coming up behind the mountains and the world around him alive with song birds; a spirited horse between his knees, its breath coming short and fast, cattle moving out in front of him, raising dust; sitting in a smoky bar, the taste of cold beer, fanning four aces across green felt, raking in a big pot; a pretty girl lying naked and willing across his bed—each snapshot implying desire, promise, pleasure, fulfillment.

Ty had a sudden urge to run over to the Oregon coast. He had been to the ocean only twice in his life. Once when he busted out and went his own way and the other must have been for some special occasion because it was the only family vacation he remembered.

That time the Battle family had checked into a motel overlooking the blue-green sea. Ty and Cole slept in their own room, and in the morning they slipped away undetected and went to the beach. The tide was out, revealing a long stretch of wet sand. Ty took off his shoes, stood bare-footed, pant legs rolled to his knees and allowed the bone-biting coldness of the saltwater to sting his skin. The sand shifted beneath him and threatened to wash him off his feet.

There were tidal pools, and Cole had led the way, moving fast, jumping from rock to rock with an agile grace that Ty could not match. There were anemones, brightly colored starfish, red kelp and brown shells. As the boys played, they never noticed the onrushing tide until it was too late and the only escape route was straight up a rocky cliff. They started up the headland climbing like a couple of crabs.

Beneath him, Ty heard the sinister sea booming and sending spray up the cliff that, like long, skinny fingers, threatened to drag him down. He sensed the sea wanted him, and if the water succeeded and pulled him down, the current would sweep him away and the soft mouth of the ocean would suck the life right out of him. In that moment Ty visualized his mother standing over his lifeless body, crying so desperately her sobs burst forth like uncontrollable hiccups. Frank was there, too. He was regarding Ty with calm indifference as if the only emotion he was capable of expressing had to be anger or nothing at all.

There, on the face of the rock, Ty became scared. He froze, could not move and called out. Cole reached back, extended his hand, told Ty to grab hold. It was the most difficult thing Ty ever did, to give his fate over to another, but he let go of the rock, and he and Cole locked hands. Cole saved him.

Thinking back on it, in the panic of the struggle up the cliff, Ty remembered Cole becoming as hard-edged and determined as Frank. He seemed to say, *"Fight the battle, give it your all: win or die trying."* That was the same philosophy Cole shared with his father.

Ty and Cole saw a lot of things differently. Cole saw the ownership of the ranch as a right and as a measure of pride and self-worth. Ty's way of thinking was—you can own something, but that something owns you back. Buy land and be bound to a mortgage. Take out a loan and the banker has you by the short hairs until the interest and principal are paid in full. Fall in love, get married and the leg trap slams shut. You ain't never gonna get free until one of you dies, or divorce releases the grip of the iron jaws.

When Frank was alive, he was a slave to the ranch. The only time he ever got away was to travel to bull sales or meetings, otherwise he was as predictable and unmoving as a hunk of rimrock. The only gamble he ever took was on the uncertainty of the price of cattle. When it came to property, he had confidence land was always a good investment. He had the patience to make it work, to outwait the seller, and when the price was right, Frank stepped in and plunked down cash.

The fact that Frank only took calculated risks was probably why Ty rebelled, and in his wanderings, took up playing poker. Not poker for fun, or matchsticks, not even a penny-ante game, but high-stakes poker for real money. There were times, if Ty got on a roll, that the pot was so big, it'd cause a grown man's asshole to pucker and sweat to roll over his ribs.

Ty got his introduction to high-stakes poker while working grain harvest in the Palouse country of Eastern Washington. He was employed by a farmer who coaxed wheat from two thousand acres of topsoil and whatever moisture Mother Nature grudgingly provided. The minute harvest ended, the farmer threw himself into having fun—drinking and gambling—with the same single-minded intensity as when he worked.

Ty was in the bar the night the farmer bet his entire harvest check on a high spade flush, pushed a mountain of chips and cash into the center of the table. With the roll of his hole cards, the farmer doubled up.

For Ty it was not so much the singular act of winning or losing but the reckless courage it took to play the game, to risk everything, stare the other man in the eye and call. *"All in."* No beating around the bush. No bullshit. Just guts. *"All in."*

After that night, Ty began playing cards in the back rooms of seedy country bars where the fix was on and the regulars predetermined the outcome. Ty might win a few hands, but he always lost the big pots, causing the local-yokels to shake their heads and lament how tough it was when a fellow's luck went south. They never openly cheated but knew when to hold and when to get out of the way. They ganged up on Ty, one-twoed him, and after he was forced out, they played cutthroat for his money.

Ty learned by losing. Each time a card was turned it added to his education. At first he played the odds but soon learned the real difference in winning and losing was in playing the players: observing how men react to good cards and bad cards, reading an opponent's face, mannerisms and emotions—the way an artery will pound in a man's neck, a muscle twitch, an eyelid blink involuntarily—each subtle, and not so subtle, revelation proving whether a boat was filled, an inside straight missed, or the nut flush picked up.

Ty was addicted to the idea of pulling up stakes and heading off to Reno, Winnemucca, or some two-bit town between here and there where a game was going on, and he could slap down a roll of Ben Franklins and gamble. Jesus, he needed that surge of excitement a big game brought, needed it to feel alive again. Instead, he took a deep breath, ratcheted the handle on the come-along with more force than was necessary, pulled the barbwire taut and tied it off.

Stormy had never seen a chipmunk before coming to the ranch. And now he sat on the steps of the log house eating a sandwich and watching a chipmunk scamper close to grab bits of bread he tossed on the ground. At first the black-and-white striped animal had scampered away with the bread in its mouth, choosing to eat in private, but it soon was feeling more comfortable and sat on its haunches, holding the crust in its little paws and nibbling with swift chewing motions.

It was a fun game for Stormy, to tempt the chipmunk to come even closer. He held a piece of bread in his fingertips and laid his hand where the marbles spelled out the letters of the Battle children's names. The chipmunk, his tail flicking back and forth at a rapid rate, came nearer, and nearer, and nearer.

Stormy kept very still, did not even breath until he finally had to and that frightened the chipmunk. He shied but soon returned, inching closer. With a motion so quick the eye could not perceive it, the chipmunk stole the bread and dashed away.

This so excited Stormy he ran inside to tell his mother, settling instead for Iris, telling her, "He ate out of my hand. He really, really did. Right out of my hand."

"What did?" asked Iris.

"The little chipmunk."

"Tell me about it," said Iris. She pulled up a chair so Stormy could sit, but he was too wound up to sit.

"I held a piece of bread, and he grabbed it away from me so fast I didn't even see him do it."

Stormy ran to the screen door, peered outside, turned back and with sadness etching his voice said, "He's not coming back."

"Oh, he'll come back," promised Iris. "You go out and wait. Be patient. He'll come." She got up, went to the cookie jar and opened the lid. "Here, take a chocolate chip cookie with you. Chipmunks love cookies. Better take one for yourself, too. It'll make the wait a little shorter."

Stormy took a cookie in each hand and went outside, making sure the screen door did not bang behind him. He sat on the bottom step, munched one cookie and waited. Birds sang in the towering poplars, a bull bellowed from the timber, cows mooed and several magpies swooped low on their way to the barn. Stormy followed their flight with his eyes. After that he remained motionless for the longest time. Finally, just before he was about to give up, the chipmunk reappeared. At first there was only a hint of movement in the branches of the pine tree and then Stormy saw a black nose sniffing the air, then the striped head and finally the whole body came into view. The chipmunk scurried down the trunk, came out in the open and sat up on his hind legs as if begging. Stormy guessed, if the little animal could talk, it would be telling him to throw the cookie, but Stormy remained motionless, the cookie in his fingertips. The chipmunk came closer, so near Stormy could see little whiskers twitching on the side of its face.

"I'm not going to hurt you," whispered Stormy. The sound of his voice surprised the chipmunk, its ears perked, and it looked directly at the boy with a quizzical expression. Stormy remained as steady as a rock, and the chipmunk leaned forward, and using its sharp teeth, stole a bite of the cookie and chewed it. And when the boy did not move, the chipmunk leaned forward and took another bite.

When only a small hunk of cookie remained, Stormy allowed the chipmunk to take it. After the animal had gone Stormy turned, and looking behind, saw the faces of Iris and his mother framed behind the screen door. They were smiling.

Donna reluctantly agreed to meet Cole at a downtown coffee shop. They sat at a small, round table, across from each other, on stools, where they talked quietly in an endless circle about their lost love. Cole believed, or maybe he only hoped, that at some point he could find an excuse to scoop Donna up in his arms the way Richard Geer had done to Debra Winger in *An Officer and a Gentlemen*, Donna's favorite movie, and carry her between tables and out the door of the coffee shop. It became evident that Donna did not share that same romantic fantasy because she talked about forging a new life, a life separate from him. And finally, Cole began to understand the love they shared, somewhere along the way, had become as unstable as gas escaping into thin air. He thought he could still feel it, taste it, touch it. But he couldn't. It wasn't there. And when that became tangible in his mind he lost heart and quit talking.

After Donna departed, Cole went outside and walked in the Willamette Valley evening where the wind gusted, the acrid stench of the city hugged the street, thunder cleared its throat and rain whipped down at odd angles. The city took on an ominous glow as purple as a three-day-old bruise. Advertising snippets caught Cole's eye: romance novels, one-minute rice, titanium golf clubs, motherboards, appetizers, video games, art deco furniture, up-to-the-minute news, platinum credit cards, Italian shoes, Grande Mocha Frappuccino, salon tans, pedicures, health club memberships….

As he walked he was aware of people. There were affluent men and women who moved silently and quickly, eyes straight ahead, never glancing left or right. There was also a legion of unfortunate ground troops—the homeless, destitute, needy, pathetic, wretched, weird—who mumbled to themselves and moved erratically with rough-edged intentions.

Cole found himself standing at a busy intersection. Tires of transitory cars and trucks hissed. Traffic lights vacillated between green, yellow and red. *Walk* and *Don't Walk* flashed. He tugged at the brim of his cowboy hat. A narrow stream of water ran off. The sign blazed *Walk*. Finally he walked.

CHAPTER FOURTEEN

TURNOUT, THE DAY THE CATTLE WERE STARTED ON A TWO-DAY DRIVE, had been a special occasion at the Double X for better than a hundred years. The terminus of the drive was an arid plain where the grasses came early and burned off fast. After a few weeks on the desert the gates were thrown open and the cattle allowed to graze their way into the mountains where, over the course of the summer, they were rotated through a series of pastures until, late in the fall, the changing seasons started the cattle drifting toward home and the promise of handouts over the long, snowy winter months.

On the range, the cattle required a minimum of looking after. Because natural salt was lacking in the soil, salt blocks had to be set out. The Double X used salt as a management tool, a treat to lure cattle into areas they neglected to graze because of the terrain or the fact there was more grass along the creek bottoms and in the meadows. By not putting salt in the prime grazing areas, the cattle were forced to keep moving and not overgraze any one area.

Turnout required every warm body that could ride to be in the saddle working. Cole, Ty and J.B. were riding and so were

Johnny Ritter and a couple of buckaroos out of Nevada, Tucker Blake and Waddie Wright, as well as Tex Corwin, an old fellow who had helped on the drive for 23 straight years. Tracee, who had been riding some over the past several weeks so she would not be saddle sore when the day finally arrived, was also riding. Lila Corwin, Tex's wife, was camp cook. Iris was staying home, babysitting Stormy.

Turnout morning began early. The horses were saddled and tied to the hitching rail in front of the barn where they pawed the ground and nickered, restless for the drive to begin. The word was given to "mount up" and Tracee stepped into the stirrup and pulled herself up and onto her horse. The horse threw its head and nervously pranced until the gate was swung open and the cattle began boiling down the long lane, outlined on either side by split rail fences, weathered gray and encrusted on the north face with a coating of gray-green moss. Ty rode near Tracee and nodded toward the fences. "Grandpa hand-split every one of those." With that said he wheeled his horse and rode away.

Tracee watched him go and wondered how he would react if he discovered he did not have any Battle blood pumping through his veins. Tracee wished Iris had never shared that secret with her, thinking it would have been best if she had told Ty instead. But that was silly, how could a mother ever tell her son he was a bastard born out of an adulterous affair? And Tracee knew Iris was, and would remain a puzzle, a puzzle missing many of the important pieces so that an accurate picture of her could never be realized. Why had she chosen to make Tracee the keeper of her scarlet secret?

Ty interrupted her thinking; shouting to her, "Wait until the last one goes past and drop in behind. Keep everything in front of you."

Tracee moved into position behind the last cow and calf. Her horse danced anxiously. Dogs barked. Cows bellowed. Horses and riders moved to an elusive tempo aimed at keeping an orderly flow of cattle moving down the lane, and yet chaos threatened to erupt as cows tried to turn back. But each time, Tracee was there, maneuvering her horse into position to cut the renegades off and keep the herd together.

Out in front a few leaders emerged. These cows set the pace and led the others up and out of the valley. They crossed an open sagebrush flat and cut through long fingers of dense timber. The two old-timers, J.B. and Tex, had the honor of riding point, staying ahead of the leaders and controlling their speed. On one side of the herd rode Ty and Tucker and on the other side, Waddie and Johnny. Cole moved around, wherever he was needed. He seemed to always show up in the nick of time, to push a wayward cow back into the flow.

Tracee had been given the assignment of riding drag, bringing up the rear, staying behind the cows and calves and away from the majority of the noise, confusion and possible trouble. The herd ambled onto a wide, muddy trail where frisky calves darted here and there and then hurried to catch up. Before long their friskiness was gone, and they stayed near their mothers, walking and sometimes trotting to keep pace. The ranch dogs followed at a discreet distance but soon lost interest and doubled back to their lair beneath the porch.

As the calves became fatigued, they congregated near the rear. The wingmen took turns dropping back to help Tracee and urge on the tiring calves. The trail wound through a park-like setting of towering ponderosa pine and skirted thickets of lodgepole and stands of brushy mountain mahogany. The morning wore on, the pace slowed and some of the calves wanted nothing more than to find a shady spot and lie down. The riders kept them moving to reach the noon resting spot, a place the Forest Service maps refer to as Naughty Girl Meadow, but the locals still call Whorehouse Meadow. In the olden days there had been a mill at the site and logging camps scattered throughout the forest in a 20-mile radius. A group of working girls set up a tent at the far end of the meadow with canvas partitions to make semi-private rooms. Every Saturday night the loggers and mill workers gathered at the tent, tossed down overpriced liquor cut several times with creek water, and depending on their mood and state of inebriation, they were up for one of two activities, fucking or fighting.

Lila Corwin, a woman of substantial girth, had driven the family Suburban to the meadow and had lunch ready and waiting: sandwiches, potato salad, orange juice and baked beans that she packed in a crock pot surrounded by quilts and wool blankets. The beans were still warm.

After the crew and the cattle had eaten and rested in this peaceful and idyllic meadow, the drive resumed. The cattle were pushed off the meadow and started down the trail. The point men regulated the speed of the drive; on the uphill they pushed the leaders to go faster than they preferred and on the downhill they used their horses to get in front and slow the leaders. Tex and J.B. were well experienced in handling cattle and shared an uncanny ability to know when a cow would try to break, where she was likely to stray from the trail, and by the time the cow began to drift in that direction, they were already there waiting for her to make her move. It was all done with subtle, unspoken signals. They never forced their horses into anything above an easy walk. Spurring a horse was an admission of failure and an unnecessary waste of horsepower. If a point man was in proper position, and doing what he needed to do to keep the herd moving as a single unit, nose-to-tail, the steady pace ate up the miles without overly fatiguing the animals.

The afternoon sun beat down, and here in the high country, the ground was drier, causing dust to billow in a rolling beige cloud. Cows bellowed, calves bawled and constantly interrupting the flow were undercurrents of sharp whistles, quick shouts and loud cursing from the men on the wings where one or several cows grew tired of eating dust, or wanted to change the pace, or to see different scenery than the ass-end of the cow ahead. But sometimes, for a few delirious moments, the swelling brown current drifted along contently and the only sounds were of hooves striking the ground, the sweet jingle of spurs and the squeak of saddle leather. Those intervals were few and far between.

The cattle drive reached Thompson Field, named after the homesteader who had originally laid claim to the land. Here, a half-section bisected by a small stream, with plenty of feed and a profusion of wildflowers, had been fenced off. The homestead shack, a rough affair of logs and split shakes, still stood as mute witness to unfulfilled dreams. It was of little use now except as a home for packrats and one sleepy-eyed owl.

Clustered around the old shack, and standing out in a colorful contrast to the lush pasture and verdant forest, were a number of domed tents and a blue-tarped lean-to converted into a makeshift kitchen. Lila had a fire going and coffee perked over glowing coals. Off to the side a big pot of chili bubbled and burped. Potatoes, wrapped in aluminum foil, were buried under the coals and a pile of rib eye steaks, two inches thick, waited to be tossed on the blackened grill. The smell of dinner was mouth-watering and the crew, after a hard day of work, pulled their saddles, turned their horses loose and congregated near a washtub where pop, ice tea and beer floated on ice.

Tracee got off her horse, unsaddled and made it as far as a grassy flat in the shade where she laid down and stretched out. Cole came near and asked, “How you doing?”

She responded with a weak smile, “My butt’s sore.”

Johnny reached into the washtub, grabbed a bottle, opened it with an experienced flick of his wrist and brought it over and handed the beer to Tracee. He said, “Maybe this’ll help. If it don’t cure the pain, at least it’ll cut the dust.”

They ate as the sunset ruptured into wild splashes of crimson and gold and after the crew had eaten their fill Tex recited several cowboy poems. When he finished Waddie took up his guitar and Tucker brought out his mouth harp, tapped it against his thigh a time or two to knock loose the dust, and the men played music. Tracee leaned against the fenders of a saddle turned upside down to air. Her belly was full and tiredness seeped through her muscles. She enjoyed the music but did not have an appreciation for the fact the same tunes had been listened to back in the days when cowboys drifted cattle from Texas to the railhead in Kansas. Tracee told herself she would close her eyes, but just for a moment or two.

Ty gently shook Tracee awake. It was almost dark. He said, “We’re set up over there. Your sleeping bag’s rolled out.” He helped her up, wrapped an arm around her waist and directed her toward their tent. She took a seat on the ground, peeled off her boots and pants, left on her other clothes and crawled inside the sleeping bag. She breathed in the smell of wood smoke and the perfume of wildflowers, sage and evergreen. Quiet rushed in but soon the distant gurgle of the creek became audible, followed by the chomping of cattle grinding grass between their teeth and finally the soft whisper of wind coursing through pine needles.

Lila banged an iron triangle to signal coffee was on and breakfast would follow. It seemed to the riders as though morning butted directly up against a pleasant evening, and yet, one after another, the crew rolled out to meet the dawn. They stepped into the timber to relieve themselves, staggered to the creek, rinsed their faces in the frigid water and then gathered around the cook fire where Lila already had bacon sizzling on a griddle. The crew wrapped cold hands around warm tin cups and drank black coffee.

“How do you want ’em?” asked Lila.

“Sunny-side-up.”

“Make mine over-easy.”

“Beat-the-hell-outta-’em.”

Eggs blurped in a sheen of grease, and then Lila was serving plates with eggs cooked to perfection, just as had been ordered, along with crisp bacon, golden-brown sourdough pancakes, with warm maple syrup and cold, homemade butter on the side.

After breakfast Cole asked Tracee, “You too sore to ride?”

“Nope. I can do this,” she said, moving a little, wincing.

Johnny playfully, and lightly, slapped her back, told her, “Well, let’s get ’em saddled, partner. We got a long row to hoe.”

The well-fed crew lined out the herd and then started down a trail leading into country more open than it had been the day before. They passed rimrock mesas, outcroppings of mountain mahogany interspersed with juniper dotted flats, and dry washes that led off toward the desert. By midmorning the sun was hot enough to make heat shimmers and cause the cows to walk with their tongues hanging low. Long streaks of saliva smeared the red volcanic soil, and the dust was so thick Tracee and the others riding drag finally had to tie bandannas around their noses in order to breathe.

The cattle traversed this dry stretch, and then, finally, a current of wind came wafting up from below bringing with it the scent of water. There was no holding back the leaders as they bypassed the point riders and broke into a trot that did not end until they were down into the swale carved by Deep Creek. Here they indulged themselves, thrusting their parched muzzles into the lukewarm water and drinking long and thirstily, ignoring the cattle behind them until, finally the force of the subsequent waves of newcomers shoved the leaders up the bank on the opposite side.

By the time the cows and calves had found each other and the calves were beginning to nurse, Lila had already ferried the men back to the ranch, and they were returning with their pickup trucks and horse trailers. Cole got out the checkbook and was in the process of writing checks, but the cowboys knew the Battle family was fighting for every dollar, and to a man, they refused to take any money. Lila only took enough to cover the cost of groceries, nothing more.

On the way to the ranch Tracee dwelled on a singular thought, all she wanted was to soak in a hot bubble bath until the soreness in her backside, and the dirt, were gone. And when she did, luxuriating in the deep tub, running more hot water each time the bath cooled, she lay there remembering the cattle drive.

CHAPTER FIFTEEN

Wood River Valley, empty now except for the saddle horses, the bulls and the replacement heifers, was a strangely quiet place. The heifers took turns wandering from the timber to drink from the creek, leaving their black baldy calves with a surrogate babysitter. The calves enjoyed frisky play, butting heads, running around and occasionally leaping into the air in their liveliness. If a coyote sauntered too close, the protective babysitter sounded a warning, and the mothers returned on the run and stood guard until the danger passed.

The bulls were a moody lot, bellowing passionately whenever they picked up the scent of a heifer, grudgingly moving around their pasture, rubbing off coarse winter hair on the rough bark of pine trees until their red coats became sleek and shiny. Whenever one bull's aimless wandering brought him in contact with the aimless wandering of another bull they roared in defiance and might butt heads and lock horns in mock battle. Once in awhile their playful ways turned serious, and then they squared off, pawing dirt, making low, guttural noises, and charging each other. When this happened the impact of their heads colliding cracked like thunder, horns rattled and the brutish beasts pushed and shoved, trying to determine the most powerful. When the winner was determined, he paraded triumphantly around while the loser moved away to lick his wounds and rebuild his damaged pride.

On the meadow the green grasses were mixed with the yellow of buttercups and dandelions, the blue of camas and wild iris, the elusive reddish-orange of Indian paintbrush and the white of yarrow. The air was busy with the happy melodies of songbirds, the whoop of sandhill cranes, killdeer trilling and valley quail calling with the same three precise notes, "er-er-errr." Swallows and nighthawks dipped and dove, swooping low to catch bugs. A jet airplane cracked the sound barrier and triggered a round of agitated caws from the crows, and a China rooster beat its wings and screeched loudly.

The men drove the tractors, pulling drags back and forth across the meadow to break up the manure piles and open up the ground. In the process artifacts from the past were exposed: arrowheads, scrapers and net weights usually went unnoticed, but each time one of the mortars or pestles worked their way to the surface, the man on the tractor stopped, dug it free and added it to those already on display at the Home Place. The perfect mortars and pestles were exhibited along the foundation of the log house, those with a crack or a chunk missing were leaned against the weathered boards of the barn, and those deemed worthless were tossed under the poplar trees.

Archaeologists claimed humans first populated Wood River Valley ten thousand years ago, maybe more. The original inhabitants hunted big game with spears, clubs and rocks, killing animals long extinct: mastodons, mammoths, giant ground sloths and long-horned bison. In addition to hunting, these people dug roots, picked berries and gathered seeds and barks. They fished the streams and lakes, and when the migratory waterfowl passed through, they fashioned crude decoys from cattails to lure the birds within range of their weapons.

Cole, seated on the John Deere tractor, pulled a drag in circles around the big fields and thought about those thousands of years of history. He tried to envision what life must have been like for the people living in the valley when Sugarloaf Mountain awoke from her slumber and became active a mere five thousand years before. He thought it was probably similar to when, in modern times, Mt. Saint Helens blew her top. He imagined a terrific explosion shooting ash and rock skyward with a deafening roar, black smoke billowing and red-hot lava oozing from fissures near the summit and spilling down the sides like hot fudge on a sundae.

The native people had been forced to leave the valley, and for decades after, their homeland, covered with several feet of ash, remained devoid of vegetation. But moisture percolated through the soil, grasses began to spread over the valley floor and on the hills brush took root and trees began to grow. Water and wind carved the landscape, dragging the finest topsoil down and depositing it on the valley floor. Insect populations returned. Fish returned to spawn in the streams. Waterfowl paused to rest on their migratory routes, and animals once again began to roam the landscape.

The native people came home, and as before, their nomadic lifestyle revolved around trapping and spearing salmon and steelhead, hunting waterfowl on the lake and big game in the mountains, gathering roots, berries and nuts and utilizing tule reeds, marsh grasses and pine needles to weave clothing, baskets, sandals and mats to cover the framed wickiups where they lived. Life for the native people, as it had been for thousands of years, was once again gentle and easy.

Then the white man arrived and the native people resisted, saying all they wanted was to live in peace in the valley protected by the great, white mountain. The invaders forced the native people to fight and soldiers and turncoat scouts from other tribes killed the native warriors, rounded up those who remained and transported them to a distant reservation. In the ensuing years, Wood River Valley, what Lewis Battle did not legally own, was thrown open to homesteaders.

The homesteaders laid claim to 160 acres of free government land—later increased to 320 acres of desert entry. They plowed the virgin soil, and for several years the rains came on schedule, the crops sprouted and harvests were abundant. But then came dry years, years when rain drowned the seeds and years when a late frost destroyed the emerging crops. There were infestations of crickets, grasshoppers and field mice. One by one the homesteaders went broke, pulled up stakes, sold out and moved on.

Lewis Battle built his ranch one homestead at a time. Sometimes he paid nothing more than a buckboard load of groceries. Once he paid ten cents an acre, sixteen bucks for 160 acres, a house and barn. Another homestead was relinquished for the price of two train tickets to Chicago.

Each time, after Lewis had acquired a homesteader's land, he promptly burned the buildings, ripped out the lilacs and rosebushes and plowed over the graves. The history of the homesteaders, who had worked so hard to make their dreams into reality, were deliberately erased from history. They suffered the same shameful indignity that the native people had before them.

However, Lewis Battle did retain a modicum of compassion, allowing a few of the old Indians to return to Wood River Valley each spring and fall. They set up camp in the meadow and fished, gathered eggs from the nesting ducks and geese and hunted deer and elk. Later, after Lewis's boy Harold had taken over the ranch, some of the young bucks came in automobiles instead of buckboards, bringing with them firewater and trouble. Harold put a stop to it, and never again were Indians allowed to camp on Double X land.

Cole remembered his father showing him where the Indian campsite had been. All that remained was a circle of rocks where the campfire burned, meat poles that had rotted off and were lying on the ground, some rusty tin cans, a crumpled fender from a Model-T Ford and a few whiskey bottles turned blue by the sun.

"Oh, that boy of yours," said Iris. "You have to see what he's done."

"What did he do?" said Tracee, wary that Stormy had caused some mischief.

"He didn't do anything wrong," said Iris. "He was my inspiration. He helped me break out of my rut, the one I've been in for God knows how long."

Iris led the way to her room and proudly showed Tracee a painting. The work was predominately blue sky, but the lower third of the painting depicted Stormy in a swing, as seen from the back, and even though the face was not visible, something was captured in the way his feet were thrust toward the heavens that communicated absolute exuberance. It was such a startling diversion from the stilted flowers Iris typically painted that, at first, Tracee was of the mind someone else had painted it.

"You did this?" she asked.

"Yes, of course I did," said Iris beaming with pride. "I saw Stormy swinging in that old swing and something came over me. I remembered the way Cole and Ty used to play there, and I felt compelled to capture in a painting that feeling of not having a care in the world, innocence and having fun. I think I did just that."

"You certainly did," said Tracee.

Iris was smiling. She had her hands on her hips. "My doctor told me to quit seeing the world with Iris's *old* eyes and to see the world with Iris's *new* eyes."

"It certainly shows," said Tracee.

"You like it?"

"Very much."

"I want you to have it," said Iris. She picked up the painting from where it was propped on a chair and handed it to Tracee. "A spiritual change has come over me. From now on I'm going to indulge myself and explore my artistic side. I've never had the freedom to do that before. Now I'm inspired."

Tracee searched for the right words to say and settled for, "Well, I think that's really great. I'll treasure this."

Iris lowered her voice, "I've already made up my mind. I'm moving to town. It won't cost any more for me to live there. Jerry Pavlinac has agreed to rent me a spare room in his store. I'm going to open an art gallery. I'll sell my paintings and some from local artists, too. You might not know this, but we have some fine artists living around Emerson. We really do. I think I can make it pay. I'll have to make it pay because I refuse to be a burden on anyone."

"That's absolutely fabulous," said Tracee. She was surprised by this and yet wanted to be positive and encouraging. "I think Emerson is probably ready for an art gallery. I'm sure the tourists will support it. When do you plan to start?"

"I spoke with Cole at lunch today. He was worried about the costs, but I assured him I'd pay my own way with my social security. We talked for quite a spell, and I told him the doctor I'm seeing said it was a wonderful idea. Cole said he thought it had *some merit*. Those were his words, *some merit*. In the end, Cole said he'd go along with it if I promised I'd keep seeing the doctor."

"And so you promised?" said Tracee.

"At the drop of a hat," laughed Iris.

"When's the grand opening?"

"Soon, I'm hoping."

"Maybe I can lend a hand."

"I'd like that," said Iris, and the lines etched in the skin around her eyes danced with her happiness.

Tracee swept the wood floor, washed windows and helped apply a coat of flat white paint to the walls. And when the interior of Iris's gallery was ready, Tracee helped sort and organize, leaning paintings against the wall, standing back to envision how they would look hanging. While she worked a few curious customers filtered in for a look around. A woman who said she was from Lake Oswego inquired about a landscape painting of Wood River Valley and Sugarloaf Mountain, and when Iris told her the price, the woman didn't bat an eye at paying two hundred dollars for the painting.

That evening, as Tracee was preparing to leave the gallery, Iris handed her a long white envelope. At first Tracee thought Iris was trying to pay her. She said, "No, you don't need to do that. I just wanted to help out."

"It isn't what you think," said Iris. This time she placed her hands over Tracee's hand that held the envelope. "I want you to give this to Ty. Make sure he's alone when you do. I hope he won't be too terribly upset with me."

Tracee took a step back. She was trying to read the older woman's face, hoping a look might reveal, or at least suggest, the contents. But there was no clear indication of what the letter might contain.

Iris continued, "I wish I could tell him in person, but I think it's better this way. Please, will you give it to him for me?"

"Of course," promised Tracee.

XX

When Tracee reached the ranch she found Ty in the living room and handed him the sealed envelope. She told him it was from his mother, and that he needed to read it in private. Without saying anything he tucked the envelope in his shirt pocket, worked on finishing his beer and finally went to his room where he flopped down on the bed, tore open the envelope and stared at the lined yellow pages. He began to read:

Dear Son,

For a very long time I have wanted to say the things I'm writing to you in this letter. I had hoped to be able to tell you in person, but I'm afraid I'm not that strong, not just yet. Let me also say, it is very difficult for me to reveal events that happened so very long ago, to put these things, and my feelings about them, into words, but I shall try.

First, let me say, when Frank died it was like a heavy burden lifted away from me. For years I felt smothered by him, or perhaps I should say I allowed myself to be smothered by him but, as you read this letter, perhaps you'll be better able to understand why I did what I did, why I allowed it. Frank and I had a relationship that, because of our actions and unforeseen circumstances, evolved from real love into something else; I don't know what to call it. We stayed together because I could never find the courage to leave him.

Frank and I made mistakes in our lives, many mistakes. We both found it difficult to forgive, forgive each other, forgive ourselves. And I was just as guilty as Frank. I suppose our mutual guilt is one of the things that bound us together.

I feel it is well past time for you to find out the truth. I'm sure what I have to say next will shock you, as it did me. I witnessed Frank kill his father. It was at branding. They had an argument. Grandpa Harold slapped Frank across the back with a rope. Frank reacted without thinking. He struck out in anger, used his fist and hit Grandpa on the temple. That's what killed him. Frank said it was an accident, that a horse knocked Grandpa into a corral post. But I saw what happened. I think Frank knew that, but he never said anything and nobody ever suspected it was murder, that Frank murdered his father.

I was pregnant with Ruth Ann at the time. She was born a few months later, and she was such a sweet thing, a perfect baby in every way, hardly ever fussed and she smiled and laughed all the time. I'd bundle her up and take her for walks and oh, how she loved to hear the birds sing and watch the horses and cattle. They came right up to us, the cattle and horses did. She had that type of magnetism with animals. I loved to dress her in cute outfits and hold her in my arms. The touch of her skin, the smell of her, was so wonderful. Like I said, she was perfect.

When she came down with the croup, I asked Frank to run us into the doctor—he never wanted me to drive—but he said she just had a cold and that she'd get better. She didn't. Her cough grew progressively worse. Her temperature went through the roof. I tried putting her in a cold bath but it was just no use. All I could do was stay with her and when she coughed and began choking I'd turn her on her side and pat her back until she'd gasp for breath. It was a terrible thing, just terrible, not being able to help.

And where was Frank? It was the middle of the night, and he and J.B. were out calving. When Frank finally did come in there wasn't much could be done. We got to the doctor but my baby only lasted a few hours. The doctor said it was pneumonia, said if we'd of gotten there earlier he might have been able to save her.

In my grief I blamed Frank. From that point forward, everything that happened, just happened. Perhaps I could say it was all a dreadful mistake but that's not true because you were meant to happen. You are God's gift to this earth—God's gift to me.

The following paragraph began, *"Frank is not your real father...."* and went on for several pages with words that were spare, direct and informative. They lacked any hint at the motive behind, or the resulting remorse and sorrow, of Iris's illicit love affair. It was as if mere words could never explain anything.

Iris's infidelity began one sunlit, airy, spring afternoon. Frank was away attending a bull sale and Iris had returned to the kitchen from putting Cole down for his afternoon nap. She was kneading dough to make bread when she heard a rig pull up out front. She glanced out the window and watched a red Cadillac convertible, ragtop down, wheel to a stop in front of the log house. A well-dressed man, wearing a western sports coat, gray slacks, colorful shirt and a cowboy hat—so light gray it could have been white—pulled his lanky frame from the Cadillac. He took a moment to look around, and then, with long unhurried strides, he strolled onto the porch and knocked on the screen door.

By the time Iris had dusted her hands and stepped to the door, the man had already removed his cowboy hat, exposing little tufts of hair at each temple beginning to turn silver. "Howdy, ma'am," he said through the screen, "My name's Lucky Price."

Iris thought the way this man stood with one forearm cocked against the doorframe, leaning slightly toward her, his image softened by the screen, was absolutely the most self-assured man she had ever come face-to-face with. He oozed self-confidence. But she remained guarded and wanted to know, "How did you get through the gate, Mr. Price?"

"It was open," he told her.

Iris recalled J.B. had run into town. He had probably left the gate open since he was coming right back. She added, "We don't get many visitors."

"Don't imagine," said Lucky. "You're more than a few miles off the beaten path." He took a quick glance over his shoulder, down the long valley, and returned his attention to Iris. "I certainly do see why you choose to live here. Don't believe I've ever been in a more beautiful valley."

"We like it," said Iris, emphasizing the "we" in her declaration. "What can I do for you, Mr. Price?"

"Ahh, call me Lucky, everybody else does," he said with a disarming grin. "Heard through the grapevine Frank Battle, I assume he's your husband...." Iris nodded. "Heard he had some extra pasture and was in the market for feeder steers. I've got a line on some, wanted to talk business with him. He around?"

Iris deliberately wiped her hands on her apron. "He's at a sale in Madras, or maybe it's Prineville. He'll call tonight. Do you want me to give him a message, a phone number where he can reach you?"

"That'd be fine," said Lucky.

Without thinking Iris pushed open the screen door and invited Lucky inside. She went in search of paper and a pencil, offering as an afterthought, "Care for a glass of lemonade, Mr. ... Lucky? I was about to pour myself one."

"Sure," he said. She motioned to one of the kitchen chairs, and before he took a seat, Lucky slipped off his coat. Under the coat he was wearing a lightweight, long-sleeved shirt, open at the collar. As he nonchalantly tossed the coat over the back of a chair Iris noticed this man's lean, limber muscles. He was the total opposite of Frank, and she blushed slightly at her comparison.

Iris was bare-footed, wearing a split skirt, a faded denim blouse and the apron. Her hair was pulled back into a loose bun. By the time she returned with paper and a pencil, she had removed the apron and put on shoes. Lucky scribbled his name and number while Iris served lemonade. She set his glass on the table and stood nearby.

"You buy and sell cattle," she said. It was more of a statement than a question.

"Yep," he said and took a sip. "Real tasty. What did you say your name was?"

"Iris. Thank you. It's fresh-squeezed."

"Iris," repeated Lucky. "And, I must say, you're as lovely as your namesake." He tossed a happy-go-lucky grin in her direction and returned to sipping slowly, making his drink last. He knew about women, had had lots of women in his time, and was blessed with a special knack for knowing when a woman had certain needs, needs that were not being fulfilled. He had a sense this woman—living as she did way out in the sticks—felt trapped, or unloved, or both. He explored the possibility by asking, "You get to town often, Iris?"

Iris took a seat in the chair across from Lucky, cocking one leg under her as she did. "I wouldn't say often. Whenever I need to stock up someone runs me in." She tugged at a few loose strands that had fallen over her face and tucked them into the sweep of her hair. She was enjoying this dialogue. Living on the ranch there were many times she longed for conversations with interesting people. Sometimes, when she went to town, she'd have coffee at the café and start a conversation with whoever happened to be sitting nearby. She asked, "So, you must be on the road a lot, looking at cattle, finding buyers, that sort of thing?"

"I am. The only days I take off are Thanksgiving and Christmas. That's it. Found out a long time ago, if a fellow wants to be successful, he has to knuckle down and work at it.

My particular line of work requires a discriminating eye, the ability to judge quality, and it doesn't hurt to be in the right place at the right time. Mostly I stick with cattle, but I'll pick up a saddle horse now and then.

"Just last week I was at the sale in Ellensburg, that's up there in Central Washington, and in the ring were burros fresh off the Nevada range. Now normally I wouldn't have any use for a burro, but a farmer I know told me he wanted one as a pet. He asked me to keep an eye out, buy if the price was right. Nobody bid on these Nevada burros, so I made an offer. The auctioneer brought down his gavel, and just like that, I was the proud owner of a dozen burros. I got on the phone, told the farmer I had his burro and went to work trying to unload the others. I didn't make a dime on the deal, but I didn't get stuck with a burro as a pet either."

Lucky smiled, showing he had perfect teeth, white and straight. And Iris noticed he was wearing an expensive watch with turquoise stones on the band. She said, "That's a beautiful watch." Lucky told her he bought the watch in Arizona and opened the throat of his shirt to show her a necklace with another turquoise stone. He raised the stone from a mat of dark chest hair.

Completely out of the blue Lucky asked, "Iris, what's your favorite time of year?"

"Oh heavens," said Iris, feeling flustered. "I never stopped to consider, well, it certainly wouldn't be winter. I detest the cold." She became sidetracked, thinking that in normal conversation she would never use the word detest, maybe hate or dislike, but never detest. What had made her say that word now? And then she was talking again, "Probably springtime. I love the smell of things growing, the blue sky, the way life renews itself."

"Me too," said Lucky. He removed a pack of cigarettes from his shirt pocket, tapped one loose from the soft pack while asking, "Mind if I smoke?"

"Heavens no," said Iris. "I'll get you an ashtray."

"Would you like one?"

"No thank you," said Iris. "I don't smoke."

When Iris returned Lucky was using a lighter adorned with hammered gold nuggets to light his cigarette. He held the lighter up so she could see it. "Klondike gold," he said. And Iris, at that moment, felt more foolish than she ever remembered feeling. Here she was, trapped in her one-dimensional life, bound to a man she no longer respected or loved, and she had no idea, no idea at all, whether the Klondike was in Canada or Alaska.

Lucky, in an off-handed manner, asked, "Did you always want to be married and settled down?"

"Not really," said Iris a little wistfully. "I had big plans. I wanted to go to college and be an artist. But things like that don't always work out,"

"I wish I had the talent it takes to be an artist," said Lucky. "What I'd really like, is to see the world like a painter sees it—geometric shapes, form and contours, light, shadows and swirls of color. Take time to study, really study, the intricate reds of a rose petal, examine the elaborate texture of a fern, the golden ruffled edges of a cloud at sunset—see beauty through an artist's eyes. That would be absolutely marvelous."

Lucky peeked in Iris's direction, saw he had hit a responsive cord, and with all the sincerity he could muster, asked, "Iris, do you ever wish, for just a day, you could be someone else?"

Iris felt herself being swept along in Lucky's comfortable cadence of words. She responded, "What I'd like is to be the featured artist at a gallery show, have all the patrons and critics fawn over my work. It would be wonderful to have that experience before I die. Do you know what I mean?"

"I absolutely do."

Having allowed this virtual stranger to discover something about her that even her husband did not know caused Iris a flutter of shyness. But what did it matter. Frank didn't care to know. "And how about you, Lucky, what would you like to be?"

"World Saddlebronc Champion," said Lucky. He knew from past experiences that, at this juncture in their conversation, Iris would be particularly susceptible to a compliment. He said, "Iris, you're a very attractive woman." And when she started to protest he added, "No, no, I mean it. What I see in you, Iris, besides your physical beauty, is that you have tenderness and compassion in your heart."

Ruth Ann's death had shattered Iris's heart. What Lucky said, or maybe it was the perceived compassion in his voice, real or imagined, triggered an involuntary release in Iris, and she burst into tears. Lucky took quick advantage of the situation by removing a handkerchief from his hind pocket and gently dabbed at her tears. The next thing Iris knew, she was sobbing out the detail of Ruth Ann's death, and Lucky was stroking her shoulders and whispering to her that everything was going to be all right. Never did he try, in any way, to inhibit her emotional outpouring.

Afterward, Lucky refused to allow Iris to feel even the slightest twinge of embarrassment at having bared her soul. And because of that she felt closer to this cattle buyer than she had to anyone in a long, long time. She asked, "Care for more lemonade?"

Lucky drawled, "Naw, but thank you. I suppose I best be on my way." He stood, picked up his coat and shrugged it on.

"I could fix you a sandwich," said Iris, grasping at any possible excuse to delay his departure.

He shook his head, told her she had been the perfect hostess, that it was indeed a pleasure having made her acquaintance, and when he took her hand, Iris felt the firmness of his grip and the way he held her hand, cradling it, and it seemed as if a tenderness, almost an intimacy, passed between them.

Lucky pulled away. He walked across the room in just a few quick strides and was out the door. He never allowed the screen to slam shut like everyone else did. Instead he held the door briefly, and in that instant of hesitation, Iris imagined he might be contemplating returning to her, but he didn't. The door softly tapped the jamb, and he was gone.

The big red Cadillac made a wide turn and headed back the way it had come. Iris stood at the screen door watching the dust cloud rise, lengthen and slowly begin to settle. She closed her fingers around the scrap of paper with Lucky's name and number on it, and brought her hand up to the soft valley between her breasts.

Iris kept the paper hidden in a secret compartment in her jewelry box and never gave Frank the message. One evening, nearly six months later—she was spending the winter in the house in town so Cole could attend kindergarten—she withdrew the note and dialed the number. Lucky answered.

She began, "You probably don't remember me, but this is Iris Battle...."

And he interrupted her, told her of course he remembered her, and that for months he had been hoping she might call. They talked for two hours. And the next night, and the night after that, with Cole tucked in bed and sleeping soundly, she called Lucky and their conversations spiraled into something with more meaning than simple friendship. The fourth night Lucky mentioned he was coming to Lincoln, a town only thirty miles from Emerson, the following day. He said he was staying at the Carolina Motel, and since it would be best if they were not seen in public, suggested she come to his motel room.

With Cole away at school Iris took the only taxi in Emerson to Lincoln and instructed the driver to drop her off at a shopping mall with the understanding he would pick her up in two hours. After the taxi departed, she walked five blocks to the Carolina Motel. When she arrived at Lucky's room, he opened the door immediately. He was wearing a broad smile, and he had a drink and cigarette in hand. He fixed another drink for Iris and they sat side by side on the foot of the bed, engaging in meaningless small talk until Iris confessed she wouldn't be able to stay long, that she had to be back when Cole arrived home from school.

Lucky set his drink aside and did the same with Iris's. She uncrossed her legs—her nylons making a soft swishing sound as they scraped together—and tried to stand, but Lucky pulled her down onto the bed and into his arms. He was the aggressor, the one in control. She felt small and awkward and had the overwhelming sensation she was falling into him, and at that point, she could not have stopped her headlong plunge even if she had wanted to.

Lucky kissed her neck with a string of kisses so buoyant and soft they wouldn't have broken the plane of still water. He unbuttoned her blouse.

"I've got to go," she breathed.

"I know," he said.

Iris gave herself to Lucky, lost herself in him, and after making one phone call to have a friend come stay with Cole, she ran away with the handsome cattle buyer. For about a week they ran hot and heavy, and then he dumped her in a cheap motel room in Twin Falls, Idaho. She had a black eye, a busted lip, and a baby growing in her belly. On the way out the door Lucky laid a hundred dollar bill on the dresser and said, "Go home."

Iris walked out onto the high bridge straddling the Snake River. She didn't think she could go home and face Frank. She crawled over the railing, stood on a strut and had every intention of ending her life, her disgrace, her humiliation. All she had to do was open her hands and push away. Simple as that—open her hands, push away –and find the peace of absolution in the selfish act of freefalling. Then, just as her grip loosened and her fingers began to unfurl, an image of Cole came to her and she knew, if she did this thing, he would grow up without his mother. Never again would she feel his embrace, kiss his forehead when she tucked him in bed, watch his face light up when he saw what Santa had brought him on Christmas morning, see him march off to school with his hair freshly combed like a big little boy. All those things, and so very many more, would never be. And that was just too much for Iris. She could not allow herself the indulgence of suicide. The fear of dying suddenly gripped her hard and fast. She seized the cold, unyielding metal, gripped it hard and for the longest time she remained there desperately clinging to the bridge, sobbing uncontrollably, her body shaking violently. But finally, she was able to regain some control over her emotions and managed to pull herself up and over the railing and return to the world of the living.

Iris used the hundred bucks from Lucky to buy a bus ticket, and when she reached Emerson, she called Frank. He drove in from the ranch, met her at the bus station and they sat in his pickup and talked. He asked what she had done. She told him the truth. At last he said, "You wanna go home?"

"Yes," she sobbed.

Frank took her back. But he never forgave her.

Frank is not your real father. You have a right to know that. Your father was Lucky Price. He could be a decent human being when it served him, but he was not the type of man I could stay with. Instead, Frank took me back. We forged a bond; I suppose you could say it was an alliance of sorts, even though, by then, our love for each other was gone. It died a long time before I met Lucky.

I suppose you will have questions concerning your biological father, but he is no longer of this earth. He was killed in an automobile accident three years after we parted company. I wish he had lived and that he had had the opportunity to get to know you, to have been a father to you. But on the other hand, Frank would never have allowed such a thing.

I live my life with remorse for the mistakes I have made, and with regret and shame for those things I was powerless to avoid. I think you have already discovered that, in this life, we sometimes choose a road, and once we start traveling down it, we have very little control over where it takes us. The best any of us can hope for is to live each day to its fullest and make the most of our God-given talents.

You are of my flesh and blood. I'm sorry for the pain this letter will undoubtedly bring you but, Ty, I think you had the right to know all this. I will love you forever.

Your Loving Mother,
Iris Battle

P.S. Son, you have as much right to the ranch as anyone.

CHAPTER SIXTEEN

THE PERFECT COMBINATION OF SUN AND MOISTURE COAXED THE timothy and blue grass to grow tall and stout. Afternoon winds blew across Wood River Valley, and the weight of the ripening seeds made the stems sway in meandering rhythms and undulate in waves that turned colors from the glitter of green glass to the burnished spangle of a freshly scrubbed copper pot. White and pink clover blossoms hugged the ground, charging the shifting air currents with a sugary fragrance, and bees and delicate sapphire-winged butterflies flitted about. The hay grew riper by the minute.

Ty almost stopped at a bar before visiting his mother but told himself he wanted to remain clearheaded. When he got to the house, he found her watching *Wheel of Fortune* on television. He waited at the door until Iris looked up and saw him. She promptly turned off the television and motioned him inside. Ty took a seat on a straight-backed chair, occupying only the first few inches, and hunched forward with his elbows on his knees while lightly fingering the brim of his hat. He said nothing. His eyes were slightly red. He did not look up.

"The letter," he said, and stopped, but the ice was broken and he went on, "The letter explains a lot. On the other hand, it tangles up a bunch of stuff, too."

"I'm sorry," said Iris.

"Why now?" asked Ty.

"Because Frank's gone. The doctor said it would be a good idea if I got it all out in the open. Oh Ty, I just couldn't keep it from you any longer."

Ty looked at her then, looked at her eyes, and her eyes betrayed her. They revealed the depth of her sadness, shame and remorse. He didn't want his mother to suffer and was gripped by an urge to go to her, give her a hug and tell her she was forgiven, and that he loved her. He wanted to do that, but instead he behaved the way a skittish horse will react when faced with something uncomfortable, he pulled back. He needed time, needed to be alone and needed to get away. He filled his lungs, expelled the sour air in a rush, stood, crushed his cowboy hat on his head and said, "Tell Cole I'll be back in time for haying. Tell him that."

"Okay," Iris answered meekly. She was close to tears but did not want to break down in front of her son. Ty got to his feet, and as he passed, she offered, "I'm so sorry."

Ty kept right on walking. The screen door swung open, and in the instant before it slapped the frame Iris thought she heard him say, "It's okay Mom. I forgive you." But she knew he never said those words. She merely wished he had.

XX

Iris forced herself to paint, working through the night on an image contradictory to her mood—a garish landscape, with bright, happy colors. The focal point was a band of wild pinto ponies at play, galloping hard along what could have been the luminescent, hard-packed sand at the edge of the world.

Ty drove directly from his mother's house to the liquor store. He bought a bottle of cheap whiskey. The clerk placed it in a paper sack and when Ty got to his pickup he unscrewed the lid, rolled down the paper and drank as he headed south. He took back roads, and when he was within sight of the great snowy fault line of Steens Mountain, he pulled over and stopped. He dropped the tailgate of his pickup and sat there drinking and thinking as the day faded and the golden sun made haloes around the sage, highlighted elaborate spider webs, before sinking into the western horizon. Twilight emerged. Heat dissipated. A light breeze stirred the air. Nighthawks swooped. Bats dipped and glided. Two does wandered gracefully through on their way to water.

In time, darkness prevailed. Stars emerged and began twinkling. Passing aircraft sent pulsating flickers of green and red. Fast moving satellites and space junk arced pinpricks of fast-moving light across the blue-black sky. And, off to the east, behind the escarpment, a modest glow grew in intensity and soon flooded the night sky with an intense white moon.

Ty watched and drank. He wondered about his father—his looks, the kind of a man he was, his likes and dislikes—and eventually came around to equating his current circumstances to what Tracee and Stormy would someday face, when Stormy had questions about his father. Then she, like Iris, would be forced to raise the curtain and expose her past. Ty thought about Frank and realized, to his credit, the man had taken Iris back into his home after discovering she was pregnant with another man's child. He would have been justified in kicking her out. Certainly he had been under no obligation to raise Ty, especially not as his own flesh and blood. But he had done just that. Ty felt his hardened opinion of Frank begin to soften, but only a little.

Ty fell asleep in the back of his pickup and awoke to the radiance of a new day coming on. He was stiff and sore and had a pounding, hangover headache. Yet he managed to drive on to McDermitt where he picked up a case of beer. He opened a bottle as soon as he was back on the highway and that seemed to revive him enough to drive to Winnemucca where he caught a room and proceeded to go on a wild toot: drinking, playing poker and availing himself of prostitutes at whorehouses on the circle. After five days of running wide-open he had had his fill, and with haying season fast approaching, he turned his pickup north and voluntarily returned to the Double X.

XX

J.B., with Stormy riding shotgun and helping as much as he could, drove into the mountains and set out salt and mineral blocks for the cows on pasture. The two of them ate lunch in the woods where a spring bubbled from the ground to fill a blue-green pool, bleeding off in a narrow stream choked with watercress. Stormy had, pretty much by himself, fixed the lunch. He was especially proud of what he had included: peanut butter sandwiches, pickles, potato chips, cookies, Skittles and soda pop.

XX

Cole and Tracee rode horseback, plunging in and out of pools of sunlight and shadows, pushing the bulls from the valley into the high country so the bulls could breed the cows. The bulls lumbered along, refusing to be crowded or to travel any faster than they wanted. Sometimes Cole and Tracee visited, but more often than not they rode together in silence, sharing the tranquil joy of being horseback in the outdoors where leaves and grasses whispered, pine and fir charged the air with the lively fragrance of evergreen, and the deer and elk moved through the timber like phantoms. A magpie swooped low, landed on the back of a slow-moving bull and feasted on bugs gleaned from the coarse brown hair.

Tracee suddenly caught the penetrating stench of a skunk. She wrinkled her nose, made a face and exclaimed, "Pew, that's horrible!"

"It's not what you think," said Cole.

"That's not a skunk? Please."

"It's not."

"Then what is it?"

"Sweet-smelling perfume from a patch of wild azaleas," kidded Cole as he fought to keep a straight face. Tracee laughed, and to Cole her laughter sounded like a bird singing.

When Ty returned, he worked with Cole to get the machinery ready for haying. They replaced worn parts, tightened loose belts, dumped old gas, changed oil and filters, and every now and then, one of them uttered a few choice cuss words when a knuckle got scraped or a wrench slipped and clanked onto the concrete floor. The welder hissed, the grinder spit sparks, and as each piece of machinery was repaired and ready for work, it was rolled out of the shop to join the ranks of a small army of equipment poised for haying.

During this time Ty never offered a single word of explanation, not about where he had been for a week or what he had done. Nor did he divulge the contents of his mother's letter. He kept that information strictly to himself. As a result, he bore the total weight of that burden—the knowledge Frank had killed his own father, his mother had borne him after an adulterous affair and that he was not a Battle, not by blood anyway. So why did he still feel such family loyalty? He didn't know.

Ty privately acknowledged his mother had force-fed him a lot of truth at once. He questioned if he had been administered a smaller dose of facts over a longer period of time, would that have been preferable? He didn't know the answer, and he sure as hell wasn't about to tackle the thorny question of entitlement, even though his mother had written, *"Son, you have as much right to the ranch as anyone."*

Ty figured he'd make his decisions about what he would do when the time was right. In the short term, all he had to worry about was having the haying equipment in the best shape possible, so that maybe, just maybe, it'd hold together—with hope, bailing wire and spit—for one more hay season.

If Ty had little to say to Cole, he had even less to say to Tracee. Their lack of communication only served to underscore the obvious fact that, somewhere along the line—it was impossible to put a finger on it and say it started here, or there—a fissure had opened between them, and like a rock split by moisture and cold, the gap between them had continued to widen. Now there was nothing holding them together.

Haying the broad meadow of the Double X had once required a full crew of men. Teams of workhorses had been used to propel mowers, rakes, wagons and pull-nets. A squadron of men cut the hay, raked it and built loose stacks that dotted the valley floor like giant loaves of golden bread. With the advent of tractors, and innovations in machinery, the haying operation had been reduced to a strike-force of swathers, rakes, balers and harrow beds. Of course the machinery was not new. Frank had never bought a piece of new equipment in his life. As a result, every machine rattled and clanked, shimmied and shook. But a few men with mechanical aptitudes just might be able to coax the machinery into performing the necessary work.

A swather is a self-propelled rotating blade that crimps the grass stems and augers them into the center where they are fluffed into a windrow that trails behind the swather like a sweet-smelling, skinny green river. After several days in the sun the hay is raked and turned so it dries underneath. When the sun and wind have extracted the majority of the moisture, the baler, pulled by a tractor, straddles the windrow gathering hay and feeding it into a chamber. Here a noisy plunger, operating with such force that each downward plunge causes the bailer to bounce on rubber tires, squeezes the hay, and every thirty seconds or so a bale, a hundred pounds of compressed hay held together by two wires, emerges from the chute and tumbles onto the ground.

Another self-propelled piece of equipment, the harrow bed, is driven up and down the long rows of baled hay. It uses a conveyor system to pick up and stack bales on a tilt bed. Each load is transported from the field, tipped into position and added to a stack. The ends of the stacks have to be built by hand, the bales interlaced, so they stand free and do not have to be braced.

For men working on a short crew like the Double X, haying is a timeless string of sun-hammered days whirling into starry nights. Sleep comes in stolen hours and is often nothing more than a couple hours nap on the hard seat of a pickup truck. Most meals are brought to the fields and devoured on the run. Machinery runs constantly, except when being fueled or greased, and when breakdowns occur, which is all too often. When there is a breakdown someone has to make a run to a parts store in a distant town or a replacement has to be fashioned by hand in the shop.

As the haying season whirled into full stride, Tracee juggled looking after Stormy, cooking, taking meals to the men, keeping house, doing chores and gardening. Any of these jobs, at the drop of a hat, was interrupted if a part was needed. Tracee, with Stormy riding along, would make a flying trip to Emerson, and if the part was not available locally, they had to travel to Lincoln, or even twenty miles farther to Ashwood.

Of all her chores Tracee preferred gardening, taking pleasure from weeding, watering and harvesting. In this work, she felt as though she was doing her part to feed the crew and helping save money.

While she gardened Stormy played nearby. He watched bumblebees fumble in and out of flowers, swallows slashing across the sky and ants ferrying food to their homes. Tracee, her face damp with sweat, sometimes watched him as she worked.

Xx

The heat of the midday sun was paralyzing, the ground cracked open and the hills turned as tawny as the flank of a lion. And yet the work in the fields continued. The hay was cut, dried, hammered into bales and the bales taken from the fields and added to the stacks. Only when the sun mercifully fell from the sky did the oppressive heat begin to dissipate and bring relief as the night air turned chilly. By morning a blanket of dew coated surfaces with a thin layer of moisture that quickly dried in the first rays of sunlight.

The heat wave triggered ladybugs to swarm and brought a swarm of pale blue butterflies that were so numerous their fluttering wings vibrated the air. The mosquitoes, having lost their homes in the tall grass, became vicious and hovered in thick, angry clouds above the men and the machinery.

Xx

Cole swung by the house with an armload of wild sunflowers. He gave them to Tracee, telling her, "Thought they might brighten up the kitchen." She thanked him, poured him a glass of ice tea and began arranging the flowers in a vase. She set the vase on the table, and as the flowers settled, they immediately began turning their shaggy golden faces, searching for the power of the remembered sun.

Tracee poured Cole a second glass of tea from a metal pitcher so cold condensation ran down the sides like tears. She asked, "Which would you rather be, invisible or have the ability to fly?"

Cole laughed. “Where did you come up with that? Sounds like something Stormy might ask.”

“Nope, heard it on the radio. They were doing a survey,” explained Tracee. “Well, what do you say?”

“Gees, I don’t know,” said Cole. He scratched the stubble on his chin. “Fly I guess.”

“You’re such a typical man, so predictable,” teased Tracee. “The radio said most men want to fly and women want to be invisible.”

“Is that true?”

“Not for me,” said Tracee. “I want to fly.”

XX

A stream of moisture-laden vapor blew in off the Pacific and hung passively in the windless night until sunrise coaxed the mist into a swirl of ominous thunderheads that soon towered above Sugarloaf Mountain. The tops of the building clouds glistened as white and fluffy as cotton candy, the underbellies mirrored the browns, grays and greenish hues of the land. Clouds boiled over, touched the sun and the sun sent down long, shivering streaks of light. Clouds gobbled up the blue sky. A cool, wet wind began to blow straight out of the west, rattling the leaves and swirling the dust around. The temperature dropped like a rock down an open well. Lightning flashed. A few seconds later thunder clapped.

Cole had been keeping an eye on the storm. He was hoping it might blow over, but as he raised his head, a single drop of rain found his face and made a tiny muddy stripe down his cheek. In dismay he looked around at the cut hay lying in the field and grunted, “Piss-poor timing for rain.”

Rain came with a vengeance and the men had no choice but to retreat to the shop. They stood inside, the double doors thrown open wide, and drank beer and watched the rain quickly settle the dust, releasing the sharp smells of the land. The full fury of the storm hit and rain drummed the tin roof, ran off and made puddles below the eaves. Lightning popped and flashed. Thunder boomed and rolled.

That evening, the men enjoyed their first sit-down dinner in a long while. After dessert, fresh rhubarb pie with ice cream, Cole stepped outside onto the porch and was relieved when he noticed that the rim of the sky around Sugarloaf Mountain was a lighter color. He checked again later and a pale evening sky shone clear, as if it had been scrubbed clean, and the evening star shone brightly. Cole went inside and told Ty, "She's blown over. But we'll have to wait a day or two for the hay to dry. That's okay. We sure enough can use the extra time to work on machinery."

"It needs it," said Ty without any genuine enthusiasm. He addressed a question to nobody in particular. "Have you ever seen such an accumulation of shit machinery in your life?"

For Cole and Ty, it was one thing to see Iris in the company of a man, but quite another to see her behind the wheel, driving Jerry Pavlinac's Ford pickup. She drove right up in front of the shop and stopped, crawled down off the high seat and stood on the apron of concrete like a gunslinger spoiling for a fight. Her feet were slightly spread and her hands rested lightly on her hips.

"So boys, what do you think?" she called, making the words seem like a challenge.

Cole crawled from under a baler, and was the first to find his voice. "Next time you come wheeling in here, be sure and honk the horn a mile or so down the road so we can find ourselves a safe place to hide."

Iris's broke into a broad grin and her posture became less aggressive. "I've been taking lessons. Jerry's teaching me to drive." Jerry came around the pickup and stood by her. She took his arm and patted it affectionately. "I passed my driver's test. I have a license but I haven't graduated to a stick shift, not yet, but I'm pretty good with an automatic transmission aren't I, Jerry?" Jerry nodded.

Iris explained, "I need to have my own transportation. I decided I'm gonna drive the Mercedes back to town.

"Want me to back it out of the garage for you?" offered Cole.

"Don't be silly," said Iris. "I know all about reverse." She laughed and moved away toward the dilapidated garage that housed the high-priced automobile.

"My, my," said Ty to nobody in particular. "Hasn't she found a streak of independence?"

"She sure has," said Jerry. He turned to Cole. "I think that psychiatrist is doing wonders for her. He's really helping bring her out of her shell."

Cole took a couple steps, raised a meaty hand and dropped it on Jerry's shoulder. He said, "If you taught her to drive you've got way more patience that me."

"She's a fast learner," offered Jerry.

Cole said, "You're a good man, and a good friend."

Iris and Jerry departed the ranch. Iris drove the Mercedes sedan and Jerry followed in his pickup. They passed the field where J.B. was raking hay. Iris stuck her arm out the open window and waved. J.B. was dumbfounded at what he was seeing, was so caught off guard he failed to wave back, just stared gape-mouthed at the dust cloud and wondered how many years had he ferried that woman back and forth to town and never, not once in all that time, had she ever given any indication she had a hankering to drive?

After a warm wind sucked the moisture from the hay, the men went back to cutting, raking, baling and hauling. They lurched from one breakdown to the next and it was a crap-shoot on which piece of equipment would throw a sprocket, blow a gasket, have a wheel bearing go out, something, always something. But with each new breakdown, life was somehow coaxed back into that particular piece of machinery. It was never fixed, merely patched temporarily.

The irony of haying was not lost on Cole. The hay was put up when the days were the longest, the weather the most uncomfortably hot, and the air as dry as bone. It was fed out when the daylight hours were short and the temperature bitterly cold. In summer a fellow longed for winter, and in the depths of winter he longed for summer.

As each field was cut and the bales removed, the river water, through an intricate system of ditches and small check dams, was turned in to flood over the land. The thirsty soil sucked it down and within a few days the grass was green again and growing steadily.

Tracee made frequent trips into the mountains, following maps Cole drew for her, opening gates and setting out salt and mineral blocks to entice the cattle onto the next pasture. If everything was going smoothly—the chores were done, the garden weeded and no breakdowns in the field—Tracee allowed herself the indulgence of saddling one of the gentler horses, pulling Stormy up behind her, and going for rides near the Home Place. She often checked on the second-year heifers and their babies to make sure there were no problems. Once she came across a bawling calf with its hind legs caught in the wire fence. With Stormy helping she worked to free the calf while a yellow-eyed coyote circled at a distance. On the way home Stormy squeezed his arms around his mother's waist and told her, "Mommy, you saved that baby. You're my hero."

Tracee reached around and gave him a one-armed hug. "I couldn't have done it without you."

"Guess we're both heroes," he said.

The steel fingers of the revolving reel fed the remnant of the final windrow into the chamber. The plunger compressed the dry hay and sent it traveling into the chamber where a synchronized whirl of knives carved it, like ribbons on a Christmas package, and two lengths of wire tied the block of hay together. With a forceful shudder the machine spit the last bale of the season onto the ground.

But the work was not finished. The top rows on the haystacks had to be sprinkled with rock salt to prevent mildew, and heavy tarps were stretched over the crowns and tied to wooden panels that protected the stacks from marauding deer and elk.

Cole, even though haying season was now officially over, spent nights dreaming of driving in endless circles, spinning swather reels, hearing and feeling the monotonous *chunk-chunk-chunk* of the baler, counting endless trips with hay from the field to the stack, fixing machinery, witnessing intense sunrises and brilliant sunsets, testing the hay for moisture content, bucking bales, rolling bales, stacking bales. For Cole, the haying season had been like a thoroughbred running a long race, crossing the finish line and not knowing when to stop. Even though the race had been won, and the haying season had been concluded, Cole's body and mind just wanted to run.

Cole looked at the long stacks of hay with a tremendous sense of pride and satisfaction. He considered hay to be money in the bank, money to be spent cautiously during the winter to keep the cows in a healthy condition and ready for calving. Hay was the hard cash of the Double X. But it seemed that damn near every time he was feeling smug about the success of the haying season, he was brought up short because he knew, if the price of feeder calves did not inch up a few cents, if the calves on mountain pasture had not grown fat and sleek, then all the hay in the world was wasted. Oregon State University would take over the ranch. The hay crop would be sold. Doc Taylor would wangle his way in and divide the Double X land into golf courses, trophy homes, ranchettes and hideaway cabins. And the OSU general fund would be millions of dollars richer.

Ty viewed the haystacks as tangible symbols of his summer's confinement. All he wanted was to see some new country: the Tetons blush with morning's first light, the Wallowas under a dusting of fresh snow, Green River, Leslie Gulch, Hells Canyon.... Christ-on-a-crutch, he yearned to be sitting in some hole-in-the-wall bar, getting shit-faced on whiskey, waking up in the morning with a hangover and trying to cure it with red beer. He craved sitting in on a game, bluffing a nothing hand and raking in a big pot. He had a burning desire to wake up with a naked waitress or a stripper ... hell, it didn't much matter as long as she was a little on the chancy side and wild as hell in bed.

Cole took a few heifers that had failed to calve to the livestock auction in Lincoln. By the time he got home, Stormy's birthday party was over and done with. When he came into the kitchen where Tracee was cleaning she asked, "You hungry?"

"Grabbed a bite in town," he said and then lowered his voice, "Is the birthday boy still awake?"

"Brushing his teeth."

"Probably shouldn't have done it, but the price was right. I got him a surprise."

"What?"

Cole inched closer. "I've been watching how he gets along with animals. I picked him up a nice little pony. Like I said, the price was right. He's old enough to have a horse. It'll do him good to take care of it. He'll learn about responsibility. I was younger than him when I got my first saddle horse."

Tracee moved into Cole with a suddenness that caught him off-guard. She planted a quick kiss on his cheek and told him, "Thank you." She dashed across the room toward the stairs, tossing over her shoulder, "I'll bring him right down."

Coming down the stairs with her son, Tracee was hit by the full impact of the gift. It dawned on her that, when the day came that she and Stormy would have to leave the ranch, what was she going to do with a pony?

Stormy, dressed in Big Bird pajamas with fuzzy slippers on his feet, rode on Cole's shoulders through the warm night. The moon lit the way, and although Tracee had grabbed a flashlight on the way out, she did not turn it on until they reached the barn and then only to provide momentary light to locate the switch. A pair of evenly spaced bare bulbs winked on. The air was charged with the rich aroma of fresh hay and sour manure.

"Keep your eyes closed. Are they closed?" Cole wanted to know.

"Yeah, they're closed. So what's my surprise?" bubbled Stormy.

"I'm certainly not going to tell you and ruin it," teased Cole. "Just be patient a little longer. We're almost there."

They reached the stall and Cole stopped. "Okay, you can open your eyes."

Stormy's eyes came open, and got wider, and still wider as he stared at a gray pony, its coat sleek and fine, mane and tail almost powder white. He finally found his voice and said, "He shore is real pretty."

"He's a she," corrected Cole. He boosted Stormy to the top rail and held him there, adding, "She's all yours. Happy birthday."

Stormy turned toward his mother with an incredulous look, wanting her to confirm what Cole had said. She was smiling. That was enough for Stormy. He believed the improbable—that this pony was really his to keep.

The pony lifted her head and Stormy reached to touch the gray muzzle. The pony's whisker tickled him. He giggled. "Can I sit on her?"

Tracee opened the gate and Cole stepped through, lifting Stormy and gently placing him on the pony's back. Stormy grinned as one hand tightly gripped the mane and the other tenderly stroked the short hairs of the pony's neck. He spoke to her in a soothing tone, "You're so pretty. I'll bet you're fast like the wind." He turned to Cole and asked, "What's her name?"

"She's your horse. You name her," Cole told him.

Stormy pondered for a moment and then beamed, "She's gray like smoke. I think I'll call her Smokey."

"Stormy and Smokey, sounds like the dynamic duo to me," laughed Cole. He was feeling good, satisfied at being the one to give this wonderful gift to such an appreciative kid. He remembered his first horse and how it had made him feel bigger, more important and how it seemed to lift him above the level of mere mortals.

Stormy told his mother, "I want to sleep with her."

Tracee laughed, "I don't think so. Not tonight."

"Take it slow," said Cole. "This is a rule you'll have to promise to follow. One of us always has to be with you when you go in the stall with her. I don't want you getting stepped on. Is that a deal? Never get in the stall alone with her. Deal?"

"Okay," said Stormy. "But someday I'll get to ride by myself, won't I?"

"Sure, someday you can," responded Cole. "But for now she has to get used to you and you have to get used to her. It'll be your responsibility to make sure she has feed and water, and you need to take care of her feet and brush her. When you can do all that, we'll teach you how to put on the bridle and saddle and you can learn to ride."

"You'll do that? You'll teach me?"

"You bet," said Cole.

"And now you need to get to bed," said Tracee.

Stormy flung his arms around the pony's neck. "I love you, Smokey," he said.

CHAPTER SEVENTEEN

THE WANING SUN SET BEHIND SUGARLOAF MOUNTAIN, AND IT WAS like a holiday at the Double X. This day marked the official changing of seasons and was the signal to begin the fall roundup, gathering the fat cattle off the mountain range and driving them to the safety of the valley floor. The best yearling heifers were to be separated and saved for replacements while the remaining crop of calves, both heifers and steers, would be weaned and sold. And if the price was high enough, and the calves weighed enough, then the Battle family would be able to continue ranching.

Over the course of the summer, the cattle had been rotated from one pasture to the next and now, with the gates to the valley open, some of the more manageable cows were beginning to find their way home. Upon reaching the valley floor they stuck their noses in the air and bellowed back in the direction they had come. Within a few minutes, other cows, calves tagging obediently along, charged from the pine forest, nostrils flared, tails raised, trotting like a band of Clydesdales pulling a beer wagon. They loped down the lane and into the field, feasting on the mellow tang of timothy and blue grass and the candied sweetness of clover, ignoring the pesky flies and mosquitoes.

In the morning, as the sun began to lighten the eastern sky, the Double X horses were trailered to Dragget Meadow. The meadow was named after John J. Dragget. He had come to the country in the early days and attempted to establish a stage stop on the road connecting Emerson to the mining claims high in the Blue Mountains. John brought in a small mill, logged his property, cut lumber and built a two-story structure with nine rooms for his guests. Each room had a fireplace. But before he could entertain his first paying customer, a fire swept through the area, destroying everything. John never rebuilt. He moved away. And now, even though there were no Draggets in the country, the name lived on.

After the Double X riders had mounted, Cole instructed J.B., "How about if you make a swing around Hat Point," and then turning to Ty he asked, "Want Reid or Copeland?" referring to two drainage creeks.

"You three take Copeland. It's a little easier going," said Ty. "I don't believe I feel up to babysitting, not today." He reined his horse away.

Back at the Home Place, Ty had spoken his mind; said roundup was no place for a 6-year-old kid. Cole reminded him they were both hardened veterans by that age. But Ty was having none of it, said there was a lot of difference, that they had been raised horseback while Stormy was a greenhorn who was liable to fall off his pony, get hurt or become lost.

Cole had promised Stormy he could come along and had resigned himself to being the responsible party. Before they started riding he told Stormy, "If we get separated and you can't see me or your mother, I want you to rein up and stay put. Don't move. I'll find you."

Next Cole turned his attention to Tracee. "This is big country. If you get turned around you can go a long way before you hit a drift fence or a road. Basically, what we're doing is riding up this hill, crossing over the top into the next drainage and making a sweep down the draw. We want to keep any cattle we come across out in front of us. We drive them to the meadow where we'll wait for the others to bring in whatever they find."

The horses were eager to work. They lunged up the face of the ridge and dropped down the far side. In the bottom of the draw ran Copeland Creek, a thin stream of water meandering through thick tangles of cottonwoods, aspens and willows. Most of the leaves had already lost their green snap and were beginning to turn a pallid yellow. Cole took the far side of the creek, Tracee and Stormy the near side, and after having traveled less than a half-mile, there was considerable snapping in the brush. Every once in a while a calf bawled or a bull bellowed. Near the tail-out Cole rode into the thicket, whistling and shouting, driving the stock into view.

Cole counted twenty-seven pairs, and two range bulls. The calves, milk and grass fattened, looked to be in the peak of condition and that pleased him. The bulls, having had their harem disrupted, were mad and turned on each other, butting heads, kicking up dust, pushing and shoving. They soon tired of their personal war and drifted onto the meadow with the cows.

Cole rode to Tracee. She was mounted on a paint horse she was fond of riding and Stormy was beside her on his gray pony. Cole asked Stormy, "What do you think of roundup so far?"

"Fun," exclaimed Stormy.

Tracee was watching Cole. He leaned a forearm nonchalantly on the saddle horn and she thought he looked to be in his element. Her thoughts were cut short.

"Lot more riding to do," said Cole, turning his attention to Tracee. "This is fairly easy country but we'll get into some that's more like a survival course. You'd swear a cow could never make a home in such sparse conditions, but they do."

Tracee looked around, drinking in the beauty of the land: the sky dotted with puffy white clouds, glittering groves of aspens, broad meadows the color of jade, high hills and deep canyons. She sighed and said, "I can see why you love this ranch. It's like stepping back a hundred years into the days of the Wild West."

Stormy intruded, "Can I gallop Smokey?"

"Don't think you better," Cole told him. He smiled at the boy. "You don't want to spook the cattle. You're better off riding slow, taking it easy, not getting in much of a hurry. There'll be plenty of time to gallop, but not right now."

Later in the day Tracee and Stormy returned to the horse trailers. Stormy took a nap and Tracee read a book. The country Cole would be riding next, up Willow Creek, was too steep and rugged for Stormy.

As he rode, Cole thought about what Tracee had said, that the ranch was like stepping back a hundred years, and it occurred to him that the American West was actually won in one long lifetime—between the Lewis and Clark overland expedition and the last Indian battle at Wounded Knee. In that long lifetime the buffalo were killed, the Indians rounded up and confined on reservations, the western lands thrown open for anyone wishing to claim a free homestead, and the coasts were linked by telegraph lines and steel rails. All this came about in less than a hundred years.

Buffalo Bill had put this exciting era of history together in his Wild West show—an odd collection featuring a few shaggy buffalo, horses, longhorn cattle and famous marshals, pretty whores, pony express riders and noble savages in war paint. Cole could only imagine the impression the shows made on those in attendance when presented to eastern audiences, and those in England, too.

In truth, the romantic life of the free-roaming cowboy was a myth. It was only for a couple short decades that drovers lived the dream, driving cattle from Texas to the railheads in Kansas, and even then the cowboy was governed by economics. Cowboys were little more than poorly paid laborers working for rich cattle barons. In less than twenty years, fences split the open range and squatters had laid claim to every decent waterhole.

Life on the Double X was never going to be like stepping back in time. That was impossible. But Cole figured he could live with the compromise; of having one foot firmly planted in the past, and the other squarely in the present.

XX

Each of the summer ranges had to be ridden, and any of the cattle that had hung up there had to be rounded up and driven in. A dozen pairs were brought in off McGraw Gulch, twenty-three pairs were gathered from Burnt Creek, sixteen pairs came off from Power's Meadow and thirty-six pairs were brought in from Baldy Butte. And so it went, the riders sweeping the country: hitting the water holes in the heat of the day and again in the evening when the cattle drifted in for a drink, driving the brushy draws and fighting through the high mahogany thickets where cattle tended to congregate to escape the irritating small black flies and the big, mean-spirited horse flies that draw blood with their bites.

When the sun was directly overhead, the riders rested and ate lunch, sitting on windfalls and watching nuthatches move up and down trees searching for insects, phoebes and towhees scratching the ground, turning leaves, probing for seeds, yellow finches, as lively as sparks, flitting through the dark green forest. Sometimes a breeze made the aspen leaves flutter, and occasionally a deer or an elk sauntered into view. A coyote might come for a look-see, and likely as not, a stellar jay would be there to scold it for its intrusion. Each time a scrap of bread crust was discarded, an army of ants appeared and attempted to carry it home on their backs. A tired rider might lie on the dry, cool ground, tip his hat over his eyes and try to catch a few winks; his horse standing nearby, lower lip drooping, eyes half-closed, a hind hoof tipped, fast asleep.

The riders were working under a strict time limit and the work progressed at a steady pace. Hunting season was just around the corner and the cattle, for their protection, needed to be gathered and brought in to the safety of the valley floor.

The annual deer season brought a hoard of trigger-happy outsiders who crept around the public roads surrounding the Double X ranch in caravans of pickups, jeeps, four-wheelers and motorcycles. They were armed with high-powered rifles, cases of beer and fifths of whiskey. They shot at glimpses of bucks and any sound in the brush was considered fair game. They dressed in fluorescent colors so as not to be mistaken for their quarry, and for most, this was as close as they would ever get to an actual live combat situation.

Hunting season made it too dangerous for a rider on horseback to be in the woods and the Double X crew made the most of this time. They worked cattle in the corrals and any dry cow was cut out, given a pregnancy test, and if barren was sold. A cattle ranch could not afford to carry non-producing freeloaders on its payroll. Replacement heifers were selected and though Cole tried to be diplomatic, asking Ty and J.B. what they thought, he had a good eye and usually made the final decision. When he chose a replacement heifer, he looked at the mother to determine if she had good physical qualities and if she was a good milker. Then he cast a critical eye toward her calf, judging its size, straightness of back, confirmation and coloration. The one daunting question he had to answer in the selection process was, in his estimation, would this heifer throw calves that were fast gainers with high grade meat? If so, Cole nodded his head, and the calf was run into a holding pen.

All the range bulls had been accounted for and were separated from the other stock in the bull pasture. But the ranch was still short thirty-seven pairs of cows and calves. Six pair showed up at the barn, and the next day three more pair wandered in. When deer season finally drew to a close, the crew made one last sweep and found fifteen pair hung up on Goodlow Meadow, which left a balance of thirteen head missing. Cole thought to himself thirteen was an unlucky number and wondered if that would be what tipped the scale and caused them to go in the red. But he kept this thought to himself because, he feared, even mentioning the fact might bring bad luck to pass.

XX

The Double X crew, along with outside help from Tex Corwin and Johnny Ritter, were ready to sell and ship the cattle. Cole had broken the news to Stormy the night before, being as gentle as he could, saying the work of separating cows and calves was dangerous and that Stormy had to wait until he was older before he could lend a hand. But, in the chill of morning, Stormy was there, perched on Smokey outside the corral, watching everything that transpired, drinking it all in so, when he got his chance, in a year or two, he would be ready.

As soon as the calves were separated from their mothers, the bawling began. The air clamored with their unhappy noise. Men on horseback rode through the milling calves, easing a few that were too small for weaning back onto the pasture to find their mothers. In the corral the steer calves, the heifer calves, and the bull calves were separated and held in adjoining pens. Steers typically fetch a higher price than heifers because, in a feedlot, steers gain weight at a faster rate. But the Battle operation was unique. The purebred Hereford heifers were prized and worth a premium for the calves they would throw, as were the bull calves because of their ability to father hundreds of offspring.

That night Wood River Valley echoed to the discord of the separated cows and calves. The hungry calves bawled and bleated. The cows were in pain from engorged udders. They lowed and bellowed. The clamor continued all night long, and throughout the next day.

XX

The cattle buyers arrived in time for dinner, and after indulging themselves on Double X steaks and all the trimmings, they climbed on the corral railings and pointed to the calves they wanted. Cole tallied every sale, and the crew ran the purchased animals into holding pens. As the last few calves were being separated, as if on cue, a deep-throated rumble signaled the arrival of a convoy of trucks and trailers. They were silver, long and shiny, double-decked and brought with them a cloud of dust that settled over the penned cattle like a rolling fog. Within minutes of their arrival the first truck had jockeyed into position at the head of the chute. The riders pushed a group of steers onto the scale. They were weighed as a group and herded onto the truck. The number of cattle, their sex, and weight were recorded twice, once by the buyer and once by Cole, who jotted down the numbers in a leather-bound notebook he kept in his breast pocket. The state brand inspector was on hand to check each calf and make sure it carried the proper identification. The drivers, a bleary-eyed bunch, had absolutely no interest in the cattle or the goings-on in the corral, pens or loading chute. They gathered in front of one of the big rigs to discuss those things important to them: the miles they had driven, storms they had barrel-assed through, raw horsepower, foot-pounds of torque, speed traps, women of easy virtue, good food and fights they had won.

Back in the pens and loading chute yearling calves bawled, horses whinnied, men shouted, dust boiled. There was the constant clamor of hooves striking the metal scale, the wooden ramp and metal again as the calves were forced into the bowels of the trailers. When one tractor-trailer had been filled, it departed and another quickly took its place at the head of the chute. The only lull in the constant flow of cattle was to clean the scale of an accumulation of manure. With the calves in distress, every minute of delay caused them to lose weight, so the crew worked quickly to make sure the swelling brown stream kept moving.

Finally, as the sun made shadows long and distorted, the last truck in the great aluminum caravan pulled away and headed down the road. The bulls were to be sold at an upcoming auction in Fallon, Nevada. A ranch in Texas had purchased most of the heifers. The black bally steers and heifers were being sent to Red Bluff, and the Hereford steers were split between several buyers, the majority going to the J.R. Simplot feedlot in Idaho where they would be fattened on cull potatoes. The carcasses would be sold through the Albertsons chain of grocery stores. The rumble of the last truck faded. The sun settled into the southern flank of Sugarloaf. Clouds massing in the west turned red but quickly tarnished to a washed out pink.

Tracee was alone at the far end of the corral. Johnny Ritter rode near her and said, "What's the deal, don't that old man of yours ever take you out on the town? I've looked for you at every dance, all summer long. Thought maybe I could steal a slow dance but nothin' doin'. Sweetheart, you've done broke my heart." He tried to look sad.

"We've been busy."

"Busy don't cut it," teased Johnny. "Busy should never keep a pretty gal like you from havin' fun. If he won't take you out dancing maybe I should. Ya know, there's a dance tonight, wanna go?"

Tracee said, "I just wanna go to bed."

"Sounds like something I could be talked into," said Johnny with a grin, revealing two rows of dusty teeth.

"Johnny, you seem like a nice guy," said Tracee. "But really, I'm not interested. Nothing personal."

Johnny, refusing to give up, said, "Maybe some other time."

"I don't think so," responded Tracee. She turned away, found Stormy and shepherded him toward the house. Johnny shook out a cigarette and lit it. He squinted when the smoke hit his eyes, but he never stopped staring at Tracee. Half under his breath Johnny muttered, "All them potatoes and no meat. What a goddamn pity."

The evening meal was stew that had simmered all day in a crockpot, corn bread and a green salad Tracee had tossed together at the last minute. Ty came in and was more interested in drinking than eating. After his fourth beer he fell asleep in Frank's chair without eating a single bite of dinner. When Cole came in he washed up, and then he too had a beer, but he sat at the table and ate. Tracee joined him.

Around bites Cole said, "You've done more than your fair share around here. I always look forward to what you are gonna fix. You're one hell of a fine cook. And you roll up your sleeves and work like a man."

"Thanks," said Tracee, breaking into a smile. "Nobody has ever said that before—that I work like a man. I'm guessing it's a compliment."

"Believe me, it is," said Cole. "I don't know how we'd have got along without your help. I just want you to know how much I appreciate everything you've done to help out. Don't believe we ever had as good an all-around hand—from cooking to working cattle—as you. Never."

Cole had wanted to say more, but he left it at that, hoping she knew that he thought a lot more of her than a "good all-around hand" or a gal his brother happened to meet along the road and drag home. He considered her and Stormy an integral part of the family, but never confided that to her. He thought his personal feelings were best left unsaid.

CHAPTER EIGHTEEN

A YEAR HAD PASSED SINCE FRANK BATTLE CROSSED TO THE FAR SIDE of the fence. Some claimed the mean old bull of Wood River Valley burned in hell and others figured, on his wild ride from the ranch to town, he most certainly had asked God's forgiveness. When, over a beer, the question was posed to Ty, he shrugged and said, "I don't give a rat's ass either way."

And now, at long last, the day of reckoning had arrived. The accountants from Hanby, Rowe & Fitzgerald had added up the numbers. The attorneys had deciphered the legal mumbo-jumbo. A decision was about to be rendered on whether the Battle family would continue to run the Double X as a cattle ranch or whether it would become a valuable asset belonging to Oregon State University, and most probably, developed by Doc Taylor, or someone like him.

Whichever way it went, the final decision was likely to end up in court. If the Battle family won, OSU might choose to file an appeal. The Battle attorneys had advised the family, if OSU won, the will should be contested on the grounds it was invalid because Frank had suffered from diminished capacity and was not in his right mind at the time of the signing. In either case, if the decision was left to the judicial system, and the verdicts were appealed, it could take ten years to settle the matter. By that time the lawyer fees would eat up a big chunk of the value of the ranch, and if they played it right, maybe the whole damn thing.

Cole recognized that ranching was a gamble. If the cows sloughed their babies, or if disease swept through the herd, or if the rains didn't come, or if they came with a vengeance, then it was the bank foreclosing and raking in the pot. Cole concluded a man, a family, ranched because it was a way of life, a life they loved. He also knew the only time a rancher ever profited financially was when the land was sold to a developer.

Seated at the head of Mr. Sandlin's wide conference table, made of some exotic wood and surrounded by impressive chairs, was a pair of senior accountants from Hanby, Rowe & Fitzgerald. They were dressed like identical twins, wearing white shirts offset by red ties. A small mountain of papers, neatly confined to folders and presentation reports, sat on the table in front of them. To the accountants' left, was a representative from the Acquisition Department for Oregon State University, as well as an attorney representing the university's interests in the matter which, in future case files, most likely would become known as Oregon State University vs. the Battle Family, et al.

Directly across from the university's delegation, the chair nearest the accountants was unoccupied, and awaiting Mr. Sandlin, the Battle family's attorney. Cole, wearing a clean pair of blue jeans and a blazer from his previous life as a real estate broker, sat in the next chair. His pale blue shirt was open at the throat. A year spent in the weather had turned his skin a leathery brown and he rested thick forearms on the table. He worked to radiate a confident attitude although inside he felt none of that confidence. In the next few minutes, all this might play out the wrong way, and then what the hell was he going to do? There was always the possibility he could get back into real estate, but from the side of the fence he was on now, he knew how damn hard it was for a family to have to let go of their ranch or farm. He no longer wanted any part of buying and selling failed dreams. He told himself he could always go to work for a big outfit, run a ranch, but that would be nothing more than a job. A couple minutes more ... the wait was killing him. He occupied the time rehashing the past year in his mind: cruising the pregnant cows like a submarine patrolling the coast, checking for signs of labor, glassy eyes, swollen bags, infections, drooping ears, lameness, prolapses. He knew that missing a cow's distress might, in the long run, cost the animal its life. And losing a cow was a heavy hit because you not only lost her, but you lost her calf as well. And he remembered feeding out on cold mornings, the cattle drive, haying, playing chess with Tracee, the look on Stormy's face when Cole gave him the pony.... He viewed these events from the past year like he was looking at snapshots in a photo album.

Ty sat beside Cole. He was in desperate need of a haircut and a shave. Tracee had tried to convince him he should at least put on a clean shirt, but he hadn't given in to her wishes. His blue jeans were old and faded, his boots caked with manure and he wore his sweat-caked cowboy hat pulled low over his eyes as he leaned back on two legs of the expensive chair. He had told Tracee, "It doesn't matter how I look, or how I dress, it's all about numbers and those accountants can make it come out any way they want. You can't tell me someone hasn't already slipped them a shit-pot full of cash."

He had no real interest in any of the wheeling and dealings. He only wanted out. Once the decision was rendered, it meant one thing to Ty—he had kept his word, fulfilled all his obligations, pitched in and done his fair share—now it was over. The chips could fall where they may. If the ranch stayed in the Battle family, Cole could hire someone to take his place, but sure as hell Ty was not signing on for another tour of duty.

Ty's relationship with Tracee was another matter. He wanted to escape from that, too. The fire of their relationship had cooled to the point that not even a tiny spark remained. They wanted different things from life. She wanted to settle down, sink roots into the ground, raise her son and be a mother. More than likely she had designs to be someone's wife. None of that appealed to Ty. He was anxious to get back on the road. For Ty, the enticing part about mobility was that when problems entangled a fellow he could pick up, move on, and it'd be awhile before the same old problems caught up with him.

Iris sat next to Ty. She had asked Jerry Pavlinac to accompany her to the meeting, telling him, "I need you. You're my strength." She insisted Jerry sit beside her, and when he did, she smiled like a schoolgirl at the prom. Her eyes had a sparkle, and to anyone who had known her, it seemed she looked the best she had in many years. Whatever the cause for her happiness, it seemed her current life suited her fine. Under the table, and unseen by the others, she took hold of Jerry's hand, squeezed it and placed it on her lap.

Tracee and Stormy occupied chairs against the wall. Stormy looked the part of a little buckaroo, wearing boots, a red vest and a straw cowboy hat. All he needed to complete the outfit was a pair of six-shooters. He once owned a pair, but they were lost when they moved to the ranch.

Tracee was wearing a yellow sundress, so bright it all but shouted, "Summer!" But she was not nearly as carefree as her dress portended. She was worried, had dreaded this day because her entire future seemed to rest on the decision to be handed down in this room. If the Battle family won, she might be asked to stay on. She had done a good job this past year; Cole had told her so, but there were no guarantees. If the Battle family lost, she had to come up with Plan B and that was to find a job, and a place to live for herself, Stormy and the pony. They were staying together. There was no doubt about that.

Tracee, as she watched Stormy blossom into a real person over the past year, had experienced the joys of being a mother. She wanted to continue to nurture him, and if she could, she wanted them to live on a ranch. Maybe she could find work as a ranch cook or maybe even as a cowgirl. She enjoyed both, but being outdoors appealed to her more. Tracee pictured her future like a balloon floating over the landscape. There was no telling where she might land, but she knew for a damn solid fact she would.

J.B. came in late, pausing in the doorway, not sure of where he should sit. He removed his hat, and the whiteness of his forehead stood out from the brown of his face like neon. He shuffled over and took a seat beside Stormy. He reached out and patted the boy on the leg and said in a raspy whisper, "How ya doing, little man?"

In a loud voice Stormy responded, "I'm a cowboy. But I don't have no guns." He slapped his hips to add emphasis to his dilemma and everyone in the room, except for the accountants, smiled.

Mr. Sandlin remained in his private office. He was a no-nonsense man who enjoyed brevity but also derived immense pleasure from manufacturing drama. He gathered an envelope and other papers, added them to a manila file folder and finally got up and walked down the hall. He breezed into the conference room proclaiming, "Sorry to keep ya all waiting." He slid onto the chair beside Cole and slapped the manila file folder on the table. His elbows kneaded the armrest and he touched his fingertips together several times. He seemed momentarily lost in thought, then peered over his reading glasses, which had slipped most of the way down his nose. He looked to his right, and his gaze paused at each member of the Battle family, as if sizing up that person, making sure they were ready for the upcoming revelations, continuing on to the next individual and ending with Jerry. He was surprised Jerry was there, but did not let on. Finally he turned to his left, toward the accountants, and addressed them by asking, "Have you gentlemen reached a definitive resolution in this matter?"

The first accountant said, "Yes sir, we have."

"Pray tell," said Mr. Sandlin a bit of irritation showing in his voice. "And can you dispense with all the qualifiers on how you compared expenses against income to determine, in your considered opinion, whether a profit was attained? We are not particularly concerned with your meticulous calculations, only the end result. And, the bottom line is?"

The first accountant tapped a forefinger on the stack of folders and presentation reports. He drew a breath and said, "The bottom line shows a slim profit, but a profit none the less."

He had planned to say more but Mr. Sandlin held up a hand cutting him off. "And do you concur?" asked Mr. Sandlin to the second accountant.

"Yes, sir," said the second accountant.

"Very well," said Mr. Sandlin, "The two of you may go. Thank you."

The accountants gathered their paperwork and departed. As Mr. Sandlin moved to the head of the table he invited the representatives of the university to stay, advising them that the upcoming matter might have a direct bearing on the legal aspects of the case. Then Mr. Sandlin turned his attention to the folder in front of him. He opened it, and with a flourish, removed a long white envelope that he held aloft, between thumb and forefinger, as if this was the beginning of a magic trick. He laid the envelope on the table and began working the blade of a small pocket knife he had withdrawn from his coat pocket, under the seal.

"As each of you are already acutely aware, Frank did leave a valid will," said Mr. Sandlin. "However, a few weeks before his unfortunate death, he came to my office and said that he wished to amend that will, adding a stipulation that the existence of this amendment was not to be disclosed until one year had passed from his death, and then only if the family continued to operate the ranch according to the conditions of his recorded will.

"I do not know the specifics of this amendment although I did witness his signature. Frank dictated this letter to my secretary and specifically asked she take it down word for word, and that the contents be kept strictly confidential until such time as the conditions I eluded to previously were met.

"As your family attorney, I want to assure you this amendment takes legal precedence over any and all previous wills. This document reads as follows..."

Mr. Sandlin withdrew two typed pages and in a voice solemn enough for church, he relayed Frank Battle's final thoughts and wishes.

> *"Dear family,*
>
> *"I'm dictating this here letter to the secretary in Bob Sandlin's office. She promises to take down every damn word I say, so here goes.*
>
> *"I haven't been feeling all that well of late, and I want to have everything spelled out legal-like. I've instructed Bob Sandlin that, if something should happen to me, not to give this letter to you, not to even mention its existence, until one year has passed. So, if you are reading this now it means I've gone to the big roundup in the sky. It also means you have spent the last year busting your butts to show a profit and not lose the ranch to Oregon State University.*
>
> *"I imagine you've cussed me for putting that stipulation in my will. You probably took it as a threat to your inheritance. I'm sure, for this and many other things, there have been times you thought I was the meanest SOB in the world.*
>
> *"You probably want to know why I did it. The answer is simply because nothing was ever handed to me. I worked like a dog for whatever I got. Nothing came easy. Nothing came without a price attached. Sometimes that price seemed awful damn steep.*
>
> *"Looking back on things—maybe I was a bit of a hard ass on you boys. Maybe I expected too much from you. But I always justified it because I never once asked more from you than I was willing to put out myself. Besides that, nothing builds a fellow's character like a struggle.*

"Iris, if there was one change I could make, it would be that our baby girl had lived. Her passing was a tragedy. The Man Upstairs called her home and there probably wasn't much we could have done to change His mind.

"Cole, even though we never talked about it, I know that when you came back from college, you expected to take things over. But the Double X was my life. I sacrificed everything for it. What the hell was I supposed to do, take up golf, buy a motor home and travel around? I wasn't ready to step down. If it happened today things might be different. Maybe. Hell, I don't know.

"Ty, you were a good worker but you always had a wild hair. You were looking for an excuse to light out of here. I knew you never wanted to be tied to this ranch. You always did have wings on your boots.

"I did the best for all of you I could. We had some rough times, but we had some good mixed in here and there, too. I wish I could have handled some situations a bit different, but all that's water under the bridge. If I had it to do all over again, I'd try to have a little more compassion, and once in a while try to put your feelings into the mix. But since you're reading this letter, it means there ain't gonna be any second chances.

"So, this here will be my final will and testament. I have worked all this out so that it meets the legal requirements. To put it simply, I formed a corporation and gifted stock to each of my beneficiaries. I also established a fund to take care of any remaining inheritance tax. I don't want the beneficiaries of my estate forced into selling off land, or having any shit-for-brains bureaucrats involved. The government would run the ranch into the ground in nothing flat.

"The division of my estate shall be as follows: Cole, I want you to have the ranch and run it because that was always your dream. You'll be entitled to one-half the land, cattle, chattel and one-half of any profits. The other one-half shall be divided equally between Iris and Ty. There will be some years where there isn't much to split and other years when there are a few beans in the pot. I don't want any of the land sold. I want the ranch to stay intact. It's a good outfit the way it is. If you don't want to operate it as a working cattle ranch then Oregon State University takes over, lock, stock and barrel.

Rick Steber, the author of more than thirty books and sales of more than a million copies, has received national acclaim for his writing. His numerous awards include the Western Writers of America Spur Award for Best Western Novel, Western Heritage Award, Benjamin Franklin Award, Mid-America Publishers Award, Oregon Library Association Award and Oregon Literary Arts Award. Two of his books have been optioned to movie production companies.

In addition to his writing, Rick is an engaging Western personality and has the unique ability to make his characters come alive as he tells a story. He has spoken at national and international conferences and visits schools where he talks to students about the importance of education, developing reading and writing skills, and impressing upon them the value of saving our history for future generations.

Rick has two sons, Seneca and Dusty, and lives near Prineville, Oregon. He writes in a cabin in the timbered foothills of the Ochoco Mountains.

put out his hand to Cole, and as they shook he leaned in close and said, "She's a great gal. Take care of her." He turned away and gave Tracee a passing, one-armed embrace, saying to her, "I'll think about you when I'm lying on the beach in Mexico." He turned his attention to Stormy, pulled off his hat, tousled his hair and gave him back his hat, saying, "See you down the road, cowboy." And then, with a lively spring in his step, Ty strolled to his pickup, fired it up, chunked the transmission into low, released the clutch and started moving forward with no destination in mind.

Cole and Tracee turned and began walking together, side by side. Stormy came running up from behind, grabbed hold of their hands, and in wild exuberance swung his feet up and off the ground, completely trusting they would never let him fall.

THE END

"Iris, if you should remarry, and can get along on your own, then your quarter shall go to J.B. along with the stipulation that when he dies it reverts to Cole. J.B. has been a hard worker, and no cowhand was ever more loyal, or deserving. No matter what happens, make sure you find a place for him on the ranch. These are my wishes. I want it plain and simple and no bullshit that involves lawyers and the courts.

"I hope that during the last year you've all learned something more than you thought you knew about the cattle business and something about yourselves, too. I wish I could have been there to watch. I'm sure you struggled. I think you probably made a go of it. My hat is off to you for sticking together.

Frank Battle

P.S. I never happened to mention it, or if I did it was a long time ago, but I love you all."

Mr. Sandlin folded the pages and tucked them inside the envelope. He turned to the representative from Oregon State University, "Guess you're out of luck." They rose and quickly departed.

After they were gone Mr. Sandlin spoke to the Battle family, saying, "If you have further questions or need clarification of anything, please do not hesitate to call me." With that said he stood, picked up the file folder and left the room.

Iris went around the room, hugging and congratulating each of them. When she came to J.B. she leaned toward him and whispered so only he could hear, "Jerry and I have set the date. You and the boys take care of the ranch." She walked from the room arm in arm with Jerry and when she reached the Mercedes parked at the curb Jerry opened the door for her and Iris slipped behind the wheel.

J.B. went directly to the nearest bar. He was a landowner and wanted to show it by buying the house a round. Five minutes passed and the others emerged from the attorney's office. They stood awkwardly, facing each other, and then Ty